RHODE TRIP

L.B. DUNBAR

Graphic Cover Design: Booked It Design

Editor: Melissa Shank

Editor: Evident Ink

Proofread: Gemma Brocato

Proofread: Karen Fischer

OTHER BOOKS BY L.B. DUNBAR

<u>Sterling Falls</u>

Sterling Heat

Sterling Brick

Sterling Streak

Sterling Clay

Sterling Fight

Sterling Touch

Sterling Stone

<u>Chicago Anchors</u>

Elevator Pitch

Catch the Kiss

Parentmoon

<u>Holiday Hotties (Christmas novellas)</u>

Scrooge-ish

Naughty-ish

Grouch-ish

<u>Road Trips & Romance</u>

Hauling Ashe

Merging Wright

Rhode Trip

<u>Lakeside Cottage</u>

Living at 40

Loving at 40

Learning at 40

Letting Go at 40

<u>Silver Foxes of Blue Ridge</u>

Silver Brewer

Silver Player

Silver Mayor

Silver Biker

<u>Sexy Silver Fox Collection</u>

After Care

Midlife Crisis

Restored Dreams

Second Chance

Wine&Dine

<u>Collision novellas</u>

Collide

Caught

The Sex Education of M.E.

<u>The Heart Collection</u>

Speak from the Heart

Read with your Heart

Look with your Heart

Fight from the Heart

View with your Heart

The Heart Remembers - a sequel

BOOKS IN OTHER AUTHOR WORLDS

<u>Smartypants Romance (an imprint of Penny Reid)</u>

Love in Due Time

Love in Deed

Love in a Pickle

<u>The World of True North (an imprint of Sarina Bowen)</u>

Cowboy

Studfinder

THE EARLY YEARS

<u>Legendary Rock Stars Series</u>

<u>Paradise Stories</u>

<u>The Island Duet</u>

<u>Modern Descendants – writing as elda lore</u>

*For those who feel the call of a highway.
Let's take a road trip.*

*WARNING: Off the page reference to suicide; fear of potential
suicide; and NOT a cheating book, although adultery is surmised at
first.*

"All that is gold does not glitter.
All who wander are not lost.
The old that is strong does not wither.
Deep roots are not reached by the frost."
– J.R.R. Tolkien

1

Playlist: "Girl On Fire" – Alicia Keys

[Lindee]

There is something about the open road that soothes my soul.

And I've been on the road often in my forty-two years.

Maybe a bit of my absentee father resides in me. A need for escape lives inside me.

I can never decide if my admiration is the sound of eighteen wheels whirling on a highway, or just the swish of another speeding vehicle passing by me when my windows are down, and the wind tosses around my hair. Maybe it's the fresh scent of wide-spread land, the dense fragrance of forests, or the tangy nose-burn of asphalt.

Whatever it is, the road is a balm.

And the newest stretch I drive isn't a straight line, but a

twisting, turning ribbon through thick trees with a sharp drop off to my right and boulders to my left as I climb the mountains of Tennessee and cross into North Carolina.

I'm on two missions.

My first goal is to master this road, famous for motorcyclists and high-speed enthusiasts. I'm not a cyclist, but my Jeep was made for this kind of terrain. Spring is in the air and the leaves in the surrounding forest are just starting to bud. The highway before me is an S-curve, slithering like a snake which makes its name almost appropriate—The Tail of the Dragon. Route 129 is twelve miles long with 318 curls before I hit Deal's Gap, the official start or finish line for travelers on this elusive highway.

As for me, I'm clutching the steering wheel like it's my last gin and tonic on a hot summer day, and strongly questioning my sanity.

The second purpose in taking this difficult strip of road is that it was the best route from point A to point B despite all the hairpin curves. A lodge in Robbinsville is my destination. Once owned by an aluminum company and the location is now a traveler's delight near hiking, fishing, and white-water rafting in the Appalachian Mountains. I'm a bit of a hotel restoration expert. I don't have a degree in interior design, though. I just sort of fell into the path of rehabbing and I love short-term stay locations. Homes converted into bed-and-breakfasts. Motels rescued from ruin. Historical landmark hotels returned to their glory. I love a secret hideaway tucked into the landscape or a small-town treasure. Whatever the case may be, the concept of never staying long in one place is who I am.

Only, I'm growing older, wiser and, frankly, a little weary of never having a place to call my own. As I travel often, anything of great value is at my mother's home. I don't visit often, and I prefer it that way. My mom can be domineering at times, complacent at others, although she's the only parent I've ever had.

That's a story for another day.

Today, the breeze ripples through my open window and I hold my breath around another slinky curve. Motorcyclists are slowed by my pace, and I wave my arm out the window, signaling them to pass. I'm not in a hurry. I'm only trying to prove something to myself. I can tackle anything, like bumps in a road, or in this case, the curling of one.

The Iron Dragon is a marker that coordinates with the beginning of the highway headed north. I'll take a picture on my return trip. Tomorrow, I'll be meeting my sisters at a cabin in the Tennessee Valley. This is a new thing for the Fox sisters. In an effort to reconnect, we'd decided to meet up once a year in a location none of us have ever visited. As this was Mae's idea, we let her pick our first location.

For tonight, I'll be staying at the Opatoc Hotel here in North Carolina.

When I pull into the parking lot of the lodge, a deep breath escapes me. My hands still clutch the steering wheel and my fingers ache as I peel them away. My arms are tense. My shoulders tight. The perilous drive was both exhilarating and exhausting, and yet a strange hum vibrates within me. I tackled the Tail. The loops and bends of this road deserve mad respect, and pride fills me that I can add this road to the long list of many I've traveled.

As I exit my Jeep, I inhale crisp, mountain air that's ripe with sunshine. My legs are shaky. I need a Coke, or perhaps something stronger.

Arriving at reception, I learn my room isn't ready which is fine with me. I don't want to be indoors. The day is a comfortable sixty-something degrees and in my sweater, booties, and jeans, I'm sweaty from the taxing drive. The receptionist mentions there is a patio located beyond the gift shop, and I head in that direction.

Once outside, I descend a set of stairs that leads to a stone patio. My legs continue to wobble as I step downward, and I breathe deeply to calm myself, willing the damp mountain scent to settle into my lungs. In the early spring, no flowers are in bloom, but swatches of freshly turned soil suggest plants will soon blossom along a brick wall bordering the patio. Before me, a river of crystal-clear water gently rushes over a picture-perfect display of river rocks in varying tones of brown and gray. Beyond the river, the forest stretches skyward, trees are laden with springtime buds.

The spot should feel serene but I'm too keyed up to relax.

Wrought iron tables are clustered near the base of the stair-case. A few patio heaters are interspersed among the tables and there are people seated nearby. However, I veer to the right where a series of plastic Adirondack chairs sit with their backs to a rock wall. Each seat faces the river, and a man sits in the farthest one.

His long legs are stretched out before him and casually crossed at the ankle. Thick boots cover his feet. His pants are a Carhartt-brown color, and he wears a thick sweater with the sleeves pushed up to his elbows. His hair is a dusty mix of light brown and gray. His jaw is covered in the same combination. When his eyes momentarily meet mine, I'm struck by their smooth whiskey-color.

"Mind if I sit?"

"Suit yourself, sugar." His voice is as thick as his thighs and sends a ripple up my spine that rivals the river before us.

I drop onto a chair three away from him and tip back my head. The sun is behind me, but the warmth still covers my cheeks. I sigh once. I exhale slowly. While I will myself to sit still, my body won't settle. Everywhere feels tight, like a rubber band wound and ready to snap.

A waitress approaches. "Can I get you something to drink?"

"I'd love a soda." I don't know why I drag out the word or even call it such a thing. My sisters are both Midwesterners and call the carbonated drink pop. I typically follow their lead. As the youngest of four, and the last sister of three, I've been in their shadows most of my life. Maybe that's another part of my need to keep moving. Outrunning their successes. Trying to create my own.

The man beside me chuckles and I turn in his direction, taking another glance at his profile. The wave of his hair. The thickness of his beard. The long length of his body, relaxed and slouched in a plastic chair. A chunky gold ring circles his left ring finger.

Married.

Quickly, I turn away, glancing at my naked fingers. Vacant like the promises once given to me.

"Have you ever done something completely out of character?" I blurt, not directing my gaze at the man but staring at the simple river as it tumbles over rocks, like a rushing melody.

"Pardon me?"

I turn toward him, noting how he leans his arm on one rest, elbow bent. His beard-covered chin tilts in my direction.

I shift, facing him better. "Out of character? Something extreme. Something no one would expect of you." Staring at him, hopeful he knows what I mean, I surmise almost instantly he's done more than I've ever dreamed. His size. His casually confident posture. His heavy boots. At a glance, he's a man who has more experience than me in everything.

His thumb pushes at the hefty ring on his finger. The gold glints in the afternoon sunlight. "Sure," he mutters.

Twisting back in my seat, I face the river again, uncertain why I've asked him. Unclear what I expected in his answer.

He clears his throat. "Have you?"

Have I? Have I ever done anything beyond what my family has come to expect of me? There was that blip in the past, but I don't talk about it all these years later. From then, I've buried myself in work, desperate to prove myself. Eager to outrun my decisions.

I don't answer the stranger, only offer a shrug, narrowing my eyes at the river. Without looking at him, I feel his gaze on the side of my face.

Silence fills the seats between us, but the race of the river grows louder. Or maybe my heart is finally settling, the rush no longer pulses in my ears, allowing other noises to intrude.

Like the rustle as his body shifts, even though he is several feet away from me.

The scrape of his heels on the cement beneath his feet.

The creak of the chair under his weight.

He clears his throat again. Then he stands and the plastic legs of his chair drag over the stone patio.

Sound surrounds me.

And something inside me doesn't want him to walk away. A man I don't know, and isn't offering conversation, is someone I wish wouldn't leave me alone with my rambling thoughts.

The waitress returns as the hunky stranger passes before me without a word. I reach for the tall glass of Coke on her tray while my gaze follows his retreat. He's tall as I suspected. My eyes trail down his solid back, hook on the thickness of his leather belt, and then fall to his backside.

Nice.

"Want to run a tab?" The waitress's question pulls me back to my seat.

I shake my head.

"I'll be back, then." She leaves to retrieve my receipt and I stare out at the water again, feeling a weird hollowness from the absence of an intriguing stranger and the emptiness of the space he left behind.

Within minutes, another man arrives and takes the chair beside me despite three other vacant ones. I hardly glance up at him.

"Beautiful day, eh?" His voice isn't nearly as appealing as the man who just walked away.

With a dismissive nod, I sip at my drink and hum a response. The space to my left is populated with people lingering at patio tables. The waitress will be back momentarily. I'm not under any immediate threat, but I'm strangely uncomfortable with this man sitting a little too close to me and I don't want to talk to him.

Call it female intuition.

"Come here often?"

Turning in his direction, I take in his red-rimmed eyes and thick jowls. His lips are moist in an unappealing way. I hold still despite the shiver trickling down my spine.

I shake my head and reach for my phone which I'd set face down on the armrest. Maybe my room is finally ready. Still, I hate feeling like I need to walk away when I was here first. I don't want to hide in my room because this man is too close. I don't want to give up the desire to relax and a will to chill.

Not that I was chilling. Seconds ago, I'd been a chatterbox asking questions I hadn't expected to be answered by a different stranger.

Had I just driven off the other man? Had I disturbed his peaceful moment? Did he think I was hitting on him?

The truth smacks me in the forehead.

I stare at my phone, feeling bad for having chased him away, or potentially making him uncomfortable.

The man beside me now leans over his armrest, upper body shifting toward me and the fine hairs on my neck lift. I arch away from him, digging my side into the corner of my seat and hoping he'll take the hint. My eyes remain lowered, unfocused on the open screen of texts from my sisters.

"Let me buy you a drink."

I turn toward him, attempting to be polite, and lift my glass. "Thanks, but I'm good."

His eyes roam my face and lower toward my chest. Quickly, I turn away. My breasts are large for my small frame. A curse or a blessing is debatable at times. The force of his stare has me shifting in my seat, adjusting my sweater which doesn't expose any skin, but still, I tug at the material as if it will disguise my physique.

In my peripheral vision, a presence draws near, and I glance up to see the original stranger returning. His eyes catch on mine, and I hold that whiskey gaze. He walks with determination, boots thudding on the cement pavement. His attention doesn't leave my face. I should look away and yet I can't seem to pull my gaze from his.

He reaches my chair. "Sweet thing." With his eyes focused on mine, speaking a language I can't read, he lowers before me, knees creaking as he balances on his haunches. With my phone still in my hand, as if it's a shield to protect me from the stranger sitting too close to me, this man reaches for my other wrist. He gazes at me as he lifts my arm and twists it the slightest bit. The lazy sweep of his thumb over the tender skin of my inner wrist settles the quake I hadn't known was present. Then his mouth presses there. His lips linger. His eyes hold. A new vibration develops, one rippling up my arm and into my chest, like the rapid flapping of dragonfly wings, hovering in mid-air. The buzz is a pleasantly welcome effect of his kiss.

Heat rushes over my face.

I don't understand what exactly is happening here until the man on my right grunts and hefts his body out of the chair beside me. He stalks past my sudden savior, who is still watching me, holding my eyes like I'm a prisoner to his will.

And suddenly, I want to go anywhere he'll take me.

2

Playlist: "Sweet Thing" – Hozier (Van Morrison cover)

[Thad]

I don't know what possessed me to look back at her.

Sitting there, taking a moment to collect my thoughts, her small frame collapsed in that chair like she was an elephant instead of a mouse of a woman who couldn't weigh more than a buck-fifty. Her features were delicate. Her breasts stacked.

And I shouldn't have been looking at her.

Have you ever done something completely out of character?

She had no idea the things I'd done in my lifetime. The places I'd been. The roads I'd traveled.

The most recent journey could have been life threatening, but thankfully, the final prognosis had been positive. Life was still ahead of me.

Coming here had been a momentary reprieve for what I was about to face next. Plus, I needed to check on the cabin. My grandmother wanted me to make sure things were in order. The cabin was one of many real estate investments she owned in these mountains. She was a wily woman at ninety, always saving her pennies for the future while sinking dollars into places for her retirement.

She's been retired for three decades.

All thoughts of Gran had shattered when that woman plopped down three chairs away from me. I'd wished I'd had more to say to her, but I was a man of few words. She kind of crashed into that chair, making her sudden presence known. Except her presence felt like a quiet storm; one slowly tumbling in to cool off a warm day. I wanted to speak but I was tongue-tied by the angle of her neck as she rested her head against the seatback. Her face tipped toward the sunshine. Her skin looked soft, tempting even, and my lips twitched with desire to explore the smooth expanse. In the flash of a glance, I'd noticed the blue in her eyes, alluring and bright, and full of hidden promise.

I should have answered her question with some truth. Only, I'd had a little too much honesty lately.

Still, I looked back once I'd topped the stairs leading to the gift shop. My room for the night was a lodger's cabin on the other side of the parking lot. The main hotel had been booked when I pulled up earlier in the day. The space seemed excessive for such a short stay, but I took it.

One night.

With my eyes focused on her, her shoulders were suddenly hunched forward, focus aimed at her phone. A man had taken a seat beside her, aggressively leaning toward her. She pulled away from him, raising her glass in a dismissive way. Maybe she was toasting something he'd said. Giving him a *cheers* in celebration. However, the angle of her body suggested she wasn't interested in him.

And it shouldn't be my problem.

The waitress who'd taken my drink order earlier nears and I hold up my card. "Put her soda on my tab, too." I nod in the direction of the woman who holds her phone.

Why isn't she looking at the river like she had been when I was seated near her? Why isn't she enjoying the fresh air and the soothing sound? Her body language answers my questions, and I return toward her, leaving my credit card with the waitress for the moment.

Something extreme. Something no one would expect of you.

I'd answered her that I had done extreme things in my life. However, as my feet carried me back down the stairs, I wasn't certain I'd ever done anything crazier than what I was about to do. Damsels in distress were not my forte. I didn't know what my type was anymore. The last thing I needed, or wanted to do, was become involved with someone.

Still, something about this woman called to me, or at least, the way she was clearly trying to avoid the guy beside her spoke volumes.

Then her gaze hit mine, and like metal pulled to a magnet, I couldn't turn away. Those blue eyes were sky worthy and ocean deep.

She didn't flinch when I lowered before her. Didn't stir when I cupped her wrist. She didn't slap me when I kissed her tender skin.

Her eyes locked on mine, holding me like a huntress scoped in on her prey.

Bang. My heart staggered. My lips tingled. Her smile froze me in place.

"Thank you," she whispers as the too-close-to-her-man hustles away behind me.

"You look like trouble," I mutter.

"The best kind." Her eyes widen, surprised maybe by her own words. Then she giggles, sweet and girlish, while the fine lines by her eyes and mouth suggest she isn't a child. Her body certainly says she's all woman. And her acorn-colored hair would look pretty wrapped around my hand as I tip her head back and kiss her neck.

"I don't know where that came from," she admits once the tinkling of her laughter settles.

"You looked uncomfortable."

She shrugs. "Just a little. I was getting ready to leave if he didn't."

"You here on your own?" My brows pinch. A pretty thing like her shouldn't be traveling solo.

"Work thing." Her shoulder shifts.

"That isn't what I asked."

She hesitates a moment while I'm still caging her in, hands resting on the armrests, bracing my upper body over her. For a moment, I wonder how she'd look if I lowered to my knees, tugged off her jeans, and spread her thighs. An inhale from that kiss told me she smells citrusy and sweet. I bet she's tangy in other places.

How long has it been since I've tasted such sweetness? How long has it been since someone wrapped their lips around my dick? If I press off this chair, standing to my full height, she's going to get a sight she probably doesn't want to see, because behind my zipper my body is reacting in a visceral way to her. And I'm relieved at the thrill tightening my balls.

"I'm only here for the night," she says.

Those words are hard-rock ballad lyrics to my ears. When was the last time— *It doesn't matter*.

The next words out of my mouth aren't what I expected to say any more than I expected to rush to her rescue. "Take a ride with me."

"A ride?" One brow arches, emphasizing a gleam of brightness in her crystal-water blue eyes. She's cute in a pixie sort of way. My fingers twitch as I study her hair, wanting to feel those waves and curl them around my fist, take a turn at her neck, then her jaw and her lips. I'd linger on her skin before I'd take a nip of her soft flesh.

And I need to settle my thoughts if I want her to spend some time with me.

"On my bike."

"You haven't even told me your name." She snorts. Not the most attractive sound, but still . . . cute. "And I just tackled The Tail of the Dragon, so I think I'm all set."

It's my turn for a brow to tweak upward. "You rode the Tail?" That road can be unforgiving. I've known a few bikers that didn't complete the run and graced the Iron Dragon—a statue of bike parts—in a show of shame. I also know a man or two who didn't survive the highway because of stupidity.

"Drove my Jeep down it."

I huff, tickled by the bravado in her tone.

"Don't knock it. Remember? Doing something out of character. I'm afraid of heights." The admission comes too easily. The strength in her voice almost negates her fear.

"We need to continue that wild side streak, then," I tease, lowering to my haunches again. My knees crack as I squat. My boots support my backside. My body isn't made for this position but I'm not ready to separate from her. I want her on the back of my bike.

"Don't mock me." Her lower lip pouts. The expression is another version of her cuteness. She's flirty despite her attempts at putting me in my place.

"You can call me Roadster." The name feels foreign after all this time. "Just a little ride, sweet thing. Down to the dam and back." *The Fugitive* was filmed not too far from here. I love the dam and haven't been there yet today.

She hesitates, tipping her head to the side. "Let me see your driver's license."

I tilt my head. "You don't believe I'm old enough to drive?" With plenty of years behind me at forty-five, my driving record is perfect. There are worse things in my past.

She laughs again, lyrical and sweet. *Damn, she's cute.*

"Not for your age. For protection."

My brow hitches again but I reach for my wallet. A different form of protection is in there only because my cousin suggested I start carrying condoms again, like a zealous teen.

Snagging my license from my fingers, she hardly looks at the information before snapping a picture with her phone.

"Hey." Instantly, I tug the small rectangle back and return it to the leather holder.

"I'm texting my sisters. If something happens to me, they'll know who I was last seen with." She quickly types and closes out of the messaging app, giving me a look like she's pleased with her smart caution.

I scoff. "Afraid I'm the murdering type?" I might have killed a man for less in my past, but I wasn't interested in hurting this fiery spitball before me. I just wanted a little time with her.

"Now that you mention it, I might be." Her crooked smile suggests otherwise.

Are we really doing this? Am I actually putting a cute-as-fuck stranger on the back of my bike?

She holds out her hand. "Lindee Fox."

Since I wrist-kissed her, I'd say we're past the formality, but I take her hand and don't let go. "Well, Lindee Fox. Let's take a little road trip."

"Pun intended." She leans forward, and I stand. Damn knees cracking again. Still holding my hand, her fingers feel tiny in my palm but not small. Nope, this little wisp of a woman isn't an elephant, but she's definitely a force larger than her frame. Her name says it all. She's a vixen, tempting me to do something completely out of character. At least, out of character for the past thirteen plus years.

And the heat crackling up my arm reiterates what I've already suggested.

She's going to be trouble.

3

Playlist: "Born to Be Wild" - Steppenwolf

[Lindee]

"Wait." I stop us both the second my fingers touch the ring on his. "Are you married?"

Is a perfect stranger going to give me an honest answer? I'm typically a good judge of character. Hence my apprehension about the man sitting too close to me on the patio. Still, eying Roadster, I wonder what his story is. Something inside me whispers he's trustworthy when I don't need to trust him. Trust is for long-term relationships, which I don't have. I only need this truth.

He pauses, releasing my hand, as he looks down at his. He flexes his fingers, splaying them apart. His knuckles are scarred, a sign of both strength and manual labor.

"This?" He swallows hard. "This ring belonged to my Pop." He glances up at me, whiskey eyes dimming a bit. Sadness answers a question I don't ask. The past tense in his statement hints his grandfather isn't alive anymore. Neither is mine.

Grandad was the only father figure I had, and I loved him like the dad who had been missing all my life.

While I sympathize with the sorrow in his eyes, with his loss of someone special, we don't need to share our sad stories. He's offering me a motorcycle ride, and I'd like to take the trip. He's right. Might as well continue to entertain my impulsive side.

When he tips his head, I follow him. His strides are longer than mine and I walk fast to keep up. As we near the stairs leading up from the patio, he pauses and sets his hand on my lower back. The waitress approaches us with his credit card, and I reach for mine tucked into my back pocket. I'd left my entire purse in the Jeep.

"I got it," he states.

"You didn't have to do that."

"Don't ever do anything unless I want to."

The philosophy is one I might have lived by for a little too long. The list of regrets in my life might be short but the depth is deep and painful.

We cross through the gift shop and leave the lodge. As we stride into the parking lot, I'm suddenly second guessing my decision. Is this smart? Is this safe? Then again, I've lived the safe life too long.

Never staying in one place is safe. Never getting attached is another.

Roadster taps the seat of a giant two-wheeled mean machine that was a study of dark leather and polished chrome. I'm not a motorcycle aficionado, but I recognize the Harley Davidson logo. This bike screams power and speed. A hint of gasoline, oil, and something sweet lingers in the air around it. Roadster picks up a helmet and hands it to me.

"What about you?" I ask.

"We aren't going far. I'll be careful."

A pause falls between us.

"Ever been on a bike?"

I shake my head, wondering once again what I'm doing, why I'm doing it. A tremor ripples up my body, but I don't want to be afraid. It's time for a few changes in the life of Lindee Fox. Not that a motorcycle ride will redefine mine, but a new journey always begins by facing forward and skipping the rearview mirror.

Roadster nods. "Okay. A few rules. Hold onto me. Lean with me, not in opposition." He tips his body to demonstrate his point. "I'll keep it slow, since it's your first time."

The statement sends another ripple through my body, one sharp with the sexual crackle in the innuendo. Or is that my imagination? His voice is a sensual glide over my skin. Could a man like him go slow? Be patient? Neither seems important as I try to focus on what he's saying not the way it's said, like a rough caress over sensitive folds.

How long has it been since I've been touched by someone else in such a place? *Too long.*

And now my brain is thinking other things, like if certain parts of his body match the stature of his height or the length of his fingers. There's something said about a man with big hands. Or is that large feet?

"Lindee?"

"Yeah." I shake my head, flinging away all thoughts of parts on him I'll never see.

"You still with me?"

"I'm still with you." For reasons I can't explain, I trust this stranger who interrupted an awkward situation by the river. In a sense, he's giving me a second chance after I'd felt guilty for rushing *him* off.

Roadster slings a thick leg over his bike and then holds out a hand. Taking it, he firmly hangs on to me as I struggle to tuck myself behind him.

"Keep your feet on those pegs. I don't want you getting burned, sweet thing."

Too late. Even a short, steady ride with this man is going to scar me in a way I can't define. With my arms sliding around his solid waist, he tugs at my forearms, encouraging me to hold tighter.

The engine roars to life and the seat beneath me rumbles. As my thighs press at the outside of his, I hope I don't embarrass myself because of the sudden vibration against a sensitive spot.

He glances over his shoulder and yells above the engine. "Hold on, sweetheart."

He had no idea how dangerous it might be to hold too tight to him.

However, as he rolls forward, gliding out of the parking spot and leaning as we turn before hitting the road, the thought disappears.

I'm a lost soul and I've never been found because I don't hold onto anything but memories.

4

Playlist: "Take Your Time" – Sam Hunt

[Thad]

When I asked Lindee to take a ride with me, I didn't think she'd agree. I hoped but didn't know for certain. I was out of practice at asking a woman for things. Things I wanted. Things I needed.

With this sweet thing on the back of my bike, I suddenly felt free of everything. Every worry. Every issue. Every thought. We breezed along the curving highway, past the dam I initially sought. We'd catch it on the way back. For now, I just wanted to ride with my bike beneath me and a woman at my back. Her thighs outlining mine. Her arms around my waist, holding onto me like I could be her salvation. Her head on my shoulders, at ease behind me.

The forest around us was still relatively stark, not quite

completely awake from a winter's nap but signs of impending spring were everywhere. Soon, this road would be shadowed by a lush canopy of greenery and a sharp scent of pine and earth. A new season would bloom.

That's how I saw my future. Change was coming, and I was relieved, like a fucking bud on a tree ready to open and unfurl its leaves.

But none of that was on my mind as I drove us along the North Carolina side of US-129. Lindee had already mentioned she'd been on the Tail, and I wasn't looking for something that involved high concentration and elevated skill to master. I just wanted to ride.

With the powerful vibration of machinery beneath me. With wheels spinning, carrying me away.

At some point, Lindee's arms slowly slipped free of me. Her thighs tightened instead, squeezing the outsides of mine as if to steady her in place. Then her arms spread wide, and she tipped back her head, letting out a rich, melodic laugh. A mix of battle cry and freedom scream.

Damn, she was a dream.

Her easy trust in me makes me smile.

In my rearview mirror, I watch her hands dance in the wind before wrapping around me, quick and tight again, like a bird folding its wings to its chest, protecting something.

That something was me.

If I was a less sensible man, I would have kept driving. Driven until the road ended. Until Lindee was tired of me, but I didn't want her exhausted. Not yet.

Pulling off on a narrow strip along the road, I slow to a stop.

Her arms stiffen and I'm quick to rub my hand over her wrist and dig my fingers between hers in reassurance. I don't want her to be afraid of me.

If anything, I'm frightened of her. I'd been with the same

woman for more than a decade. Touching someone new, feeling her skin beneath my palm is foreign and soothing. Sweet even.

"Why did we stop?" she yells over the engine, still rumbling loud and angry beneath us.

Glancing at her over my shoulder, I state, "As far as we go, we'll have to travel back."

She nods.

"I promised we'd stop at the dam, and we flew by it earlier." I pause, disappointed that we need to turn back. "Still with me?"

"Still with you." Her confident response is another show of trust and the extra squeeze she gives my midsection secures the bond.

Cautiously turning us around, I head back toward the dam, not wanting to rush but also unable to keep my Harley slow. Before I know it, Cheoah Dam is in sight. We park and Lindee braces on my shoulders to hike herself off the bike.

Although her feet are on steady ground, she wobbles. "Whoa"

I catch her waist at the same time she reaches for my shoulder again.

"Shaky legs?" I tease. "First ride can have that effect."

"The vibration. I think I might have—" The abrupt halt of her words and a deep redness on her cheeks tells me everything. It's a little unlikely, but I'd once heard a woman can orgasm from the rumble of a bike.

Is she that sensitive?

My dick leaps to life at the notion. The sensation is a relief. Everything down there still works after all.

With Lindee's eyes locked on mine, I slowly smile. I'd love to know more about her and a spontaneous orgasm but the heat on her cheeks doesn't allow me to embarrass her. She's too sweet and I want to learn more about what sets her off . . . later.

Without releasing Lindee's waist, I nod in the direction of the dam. "Let's have a look."

Swinging my leg off my bike, I press my hand to Lindee's lower back, guiding her forward to a spot for better viewing.

The thunderous sound of water swells as we approach, and we pause to take in the magnitude of a structure holding such a powerful resource back.

"Harrison Ford made that jump look easy." Lindee whistles in awe of the famous actor and his daredevil feat in *The Fugitive*.

"Not certain a man could really survive a jump like that." I hate to burst her bubble, but a dummy was tossed over the edge, not a stuntman.

For a moment, Lindee appears transfixed by the water plummeting from the dam and pounding into the lake below with an angry roar.

"Next to a fear of heights, bodies of water scare me," she says, still transfixed on the powerful water pooling below us. Her voice is low and I'm not certain I've heard her correctly at first.

"Nothing to be afraid of here." I rub a hand up her spine and squeeze the back of her neck once.

"You never know what's beneath the surface." Her statement is hollow, utter fear laced in the admission.

I stare at her while she stares at the unrelenting river colliding with the pool below. White cap waves riot as water crashes against water.

Lindee visibly shakes herself. Shoulders wiggling, eyes closing, before she glances over at me and timidly smiles. "It is beautiful, though." Wherever her thoughts went, she let them go.

Beautiful *and dangerous*, she doesn't say, but I read it in her momentarily sad eyes. Then her smile grows, and those eyes flick back to light and easy.

She's beautiful and going to be dangerous for me. Because a woman like her isn't someone you easily leave behind.

Turning her head, she breaks the gaze we held. "Should we head back?"

I'd like to think I hear hesitation in the question. A need to stay a little longer. Maybe run away together. The thought is ridiculous, but hadn't I already thought it? Could I ever ride off into the sunset and leave all I had behind?

Already did that once. Wasn't likely to happen again.

Change might be on the horizon, but it didn't mean an absence of responsibility.

Still, I wasn't ready for my time with Lindee to end even when I offer, "Sure. We can head back."

Swallowing around a thickness in my throat, I wave for Lindee to lead the way back to my bike, watching her ass move in those skinny jeans. The soft sweater slips from her shoulder and her low boots shouldn't be sexy but somehow complete the package.

The one I want to unwrap.

Can I pull off a one-night stand? It's been a long time since something like that has happened.

Then again, isn't that what change means? Something new? Starting fresh?

Swiping a palm down my face, I will myself to chill.

Escorting Lindee back to the bike, I lug my leg over the seat and catch her at the waist again before she hops on.

"Thank you." My gaze locks on her eyes. Damn, a man could get lost in that sky-blue color.

As her lush mouth curls, I watch in wonder, curious how she might taste. Curious how those lips would feel wrapped around a part of me.

Fuckin' stop.

"The pleasure has been all mine." With a wide grin, she places her hand on my shoulder and climbs behind me. Her arms give me another tight squeeze, like a back hug, but as we take off for the hotel, she loosens just the slightest when I really want her to hold onto me a little longer.

ONCE WE'VE PARKED, I follow Lindee toward the main entrance although my cabin is in the opposite direction. She steps toward the small gift shop which we'd have to walk through on our way to the back patio.

Say something. From all my years of singlehood, I should be better at this, but it's been so long. Asking a woman to have a drink. Asking her if she'd like to share a bed. I'm fucking tongue-tied.

Lindee has this cool-woman vibe, mixed with it-ain't-gonna-happen, and I should be walking away. Still, I follow her.

"Souvenir?" I question as she picks up a silver cuff bracelet with a little clasp.

"Retail therapy," she teases. "Actually, I always purchase a memento on an adventure."

"Isn't that a souvenir?" I laugh.

"Nah. Souvenirs you stick on a shelf and never think about or stuff in a box in the back of the closet. A memento marks the occasion as something special, unique. And something functional like a bracelet will remind me of where I've been. Who I've met." She gazes up at me.

The color of her sweater enhances her eyes. Summer sky. Deep sea. Sapphires. Poets could write poems about that color and all I can muster is they match springtime bluebells which will soon bloom.

"So, what's the next adventure for you?" Curiosity gets the best of me.

She shrugs. "Never know where the road will lead." A laugh follows her declaration. The melody is like a gentle creek in comparison to the rush of water falling from the dam. "I make a habit of never looking in the rearview mirror." Her hands come up and motion forward like a person on a tarmac directing a plane. "Only face forward."

Huh. If only it felt that simple. The road ahead of me was bumpy but the one in the rearview mirror had practically been a field of land mines. I was looking forward to a smoother ride ahead despite a few predictable speed bumps.

Lindee turns for the cashier station and makes her purchase. She dismisses a bag and twists toward me. I've followed her once more.

"Help me put it on?" She pulls up her sleeve, exposing a delicate wrist with a semi-colon tattoo. My eyes lift, seeking her face. Does this symbol mean what I think it means?

Gripping her wrist, I swipe my thumb over her tender skin and the blue river of veins. No scars feel present.

"It's not what you think," she says, watching my thumb trace over the ink. "And I don't owe you an explanation."

I blink. Her words aren't harsh but hold a sharp warning. She might have taken a ride with me, but she doesn't owe me her history. Hell, I certainly don't want to share mine. I just wanted some time with her. Still, I'm shaken by the possibility of what this tattoo could mean.

Lindee holds the bracelet from the underside and my fingers shake as I fumble with the delicate clasp before the latch catches. She flips her wrist again and straightens the silver cuff.

"A dragonfly," I chuff. Not exactly what I'd expect but then again everything about her has been unexpected.

"It's perfect. I just drove the Tail of the Dragon. Plus, dragonflies are notorious around rivers. They hover for a bit and then flit away, like me." She spreads her fingers and waves her hand higher and higher in the air mimicking the insect. "They're a symbol of transformation. A change is coming."

We both stare at the metal wrapped around her wrist engraved with the double-winged creature.

"Perfect," she whispers.

She certainly is. And I wasn't ready to let her flit away from me.

Not yet.

5

———————

Playlist: "Chasing You" – Morgan Wallen

[Lindee]

After Roadster saw the tattoo, his demeanor shifted. His eyes couldn't pull away from the ink until I tucked my new treasure beneath my sweater sleeve.

As I told him, it wasn't what he thought, but I didn't owe him an explanation.

Harris wasn't someone I easily discussed or often shared with anyone, least of all a stranger.

With the refreshing ride behind us and this awkward moment between us, the time felt right to part ways.

"I should probably see if my room is ready."

Roadster nods again and points toward the registration desk.

"Actually, I need to grab my bag from my car."

He stills, glancing at me with those whiskey eyes that'd

make an alcoholic crave a drink. I don't even like the amber liquor, but I'd sip if he asked me.

Or maybe not.

Thoughts of Harris are a good reminder it's time to stop sleeping around. Time to settle down. Time to invest in me.

"I'll walk you out." His offer is sweet. He hasn't taken my hint that we should separate and I'm almost relieved, but I don't know how to ask him to linger a little longer.

Should we grab a drink? Should I just ask him to my room?

I'm not certain I can handle just one night with this man. Despite his rough and tumble appearance, he has deep devotion and cuddle commitment written on him and that's something I never allow myself to read. I love a good romance novel, but the real thing is not for me.

Then again, his quiet calm and rugged appearance hints that he's not a cuddler and I'm simply projecting on him what I've been struggling to ignore for the past few years.

I'm lonely.

That's what a sense of wanderlust and work-related travel hope to cure. Never stick in one place and the loneliness can't settle in.

In silence, we walk toward the parking lot. The sunshine and warm breeze of the day has drastically shifted to cold air and gloomy clouds. I open the hatch on my Jeep and remove a small bag, tugging it up my shoulder.

"Looks like rain," he says, lifting his head and glancing up at the sky, and that's my cue that we should part ways. Weather isn't a topic; it's a filler.

Too bad, as I've enjoyed every second with him.

"I have a cabin up the hill." He hitches his thumb over his shoulder, emphasizing the single standing structures on the opposite side of the parking lot. Is that an invitation or simply a statement?

When he doesn't say more, I point at the main building. "I have a room in the hotel."

As if the heavens realize this moment is steeped in ridiculousness, the sky opens, and rain begins.

And still, we don't move.

Our eyes lock. Our feet planted.

He watches me and then he tugs his sweater off his head. A sane woman might shout over the deluge, questioning what he's doing, but I'm mesmerized by the appearance of a collarless flannel shirt beneath the outerwear which he quickly unbuttons.

Suddenly, he's bare-chested in the cold rain and wrapping his shirt around me. I'm tongue-tied at the display of bright ink down both his arms and the rivulets of water cascading over his skin.

"You're getting wet," he shouts.

He has no idea. I'm soaked in places the rain won't reach.

With his shirt draped over my shoulders, his hands remain a second before he slides them to the side of my neck. His thumb presses at my chin, forcing me to look up as he's taller than me.

"Today." His Adam's apple bobs. "The pleasure was all mine."

I hold my breath waiting on a kiss.

A kiss that never comes as he releases my throat and steps backward. "Get inside," he demands, staring at me with nostrils flaring and chest heaving.

Everything in me suggests I toss myself at him, climb him like the tree he is and never let go.

Then lightning strikes, illuminating the sky and rattling the earth. It's his place or mine and I make a drowning woman's decision.

I run away as if I can dodge raindrops and heartache.

Once inside my room, I collapse against the door. I hardly remember registering but my hands shook as I took the old-fashion metal key attached to a plastic hexagon with the hotel's name imprinted on it.

Shit. I tap my head once against the heavy wood behind me before venturing farther into the room. Dropping my bag to the side of the bed, I slip his shirt from my shoulders, inhale the rain-soaked scent and strong woodsy fragrance.

Why did I run? Why can't I stay still?

Shaking off the questions, I set his shirt over the heater which has kicked on. The day might have warmed up, but the mountain night will be cold. I'm chilly and I can't seem to stop the sudden tremble, a sign I've walked away from something big. Or something that could have been.

Needing a shower to settle my nerves and warm my skin, I enter the bathroom. My thoughts scatter when I'm under the hot spray. A shower meditation that focuses my senses on the water cascading over me, calms me a little bit.

I'd said I was afraid of water. He saw the semi-colon on my wrist. But I didn't want to think of Harris. Not now. Not here. I wanted to linger a little longer in what could have been with a tall, sexy silver stranger. The shower only reminds me of the rain sluicing over his broad shoulders, firm chest and tight abs, and the possibility—the lost opportunity—to kiss a man during a storm.

The desire pooling low in my belly and the ache between my legs could easily be taken care of by myself, but I don't. I savor this fantasy of him, of us, and the sensual thunder momentarily rumbling around us.

When the water grows cold too quickly, I exit the shower and head for his shirt. The heater has done the job of drying it and I slip the well-worn fabric over my shoulders again, buttoning up the middle. The item is huge on me, so I roll the sleeves then comb my fingers through my long, damp hair.

I'd just placed the towel on the hook inside the bathroom when a knock comes to the door. I'd ordered a burger to be sent to the room when I signed in, although I wasn't certain I had the stomach to eat.

Flinging open the door with not a care for my attire, I freeze at the sight before me.

"You," I whisper.

His chest heaving. His hair soaked. His arms stretch from side to side of the door jamb, as if holding himself back. "Look me in the eye and tell me to walk away and I will."

I've barely shaken my head, signaling I can't do it. I can't tell him to leave. And he's on me.

Solid hands are on the side of my neck. His forehead presses against mine. And then his lips, hesitate at first, as if dipping his toe into water, testing the temperature. Measuring the river rushing inside me as safe, his mouth opens and the sweep of his tongue sets off a waterfall of desire, rippling straight down my center to a place already raging with wetness.

I'm moved backward and the door is kicked shut with his mouth still on mine. We travel a few steps before he stops and pulls back.

"You." It's a single word full of so much meaning. A definition I don't need to know but somehow understand. He's going to wreck me in the best kind of way. Despite all the promises I've made myself, that I wouldn't have another one-night stand or fool around with a short-term someone, my vow rips into tiny shreds and blows away in the nonexistent wind.

"You're wearing my shirt." He stares at me. Hands slip from my neck to my shoulders and then down to my wrists which he spreads to open my arms and take a better view of me.

"I wasn't ready to let you go."

Those whiskey eyes of his burn a dark amber before his

mouth is on mine again. His kiss is the drowning I fear in deep water and the danger beneath the surface, and at the same time, he feels like a breath of fresh air after resurfacing. I'm not gulping or struggling but melting into him.

We kiss hungry and deep. Chests heave, fingers roam when another knock comes to the door.

"Expecting someone?" He pulls away.

"Date with a burger."

Roadster releases me and I walk to the door. A young man enters the room, sets the tray on the dresser and stands aside. I'm headed for my purse for a tip when Roadster hands over a bill. He nods at the kid who promptly exits.

"You didn't need to do that."

"And you shouldn't have answered the door like that."

Of all the misogynist things to say. I'll answer the door how I please, dressed how I please. "Like what?"

"Like you've been thoroughly kissed and ready to be fucked."

Well.

With eyes focused on me, he adds, "Sweet thing, let me make you my fantasy tonight."

I hardly know this man and his fantasy could be anything, but there's something safe about him. I feel it in my toes and the way he's hooked on my eyes, almost begging me to be his.

"Okay," I whisper. Not because I'm frightened. Because I'm scared out of my mind that he'll be a dream come true for me, too.

He steps over to a small boudoir chair in the corner, takes a seat, and engulfs the tight space. Nodding at the burger on a tray, he asks, "Need to eat?"

Yes. Him. "Later."

The word gives him permission to begin whatever it is he wants from me. "Come sit on the edge of the bed." He points at a spot opposite him.

On shaky legs, I climb the raised bed and straighten his oversized shirt.

"Unbutton to your belly."

My heart hammers as I take my time to open the buttons to my waist. With the rise and fall of my chest, one side slips off my shoulder, but I catch it by bending my elbow and crossing my arm over my breasts.

He shifts in the chair. Elbow on the rest. Fingers raised to trace his lips. "Did you touch yourself in the shower?"

Shaking my head, I squeeze my legs together.

"Let me see what you'd do, sweetheart. Start at the top."

The rugged tone of his voice and the subtle command heighten my arousal.

Have I ever put on a show for a man? I can't recall and it doesn't matter as the heat in his eyes makes me burn to please him.

Sliding an arm across my upper chest, I slip my hand inside his shirt, brushing back the material to expose one breast. Gently, I cup myself, giving the achy swell a squeeze before slipping up to the nipple, and pinching the hard, peaked nip.

I've never been so turned on in my life.

His reaction—a hand clenched on his thigh—is even more empowering. He holds himself back, showing great restraint while his blatant stare confirms his desire to touch me. He hisses, watching me, wanting me.

Releasing the heavy swell, I slip my hand lower, taking my time to smooth over my belly and disappear beneath the material covering my lap.

"Spread your legs," he whispers, growly and rugged. Widening my knees scoots me to the edge of the bed. The tails of his shirt fall between my legs, covering me.

"Are you wearing anything underneath my shirt?"

"Nope." The breathy answer has an extra hitch as my fingers delicately brush over sensitive flesh.

Am I really doing this for a stranger? *No, this is for me.* He's giving me the power to please myself while his hungry eyes devour me.

"Let me see." His rough voice is low, like the soft waters of the river outside, rushing over smooth boulders. Desperate for movement, struggling with the speed.

With my opposite hand I tug a portion of his shirt up my thigh, but my other hand is still hidden beneath the warm flannel. The section fallen from my shoulder slips to the crook of my arm again, fully exposing a breast.

"You're a goddamn fantasy, Lindee." Every word is a punctuation on how I'm mesmerizing him when I'm the one under a spell. I'm so turned on I can hardly breathe.

"Tell me you want me to taste you."

"I want you to taste me."

It's surprising how quickly a man of his size can move out of a fragile chair. With stunning grace, he falls to his knees in front of me. He's the perfect height to bury his face between my thighs and inhale at my flannel-draped center.

"I'm a starving man," he whispers to intimate places. Then thick hands cover my thighs and press the material upward, revealing me to him. He closes his eyes, and inhales deeply again, like he smells something delicious.

When his tongue laps along my seam, I nearly combust. The air around me crackles like the lightning outside the windows, illuminating the sky. My flesh prickles with jolts of pleasure and shocks of delight. The zap of sexual desire causes me to fall back, catching myself on my hands to keep me steady. When all I really want is to fall apart against his mouth.

He's a rush of energy with his fingers dipping into me and his tongue exploring. I soften into the wonders of his mouth. The sensation is too much yet I never want it to end. Falling to my back, I lift my hips, eager for him to continue. To give me more. I'm out of my mind, drowning into a sweet abyss under the talent of his tongue, the sip of his lips, and the sounds of him taking what he wants from me.

When my body gives him what he's begged of me, I'm the one left hungry for more.

As he pulls away, I scramble upright with weak limbs. A single hand on his cheek tugs him upward, telling him I need him to stand. With the musky scent of me on his mouth, he leans in to kiss me as he moves to his full height.

I'm going to make him my fantasy next.

Unbuckling his belt and tugging at his zipper, the bulge in his pants begs me to make him mine. I shove at the sides of his pants, pushing his underwear down with it, and then glory and goodness is before me. He's a work of art, and I've studied a lot of male art over the years. He's a masterpiece.

Drawing my fingertip along his length, he hisses. As my fingers fist around him, he groans. I tug hard at his thick shaft and his hands come to the sides of my neck.

"It's been a long time."

His comment surprises me and I glance up to find his eyes focused on my hold.

"Tell me more of your fantasy."

"You." His whisper is rough. "You. Here." He thumbs my lips, tugging down the lower one.

"And here." He runs a fingertip between my breasts.

"And down here." His fingers tease my wet center.

Yeah, he's going to have it all and the pleasure is going to be all mine. Leaning forward, I lick around the crown of his length then press a kiss to the damp tip.

A strangled curse comes from him. I adjust my grip and then open wide, slowly taking him in. He jolts forward, rushing to the back of my throat and I jerk back.

"Sorry . . . just . . . sorry." Soothing fingers swipe into my wet hair and catch on the roughly combed strands. His fingers fist but he isn't guiding me so much as holding on, steadying himself, as I take control and suck him like a savored treat. He's gifting me his body and I want to play for a bit.

A few long and another uncontrolled thrust happen before he pulls free of my lips.

"Not in your mouth."

I understand what he means. I'm eager for him inside me as well.

While I sit on the bed, he gives me a little show, tugging off a fresh long sleeve T-shirt. No second shirt covers his body like the flannel I wear. His barrel-like chest is on display for my touch, and I press my palms over his warm skin and skim upward to toy with the hairs on his chest.

"I like that." River rushing over rocks again. The sound makes me shiver in a good way.

He kicks off his boots and removes his socks, then lowers his briefs and pants. I reach for the edge of his flannel on my body.

"Keep it on. I want to fuck you wearing my clothes." He pauses. "I want to think of this moment when I wear that shirt again. Smell you in the fabric. Feel you as it touches my skin."

Okay then.

For some reason, my gaze catches on that mammoth ring on his finger. "You're not married, right?"

"Already told you, I'm not." He doesn't hesitate in his response and reaches for the chunky, thick ring, tugging it off his finger and setting it on the stand beside the bed.

Then, he gently pushes at my chest, forcing me to my back. He climbs over me and straddles my ribcage, just below my breasts.

"Want to fuck you here." He drags a finger between my breasts which are both exposed as the material of his shirt slid open.

I watch as he places his heavy shaft in the valley between my breasts and then molds them together, wrapping his dick between the weight of them. His eyes close a second as he slides back and forth. I take over, holding myself for him to glide between. The position doesn't do much for me other than watching the euphoria on his face.

Then he reaches around his backside to touch me. Thick fingers rush inside me and slick out again. His thumb swipes at my clit.

"Oh God," I groan. What's happening here? What's he doing to me? I'm winding up again which never happens.

"You," he grunts. "This body." Praise is in the minimal words.

He removes his fingers and slides off my body, standing beside the bed a second before reaching for his pants.

Condom packets appear and he tosses them to the nightstand.

"Want you to ride me, sweetheart."

With a nod of consent, he climbs the bed, props himself up by pillows against the headboard and rolls on a condom. The display has me salivating. When I climb over him, he places his hands at my neck, and tugs me to him for a deep kiss. Despite the wet at my core and the strain of his length pressed beneath me, we kiss long and lazily before his hands come to my hips, guiding me up and then over his length. Taking him into me slowly, he stretches me like no one ever has.

"You," I stress. He's a fantasy. One I'll dream about for years after this night.

Once he's filled me to the hilt, we pause, and I take a breath. He's deep in this position, different and deliciously filling.

"Whenever you're ready." It's a hint he wants me to move, but he'll wait for me to adjust to him. I tip my hips upward while resting my forehead on his.

As I drag up his thick length, he groans. "Lindee." Awe. Shock. Bliss.

Down I go, drawing him into me and he grunts. Back and

forth, we move. Building up to be torn down. With his thumb on a sensitive nub and the tension in our movements, I'm going to crumble again.

"Roadster." I choke, breaking it into syllables.

"That's it, sweet thing. Give me everything."

I slam down on him, taking a moment to let loose a second wave. My fingers dig into his shoulders, as I arch back, glancing where he's disappeared inside me, joining us as one.

"Prettiest sight ever," he marvels.

I look up at him, finding him staring at the same spot before he meets my eyes. Then he's kissing me again, hard and desperate. A man on the edge of losing control.

With his mouth still on mine, he tugs me up and off him. I'm confused for a half a second before he's guiding me to spin, placing my back to his front. My gaze catches on a mirror opposite the bed.

Roadster is moving behind me, folding those powerful long legs underneath him and pressing me until I'm on all fours. Our eyes meet in the reflection.

"This okay?" His question is asked while his heavy length falls against my backside, nestling between the crack. Then he's sliding downward and notching his tip at my entrance.

"Yes." I'm nearly begging him to reenter my body. With a sharp surge, he rushes forward, and I catch myself, fingers fisting in the bed covers. Our gazes collide in the reflection once more before he's pulling back and thrusting forward. We speed up until the mattress is quaking, and the headboard rattles on the wall. He reaches around me, touching me again on oversensitive folds.

"I can't." I'm breathless. I've never come three times in a row.

"You will." He hammers into me, drilling in his demand until I break once more. Pure bliss. Then he stills, buried deep within me. Like the storm outside, he thunders a cry while his fingers dig into my hips, holding on as if lightning struck. He pulses and pumps and rains his release.

Then he collapses over me, smothering me against the mattress.

He slides left and rolls me right to face him. Once tugged to his chest, he wraps his arms around me, holding me tight against his heated skin.

"Lindee." He breathes out my name like he's memorizing it. "I'm going to need you again."

I chuckle into his chest. I don't know if I have more in me.

But when we shower together, he proves me wrong.

The night turns out to be memorable in more ways than one.

6

FOUR MONTHS LATER

Playlist: "Hotel California" – The Eagles

[Lindee]

"I bought a motel."

The Fox sisters have reunited through a video call and my announcement echoes through my computer screen like I've shouted it off a mountain.

Moments of silence follow filled with blank stares and blinking eyelids as Jane and Mae process what I've just announced.

Me, a business owner, when I hardly owned more than my Jeep.

"What?" Mae is the sister closest in age to me.

"Why?" Jane questions at the same time in her bossy oldest-sister tone.

My answer is multifold and difficult to explain. Since the start of a new year, I'd been feeling restless to settle down. An opportunity came up, I'd decided it was time to stop being a Wandering Wendy. Or in my case, *become* a Lingering Lindee.

"It's time to own my own place. Stop fixing up properties for others and make something for myself."

I'm hopeful both my sisters understand. Mae worked for years under her ex-husband's mismanagement of his family's landscaping company and eventually dug out her own corner of business in Mae's Flowers, a garden center. Jane has always worked in corporate America beneath others until she got under the skin and into the heart of her boss, who has since become her husband. Now, she's the economic development manager for an entire small town.

And both are happily in love. Something that is nothing more than a wispy memory for me now.

Via the camera on her iPad, Mae continues to watch me. She's the easygoing, life is all daisies, sibling, although her first marriage wasn't full of hearts and flowers. Jane is the more serious sister, taking on a mother-hen role when we were younger. Our personalities are the most similar as we're both strong-willed women.

I don't think I look like either of my sisters, but everyone claims we have the same blue eyes and brown hair. However, we're a sliding scale of earth tones for hair color, ranging from darkest in our eldest sibling, Garrett, to light acorn for me. My eye coloring is more sky than the sapphire depth of my sisters while Garrett, as the token male and only brother, possesses deep brown irises. Mae is shorter and curvier, while Jane is willowy, tall, and sleek.

And all this is to explain, that I don't feel I resemble anyone in my family physically, and I shouldn't.

"Where?" The sharp question from Jane snaps me from my comparison of our physical traits.

"About forty-minutes from Wrightwood." The small mountain town was perfect for hiking and fishing, plus close to a local ski hill with a pricey resort. I'm hopeful my little motel will be cost-efficient for ski enthusiasts and summer adventurers on a budget.

"You're moving to West Virginia?" Mae's shock doesn't surprise me. Of all the states I've been to, why West Virginia, right? But there's something comforting about the place where rolling hills turned to gentle mountains. Plus, I'll be closer to Jane who recently moved to West Virginia and started a family. Maybe Mae's issue is she lives in Michigan, which is quite a distance from here.

"It's beautiful." Waving toward the window, it's hard to miss the deep green trees and climbing peaks.

"Does this have anything to do with what happened four months ago?" Shrewdly, Jane narrows her eyes at me.

"My decision has nothing to do with him . . . er, that situation." I glare back at her. Of all people, Jane would understand. I'd made a colossal mistake. A sexually satisfying, flip my heart, make me feel invincible decision that popped like a child's balloon on sharp blades of grass.

"I still think you should have looked him up," Mae adds, shrugging.

When I sent my sisters an image of his driver's license, I'd hardly glanced at it myself. I was too busy taking the picture and then messaging my sisters to read the fine print of his name. When everything fell apart the next day, I opened my photo app, selected the last image, and tapped the trash can to delete him forever without another look at his stupidly handsome face.

I can be purposefully absentminded about things, especially when there are events or people I wish to forget.

That night had been a one-night stand. And oh boy, had I been stood up. I can still recall collapsing in the shower of the cabin-rental I was sharing with my sisters, scrubbing off his scent, his touch, and his memory.

If only that had been effective.

For some reason, that night just won't disappear from my mind.

"But ..." I sigh. "I can't say that night didn't give me perspective. It's time to settle down."

"You're getting married?" Mae's brows arch upward.

"Not that kind of settled. Or maybe it is that kind. I'm settling into me." I square my shoulders, wanting my sisters to understand. All their lives, they've had direction. Mae wanted to be a wife and a mother, and once she obtained those things, she dug another niche for herself and opened her own business. Jane has always climbed the corporate ladder, wanting a partnership at the top. Now, she's running an entire village and she's the boss. I have nothing to show for myself but a scattering of vacation spots across the continental states that I renovated but didn't retain as mine.

"Can you afford this?" Jane, ever the practical one, gives me a concerned look.

"Garrett is going to help." I didn't want to ask our eldest brother for a loan but Garrett's an investor by trade. He looked at the details of the purchase agreement and he offered financial assistance before I had to ask. In his words, it was a sound investment and for a small percentage in the future profits, he gave me a huge chunk of money to get started on the necessary renovations.

Garrett has also undergone some life changes in the past few years, splitting his time between California and Georgia with his wife, Dolores. He understood the need to have something for himself, not always being a part of someone else's business plan. Their future is starting to thrive.

"What can we do to help?" Mae slowly smiles, dismissing all concerns at the mention of Garrett.

"I have everything all set. I already have possession and I meet with a contractor next week." I pause, sighing. "In the purchase agreement there was only one stipulation. I had to use the previous owner's relative to do the construction work even though he doesn't live nearby. I had trouble connecting with him, but finally received an email that he'd meet me on Wednesday."

At first, I was a little nervous about this arrangement. Garrett even agreed it was an unusual request, but he'd researched the man's construction firm, and while small, it was reputable. The company had worked in a variety of locations in and around the Allegheny Mountains.

"What's the name of the place?" Mae asks, continuing to be easygoing about the project.

"What's its name?" Jane interjects, picking up her phone to do her own investigation.

"Mountain Motel."

Jane instantly cringes at the lack of originality. "It sounds like a rent-by-the-hour place."

"I might need some marketing assistance." Hopefully, the request will bring Jane on board with my future endeavor.

"I like it." Mae gives me a warm smile. "It's right to the point."

"Who's the construction firm?" Jane asks again. Her brother-in-law is also in construction locally.

"I don't know the firm's name, but the owner's last name is spelled R-h-o-d-e, pronounced like road, the kind you drive on. His first name is Thaddeus." The name rolls off my tongue like a decadent treat, one full of sugar and capable of clogging the valves to my heart but deliciously savored. "He goes by Thad."

I've only heard his name a few times but each time it sounded more and more familiar, as if I should recognize it somehow. I mentally see it typed out in simple font, but I can never quite make out where I might have read the name before.

Thaddeus Rhode.

Well, Thad, you and I are about to have an adventure together.

7

———————

Playlist: "Unforgettable" – Nat King Cole

[Thad]

I wasn't keen on a project in West Virginia, but my grandmother deemed the job necessary. She'd been setting her ducks in a row as she loved to cliché, and according to her, her ducks were scattered. The cabin in Tennessee. The motel in West Virginia. A house in North Carolina. Her place in Kentucky. The woman loved real estate and mountainous areas.

Admittedly, I liked these mountains as well for the clean air and open road. Being in construction didn't always allow me to ride my Harley to work, though.

Neither did trying to impress the new boss by bringing her coffee.

Unbidden hope fills my chest.

I'd learned the motel had been sold to a young lady, as Gran called her. She had experience in hotel restorations and was looking for an investment property. The single story, twelve room motel, with a separate duplex and one cabin that sleeps eight was going to be a challenge, even if the new owner had design knowledge. The place was in a sad state and its use has been even sadder over the years. However, the setting was picturesque. In the summer months like now, the color around the place is rich dark greens and sturdy pine-shades.

When Hobb Hill opened their splashy resort to match the upgrades to their ski hills, Mountain Motel took a hit. Once a posh stop along the highway, complete with a cozy restaurant and a classy bar reminiscent of a time when crooners crooned, it just looked forlorn now.

I hated that Gran was slowly selling off her properties.

"Want to leave you a bigger estate," she'd said, patting my cheek like I was still twelve. As if I needed the money, when I didn't. What I truly hated was thinking about her passing anytime soon. She'd claim she never had a bad day in her ninety years. I doubted any life could be that flawless especially when both of her children and a grandchild passed before her. Not to mention the absence of Pop.

My life certainly wasn't perfect, and the past two years had been another test of my will. Being ill unsettled me, however, I am better now in mind and body, and I was looking forward to the future.

The once smooth drive was broken and cracked in places like a meteor shower hit it. I park underneath the carport near the entrance. The lobby is circular with floor to ceiling windows, giving the space a retro architecture vibe. One famous for roadside stops with swirling neon signs and big band sounds. I'm still not certain if the new owner wants to restore the place or tear it down and start fresh. I'd be nostalgically sorry to see it razed to the ground and some modern monstrosity built up. Then again, one reason Gran sold to this particular woman was because her vision was for renovation, not demolition.

"She's going to breathe new life into an old soul," Gran had pointedly told me. I didn't miss the suggestion beneath her words.

My forty-five years aren't young but I'm more youthful now than I've ever been. Funny how that happens. I'm grateful to have lived this long, especially when others younger than I am now have passed.

As I pull the long handle of the front door, a wave of dust and mold hits my nose. Shit, maybe demolition should be an option but I'm still hoping that's not the case. I used to visit here as a kid before my immediate family was severed in half. Then I'd visit with teenaged friends. Once with a girlfriend or two in my twenties. The memories were almost as musty as this lobby.

In the emptiness of what was once the lobby-restaurant-bar combination, the clunk of my boots should startle a woman whose back is to me. In a form fitting skirt, cut just above her knees, the backs of her legs are sexy as hell, accentuated by a pair of heels. Her backside is the perfect handful, although I really shouldn't be checking out the new boss.

Memories stir of a night four months ago, when I met a woman with a similar build. One that called to me, sat behind me on my bike, and then gave me a night I haven't forgotten.

"You're late."

My mouth falls open, about to protest. I have six minutes to spare and that's even with the stop to purchase coffee for her.

Only then, with her back still to me, her body angled forward over a makeshift worktable, a muffled voice responds to her comment. A phone is face up on the table and someone objects to her complaint.

"Just stay there," she says, causing me to stop in my tracks, despite the fact she still hasn't turned to face me. I'm not certain she's even aware I'm present, and I don't want to startle her. However, being female and alone in this abandoned building, she probably should have had the door locked until I'd arrived.

"I'm just nervous." She stands taller, shaking out her hands at her sides.

The hourglass shape of her body sets my blood racing, stirring up more memories. That voice has haunted my dreams.

Could it really be her?

I shake the thought. What a clusterfuck that night turned out to be. I'd never felt so elated and then deflated in a matter of twenty-four hours. She wouldn't listen to my explanation. She didn't want the truth. I took the night for what it was. A reawakening in more ways than one. My dick worked. My head cleared. And my heart might have cracked open a little bit.

"I know. I know," the owner whines at whomever is on the receiving end of the low speaker.

Standing still, I continue to hold two coffees in a to-go carrier with a white bakery box between them. I don't know if she even likes donuts or not, but who can turn down Tiny Bites. The mini donuts are melt-in-your-mouth goodness. Plus, I want to butter her up because I have a few ideas for this place myself.

"I just—" Her voice carries as she spins and abruptly stops. Her hand flattens on her chest. "You?"

Her strangled whisper is a cry of alarm in this cavernous room, mingling with a hint of her breathy tone once near my ear.

You, she'd stammered then. Her thoughts cutting off as I'd slid into her.

"Lindee." I choke, pleased while surprised. I'd dared to hope I'd get the chance to see her again but still didn't want to believe it could be a possibility.

"What are *you* doing here?" Her hands grip the worktable

behind her, as if steadying herself from the shock of seeing me again.

Okay, she isn't pleased to see me, but she shouldn't be surprised.

A muffled sound comes from the phone on the worktable.

"The construction guy is here." Spite fills Lindee's voice, similar to her anger the following day. The morning after the most unforgettable night of my life.

My shoulders stiffen at the derogatory note in her voice. "Yeah, the construction guy." *That's me.* Fuck that if she thinks she's better than me as the owner of this place. She's probably never lifted a manicured finger in her life. Then again, I remember her nails, short and trim, clawing down my back, desperate for me to fill her.

"I can't believe this," she mutters, hanging her head and shaking it.

"It was in the purchase agreement." I lower the beverage carrier. In the buyer's contract was a clause that stated my firm needed to do the renovation work. Gran was adamant we manage this project.

"I didn't know it was you," she whispers, looking back up at me before narrowing those bright blue eyes and shifting her gaze to the side.

How could she not know? She'd taken a picture of my driver's license.

Unless she dumped the image the morning after, swiping me and that night from her memory.

Could she forget so easily?

Would she renege on this purchase?

Gran would be crushed. She really wanted this *young lady* to have the property.

"Lucinda Marie Fox," I state. *Lindee.* Her name had been plain as day in the email she'd sent me and I dared to dream, while afraid to hope, that she was *my* Lindee from one night four months ago.

A muffled cry fills the space between us, and my new boss tilts her head toward the phone. "I'll need to call you back." With a finger jab, she shuts off the device and glares back at me.

With her firm ass against the table, she crosses her ankles. Those high heels look like killers and aren't proper attire for a worksite. Then again, maybe she's dressed to kill in order to exert her authority as the owner of this place. Either way, she has my attention.

And a strong desire rises in me to drop these coffees, rush her, lift her, and spread her out on the workspace behind her and remind us both of that night four months ago.

8

─────────

Playlist: "I Hope" – Gabby Barrett

[Lindee]

I cannot believe this.

Thaddeus Rhode. *Thad is Roadster?* What are the chances?

Considering my luck with this man, nothing should surprise me. After the most intensely sexual night of my life, the next day he shattered the fragile euphoria of our time together.

I peer around his shoulder, looking for someone else. "Where's your wife?" The bitterness in my tone cannot be masked.

His broad shoulders fall. A carrier with two coffee cups and a white box is in his hands. "I told you. I'm not married."

I know what he told me, and I don't believe him now any more than I believed him then.

My gaze falls to his left hand. The ring finger is missing the lion-faced hunk of gold that I believed was his grandfather's.

Lies. This man was full of bullshit, and I didn't have time for it. I had a motel to restore and a schedule to keep. So, why was he standing here looking like a wounded big cat and sexy as hell despite the guilt on his face?

"Look." His tone sharpens. "I'm telling the truth. I wasn't exactly divorced that night, but I wasn't married either."

"I don't even want to know what that means." I turn my back to him, steadying myself on the plywood over work horses that is my current office. Staring blindly at the plans laid out on the table, the image blurs.

This is my dream and he's ruining it.

I can't work with him. I can't see his beautiful face and those penetrating eyes every day.

Taking a breath, I stand taller in the heels I borrowed from Jane. She'd convinced me I needed to set the tone with this new crew. One I hadn't hired but was stuck with as a condition of my purchase agreement.

"*Show them who's the boss,*" she'd warned before slinging a pair of her best shoes at me.

I didn't dress like this. I was a jeans and shorts woman like Mae. But Jane was the one with the powerhouse wardrobe and the confidence to match it. It wasn't that I lacked assurance. I could hold my own with a construction crew. A little flirt. A lot of sass. No one ever questioned I was in charge.

But the man I've just turned my back on has me questioning my sanity. I'd certainly been crazy for him that night.

The bed. The shower. Even that antique chair in the corner.

I couldn't get enough of his hands on my skin, worshipping my body with his lips, his tongue, and his fingers.

Pressing my index finger and thumb to my forehead, I scrub away the fantasy of his masterful dick.

I'm such an idiot.

"Sweet thing."

"Do not call me that." I spin to face him, pointing a finger at his suddenly too-close body.

Reaching around me, he sets the coffee carrier on the makeshift desk behind me.

"Lindee." He breathes out my name like he did that night, only exasperation mixes with the tension in it. "Jasmine and I—"

Of course, her name was something cool despite her not looking like a sweet, delicate flower.

"Stop." Holding up my hand, I emphasize how very much I do not want to hear about her. The raven-haired woman on his arm the following day, announcing to me and my sisters how she was his wife.

Roadster—*Thad*—and I stare at one another. That whiskey gaze pleads until his eyes catch on my wrist.

"You're wearing it."

Quickly, I cover my wrist with my other hand as if I can hide the silver cuff with the dragonfly on it. I'd told myself to throw it away. I promised I'd never wear it again. But today felt like a good day to shrug off the negative memories and remember the positive of this symbol.

Transformation was happening. I wasn't a meek butterfly but a force to reckoned with.

Dismissing how he stares at my wrist and the question in his eyes about the bracelet, I speak.

"Mr. Rhode, you and I, unfortunately, need to come to an agreement. I'm not certain why you were part of the contract to buy this place but there has been a grave mistake. And now, I'm the owner of this property. So, you're . . ." I choke around the word. "You're fired."

He balks, head snapping back and eyes blinking. "Fired? On what grounds? I haven't even started work."

"Inappropriate behavior." It's the best I can come up with

because I can't think on my feet in these too high heels before the man clogging my senses by standing too close to me, filling my nose with that woodsy scent of him and a hint of rain.

I must be imagining the latter because it's a perfectly sunny day today.

"We have a contract," he reminds me.

"Contracts are meant to be broken." Like the vows he made to another woman. "You should know."

His eyes narrow. The whiskey in them the color of flames.

"I'll find another team." Jane's brother-in-law Myles had offered his services. He owns a construction firm with an excellent reputation plus I've seen his work in all he did to rebuild Wrightwood. That small town is going to benefit from my little venture here as well, as there aren't many hotels in the immediate area and only one other motel that does rent by the hour as Jane accused of my new place.

My motel.

Thad stares at me, his lush lips pressed tightly together. Damn him for being so tempting. Looking too sexy with the mix of sawdust and snowflakes in his beard surrounding that mouth of his.

"Fine," he mutters. He straightens to his full height which is rather imposing and folds his arms over his chest. I note the tightness of the T-shirt he wears. His arms are covered in ink that I didn't explore enough on that night.

Today was only a meeting. A moment to discuss plans and agree on a process. I wanted to tackle the winter cabin first, giving me and any family who comes to help a place to stay while I finish the remainder of the project. I'll be living in a camper out back in the interim. I've slept in worse places.

Like a comfy hotel bed with a burly man at my back and his arm over my waist like a comforting blanket.

Lies.

I sniff. I sneeze. This place needs a good airing out. In an unladylike manner, I swipe at my nose, preventing the inevitable drip.

Thad reaches into his back pocket and pulls forth something. "Here."

Is that . . . a handkerchief? Actually, it's a bandana but he's offering it to me like an old-fashioned snot catcher.

I wave off the gesture and sneeze again. Then another sneeze attacks.

"Are you allergic to something?"

Yeah, men who are liars.

"Just sunshine sneezes," I wave my hand through the dust motes floating in the shaft of light coming through the floor to ceiling windows in the lobby. This place has so much potential, and I was excited to begin before this encounter.

Achoo. "Goodness."

Thad chuckles. "Did you just say goodness like an old woman?"

"Did you just hand me a handkerchief like an old man?"

His lips tighten again, giving me a quizzical look after the heated sarcasm in my tone.

I sneeze once more.

"You need some fresh air." With a hand at my elbow, Thad tugs me toward the front door.

"I'm fine." I huff, attempting to pull my arm free from his grasp. A touch that sends heat up my arm and reminds me of him stroking sensitive places on me. "Don't pretend to care about me."

Thad halts, spins on his work boots, and faces me. "I do care about you. In fact, I wish I didn't. I wish I could get you out of my head, sweetheart." He harshly pats his head and raises his arm higher.

There's no warmth in the endearment. No flirt in the demand.

I could say the same to him. *Stop being a fantasy that plays on repeat in the dark of night and loneliness of my bed.*

Instead, we stare at one another before I state, "I can't work with you." I can't pretend his eyes don't make my knees weak. Or I don't want his mouth on mine again. I can't work beside him day by day and deny the reality in my head, that I want him again.

"I brought you coffee, boss. And donuts." He nods at the containers on the worktable. "I'll be back tomorrow."

"I fired you," I remind him.

He simply shakes his head and turns away again, giving me a nice view of his backside as he retreats, just like he did the morning after that incredible night.

THROUGHOUT THE DAY, I had more sneezing attacks as I puttered around the motel taking note of all the things I needed to do and developing a few additional ideas. By evening, I have a subtle ache at the bridge of my nose and watery eyes, but I'm fine.

Just fine.

Especially since Myles Wright agrees to meet me for a drink at Trophy's, a sports bar in Wrightwood. The small town is forty minutes away but worth the drive to clear my head and realign my thoughts.

Myles's help feels imperative. "I need a construction crew."

We sit side-by-side inside the enclosed balcony on the back of the bar overlooking the Kanawha River. A rough-cut countertop runs the expansive length 1f the floor to ceiling window offering an excellent view of the rainbow bridge crossing the river.

"Don't you have a contract with someone?" Myles has a

rugged voice that matches his twin brother, Mach, who happens to be my sister's husband. While identical, there's still enough of a distinction between the men despite sharing silver streaks through the midnight color of their hair and beards. They have the same deep-set eyes, but Myles's are even sadder than Mach's once were, although his overall personality is much brighter than his brother's. He's someone I definitely would have considered sleeping with, but we both have a sorrowful void within us. And sad plus sad does not make a happy outcome.

Myles and I are just good friends.

"I can't work with him."

"Why not?" Myles lifts his beer for a drink.

My hands tighten around a gin and tonic but there's no taste to the typically refreshing drink. My throat hurts and the cool liquid isn't soothing the ache.

"History."

Myles swallows hard and turns his face toward me. "It's difficult when the past rises to haunt you."

A former lover from when Myles was young has recently returned to the area. They share more than their romantic past, though, and I sympathize with his plight although Myles doesn't know anything about Harris. He means Thad is my haunting memory, but he doesn't know the details there either. Yet.

"So what happened?" Myles studies me. Something unique about him is he's an observer and a great listener.

"I was a complete idiot, trusted a stranger, and then had my heart stomped on like a foolish schoolgirl when it was only a one-night stand." One night when my world was rocked by the comfort I found in *him,* and the desire to see him again when never before have I looked back with longing.

Myles hums, introspective a moment. "One night is never really one night, is it?" He gives me a cheeky grin and I'd push at his shoulder if I had the strength to lift my arms. I feel a little achy all over and I haven't even started demolition work.

"So, you slept with him one night, and then you saw him again?" Myles hesitates on the timeline.

"He owns the construction firm built into my purchase contract."

Myles blows out a breath and shakes his head with a sympathetic chuckle. "Tough."

"He deceived me." I lower my voice and my head. I'd been a fool.

"How so?"

"The next day, I met his wife."

9

———————

Playlist: "Never Wanted to Be That Girl" – Carly Pearce
& Ashley McBryde

[Lindee]

Four months ago, I'd had the most incredible night of my life. This mysterious motorcycle man knew how to ride a woman's body. Coasting curves and ravishing roads, he was a master. I'd never been so oversexed and fully satisfied in my life.

And when he slunk from my bed in the morning, I watched in silence as he dressed and then slipped that giant ring back on his finger.

His gaze held mine, as I lay lazy and replete among rumpled sheets.

"You've been a dream, sweet thing."

He had no idea the kind of fantasy he'd been for me.

"Thank you." His voice softened. His expression saddened. "Stay out of trouble, Lindee Fox."

"You too, Roadster."

It felt like the saddest goodbye I'd ever said. Then I watched him walk toward the door, taking one final glance at the strength in his back and the firmness of his ass. The door clicked shut with his exit.

Like a schoolgirl having just spent the night with her dream man, I turned my face into the pillow, giggle-screamed, and kicked my legs in excitement.

Wow. What a night.

Then, my alarm went off, startling me from my happy-sex dance and I slapped at my phone, noticing a text from Jane.

Be there in an hour, *I'd typed in response.*

I was meeting my sisters at a cottage in Tennessee, on the other end of the Tail of the Dragon. The ride should have taken forty-five minutes to retrace over the highway, but that hadn't left time for a shower. Instead, I quickly did the minimum—brushed teeth, hair in ponytail, deodorant, dress. The scent of Roadster was all over me, and I wasn't eager to erase him yet.

Once on my way, I'd messaged Jane again.

Only after officially exiting the Tail in Tennessee, I took a wrong turn somewhere. Maps on my phone was not working thanks to spotty reception, and I circled back to the same location twice. I have no sense of where I was or where I'd been. Eventually, I ended up at a small convenience store on an unfamiliar highway but retraced my drive once more up to the crest of the mountain before finally asking two hikers if they knew where I was and how to get back to the valley where I intended to meet my sisters.

They directed me along the top of the ridge, toward the convenience store once more, where I should get better reception, but they also told me to go right at the store and continue east.

Near tears, I was three hours late.

"Where have you been?" Concern filled Jane's face as I exited the

Jeep. She stood on the low porch of a humble log cabin. Mae had booked this place for us. I'd arrived a day early so I could drive the Tail and scope out the Opatoc Lodge for inspiration. I already had a plan to purchase my future motel.

"Are you alright?" Mae had asked from her seat in a willow-back chair, eyeing me with worry.

Panic had set in and then frustration as I wove up and down the same roads only to eventually discover that I'd been fifteen minutes from the cabin at one point but turned around when nothing looked familiar.

"Yeah, I got lost and I'm—"

"Okay, the shower should be good now." A man walked out the front screen door, holding the wooden frame so it didn't spring back and slam the jamb. After righting the door, he glanced up.

Our eyes locked.

"Roadster?" A moment passed as I registered that the man whose scent was still lingering on my skin was standing before me when I never thought I'd see him again. My thighs clenched. An ache still apparent after a night of him between them. Confusion settled in, trying to merge the sexual being of the night before with the solid form who stood on a cabin porch an hour away from where we'd met.

"Lindee?" A spark filled those whiskey eyes, reminding me of candlelight.

But then, the screen door screeched open again. This time it smacked against the jamb like a thunder crack before a storm. A woman wrapped her hand around the bulging bicep of the man I'd slept with last night. Her long, dark hair was midnight-colored and beautiful, but the fluorescent orange of her fingernails created a violent contrast.

My gaze darted to the giant diamond and gold band on her ring finger.

"Do you two know each other?" Her voice clawed down my skin.

What had I done? What had *he?*

The shake of his head was so minimal I almost missed it. He could have been flicking back his hair, if it were longer. Or swishing away a fly annoyingly buzzing by his face.

"No," I whispered as a lump formed in my throat. A lump the size of a boulder threatening to roll me over and press me into the porch boards. "I must be mistaken."

"But you called him Roadster?"

Jane stepped forward. "So the shower?" Her feeble attempt to shift topics and break through the sudden tension was noticed by all.

"It was just a valve turned off. Sorry about that. Everything is in working condition now." The thickness of his voice had me closing my eyes, willing away the memory of his rugged tone telling me what to do and asking me what I wanted from him.

Here? He'd blown on tender folds, causing me to shiver in the air-conditioned room.

How about here? He'd pressed his fingers forward, entering me, spreading me, prepping me for another round.

Like that? He'd teased me, knowing from my body's response I loved every touch, every lick, every motion.

"Well, if that's all then, my husband and I will be on our way." The woman hitched up a shoulder and gave a little giggle as she looked dreamily at her husband.

I hadn't taken my eyes off him either.

"Perfect," I'd snapped. "I'm going to check out that fixed shower."

Brushing passed him, but not far enough away, his hand twitched outward, fingers tickling mine. I tucked my hand to my chest and rushed inside the dim cabin. The staircase was feet away from the entrance and I raced upward, taking the steps two at a time.

Behind me, I heard Roadster say, "I forgot a tool. I'll be right back."

The screen door squeaked open as I stepped into my designated bedroom. With shaky fingers, I dumped my tote and grabbed my travel bag of necessities. Spinning toward the door, I was trapped.

"Lindee." His voice was low, hushed and deep. "She is not my wife."

Clutching my toiletry bag to my chest, I snorted. "Her words and that set of rings on her finger say otherwise."

"It's not what you think. We aren't together anymore. We're—"

"Sweetheart?" A saccharine sweet cry crawled up the staircase, calling out to him.

I cringed and closed my eyes. He'd called me the same term.

"Lindee, please. I'm not married."

My lids flicked open. "What you are is a liar."

Despite his large stature blocking the door, I nudged him with my shoulder, forcing him back into the hall and wedging myself past him for the bathroom only steps away.

"Just let me explain—" But I was already closing the door, keeping my back to him. Anger filled my veins. Betrayal stabbed my heart.

He'd been so convincing. He'd seemed so trustworthy. I'd always been so good at deciphering the truth in a man about his status. Single. Married. Or other.

But this man had stumped me. Fool me once; shame on him. So much shame.

With the door closed and my back pressed against it, I tipped back my head.

Let him explain? He'd have some explaining to do alright . . . to his wife.

With shaky fingers, I undressed, tugging at my shirt and fumbling with my jeans. My legs gave out and I sat on the closed toilet to remove the denim, along with my boots and socks. Once inside the shower, the peppering spray prickled my skin, turning my flesh red.

I'd been the other woman and I felt sick. I wanted to beat my fists against the tile and scream in rage. How could this have happened?

Even more frightening was when tears struck, heavy and thick. A waist-bending sob crept up my throat, and I slid to the shower floor, tucking my knees to my chest as I cried like I hadn't cried since I was twenty.

When my heart was first shattered.

10

Playlist: "Back to Black" – Amy Winehouse

[Lindee]

"**F**uck," Myles hums. With his body shifted toward mine on his stool, he's been listening to me share my story as I stared out at the signature rainbow-shaped bridge of Wrightwood.

Hope. I'd had so much that night. So much today when I thought I was meeting an honest man to help me make a dream come true.

I rub my fingers over the dragonfly cuff I haven't removed yet. "And that's why I can't work with him."

Myles's expression is somber.

Unfortunately, my sisters learned everything in the aftermath. I'm typically good at keeping these kinds of dramas to myself. I'd already caused enough when I was twenty. But that situation with Roadster, happening the day after a wonderful night, wasn't something I could avoid talking about, especially when I exited the bathroom to find Mae leaning against the wall opposite the bathroom and Jane seated on a couch in an alcove den at the top of the staircase.

Mae reached for me, pulling me into a hug I hardly felt at the time. Jane gave me a sympathetic look. Both waited me out until I spilled what had happened.

I'd slept with a married man.

And I struggled with his appearance at the cabin.

"When we called the host who owns the property and explained about the shower, she told us her grandson would be here within an hour to fix it," Mae had explained.

Jane added additional details which simply confirmed what I'd already learned about the woman standing beside Roadster. *"She'd told us she was on a reconciliation retreat with him."*

Reconciliation.

The rusty knife pricking my chest had sliced my heart open, leaving me raw and wounded in a new way.

"I get it. Let's look at the contract tomorrow," Myles states. "There must be some kind of clause or loophole that allows you to let him go and hire your own construction team."

"Thank you, Myles." I pat his thigh and sniffle. Tears aren't in my watery eyes but my nose burns.

"Sounds like you're coming down with something," he chuckles.

"It's nothing." I wave. "Just a dusty old motel in need of love." *Like me.*

"Wear a mask and open some windows." He sounds a little too much like my earlier visitor.

The man I do not intend to see tomorrow despite his warning that he'll be back.

~

A SHARP RATTLING of aluminum on aluminum rouses me. A determined masculine voice accompanies the rattle. "Lindee?"

"Go away," I mumble into the bed pillow beneath my heavy head. My mouth is dry. My throat drier. Hell has taken up residence in my body. I'm not hungover; I'm sick.

"Sweet thing, I know you're in there. Open up."

"I'm sleeping," I mutter although the words aren't more than a strangled whisper. Snuggling underneath the too-heavy-for-July blanket, I shiver. I'm freezing.

The hammering on the camper door continues, though, and before he pulls it from its hinges, I gingerly exit the bed, wrapping the thick blanket around me. My legs are shaky as I stumble down the narrow aisle to unlock the door.

"What?" I gargle, pressing the door open.

Thad stumbles back. With a baseball cap on his head and a well-worn oatmeal colored T-shirt, he looks fresh and spry for morning. Or is it afternoon? The bright sunshine causes me to squint as it accelerates the thumping in my head. The blinding rays suggest it's later in the day than I think.

"What's the matter?" He tilts his head, narrowing his eyes.

I'm certain I look like shit, and I don't care. Without another word, he's filling the entrance and placing a hand on my belly to gently push me backward.

"It took me days to find you. Are you living in this camper?"

"Do not disrespect Karen."

"Karen?" he scoffs.

"Yeah. The camper. Karens get a bad rap as high maintenance, suburban moms in exclusive neighborhoods driving giant SUVs. This Karen is a bad*ass* who is chill and seen her share of the road." I'll leave that final part up to him to interpret, but my little respite is a modernized vintage Airstream with a dove-gray interior and shiny chrome exterior. It's beautiful, even though the gleam from the aluminum is currently searing my eyes.

"And what do you mean days?" I saw him yesterday. Then I met Myles for dinner last night and . . .

How did I get home? I wasn't drunk. In fact, I hardly drank because my favorite gin and tonic had no taste to it going down my sore throat.

"I came here yesterday and searched all over for you but never saw your Jeep. This morning, though, it was parked out back beside this thing . . . er, Karen."

I bend my aching body for a better view out the front window. Yep, there's my Jeep but I don't recall driving home. Did Myles give me a ride back here? *He's such a good man.*

The thought has me snapping my head upward which makes me wince beneath the weight of the blanket over my shoulders.

"What do you want?" I sound like a protective dog thanks to my sore throat. Maybe I should get one, seeing as I am living in this camper off a highway.

"Look." Thad sighs and removes his baseball cap. He scratches the top of his head and then replaces the cap. He's so tall he slouches as he stands in the camper. He's also broad, so he's taking up a lot of space in the enclosed quarters. I'd have a nice inhale of his woodsy-rain scent if I could breathe through my nose.

"I understand why you're unhappy with me."

I choke-laugh which leads to a small coughing fit. With a tremor in my body, I take a seat on the bench at the dining table.

"Are you alright?" Concern fills his rugged voice, but I dismiss him.

"It's a summer cold. I'm fine."

"I know you don't want to work with me, but I have a crew counting on me. They've traveled here and they're prepared to work for eight weeks straight. We need the work."

Funny, he didn't say money. From my brother's investigation, Thad and his crew have been steadily busy. He could easily find another project.

I exhale and the ache in my chest trumps the pain in my lungs.

"We have a contract but it's more than the contract. This place is important to me."

The effort it takes to lift my head shouldn't be this difficult, still I watch as Thad narrows his eyes and turns his head toward the door like he can see the motel from his position.

"My family owned this place for decades. My grandmother, specifically. We came here as kids. I've been here as a teen . . . with friends. Hell, I've even brought some girls—" He stops short and twists his head back in my direction.

At the mention of his sexual history, I scrunch up my stuffy nose. I hate that my first thought is *which room*? We don't have a Room 13, but I can mentally mark another room as unlucky and haunted.

"Anyway. I don't want the work to go to someone else. Call it sentimental attachment. I want to see this place restored to its glory."

"What if I want to knock it down?"

Thad observes me for a long minute, almost scrutinizing me. My bedhead. My puffy eyes. "You won't."

Dammit, he's right. There is just something special about this place and in my mind's eye I can see its potential.

Summer visits.

Spring breaks.

Winter weekends.

Add in the fall review, when the trees change color and leaf peepers arrive, and I have four seasons of beauty surrounding the quiet of this place.

"I didn't know your grandmother was Vanessa Rhode."

"Nessi. Yeah, she's my dad's mom." He proudly nods.

There is so much I don't know about this man. He's the very

definition of a stranger. A mystery. And I'd give him more thought if any of my brain cells functioned.

"Are you sure it's just a summer cold?" Thad steps forward and places his hand on my forehead. I'd flinch away but the coolness of his thick palm feels good on my hot, clammy skin.

"Lindee, you're burning up. Have you taken anything?"

"I don't do drugs," I defend.

"I mean Tylenol or something for your fever."

Do I have a fever? Sore throat. Aches. Chills. I'm a walking billboard for flu medication. Being that I'm hardly ever sick, I don't have medicine readily available. I'd popped my last two acetaminophen the other night.

"You said days. *You've been looking for me for days.* What day is it?"

"It's Friday."

I've been sick for nearly two days. Shakily, I press myself upward with the aid of the table and stand. "I need to call Myles."

"Who's Myles?" His tone is sharp, demanding even, when he has no right to be. With narrowed eyes, he watches me.

"How did my car get here?" As if Thad would know. "I need to figure out how my Jeep got here."

"Lindee, you need medicine." Thad stretches for the compact kitchen cabinets, opening two at a time. I should scold him for invading my privacy and searching them, but there's nothing of significance up there. Paper plates and napkins. Miscellaneous spices.

"Have you been eating?"

"I eat."

"That isn't what I asked."

The statement reminds me of when we met. He asked me if I was traveling alone. Oh, the irony, as he'd been the liar.

"I just need a nap." There isn't enough space in the too-cramped quarters to get around him and I end up wedged between his broad body and the dining table.

"Lindee, you need more than a nap. Maybe you need a doctor."

My eyes close as he brushes his hand over my inevitably greasy hair and pauses at the side of my neck. The soothing touch is too much. I don't want him to placate me despite the comfort. My heart hammers. My pulse throbs. Even as sick as I am, my body is reacting to him, and I hate myself.

Rest. He has no idea how much I want to settle down. Plant roots and stay still for a little while. I *am* tired. Tired of the road, the travel, the different places. I never, ever thought I'd feel that way, but I want to live in one place for a while. If I leave again, I want a place that's mine to come back to. A place to call home.

"Is a motel really a home?" Mae had asked when I tried to explain myself. My sister had been settled for so long in her small town she has an opposite opinion. She longed to travel the open road and see all she could see. She'd started a quest in her forties, and I couldn't be happier for her. But we are antonyms, and I'd like to be the one to stay put for a bit.

Ignoring Thad, I squeeze out from against him and head for my bed. The sheets don't look very inviting in their wrinkled state, but I just need to lie down again. The mattress takes up most of the space in this room and I collapse on my side.

At the soft click of the camper door, I close my eyes.

Good. He left.

Everyone leaves.

But as I drift into restless sleep, I wish Thad had stayed.

11

Playlist: "The Good Ones" – Gabby Barrett

[Lindee]

When I wake, the camper is dark, and a wall of heat is at my back. I'm burning up.

With a sharp kick, I wrestle to get the blanket off me, but my heel digs into something hard and fleshy.

"Oof."

Quickly twisting to determine the obstruction, I find a boulder of a man resting on his side behind me. "Thad?" I croak. My throat is still sore.

"Sweet thing, you okay?" A heavy hand cups my hip.

"I'm hot," I groan.

He softly chuckles in the darkness. "That you are, sweetheart. But it sounds like the fever might be breaking."

I try to roll completely to my back but he's a wedge keeping me on my side. "What are you doing here?"

"Don't you remember? I left to get you medicine and some food. Came back and made you sip some soup and take Tylenol."

I thought I'd been dreaming. "Then you decided to just climb into bed with me?"

"You kept telling me how cold you were." His hand skims over my hip. "You're wearing my shirt."

The statement holds questions I don't want to answer. I should have shredded the fabric into pieces or used it to start a bonfire when he left it behind, but I didn't have the heart to destroy it. There was no point in ruining a perfectly good shirt, especially one nice to sleep in. The material is extra soft. And by washing the flannel immediately after he left the cabin that morning, I eliminated his scent.

Feeling snarky, I say, "Maybe I'm wearing it like the scarlet letter. It's a reminder of how ashamed of myself I am."

The jab is a low blow but he's the adulterer and I'm his guilty, although unknowing, partner in crime. When I consider that I hate us both.

Thad blows out a breath. "Phew. I don't remember you this mean."

Instantly, I feel contrite. It isn't in me to be ruthless toward others. Typically, I wouldn't stick around long enough to hurt someone. But lashing out at Thad seems to be my thing because I'm confused by his presence and frustrated that I might like him here.

"Sick or not, I like you in it." His voice is low, the pain in it evident.

I've hurt his feelings. Well, he hurt me when he lied to me about being married.

I huff and roll to my side again, feet removed from the blanket, legs bare and exposed to the summery night air.

"You didn't have to stay," I whisper. He probably shouldn't

have stayed. Somewhere there's another woman waiting on him.

"Nowhere else I wanted to go."

He's so good with the perfect lines. Thoughts race through my head. "Do you live around here?"

"My house is about an hour away, east of Lexington, Kentucky."

Silence falls between us. I'm not up for this conversation but it seems like it should happen sometime. "What were you doing in North Carolina?" Why was he at the lodge the night I was?

Thad sighs and the shift of the mattress behind me suggests he's rolled to his back. "Really want to talk about this now?"

"I really don't want to talk about this ever, but I need answers. I deserve them." Especially as a sneaky part of me wants to believe in him. I can't explain, not even sure I like this feeling, but I want to trust that Thaddeus Rhode isn't a bad guy. That he wouldn't cheat on a wife.

Plus, I need him to fulfill the contract and restore the motel.

Sentimental attachment. Why do I have to be a person with the same trait?

"And it feels like I have time on my hands." I'm not getting out of this bed yet, and in the middle of the night, we aren't starting work on my renovation project.

"You should rest more."

Actually, I'm restless, plus sweaty and hungry. I've slept a ton, but I don't mention these things. Staying still, my stiff body language tells him it's time to talk.

"I needed a night."

In some ways, I understand the simple statement. A night off. A night to clear his head. A night to get lost in someone else. But the idea agitates me.

How could he do that to his wife and why the hell is he in bed with me now?

"Why are you here, Thad?"

"For the job on the motel."

"No, I mean, here. In Karen. With me."

He rolls back toward me and wraps his arm over my waist. "Saying I'm in Karen sounds a little wrong." He chuckles against the back of my neck, making my skin pebble. "And I'm here with you because you need me."

I don't need *him*. I don't need anyone. I've taken care of myself for forty-two years.

Maybe not very well, and certainly not when I'm sick, but I'm doing just fine on my own.

It's a lie I tell myself too often lately.

"What about Jasmine?" Her name is a choked whisper and I close my eyes. Shifting forward, I put distance between us, suggesting Thad shouldn't be touching me, dangling his arm over my waist, and brushing his leg along the back of mine.

"I told you I'm divorced." His defensive tone is edgy, determined, maybe even a little angry.

"But you aren't." I shiver, as a creepy, crawly sensation travels over my flesh. Why are we still doing this dance?

"Lindee," he groans, flattening his hand on my belly and then dragging himself to my back to press a kiss to my shoulder. "Can we talk about this later?"

His refusal for more details is frustrating and only builds my suspicion. He shouldn't be here with me.

Thad sniffs. "No offense, sweetheart, but you kind of stink. You need a shower. Wash off the fever sweat."

If I thought he cared about my well-being, I'd be touched, but I recognize the avoidance tactic.

"Actually, I'm hungry."

"Yeah?" He pops up behind me, perching on an elbow, and I twist to look over my shoulder at him. Darkness surrounds the camper, but a low light glows behind him. Did he leave a light on for me?

"What can I make you? Soup? Some toast?"

Before I can answer, he's throwing back the covers and leaving the bed, eager to make me a simple bowl of soup. The view of him in dark-red boxer briefs that hug his fine ass is very nice. The muscles in his back are honed, causing a deep ridge along his spine. He flexes and his shoulder blades are defined. A large tattoo covers them. His arms are covered in designs as well and I wish I'd inspected him better that night.

I wish I'd seen the hints that he couldn't be mine. He belonged to someone else.

Thad turns and opens cabinets again before starting the gas stove. In the middle of the night, he's busy at work pouring soup in a pot and placing bread in the toaster. He went to the store and bought me those things. He administered fever medicine and warmed my body with his skin when I was cold.

Dammit, I do not want him to be a good man at heart.

Why did you need that night, Thad? Why did you spend it with me?

What's your story, Thaddeus Rhode?

12

———————

Playlist: "The Night We Met" – Lord Huron

[Thad]

Despite the dimness in the kitchen area, Lindee is watching me. The space is tight in this vintage 1950 Airstream, renovated with modern appliances and updated décor. If she owns this thing, this Karen, it set her back a pretty penny. Then again, she must have money as she bought a motel that needs extensive renovations.

As I explained to her, the motel has sentimental value to me. I don't like seeing Gran dissolve her holdings, but the properties are hers to do what she will with them. I'd have bought the place myself if I hadn't given Jasmine the house in the divorce.

However, I didn't know anything about running a motel. My construction company was less than ten years old, and we needed the work to keep us moving forward. Gran knew this and that's why she shrewdly wrote me into the sale of the place. Fixing up a motel would look amazing in our portfolio. There's also a clause in the purchase agreement that states if the current owner ever wishes to sell, I have first right of refusal to purchase. I think Gran hoped I'd fall in love with the place and keep it.

I'm hoping Lindee stays for a while but if she ever decides to leave, I want first dibs on this place.

As I slouch beneath the low ceiling, Lindee approaches the cramped kitchenette. She's wearing my shirt. The shirt I asked her to keep on when I first touched her, kissed her, fucked her. Then we moved to the shower, where I removed the flannel and got my first full view of her body. Large breasts, subtle curves, and the softest skin.

Despite her snarky comment about the shirt, that was like a sharp jab to my chest, I meant what I said. I like seeing her in my flannel. It's another reminder of that night.

Lindee was a dream. That night a fantasy.

I didn't trust that I *could* have sex. I didn't believe in myself or my body. Four months back, I was still in a tough place physically.

I'm better now. I credit Lindee with the shift. She lit something inside me that night and I proved to myself I could move on.

While Lindee's current flu is common, I still hate that she's sick. No one knows better than me, you don't blow off a fever.

"You're right, I should shower."

The camper shower is exposed to the bedroom area, with a rounded ceiling overhead and a narrow rectangular tub, I'd never fit in. It'd be like splashing water on my face from a sink —a wakeup call, but not a cleansing. With Lindee's smaller stature, she'll fit just fine.

"I'll stay out here," I state, knowing if I get a glimpse of her naked body, I'm going to have another hard-on, something I've been fighting every time I'm near her. Like right now.

"I just have one more question for tonight. If you live an hour away, would you be commuting here? That seems excessive. I can find a local construction company."

I twist only enough to look at her over my shoulder, continuing to stir soup, so I don't reach for her and shake her shoulders until she hears me. I'm not married anymore. And I'm not leaving this job.

I'm also holding this position, so the bulge in my briefs is trapped between me and the stove and not full on in her face.

"I'll be staying at another motel nearby."

Lindee gasps. "Are you at Hobb Hill?" Horror fills her adorable, but still a tad pale, face.

I snort. "I wouldn't give that resort a dime. The mystique of that place vanished when the ski hill was upgraded, and the fancy lodge was added."

"Are you at that rent-by-the-hour place off the highway?" Her smoky voice, which is sexy as hell mixed with her cold, rises. "Are you sleeping with the enemy?"

"Enemy?" I laugh.

"Just answer the question."

"Sweet thing, that place is not going to be competition for you. And neither is Hobb Hill once we are done with Mountain Motel." I wink at her.

Her shoulders relax. Her face softens. For the first time since that night, she isn't giving me a pinched look like I'm gum stuck to her shoe. She's so fucking pretty, even with greasy hair and a pillow crease on her cheek. Her eyes are bright. Maybe a little too bright from the fever, but still blue and beautiful.

I knew she'd be trouble for me. The best kind of trouble, like she said.

"And I'm not sleeping with anyone but you."

She leans against the privacy door for the toilet. "Thaddeus

Rhode, I do not know what to make of you." She pauses. "Or should I call you Roadster?"

"Yeah, about that." I chuckle again. "I thought it best if we didn't share names, so I gave you my road name from a million years ago. When you told me your name, I couldn't U-turn. Plus, I kind of liked the sound of an old name on your fresh tongue."

"Being charming with me will not get you anywhere, Mr. Rhode," she warns but a timid smile curls her lips. Lips I desperately want to kiss and right the wrongs she thinks I've done to her. I can explain myself but as she won't listen, I have other ways to prove myself.

"You can call me Thad. Or boss, whichever you'd like." I wink.

She huffs out a throaty chortle. God, I want to make her laugh.

"I'm the boss."

"Yes, ma'am." I smile.

"And now there will be a big deduction from your first check for calling me ma'am." She stands upright again and folds her arms over her chest, pushing up the lush breasts I had in my mouth once. The buttons on my shirt are open a few too many and the lift from her arms exposes a tight crease between the swells. The place I had my dick, rubbing between those tempting breasts.

Something else catches my attention and I nod at her wrist.

"You're still wearing it." I remember her telling me how she bought mementos, not souvenirs. *Souvenirs you shoved in closet, but a memento was for a memory.* Did she stare at that dragonfly cuff and remember our night together? Why is she wearing it now?

Just like she's wearing my shirt, that night might have meant more to her than she's letting on.

What is your story, Lindee Fox?

I bet she thinks about that night. How our bodies buzzed together. How she hummed under my touch. How she—

"Thad?"

"Yeah." My voice is too hopeful as she interrupts my thoughts.

"You can't sleep with the enemy." Deflection. I'm a master of deflecting what I don't want to discuss, but I'll let her nonresponse about the bracelet slide.

"I told you I'm not—"

She holds up a hand, allowing her other arm to drop. "It isn't beautiful yet, but you can stay in a motel room here." Her brows pinch. "What about your crew? Where are they coming from?"

I stop stirring the soup and face her full on. "Does this mean I'm no longer fired?"

Her gaze drops to the bulge in my briefs, firm and thick, and threatening to burst above the waistband.

She flicks her eyes upward, holding on mine a moment. Her cheeks are pink, and I can't decide if the color is from the fever, embarrassment, or something more . . . like desire.

"You're on probation."

Hope fills my chest. "I have two guys I work with and others on standby for specifics like electric, plumbing, and HVAC." Duke and Manor need this project, too. It isn't about the money. We have other reasons to work.

"Each of those guys can have a room, too. Or all of you can stay in the duplex although I wanted that to be my second project."

"What's the first project?" Hands coming to my hips, relief washes over me that she's not kicking me off this job.

Her gaze falls to my briefs again but quickly flits upward. "First thing is a shower." Giving me her back, she returns to the bedroom. It doesn't have a door, and she hollers back to me. "You'll stay out there, right?"

Is there hesitation in her voice? Does she want me to stay more than she wants me out of her life?

"I'm not going anywhere, sweet thing."

"You really need to stop calling me that," she mumbles before the water starts running.

Yeah, not happening. I like how her eyes spark when I call her sweet.

And I want to hear the brush of her breath in my ear when I touch her again.

13

———

Playlist: "Suspicious Minds" – Elvis Presley

[Lindee]

S howering takes all my energy, and I sit listlessly at the compact dining booth to eat soup and half a piece of toast. Thad simply sits across from me, watching me. Finally, I admit I can't stay upright anymore, and I need to return to bed.

"Just for a little while," I tell him as I slip from the bench seat and turn toward the bedroom. He was respectful of my privacy while I showered and he was sweet to make me soup and toast, but now, I want my bed for blankets and comfort.

"Let me tuck you in." He follows me. At some point, he slipped into a pair of jeans but didn't bother buttoning them at the waist, giving me a hint of the maroon waistband slung low beneath his abs.

His body is a fantasy waiting to happen.

Only, I won't be making that fantasy a reality with him again. Thad's right. I need him. With sentimental value on his mind, he'll be dedicated to the work that needs to be done on the motel. Myles's company is too busy to take on a last-minute project, plus he wants to take a vacation this summer. He deserves a break, and I can't ask him to give up the time he's set aside for it.

I still don't trust Thad but as I won't be sleeping with him again I don't have emotional expectations from him. As long as he does the renovation on the motel in a timely manner, that's all I want from him.

And if I tell myself this often enough, I might believe me.

Thad bends a knee on the mattress and cocoons the covers around my body, forcing a giggle to escape me. He's kind of ridiculous as he shoves the blanket around me, making certain I can hardly move.

"Here." He sets the television remote near my pillow. My phone is already nearby. "If you wake up, just hang out. Watch a movie or binge a series." He hesitates as he stands upright. "I won't be back until Sunday night."

"You're already taking the weekend off?" My brows pinch. *What the heck?*

He scratches at the back of his neck. "Yeah." Shifting his gaze to the side, he brushes me off. "You need more rest."

More avoidance. More suspicion.

My mouth falls open ready to ask him where he's going, who he'll be seeing, but I quickly clamp my lips shut. It's not my business if he returns to his wife. He *should* be with her, not me.

And if I weren't already closing in on myself, I'd want to burrow into my pillow and scream.

Why did I let him sleep behind me again? How could I take comfort in his touch?

At least, this time it was only sleep.

The thought doesn't make me feel better. Shame washes over me again.

With a soft kiss that lingers a little too long on my forehead, Thad leaves me alone. The camper shakes a bit under his movements and then the door opens and clicks shut. The silence surrounding his departure leaves me hollow, but I close my eyes and fall into the first peaceful sleep I've had in days.

WHEN I FINALLY PULL MYSELF from bed and make myself another meal of toast and soup that Thad had bought me, I find an envelope on the camper table with a sticky note attached. Thad's phone number is written on the note, but the contents of the envelope make me furious.

And because of it, I'm a pot of stew ready to boil over by Monday morning.

"What is this?" I snap, rattling the papers in my hand as Thad enters the vacant lobby with a to-go carrier of two coffees and a small bakery box. Previously, he'd brought me Tiny Bites, these incredibly delicious donut delicacies that have heavenly toppings. I hadn't been able to truly enjoy the first batch because I wasn't feeling well that day, but this round I plan to devour.

After I get some answers.

"Good morning, boss." His smile is wide. His voice deep. He looks rested, almost jubilant.

"Thad," I grunt, holding the pages higher and shaking them once more.

"Did you read them?" He sets the cup holder on the makeshift worktable and lifts a to-go cup toward me.

While I'm not one to turn down what I consider goddess fuel, I don't want his offering yet.

"The matter seemed rather private." Lowering my arm, the

papers smack at my hip. Although he'd left them for me, I didn't have the heart to read something so personal and sensitive.

"You didn't want to listen, so I brought you proof."

Aghast, I squeak. "You've given me your divorce papers?" The man was insufferable.

Taking the papers from my hand, Thad flips to the final page and points at a line. "Did you read the date?"

I shake my head. After reading the first line, stating the purpose of the papers, I didn't scan the rest for information. Like I just said, a private matter.

He holds the page closer to me and drags his finger underneath the date. "It's the day *after* we met. Jaz and I had been separated for more than six months before everything was finalized. And technically, our separation goes back more than two years."

"But . . ." My gaze snaps to his eyes. "You were at the cabin the next morning with her."

"Jaz and I had an appointment in the afternoon."

My eyes narrow. "You told me the other day you live in Kentucky."

Thad sighs. "Okay, *Cliff Notes* version. Jasmine and I married in Tennessee. It was quicker to get a divorce in the same state where we married. I was in North Carolina, as I told you, because I wanted a night alone before this." He shakes the papers.

"But you weren't alone." *He was with me.*

"Yeah, I hadn't exactly planned for . . . us . . . to happen." He gives me a knowing grin while lowering his arm. "Something out of character, remember? Something no one would have expected."

"Nothing happened between us."

Thad's jovial face instantly hardens, and he tosses the

papers to the worktable behind me as he glares at me. "Look me in the eyes and say that to me again."

When our eyes lock, my tongue ties. I can't lie to him. That night had meant something to me despite learning he had a wife the next morning. The night had been magical, almost otherworldly. The connection between us irresistible, not to mention Thad gave me out of this world orgasms.

"That's what I thought," he says when I take too long to respond.

He blows out a breath and scratches the back of his neck. "Anyway, Jaz and I lived in Kentucky. She still does as the house is hers."

"You gave her your house?"

He shrugs. "She needs it."

"Why?"

His answer doesn't come because the lobby door opens, and two men enter with an older woman. She's striking with deep wrinkles in her face and wild gray hair that cascades over her shoulders in gorgeous waves. She glances around the open space, taking her time to inspect the sunshine dust and the muted glass windows before turning in our direction. A warm smile curls her thin lips.

"Hello," I say, clasping my hands together.

"Lindee," Thad starts. "These guys are Duke and Manor James, my cousins, and partners."

"Nah, you're the boss," one man jokes, pulling my attention to him. He has short, cropped, dark hair, and a lean stature compared to Thad. A hint of resemblance exists between them around his nose. "Hi, I'm Duke."

He steps forward and holds out a hand. When we shake, his grip is strong and his hold firm. Tattoos cover his arms.

"Hey beautiful. Manor's your man." The second man butts in on Duke's handshake, elbowing the other man to release my hand. Then, Manor is gripping my fingers and lifting them to his lips. Tattoos cover his knuckles. His gaze rises to mine as he brushes his mouth over my knuckles.

Oh, yeah, I see the resemblance to Thad in this one.

Manor's hair is pulled into a man bun, sporting streaks of gray. He's rugged looking while almost too pretty to be a man who gets dirty doing construction. His broad shoulders and tall stature mirrors Thad.

"Manor, dude," Duke muses beside him. "Excuse him. My brother has no manners despite his name."

I huff a laugh. "Nice to meet both of you."

"And this . . ." Thad steps over to the older woman and places a loving arm around her shoulder. "This is our grandmother, Nessi."

Thad guides her toward me, but this woman looks capable of holding her own. Dark eyes meet mine with warmth and questions. When she extends a hand, I capture it in both of mine.

"It's a pleasure to meet you." We didn't meet at the closing as lawyers had handled the transaction.

"I look forward to what you'll do for him."

"Excuse me?"

"The place," she nods, glancing upward and turning her head again, observing the dusty space. Those dark eyes return to me. "This one is special."

Does she mean the motel? Or Thad? I quickly peer at him and away, drawn back to the magnetism of the woman before me.

"I can't wait to get started." On that note, we have work to do and I'm not certain why Thad's grandmother is present. It's a little unprecedented to have the former owner around when a new owner begins demolition.

"Then, I won't keep you. I understand I'm here for backup."

"Excuse me?" I stammer again, glancing at Duke and

Manor who stand tall, one with a smirk, the other with a crooked smile, as they watch their grandmother.

"Thaddeus thought he might need support. Sort of proof in the pudding." A gleam fills her dark eyes. "And I'm the pudding."

"In case you needed further assurance that I am not currently married, nor would I remain married, on the night we met," Thad speaks.

My mouth falls open and remains in a chin drop. "You brought your grandmother to me to confirm you were divorced?" *Incredible.*

"Whatever convincing you need, I am prepared to bring the proof." Thad tips up his head, a smug smile on his face as he crosses his strong, tattooed arms.

"But your grandmother?" I ask, seeking confirmation that I'm understanding correctly that he asked an eighty-something year old woman to be his defense.

"Nessi knows how to get things done," Manor quips with a soft chuckle.

Watching me, her eyes soften while she shakes her head. "These boys. You'd think they can handle themselves as grown men but they're still rascals."

Duke chuckles, dropping his head.

It's evident these three grown men love this woman.

"Well, with your grandmother as your witness, is there anything else I should know?" Snarky once again, I can't believe this grandmother is defending her adult grandson.

"The only stipulation I have in working together is I need every weekend off or at least every other weekend."

"Every other weekend?" I bark. I don't anticipate being a difficult task master, but I was still hoping for the occasional Saturday push and even a Sunday here and there.

Why would a divorced man need every other weekend off unless—

"Do you have kids?"

14

———————

Playlist: "If I Told You" – Darius Rucker

[Thad]

"**Y**ou got something against kids?" With arms crossed, my defenses rise. There is one area I won't take shit and that's my children. And the sharp shock in Lindee's voice has my hackles rising.

"No." Her voice softens as she blinks twice, before emphasizing, "No, of course not."

"Got any of your own?" Duke asks her, his voice a little too inquisitive.

Lindee's expression tightens as if she's been stricken. Her hand lifts to her chest.

Fuck, I don't want to keep hurting her, yet that's all I seem to do. How she found out about Jasmine. How she's learning I have kids. Fact is, Lindee and I have a lot to learn about each other and this isn't how I planned for her to hear about Sasha,

Vicki, and Sam.

And this isn't an interrogation. We aren't here to bully her, and Duke needs to tone it down a notch.

Still, Lindee shakes her head. "No."

I can't tell if she's hurt by the question or disappointed by her answer.

"Okay, you big bullies, let's let them be for a second," Gran commands, stepping over to the antiquated fireplace. Her fingers wander the classic red brick and then her gaze shifts to the floor-to-ceiling windows. Maybe she sees in her head what this place once was. With Pop gone, each location she owns holds a memory perhaps she no longer wants to recall.

The former manager neglected this motel into its current rundown state. Being that Nessi is ninety, she doesn't travel from property to property like she used to.

Still, Gran is a fierce matriarch, pulling her offspring's offspring out of trouble and into her fold of lost black sheep. Vic, Duke, Manor, and I had been a handful. Their mom and my dad had been siblings, but their father was like a brother to mine. Brothers outside of blood.

"Look." I step closer to Lindee and lower my voice. "I'm sorry I didn't mention my kids but there hardly seemed to be a right time." Between rescuing her from the situation by the river, then taking her on a ride, and chasing her after she ran away in the rain, the kids hadn't crossed my mind.

I only had one person in my head. Her.

"Oh, I don't know, somewhere between learning you had a wife and finding out you don't, would have been nice," she sasses. Her arms cross. Her hip juts out. She's wearing pants that band at her ankle and a T-shirt that hugs her curves.

Damn, she's so cute.

And fuck Manor for pouring on the charm. He can't have her. She's mine to keep.

"I'm sorry." An apology is the best I can offer. I should have mentioned my kids. As the three most important people to me, next to Nessi, Duke, and Manor, I should have told Lindee about them, but she knows now. I'm a single dad.

Lindee's brows pinch. "And this is why Jasmine needs your house. To raise your children."

"*We* raise our children," I emphasize. I'm as involved as I can be while I live separately from them. "I have them every other weekend and two nights a week during the summer."

"And how is that going to work with you here, an hour away?"

"I haven't quite figured that out yet." As the school year ended, Jasmine and I fell into a routine. With extracurricular activities for the kids, scheduling our nights didn't seem to matter. I didn't miss a game or an event. The kids never spent a night with me, though, because of school. Now that it is summer, things have been looser, and they hang at Nessi's on my nights.

Because of Nessi, I couldn't turn down this job, and Jasmine agreed she'd be accommodating, giving me nights according to when they were available. She didn't have a choice. She didn't want to tackle mediation again. The risk of involving lawyers was dangerous for her. She had too many strikes stacked against her as an ex-wife and mother.

For the most part, Jasmine and I had an understanding. She kept her lies while I knew the truth.

"This isn't going to work," Lindee interjects.

"It will." It must. "And speaking of work, we need to get started."

Eight weeks is going to go by quickly and her goal is to be open by Labor Day weekend. Typically, the holiday marks the end of summer, but Lindee hopes to capture the attention of leaf-peepers. The information was in the business plan she'd attached to the purchase agreement. Lindee wanted Nessi to know *how* she planned to care for the old motel.

She has sentimentality in her, like Gran.

The dragonfly cuff is further proof. Moments in time are special to Lindee.

I turn and tip my head at Duke and Manor, signaling it's time to get to business. The three of us will somehow be bunking together like old times. Reminding Manor we are in our forties, not fourteen, is going to be a constant struggle.

I point at Lindee. "Did you have breakfast?"

Sheepishly, she glances away from me and shakes her head.

"That's what I thought." I hold up the Tiny Bites bakery box and shake it at her. "I don't know what your favorite is yet, so I bought a collection. And as I still don't know how you take your coffee, it's black, but I brought a variety of flavored creams and sugar."

Lindee fights a smile. "If you want to know something about me, just ask."

I smile back, liking her sass. "Nah. I like the challenge." *I'll figure you out yet, sweet thing.*

"Mind if I look around?" Nessi addresses Lindee, interrupting us and catching on Lindee's eyes. Gran is searching for something in the new motel owner. She wants to believe Lindee can work a miracle here.

As for me, I just want a chance with this woman whose hackles are raised like fists balled in the air and aiming for a punch.

I'll fight the fight with her, because something tells me, she's worth the battle.

For the next week, including the weekend because I don't have the kids, we tackle Lindee's first goal—the winter cabin.

Every day, I bring her Tiny Bites donuts until I learn her favorite is the one with white frosting and crushed nuts on the top. She eventually told me apple cider donuts are her favorite, but they won't be available until the fall. She takes her coffee with two hazelnut creamers and a packet of sugar.

My sweet thing has a sweet tooth.

The winter cabin is freestanding. The location was the original owner's home back in the late fifties. Tucked up a gravel drive, it's slightly off to the left of the main motel and mostly surrounded by trees. When Nessi bought the place, a manager was given a room instead of the three-bedroom house. Lindee wants to add a sleeping loft in a vacant attic space above the existing bedrooms due to a high ceiling in the living room.

She has a vision, and I'm liking how she isn't afraid to get her hands dirty and dig in with us. She had several items lined up already, like replacement appliances and bathroom fixtures, as well as wallpaper for the front room that replicates birch tree trunks.

Hanging wallpaper is a bitch, though, and Lindee and I find ourselves working late at night under a halogen light to hang the long sheets.

"Why'd you even want to buy a motel?" I ask from atop the ladder where I struggle to line the top of the sheet up with the ceiling.

"I did hotel makeovers in a former life." Lindee stands below me, inspecting my work.

"How'd that come about?"

"I went to school for business but wasn't certain what I wanted to do with myself. Found out I hated corporate America and took a job with a small design firm looking for task help. I'd been in theater in high school, building sets for plays, so I had some sense of layout and design. I started out painting walls and trim. Hanging wallpaper. I liked the manual work. My first assignment was a bed and breakfast renovation. I made a few suggestions outside of the designer's input and the owners liked my ideas. Word spread." She pauses a second. "One job led to a recommendation which led to another job. I've designed places all over the continental United States. I didn't mind traveling which made me a hot commodity."

I line up the paper as she continues. "I renovated boutique hotels, cabin resorts, and roadside motels, like this one. But I wanted something for me and when this place came on the market, one look and I had to have it. Plus, my sister lives in Wrightwood, about forty minutes from here."

"Your story sounds a little like mine," I say, sweeping the wallpaper brush downward to smooth out the glue and keep the paper aligned. "Had a job, then kind of lost my way for a bit. Didn't know where to turn, what direction to take. Nessi put me to work fixing up her old farmhouse. Construction suited me." With my hands busy, my mind was occupied from all I'd left behind as I tried to figure out what lay ahead. "Thus, the company with Duke and Manor."

It's the short version of a long story that isn't as simplistic as I just stated. Duke and Manor showed up a few years after I started, and both were eager to learn. We'd all been good with our hands, understanding how things fit together like a giant puzzle.

"Your cousins are nice guys." A smile fills her voice. "And they do good work."

The week has been filled with a few mishaps and lots of teasing. Lindee has kept her patience through most of it. She's also a little quirky, shaking her hips and humming a tune as she works on something. She can get hyper-focused and stay on task like no one I've ever met.

"Yeah, they're my best friends, like brothers. We were practically raised by Nessi and Pop."

"Pop?"

"My grandfather." I pause. "The lion head ring." I remind

her of the ring I'd told her was my grandfather's and not a wedding band. I didn't own a wedding band. I'd been wearing Pop's ring for years as it brought me comfort. Reminded me to stay strong. The heavy gold was a memento of old ways and good times. "I moved in with them after my parents died when I was twelve."

After all this time, a lump still forms in my throat at the mention of my parents. I quickly clear it with a cough.

"I'm sorry you lost them." The sympathy in Lindee's voice rings sincere. "Do you . . . I mean, can I ask . . ."

"What happened?" My voice hitches. Slowly, I'd need to introduce Lindee to my past. Strangely, I wanted to tell her everything, but all in due time. This story would be one of the easiest to share.

"I don't want to make you talk about it if you don't want—"

"Road accident." Thirty-three years and it still hurts to think about. A road accident, as in someone side-swiped their motorcycle. More like purposely ran into the back tire, sending the bike into a tailspin. The truth was something no kid should ever hear. The images conjured in my head still haunt me. Things like missing limbs and decapitation. Acrid bile fills my throat.

My parents had been cremated. Vic and I were told they didn't want to be planted in the ground but spread along the open road which they both loved.

Lindee is quiet a second and her silent sympathy climbs the ladder like the tendrils of a vine. "I didn't have a dad. My grandfather was my father figure."

I work my way down the ladder to a height where she can take over the ladder and wallpapering. I'd love to pull her into a hug, but we trade places without eye contact. She's been good at not looking directly at me for a week.

"Oh yeah, how's that?"

"When I was a baby, my dad took off. Never looked back on

his four kids or my mom. She kind of fell apart and Grandad stepped in."

Shit. "That sucks. Are you and your mom close?"

Lindee huffs. "Not exactly." She smooths over the paper, working at a wrinkle where I left off. "It isn't that we disagree, it's just . . . I'm different from the rest of my family."

"How so?" Watching her arm move, I concentrate on her tight, small muscles so I don't focus on her ass in shorts just above my eye level. The past few days has been a test of wills as Lindee has worked beside me in a variety of body-hugging pants and cute, short bib overalls. She has quite the collection of concert and travel T-shirts, hinting at all the places she's been.

"Let's just say everyone else has been driven and I'm not."

"I'd say renovating hotels shows some drive."

"Yeah, but moving around has given me a rep as a vagabond. I don't have anywhere I call home."

For some reason, this surprises me.

"What about River City?" Earlier this week, Lindee mentioned she was from a small town somewhere southeast in Missouri.

"Don't really consider it home as I only visit once a year during a holiday." She lowers a few rungs on the ladder.

"Is Karen your home?" Is this woman living out of a camper?

Lindee snorts. "Karen is a rental until I can make a space for myself here in the cabin. When we finish this rehab, I'm hoping to buy a house nearby. Maybe." The hesitation in her voice speaks volumes. She isn't certain she'll stay.

"Then what? Are you planning on managing the motel?"

"Don't know yet." Lindee pauses, staring at her handiwork. "I never really have a plan further than the project I'm working on."

"Are you considering selling?" My stomach drops. I'm not in

a position to buy this place yet. And the idea of Lindee leaving after our remaining seven weeks are finalized doesn't settle well with me either.

There's something about her that draws me in. Something special about her. She's mesmerizing, familiar even, despite hardly knowing her. She's always dancing around, making snarky comments, or laughing at her own mistakes. She doesn't take any mishap too seriously and she doesn't fight with any of us, although we can be a moody bunch, especially Duke if he's hungover.

"Not yet." A smile fills Lindee's voice as she concentrates on the wallpaper. "But I let the Universe guide me."

"That's a lot of faith in the unknown." Then again, I once lived that same philosophy. Riding where I wanted, when I wanted. Taking risks at will. Whatever happened happened. Then everything fell apart.

Her impulsive streak might have been one of the first things that attracted me to her. Now, I don't want her to do anything rash or in a rush.

Let's just get through seven more weeks.

Lindee moves down a few more rungs. "The Universe hasn't let me down so far."

The tone of her voice sounds more like she's trying to convince herself rather than reassure me.

We remain quiet as Lindee works the first strip of paper which resembles a field of birch trees with their distinct peeling bark and dark notches. She makes her way down the remainder of the ladder, and I move it out of the way when she can stand on her own feet. She squats to smooth the print to the floor. When she's finished, she stands and takes a step back.

I don't move and she bumps into me. With her back to my front, I place a hand on her hip to steady her and we stare at the wallpaper with long, thin trunks of paperwhite birch trees.

"What do you think?"

"I hope you'll stay planted."

Lindee twists and glances at me over her shoulder. A crease forms between her brows. "I meant about the wallpaper."

"I like it."

I like her more. And I meant what I said. I want her to stay.

15

———

Playlist: "Layla" – Eric Clapton

[Lindee]

For nearly two weeks, Thad has made cryptic comments to me, like saying he wants me to stay planted. It's as if he senses I'm a woman who follows the wind. Then again, I don't know why he'd want me here as he doesn't live in the vicinity, and he has a family. I'm not opposed to him having children but being a dad is a sensitive issue for me. This project is keeping him from his three kids and I'm not comfortable with that.

I've learned that Sasha just turned thirteen and is a handful, as teenage girls can be.

Victoria, or Vicki, is eleven and an angel in comparison.

Sam is the only boy, and at eight, he looks like his father did at the same age.

"Trouble waiting to happen," Duke had teased.

"Sasha's going to be the pain in the ass. She's more like Jaz every day and that is not good," Manor had added.

Because I was a child raised without a father, even if Grandad was the best, I feel sorry for Thad's children. Maybe I even feel guilty about keeping him from his kids, but his grandmother wrote him into the contract, making him part of the renovation team.

I'd once argued that Duke and Manor could do the job without Thad, they both strongly disagreed.

"We're brothers in a sense," Manor had told me.

"Where he goes, we go." Duke gave Manor a look to confirm their position. The three grown men have a tight history, and their loyalty to one another was unparalleled.

At one point, Jane, Mae, and I had been thick as thieves. When we were young, Jane was the second in command, underneath Mom. Which meant Jane was in charge most of the time. Our mother had checked out once Dad left. Garrett, our brother, was in a world all his own as the oldest, the only boy, and the one with the most memories of Dad before he skipped out.

I'm told my parent's marriage was not happy.

From what I know about my birth, I surmised such a thing.

The guys made quick work of replacing floors and installing cabinets in the small kitchen in the winter cabin. They were even good sports as they finished my little off-plan design to add a sleeping loft. The walls are painted. The wallpaper hung. Vertical woodwork surrounding the fireplace adds character to the main living space.

And every day, a bakery box with a Tiny Bites donut appears along with flavored coffee.

Sometimes in the middle of the day, Thad will ask me what my plans are for lunch and half the time I've forgotten to put anything together. He orders out for all of us, but occasionally a sandwich appears for me. I'm forgetful about meals as I'm a muncher, taking a break when I want but often working through set mealtimes.

Thad has also asked me to join him and the guys every night for dinner, but I pass, stealing away to a local diner or stopping at the closest grocery store and picking up microwavable items. At forty-two, I should have better eating habits, but I don't.

This is all to say . . . I don't take great care of myself and Thad's interest in my eating schedule has me puzzled. I'm not used to someone being concerned for me.

On Sunday, I miss my daily treat of a tiny delicacy and sweet coffee, but I'm in the finisher zone. Thad has the weekend off as promised. Duke and Manor worked on Saturday, but I demanded they take a break today. They suggested I do the same, but I'm in the cabin unpacking dishes and towels, making beds, and hanging pictures. This is my favorite part of a job. When everything comes together as I planned, and the space is ready for people to enjoy.

Future memories are waiting to be had here.

Moving a couch on my own isn't easy, so I'm doing this thing where I move one side a few inches and then walk to the other end, moving it a few inches, then step back to assess the space. I'm back to the right side, hitching it up a little bit to swing it a few more inches when the front door of the cabin opens.

"What are you doing?"

"Moving the couch," I strain as Thad enters.

"Let me help you." He walks to the opposite side and picks it up with ease almost knocking me over with how quickly he lifts his end. "Where do you want it?"

"Just come my way about eight inches." For some reason, our eyes lock. The corner of Thad's mouth ticks upward.

"Now isn't the time for a dirty mind," I stress as I lift my end of the new furniture.

He chuckles. "I didn't say a thing."

He didn't have to. The smirk on his face says it all.

"More importantly, why are you working?"

"I want to feel like I've accomplished something." I set the couch down, eyeballing that it is in the right position, square with the fireplace on the opposite wall. The birch tree wallpaper on either side of the wooden fireplace surround makes the room feel outdoorsy while chic and cozy.

"This entire week was an accomplishment," Thad says. "This place is going to be great again."

"Thanks," I huff, glancing at my watch to see it's just after one. "But I didn't do it alone. You guys are an excellent team. And a better question is why are you here?"

"*We* make an excellent team." Thad holds my gaze a second with another cryptic comment. "And today should be time off the clock."

"No time off for me," I announce, rounding the couch, giving it another glance, and moving the low table before it a few inches to balance the layout. "But today is your day off."

"Sweet thing." Thad catches my wrist as I stand. "Stop moving a second."

"I don't want to stop."

Thad can't possibly understand that standing still causes my thoughts to race. And lately, my mind wanders to him and that night and the things I miss about us. The way he kissed me. The way he touched me. The way we moved together.

I can't think about it. While we work together, it isn't healthy for me, or helpful. He has kids, an ex-wife, and a life I'm never going to be a part of. Not that I'm ever *involved* in someone's life. I just don't want to be an issue for Thad.

"Then take a ride with me."

"A ride?" I choke. Thad has both his pickup truck and his motorcycle on site, and the last time I took a ride with him, look what happened. I slept with him. It messed with my head and cracked open my heart. It literally fucked with me. "I don't think that's a good idea."

"It's a great idea. In fact, I'm demanding you come with me. There's somewhere I want to show you. You'll need a bathing suit."

"Thad," I groan, shoulders falling.

"I know you don't like large bodies of water, and this place isn't that. We need to hike a bit to get there, so put a suit on underneath your clothes."

The July days have been warm, and most of our work has been inside. Some fresh air would be nice and a little separation from this place might be a good idea. A hike doesn't sound too bad.

"You still haven't said why you're here." He still had the remainder of the day to be with his kids and I don't want the job or me to be an excuse for why he returned early.

"Vicki left for summer camp. Sasha wanted to go to a friend's house. With only Sam left, Nessi asked if she could have a date with him, taking him to a movie and getting ice cream." He shrugs. "And I missed you."

Dammit, he can't say things like that to me. I give him a scathing look. His cryptic comments are messing with my head as well and I need to stay focused. On task, on target, and not on Thad.

Only he crosses his eyes and sticks out his tongue, and I laugh.

"Okay," I exhale, defeated, and wave my arms upward. "How about a half hour?"

"How about ten minutes?" That crooked smile of his appears, along with victory in his whiskey eyes.

"Fifteen," I counter, crossing my arms and cocking out my hip.

"Fifteen." He winks. "Now what else needs to be moved?"

WITH THE COUCH IN PLACE, there isn't more furniture to arrange, so I leave behind the unfinished final touches of the cabin and strut to Karen.

While I change, my phone rings.

"Hey," I call out to Jane as I hit the speaker button. My sister has been checking in on my health and the project's progress over the last two weeks. She's as concerned about the work as she is my mental state. Jane understands a little bit about my predicament with Thad.

I don't really want to be marked as the other woman and I don't want to take Thad away from his kids.

"Hey you. Come for dinner?"

"I can't. Apparently, I'm going on a hike and swimming. I don't know when I'll be back." I remove my clothing as I shout and struggle into my bathing suit. *Did I gain weight?*

"Sounds like a date," Jane teases.

With my fingers on a pair of overall shorts, I freeze and scoff, "It's not a date."

"Which one is it? Duke, Manor, or Thad?"

While I've told Jane each man is handsome in his own right, she knows Thad is the one I'm most attracted to, when I shouldn't be. He's a recent divorcé, and a single dad of three kids who need his attention.

"Funny," I snap, stepping into the short bibs and pulling them up my waist. I reach for a T-shirt next and tug it over my head before hooking the overalls into place over my shoulder.

"Would it hurt to date him?" Jane asks.

"It wouldn't help."

"Help what?"

I sigh and fold down onto the edge of my bed. "How much I like him." Dammit, I don't want to like Thad, but he's funny and sweet. He's generous with his time and attentive. He takes care of me, and I want to hate it, but I don't.

"You've been single a long time." Jane's voice is knowing.

I haven't had a boyfriend since I was twenty. That's a long time to lack commitment. But I've had my work and since I don't stay in one place for long, dalliances along the way are the norm. Not dates.

"I'm not single. I'm dating myself."

Jane guffaws. "You've been dating yourself for two decades."

This is rich coming from a woman who kept things tight to the chest herself for years as she had a seven-year relationship with the wrong man and then pretended to be married to Mr. Wright. Spoiler alert— they got married for real and Mach Wright is perfect for Jane.

"I like me," I state, while a weight presses on my shoulders. I like me well enough, but I'm also tired of life with service only for a table of one.

"Yes, but maybe it's time to let someone else like you, too." Jane's advice is well-meant, but she knows why I don't let others close. Falling in love is dangerous. And I've been carrying around the guilt for decades.

"Jane," I whisper.

"What's the worst that could happen?"

I could love him.

"Okay, second worst," she adds as if she heard my thoughts.

"I don't know," I huff with laughter.

"Orgasms. Lots of amazing orgasms."

When I told my sisters how I slept with Thad, who I thought was married, pseudo-married, or whatever he was then, part of my disappointment was the orgasms. As in, they were amazing. Thad was an incredible lover and I wasn't going to experience anyone like him in my future.

I laugh harder at my sister's suggestion until the camper door rattles with a knock.

"Shit. I need to go," I call toward the phone.

"Is that Orgasm Man?"

"Jane," I admonish. "Love you."

"I love you, too," she says before I click off the phone.

When I open the door, one glance and the idea of multiple orgasms hits my brain like a hammer. Thad is dressed in jeans and a tight T-shirt plus boots. He doesn't look like a man about to take a hike but one ready to ride off into the sunset on a highway leading nowhere. His eyes crackle like burnt sunshine.

"Orgasm Man, at your service," he snarks with a bow.

"Were you eavesdropping?"

"The camper windows are open. Voices carry." He tips his head toward the bedroom portion of Karen. The window is fully cranked out.

"Still," I huff.

"Whatever you need, I'm your man," he teases.

"Okay, I renege. I'm not going on a hike with you." I reach for the door to pull it shut but Thad catches it with his large hand.

"I'm kidding. Nothing untoward will happen."

"Who says untoward, old man?"

"Me. *Orgasm* Man."

I tug on the edge of the door, but Thad chuckles and pulls harder in the opposite direction. "Sweet thing, get your ass on my bike."

Something about the way he commands me makes my skin pebble. My heart skips a beat. I want on his bike. I want on *him* again. But I squash the thought and grab my backpack.

I can behave myself. Just because I'm highly attracted to a man with a gruff voice and a body built for sin does not mean I'll sleep with him.

At least not a second time, that is.

WE HIT the highway and take our time wandering along wooded byways until Thad slows and pulls off onto a faintly visible gravel path. Good thing we're on his motorcycle, because the lane is hardly large enough for a normal sized vehicle. The space opens up only slightly into a circular clearing, matted down by parked vehicles. Trails head outward from this makeshift parking lot. After Thad shuts off the engine and dismounts, he takes my hand and guides me toward a path to our right.

Holding hands, we hike among the trees, descending a sloped footpath. A rushing sound fills my ears, growing louder the further we walk until Thad abruptly stops and I pull up next to him.

"I present to you, the smallest body of water that I know of."

Before us, a waterfall cascades into a child-sized basin.

"What is this?" I laugh, watching the water teem from somewhere up above and bubble in the shallow depths.

"When we were kids, Pop and Gran brought us here. They said it was a secret spot full of magic. When we grew older, we learned either my dad or Duke and Manor's mom was conceived in this natural pool."

I giggle at the thought of ninety-year-old Nessi and a man with a strong resemblance to Thad having sex here.

"No babies are happening here." I nod at the water while glaring at Thad.

"I'm shooting blanks now, babe. No worries on that front."

Wait, what? "You wore condoms when we were together."

"First time being with someone other than Jaz in fourteen years. Sex safety and all that."

I stare at him. "I was your first?" I don't know that I've ever been *first* for anyone, other than Harris, and I'm shocked that a sexual man like Thad hadn't been with someone else before me. I feel . . . honored.

Thad lowers his backpack to the ground and tugs off his T-shirt without looking at me. "I'm not a cheating man, Lindee. I was faithful to Jasmine during our marriage." He hesitates as he drops his shirt and loosens his belt. His eyes finally meet mine. "Between you and me, I can't say the same for her."

My stomach drops out. I'd been the one to accuse Thad of cheating on his wife *with me*, and he's just dropped this bomb. His ex-wife stepped out on him. How could that be? Thad is amazing.

"Is that why you divorced?"

"Just one of many reasons," he states, before unzipping his zipper and hooking his hands into the waistband of his jeans, working them down his legs and exposing a pair of swim trunks I wouldn't have expected on such a rugged man.

"Are those palm trees?" His swim shorts distract me from apologizing for misjudging him.

"My daughter picked them out. Real men wear pink." With that, Thad gingerly steps into the small body of water. As he lowers, I have a better sense of the depth. Thad is only waist deep when he tucks his upper body into a seated position. His arms wave through the pond.

"Coming in?" His sunshine eyes are heated, watching me as I slowly pop the shoulder buttons on my bib shorts.

"Have I told you how cute those bibs are on you?"

I shake my head.

"Want to get you out of them every time you wear 'em."

The warmth in his words or maybe the flame in his eyes makes a part of me pulse that has no business pulsing.

I wiggle the overalls over my hips and kick them off. Then stand tall and pull up my T-shirt.

"Damn," Thad groans as I stand on the edge of the pond in a bikini.

My hand covers my lower belly. I have gained some weight, although being sick last week certainly made me feel like I'd lost a few pounds. Maybe I'm just making up for a lack of appetite and overeating from energy exerted because of manual labor around the motel.

I dip my toe into the water then jerk back. "It's cold."

"It's refreshing." Thad smiles, slicing his arms through the water. He can practically reach side to side in this pool.

Lowering my foot deeper into the water, I bark, "It's freezing." Then I'm squealing as Thad lunges forward, catches my wrist and tugs me toward him. The water is a shock and I cry out again.

Thad laughs as he cradles me in his arms, settling me on his lap, keeping us shoulder level with the surface.

Wrapping my arms around his neck, I shiver. "Oh my God, you are such a liar."

"Yeah, that's another thing I'm not, sweetheart. I might not have been upfront about Jaz or the kids, but I am not a liar." His tone drops as cool as the liquid around us.

My gaze meets his. He showed me the divorce papers with a notarized date. He brought his grandmother as a witness. His cousins further confirmed his marital status.

Jasmine and Thad had been separated, but living together, until about six months ago.

Manor told me most of Thad's belongings were in a bunkhouse the guys share on Nessi's land, and the night Thad signed his divorce papers, he was there. He never went back to what is now considered Jasmine's house.

Trust me, Thad is asking as he squeezes me tighter to his rock-hard chest.

"Okay," I whisper, dropping my gaze and watching water sluice down the side of his neck.

Thad abruptly stands, taking me up with him, and causing me to squeal once again. Then he takes a step toward the waterfall.

"You wouldn't," I cry out, tightening my hold on him, tugging myself upward against his body.

"I would. And I will." With another step, he slips under the waterfall which showers us in pelting, freezing sheets. I don't dare open my mouth with another scream for fear I'll drown, so I tuck my head into Thad's neck and squeeze my eyes shut as water pummels our skin. My flesh pebbles. My nipples harden.

Thad continues to move through the water and suddenly we are behind it.

My head pops up. Glancing around, water cascades behind Thad's back, like a curtain shielding us from view. Enclosed in a small cavern, Thad sets me on the edge of water-smoothed rocks. His lower body remains in the water. With his hands on my thighs, he spreads my legs and stands between them. His fingers dig into my flesh.

"Let me kiss you, Lindee."

I should say no. I should not go down the Thad-path again, but my body is betraying me. My nipples are hard peaks from the contrast of cold water and his warm body. My center hums, and my mouth goes dry.

When our eyes meet, I don't have the willpower to deny him. His mouth is on mine in an instant, wet and thirsty. His tongue presses forward, familiar and fierce. It's as if time and distance hasn't existed from that one night to now, as if I've been kissing him all the days between then and today. We're ravenous for one another.

His mouth releases mine and he skims his lips down my chin, scraping his teeth over the hard edge and continuing down my neck. He sucks my skin, then licks along my collar bone to my shoulder. He nips me there.

"I need to taste you."

"Oh God," I whimper as my back arches and a part of me seeks a part of him.

"Lean back a little." Thad pulls me to the edge of the rock shelf and I'm able to fold back to my elbows. The surface is hard, but I'm quickly distracted when he's untying the sides of my bikini bottoms, eyes focused on the unveiling of private parts pulsing with need.

"I've hungered for another taste of you, sweet thing. Four fucking months, two weeks, and five days. Not going to wait that long again." He lowers his head and laps against my sensitive skin. The warmth of his tongue contrasts with the coolness of my flesh. After the first swipe, he proves how hungry he's been, devouring me while my head tips back and my hips thrust upward, eager for the attention he's giving my center.

Two fingers slide inside me as the tip of his tongue teases my clit. Then, I'm a rock ballad only he can play as his fingers strum and his tongue swirls to the melody of rushing water behind him. When I release, the groan of my pleasure echoes in the hollowed cave. Thad doesn't stop until my legs tremble and I'm pressing at his head. He kisses my lower belly, working his way up my body until he bites my nipple through my bikini top. Then his mouth seeks mine and he's kissing me like he took me lower.

My core presses against the warmth of his belly, needing more of him.

Only Thad pulls back and reaches for the strings to my bathing suit. He rights one side.

"Thad," I whisper.

"That was all for you, sweet thing."

"I want you," I admit and Thad freezes. His gaze catches with mine. "Let me take care of you."

"Nah, sweetheart. I'm good."

Sitting upright, I place a hand on his chest. "I don't like that. Let me reciprocate."

"This doesn't have to be tit for tat."

I cup the thick bulge in his swim shorts. "Then let it be tit for Thad."

He chuckles, deep and throaty, causing the sound to reverberate around us. I lean forward and kiss him until I'm slipping toward him and coaxing him to trade places with me.

"Sweetheart," he moans against my mouth.

"I want to taste you again as well."

Thad tugs at the Velcro holding his trunks at his waist. Then he pushes down the sides until his heavy shaft springs forward. With a gentle hop, he sits on the edge of the rock shelf, and I tug his bathing suit to his ankles.

I wrap my hand firmly around the thickness of his dick. The man is a masterpiece. Working up and down the shaft a few times, the tip weeps and I take my first lick. Salty-sweet and refreshing, I open wide and take him to the back of my throat.

"Fuck," he grunts. His hand cups the back of my head, petting me down to my neck. "That feels so good, Lindee."

My name is strained as I suck to the tip then take him deep again. Up and down I go, until both his hands are on my neck, the tension in him tight. He wants to surge forward but he's letting me lead until he can't take it anymore.

"Sweet thing," he groans before tugging me toward him, forcing him to the back of my throat and spilling down it. His arms move to his sides, bracing him as his hips gently coast upward while his release glides down my throat.

Eventually, he stills, and I make a final swipe up his length.

"Jesus, Lindee." His hands cup my cheeks, and he tugs me to him, kissing me open mouthed minus tongue. Pulling back, he rests his forehead against mine. His eyes close and I kiss his nose. Then his eyelids. Eventually, I kiss the corner of his lips and pull away.

Suddenly, I'm shivering from the cold water around my legs and the coolness of the cavern. Or maybe it's the intimacy of the moment, the romantic atmosphere and the praise in my name on his rugged voice.

I don't deserve him worshipping me.

"We should probably warm up a bit," I say.

Thad rubs his hands up and down my arms before I step back, dampening the moment.

"This is going to hurt, isn't it?"

"What is?" Thad questions as I've given him my back while he rights his bathing suit.

Him. My heart. "The waterfall," I lie.

We need to go through the water curtain to the other side in order to exit the pond.

And I'm not a person who ever likes to retrace my steps.

16

———

Playlist: "Simple Man" – Lynyrd Skynyrd

[Thad]

Something happened between the heavenly release down her throat and exiting the waterfall cave.

Lindee is shutting down before me. As we towel off and redress over our wet bathing suits, she remains quiet.

The silence is frightening. "Did I do something wrong?" I ask once our clothes are on. My hand catches her elbow, afraid to leave the magic of this location. Afraid I'll never have another moment like I've just had with her.

"It's not you. It's me."

The slap of her words stings. How many times had I said the same thing to women before Jaz?

"Tell me," I demand. What is it about her? And why is it that I can't let her go?

Lindee simply shakes her head and shrugs away from my

touch. I follow her as we hike the path back to the gravel parking plot. When we exit the trees, Duke's pickup is parked next to my bike. The guys knew I was bringing Lindee here. They must have taken the path to the left.

"Are Duke and Manor here?" Lindee's brows crease as she glares at me.

"They wouldn't have seen a thing, if that's what you're worried about." The whole it's-not-you-thing sits on my chest like a boulder. Maybe she doesn't want anyone to know we hooked up. Too late, as Nessi, Duke, and Manor are aware of how and when I first met Lindee.

"I'm not," her voice cracks. "It's just . . . where did they go?"

I pause. I really don't want to face my cousins right now, but I'm also not ready to let Lindee out of my sight. If I take her back to the motel, she's going to disappear into Karen or return to working on the winter cabin and she needs a break. She looks tired and sometimes I worry she hasn't recovered enough from being sick before she dove into working alongside us. She refuses to give herself time off.

"Let's go see." Although I already know where the other path leads.

When Pop introduced us to the waterfall, he also brought us to the river. The niche in the trees was slowly carved out from our visits. The place was a best-kept secret, but the worn path hints the secret is spreading. Gran would have bought the land if she could, but it's state property.

When we break free of the forest on this path, a flat plateau of rock formations overlooks a river down below. The drop isn't far, roughly thirty feet, which is less than half the distance professional cliff divers jump. My cousins and I were amateurs, and I haven't jumped in ages.

On the flat rocky surface is a scattering of towels and bags. I glance over toward the railway bridge that crosses the river near here. Duke and Manor are making their way to the steel structure.

"Let's jump," I turn to Lindee. This is what I need to shake off the letdown. The euphoria of her mouth wrapped around me and then the crash of her mood.

"Are you kidding?" Lindee's eyes meet mine.

I shrug off my shirt.

"You're serious." Her tone drops.

I kick off my boots. The adrenaline builds. I can't remove my clothing fast enough. Tugging down my jeans, I'm wearing only my briefs as I'd removed my bathing suit. A double layer of wetness beneath denim isn't comfortable and I'd have gone commando, but something told me to keep my knickers on.

Nessi's voice runs through my head. She's the one who taught us all to jump.

Heart first. Head second.

Listen to your heart. Let your head catch up later.

"Thad." Lindee's strained groan is mixed with something deeper, something pleading.

I'd never push her to jump, though. "Afraid of heights. I remember."

Lindee continues to watch me, eyes pleading with me.

But I need the rush. I need to savor those few blissful seconds, suspended in midair, as I fly. The thrill of water rushing over me as I dive further down. I crave the silence of the water submerging my head.

I give Lindee a small kiss on her worried forehead, then in bare feet and my boxer briefs, I turn toward the rocks leading to the bridge.

"Thad!" Lindee catches my forearm and I glance at her over my shoulder. "Don't do this. Please."

Maybe she's just worried about me.

"I'll be fine, sweet thing." I shrug out from underneath her clasp as she'd done to me by the waterfall and leap to the next set of flat rocks.

"Thad," she cries after me, but I don't look back. With another hop I'm on another plateau, then another, until I'm at the edge of the train tracks.

Cupping my hands around my mouth, I holler, "Duke!"

Manor turns back first. He taps his brother who turns around and tips his head for me to follow. These fools are balancing on the hot surface of the metal tracks, but I step from railroad tie to railroad tie until I've hit the bridge.

As kids, we'd see who could last the longest. Bare feet on hot metal. First to jump lost some silly bet.

Then as we grew older, the goal was to feel the vibration of the train, wait until it was in sight, and then jump before it got too close.

The crazy shit we did as kids.

Vic had loved it. He was the daredevil among us, typically the one double-dog-daring us to follow him.

The thought of my brother opens the hole in my heart. Glancing up at Duke and Manor, I'm grateful for both of them. Cousins by blood, brothers by friendship. They are the best of men.

"Hey," Manor calls out as I finally catch up to them.

Duke gives me another chin tip. "Last man over loses."

"What are we even betting?" I scoff.

"Tearing off the roof on the motel," Manor states.

"By yourself," I huff. "Fuck, no. I'm not taking that bet." The roof is large and long, and not a job any person should tackle alone. I've spoken to our roofer friends about replacing the thing. Visitors need a sound roof over their head and whoever inspected the motel before Lindee bought it didn't do a good job in a few areas, the roof being one of them, although she's already told me a new roof is not in the budget this summer.

"Fine," Duke exhales. "First to jump gets to fuck our boss."

"Fuck that," I choke, ready to push my cousin over. "Lindee isn't a bargaining chip."

Duke chuckles, arching a brow at me, hinting his suggestion was intended to rile me.

Manor punches his brother's arm. "What is wrong with you?"

Duke shrugs. "I like her. And I haven't gotten laid in a long time. Plus, Thad here doesn't seem to be stepping up to the challenge."

"What challenge?" I snap, falling into the poke-the-bear trap he's set for me.

"Winning that woman's heart."

"Who's talking about hearts?" Still, I glance back at Lindee who is pacing on the plateau, like she's wearing a path over the flat rock. Her hands are in her hair. *Is she talking to herself?*

Why didn't she want me to jump?

I'd like to think it's because she's worried about me, but I'm not so certain. Not after that brush off by the pond.

Plus, I'm a simple man, and right now, I'm blinded by my desire to take this risk, master this feat, and clear my head around the mystery of Lindee, whose taste still lingers on my tongue.

I tear my gaze from her as Manor says, "Did you feel that?"

The vibration beneath my feet suggests only one thing.

"Train's coming." Duke whistles, mimicking the sound of a whistle.

We haven't agreed on a bet but suddenly the three of us are hyper-focused.

"It's been a long time," I say, looking down at the water below. *Thirty feet is nothing, right?* I shake out my hands and step to the very edge of the bridge, curling my toes over the side.

"Are we really doing this?" Manor stressfully laughs beside me.

"We're doing this," Duke states from the other side of Manor. Brother-in-arms always.

With the three of us lined up, we wait until we hear the blast of a train whistle. Glancing right, the engine appears like a mirage. It's not a high-speed train coming in our direction, but a freight one, pulling heavy cargo through these mountains.

A strong horn peals a warning in the air and the bridge begins to vibrate, rumbling under the weight of the rail carrier.

"On the count of three," Duke hollers over the roar approaching us.

My heart hammers. My pulse beats in my throat. Fuck, I need this rush.

And the next thing I know, we're hurtling in tandem even though I never heard Duke count. Our bodies are in tune with one another and as I tuck my legs, my head empties of all thought but one.

Vic.

The hard slap of water shocks the hell out of me. As I plunge beneath the surface, I hold my breath, taking in the darkness when my eyes pop open. Sinking into the abyss of black before I'm pushing upward with a strong kick, I seek the sunlight glimmering like a beacon on the surface. When I finally break free, I gasp for air, shake my head, and search for my cousins.

Duke has already popped up. Manor follows me. We pause only a second, catching our breaths before we break into laughter, rich and thick.

"What the fuck were we thinking?" Manor winces.

"That was fucking amazing," Duke cries out, letting out a sharp *whoop* that echoes off the water and bounces against the boulders on either side of us.

"Fuck yeah," I call out and seek Lindee standing still on the rocks up above. A thought hits me. "Fuck, we need to climb back up there, don't we?"

Duke chuckles.

Manor blows out a breath. "Dammit, I forgot about that."

At fifteen, we wouldn't have every thought ahead. *Heart first. Head second.*

At forty-five, I'm rethinking *not* thinking this through.

"Up we go, boys." Duke starts swimming to the water's edge.

Like jumping from a bridge, I haven't rock climbed in ages either. I wasn't out of shape, but I was out of practice, and rising was always harder than falling.

Fall down seven times, get up eight, Pop would say. Eventually, Vic didn't get up.

I push away thoughts of my brother as I need all my concentration on the climb. Foot here. Hands there. With upper body strength, I pull myself upward.

We each falter a time or two, but we take our time to forge a path and climb.

The metaphor of climbing this rock is not lost on me. Each of us have been at the bottom and might have made our own trail from where we'd been to where we are now, but the three of us were beside one another along the way. The four of us, actually. Vic had been there for a while, too.

As we near the top, Duke crests the plateau first. Lindee comes into view, and I fling myself over the final edge. Manor is last, and if we were kids, we'd have been calling out jeers and pointing fingers, setting out the dare he'd lost.

As adults, we breathe heavily from the exertion and take a moment to silently celebrate that we'd made it up the river bluff.

With Manor safely on the plateau, Lindee finally speaks.

"You three"—she inhales a deep, shaky breath—"are the biggest fucking idiots." With a stomp of her foot, she spins and stalks toward the trees, quickly disappearing down the path leading to the lot.

"What's up her ass?" Manor quips.

"It's nothing," I lie, suddenly very uneasy. Maybe it was immature of us to throw ourselves off a bridge in our forties. To feel like kids again when we clearly aren't. I don't want her to fault me for something so freeing, but maybe the decision was a bit rash.

As we stand here still trying to catch our breaths, bodies slowly feeling the tension of climbing up the rocks and the sting of the water smacking our skin, I follow her retreat with narrowed eyes. I want to understand the harshness of her words, the fear mixed beneath them, but I can't if she doesn't open up to me, and Lindee is a closed book. Open for a few pages of reading and then snapped shut like a secret code is written within the text.

Duke hits me in the chest with his towel and I swipe at the mixture of sweat and river water on my skin. Gone is the feel of Lindee in my arms and against my face when I'd tasted her behind the waterfall.

The three of us dress in silence. For the time being, I skip my boots, hooking them between my fingers, and hitch my backpack over one shoulder.

"Why'd you guys come here?" I ask when we're on the move.

"Once you mentioned taking Lindee to the waterfall, we wanted to check out the river. One thing led to another. Figured we'd go to the waterfall once you and Lindee left."

We all hold memories of this place. Bringing a woman to the waterfall hadn't been one for me, though.

Bringing Lindee here was another first.

The hidden spot was a great make-out and hook-up place, but there was something sacred at that pond for me. Even if the story of Pop and Nessi having sex was more of a ploy to keep us away from fooling around here with a girl, I never wanted to bring just any girl here. Pop might have said the waters brought on pregnancy, but that wasn't what had me avoiding the place.

It was the romance of this location. Pop proposed to Gran on the rock plateau we'd just jumped from.

Never wanted to climb another mountain without that woman at my side, he'd told us, referring to our grandmother.

Then he'd toss in once more how he got Nessi pregnant at the waterfall as a scare tactic.

Even as an old guy he couldn't keep quiet about their *sexcapades*. His attraction to our grandmother was evident in every look he gave her.

I'd wanted what they'd had.

When we clear the forest, Lindee is standing beside Duke's pickup truck, hands clutching the edge of the bed on the side closest to my bike. She's lengthening her arms and arching her back, then pulling herself forward. Back and forth, she tugs her body in agitation.

"Sweetheart," I call out as we near.

She spins toward me faster than I've ever seen someone turn. Her bone-white face strikes me first. The color is completely drained from her skin. Her body vibrates from releasing the edge of the truck and her hands are tightly balled fists, nearly red at the knuckles, she clenches them so hard. Rage clashes with chilling sorrow in her eyes.

A ragged breath escapes her before she screams at me. "Stay the hell away from me."

What the fuck?

The sharpness of her tone along with the strain in it stops me short.

"What the . . ." Manor pauses beside me.

Duke remains quiet as he rounds his truck for the driver's door, but my focus is on the woman before me.

Suddenly, a sob escapes Lindee, folding her in half. She hunches forward, covering her mouth with a hand while a fist rests against her chest as if holding in pain. Heavy tears fall from her eyes, desperately weighted with hurt.

I drop my boots and lower my pack to the ground before stepping closer to her, tugging her against my chest.

"What happened?" I breathe at her ear as I cup her head in my hand and wrap my arm around the middle of her back, tugging her as tight to me as I can get her.

She's trembling uncontrollably. Worse than the tremors of her fever. This is sheer fear. Or shock. Or both.

"Sweet thing," I whisper to her hair. "Talk to me."

She doesn't answer as sobs shake her shoulders. At first her arms are tucked between us, but slowly, forcefully she shoots them upward and around my neck, tugging herself to me as if she wants to burrow herself inside me.

"What's going on?" Manor softly asks beside me.

I spin Lindee and me only enough to meet his eyes and shake my head. I have no idea what's happening here, but I don't trust Lindee on the back of my bike. I don't trust her to hold onto me despite how firmly she's wrapped around my neck.

With my hand still on the back of her head and my other palm spread over her back, I address Manor. "Can you take my bike? Keys are in the bag."

I shift my head over to Lindee's other shoulder to catch Duke's gaze. "Can you give us a ride?"

"Of course." He nods once and opens the driver's door to his truck.

Releasing Lindee's head, I scoop up her legs. Her face tucks into my neck, her sobs soften but my skin is moist. Her tears are still falling.

With Lindee in my arms, Manor opens the passenger door for me, and I set Lindee on the seat. Duke's truck is newer with a console in the middle. Once I climb in, I hike Lindee onto my lap. She immediately buries her face in my neck again and throws her arms around me. Her back is to Duke.

As best I can, I lock the seat belt around us both. I don't have to warn Duke to be careful as he drives.

The journey back to Mountain Motel is quiet. With Lindee on my lap, I pull her left arm forward. My gaze catches on the semi-colon inked at her wrist.

Fuck. She'd told me before the tattoo didn't mean what I thought. She'd also told me it wasn't my business, but I'm making it my business now. I need to know what just happened by the river, but it would have to wait until we were back at the motel.

17

Playlist: "River" – Leon Bridges

[Thad]

Once we reach the motel, Duke pulls behind the main building and stops beside Lindee's Jeep. There isn't an official drive back here, but Lindee parked both the camper and her vehicle behind the building for safety. When she'd been here alone, she was out of sight from the main road.

She isn't alone any longer, though.

"Need help?" Duke finally asks.

Lindee had quieted on my lap. For a moment, I thought she'd fallen asleep, her body relaxing into mine. But when I lifted her arm and pressed a kiss to that tattoo, holding my lips against her inked skin, she'd stiffened again.

"I got it," I murmur before offering him thanks. Manor had grabbed my bag and boots from the ground. Lindee's backpack had been on the seat of my motorcycle. Since Manor passed us on the road, letting my bike scream around us, Lindee and my things are set outside her camper.

Lindee reaches for the truck door and presses it outward, then slides off my lap and lands on her feet beside the truck.

"Thanks for the ride." She doesn't look up at Duke.

I slide out after her and close the door behind me. Lindee walks slowly to the camper, with me trailing behind her. Once she unlocks it and tugs it forward, she steps up the metal stair, pulling the door behind her.

I catch the edge before she can shut me out completely. The countermotion to her dragging the door behind her twists her in my direction.

"Go away." No fight is left in her tone.

"I'm not leaving you alone."

In a battle of wills, she tries to pull the door toward her. I tug the door back to me.

"That's exactly what you should do. Leave me alone," she groans, the fight slowly recharging in her.

"No," I growl.

"I don't want to see you right now, Thaddeus."

"I am not leaving," I snap, struggling not to battle with this woman who has me all mixed up inside and suddenly fucking scared out of my mind. I don't trust what she'll do next.

With a sharp tug on the camper door, she's forced to release it or fall into me. When she steps back, I climb into the camper, slamming the door behind me, and turning the lock.

Lindee is already walking away, toward the bedroom. With her back to me, she pauses. "Please go away." Her arms wrap around her middle.

"No." I am not leaving her until I have answers. Or until I know she's safe. I can't dismiss the ink on her wrist.

After a strained moment of silence, I step closer to her where she faces the bed. "You need to get out of your wet suit."

With her back still to me, she unclips her overalls and lowers the top. She didn't put on her T-shirt once we exited the waterfall. Her bikini looks dry, but still, it can't be comfortable. Without a glance back at me, she reaches right and tugs something off a hook. To my surprise, it's my flannel shirt again.

The afternoon was warm but once night settles in, the mountain temp will drop.

Slipping the material over her back, she slides her arms into the sleeves and tugs the long length upward to free her hands. Then she works at removing her bikini top, using my flannel as a curtain. Next, she shakes her hips to lower the bib overall shorts to her feet. After stepping out of the coverup, she unties her bikini bottoms, and lets them fall to the floor. Lindee places a knee on the bed and crawls forward until she curls onto her side with her back to me.

I have a choice. Stay or go.

Heart first. This was another leap.

Undoing my jeans and tugging my shirt over my head, I slide out of my clothing minus my briefs which had dried on the climb up the rocks. Hesitantly, I slip behind Lindee, slide my hand over the back of her arm and extend it toward her hand. Then I lace my fingers through hers. My palm completely covers the back of her hand, and her fingers clutch between mine.

"What happened?" My voice is steadier than I expected as my heart still hammers, blood coursing through my veins like the rush of that river. I brace for something awful while preparing for her to tell me she doesn't want to talk about it.

The silence is deafening as I wait her out. She swallows deep, her breath shuddering. I perch up on my forearm and press a kiss to her shoulder. Everything in me wants to strip my flannel off her and tug her to my chest, let her feel the heat of my bare skin on hers and the beat of my heart. I want to hold her tight and tell her whatever it was, it would be okay. I am here for her.

I'm afraid to leave her.

With a glance at her face, her eyes are pinched shut. Silent tears stream along her nose.

"Sweetheart," I whisper, my chest aching at the pain in her tight expression.

Her lids flip open, and she stares forward, but unfocused.

"When I was nineteen, I had a boyfriend." Her throat rolls. "He'd been mine since we were fourteen." Her voice quiets. "I was going to marry him someday."

Shit. Shit. *Shit.*

"We'd just finished our freshman year of college. He was going to be a lawyer. I didn't know what I wanted to be. I just wanted to be with him." Her voice drops. "Only him. His name was Harris."

"We were home on summer break. A group of us had been friends forever, and we'd gone to the river that the town takes its name from."

River City. I remember.

"Jumping from an old bridge was a game. Something we'd done a hundred times."

Fuck!

"Everyone knew you jumped feet first." Her voice hitches, and she gulps. Her breathing coming heavier. "Only something happened. His foot caught. Or he was goofing off as his friends were teasing him. He flipped around and fell backward. Headfirst."

I roll my lips inward, fighting the gasp wanting to burst forth. Instead, I press my mouth to her shoulder again, willing her to finish her tale.

"He was lucky to survive, they said." Lindee's voice is distant. "Grateful to be alive." The tears continue.

"Traumatic brain injury," she whispers. "They didn't know how, or if, he'd recover."

"Lindee, I'm so—"

"He lived," she interjects, her voice rising over my sympathy. "Months in a coma. Moments of him squeezing fingers, giving us hope he'd heard our prayers."

Her voice drops once more. "I begged him to come back to me. I gave him permission to leave." Her body shudders.

"They removed the tubes when he was breathing on his own. The coma continued. Then he opened his eyes."

Thank God. My body relaxes behind hers and I close my eyes. My lips still press at her shoulder.

"The recovery was questionable. Would he walk, would he talk, would he remember anything?" She clears her throat. "Would he remember me?"

How could he have forgotten her? In the recesses of his mind, I was certain whoever this Harris had been, his head and his heart recalled Lindee.

"I took a semester off. Waiting. Hoping. People told me to leave. His parents. My mom. *Live your life, Lindee,*" she mocks.

"I took another semester off, but as the months passed . . ." She licks her lips, and the tears start to fall harder. "I didn't know if I could do it. I didn't think I was strong enough." Her hand covers her face. "Him. Like that. For the rest of our lives."

She curled forward, face burrowing into the pillow.

"Hey." I didn't want to release her hand, but I did, cupping her shoulder and tugging her to face me. She refused and I didn't fight her, but I also didn't stop stroking over her shoulder and down her arm. "You were only nineteen."

What a difficult decision to make. She loved him. High school sweethearts who share friends and history. She planned to marry him one day. Yet, how do you ask a teenager to stay devoted to someone in his condition for the rest of their lives? It's a rhetorical question until it's not.

Lindee tilts her head to the side and stares toward the window again. "I'd watched these videos of women dedicated to their man. Helping him recover. Miracles of love making him stronger. It wasn't happening for us. He was the same every day."

"Eventually . . ." She swallows and licks her lips again, then swipes at her nose. "Eventually, his parents demanded I leave. They said *I* was hindering *his* progress." An edge laces her voice.

"So I left." She shifts to glance at me. "I left because I couldn't commit to him. He sensed my hesitation, and it wasn't making him better." She rolls forward again. "It wasn't him. It was me."

Her words from earlier come back to me. *It's me,* she'd said about herself when she shut down after we were together in the waterfall cave. I still don't know what caused her to pull away, but how could she believe her love hadn't been enough for someone? It's ridiculous.

Does she believe she can't commit long-term to someone or something? Does she worry she'll drag *me* down or hold me back in some way? Not going to happen.

"Lindee," I croon. "It was not you. None of what happened falls on you."

She cranes her neck to stare at me over her shoulder once more. "It was all me. I couldn't give him the love he needed."

"That's not true." No one would have expected a teenager to devote her life to someone under such circumstances. If she'd done it, she would have been hailed a saint, but she wasn't a failure for leaving him.

"I tried to go back to school. I tried to come home and visit him." She slides her left arm forward and lowers the flannel over her wrist. "My life was on pause."

Fuck.

"Did you . . . did you want to die?"

"No," she whispers, her voice cracking. "I wanted to live, and I hated myself for it."

God forgive me but *thank fuck*.

"So, he's why you have this tattoo."

"*I'm* why I have this tattoo. My life felt like it was on hold."

"But you're better now?"

Lindee glances at me. "I wasn't the one physically hurt."

"Mental scars can run just as deep."

Lindee shakes her head.

"You're incredibly brave, sweet thing." I cup my hand over the ink and circle her wrist. Then I tug her close to me once more. Relief washing over me. She's here. She's safe.

"I couldn't stay. I finished school but didn't care about the degree. Then I took that job in a city far from home. And I've been moving from place to place ever since." A bitter chuckle fills her voice. "Got a bit of my father in me, I guess."

Lindee had mentioned her dad left her family when she was a baby but learning more about him will wait for another day. This day has been emotional enough.

Still, I have one more question. "What happened to Harris?"

"He died five years later." The pain and guilt in her voice pierces my heart. I relate to the hopelessness she felt. The desire to do something, to help someone you loved wholeheartedly, and yet nothing you did could save that person. Nothing can bring them back.

"I'm tired now, Thad." Her voice travels toward the window. "And I'd like to be alone."

The strain in her voice, the pain in her tone, tells me she doesn't give her story away easily and I'm grateful she told me.

"Thank you for sharing this with me. I'm sorry that happened to you, to him. And I'm truly sorry about jumping from the bridge earlier." Had I known it would be a trigger for her, I never would have asked her to jump, nor would I have made her a witness to my foolish moment to be a kid again.

This moment was another reminder that Lindee and I had so much to learn about one another, and she was finally opening up to me, allowing me to read more of her story than just the cover and maybe a page or two inside.

Still, I say, "I'm not leaving you alone." I pause a beat. "I'll roll to the other side of this bed, and stop touching you, but I'm not going away."

She closes her eyes and scoots forward, hinting she doesn't want my touch, but she heard my words.

I don't push, even though everything in me wants to keep her close, hold her to my chest, and continue to assure her *her* feelings are valid, her pain real, and her decision not unreasonable. Most of all, I don't want her to find fault with herself. It *isn't* her.

Despite her past, she's perfect in the present.

While not fully honoring her request to exit, I take her hint. Rolling to my back, I exhale before turning to my side, placing my back to her. A river canyon of space feels like it's between us and I don't like the distance.

Fortunately, not much time passes before Lindee shifts. Her body lines up along my spine. Her hands on my back. Her face at the base of my neck. Her legs tuck up behind my knees.

She curls into me, and I close my eyes, relieved that I didn't leave.

18

Playlist: "Heart Like a Truck" – Lainey Wilson

[Lindee]

I wake with a start. I'd been dreaming about that day. About Harris.

The reality plays out like a stop-motion film in my head, with jerky clips and scratchy in sound.

The laughter of friends.

The joke of a push.

The twist of his body.

The sudden plummet.

Harris hadn't immediately resurfaced. While others jumped in after him, I remained frozen on the bridge, disbelief pinning me in place. *Nothing happened*, I kept telling myself while something clearly happened. One minute it was all teenage pranks and the next a tragedy.

Kyle retrieved Harris's body. Some girl I didn't know who

was hanging out with us that summer administered CPR. An ambulance arrived. I still hadn't moved. It didn't seem real.

Harris had hit his head. The fall had done additional damage. Lungs. Ribs. A broken arm. None of it mattered. My once lively, loving boyfriend was incapacitated.

When he died, guilt and shame kept me away from the funeral. Fear kept me from facing the people I'd run away from. Although I'd been home on rare occasions, I hid in my mother's house, avoiding anywhere I might see anyone from my past.

I'd been a coward.

Harris's mind must have felt like a permanent black hole. Maybe he heard the voices of people he once knew. Maybe he felt trapped inside a body he no longer recognized. Maybe he was blissfully unaware. But my fear was that he'd remembered. That he'd known I wasn't present, and that he'd hated me for not standing by him, keeping my distance from him and his family once I'd left.

The warmth of the solid body against mine thaws me from the chilling memories.

Thad had stayed as he said he would.

I'd lost my shit. There was no other way to describe my behavior. A full-fledge panic attack had gripped me.

I can't believe I told Thad about Harris. I never, ever spoke about him to anyone. Or confessed my shame over my decision to leave. The self-hatred and strong-hold guilt I'd carried around for decades ate at me, especially when three grown men tossed themselves from a railroad bridge triggering memories I fight to suppress daily.

As I lay with my face pressed to Thad's chest—he must have rolled toward me at some point—I inhale his mountain scent and press a kiss to his pec, lingering on his skin. Another inhale reminds me he's alive. He's present. He's here.

He stirs but I don't retreat, needing to touch him, needing

his presence to ground me. To remind me I am here. This is the present. I cannot live in the past.

Thad absentmindedly kisses the top of my head. His closed eyes and heavy breathing tell me he's still sleeping. I don't want to close my eyes again, though.

Instead, I kiss him once more, allowing my fingers to smooth over his summer-warm flesh, skim over the firmness of his muscular chest and lower to the ridges of his abdomen.

"Whatcha doing, sweet thing?" he grumbles, sleepy and coarse.

I need you. The thought whispers through my head. I don't want to need him, or anyone, but something deep inside me says I do. I need Thad.

My fingers continue over his belly which quivers beneath my touch.

"Ticklish?" I quietly tease.

Thad hums. His eyes are still shut while I explore him. I didn't mean to wake him, but I can't go back to sleep. Sleep will only bring more memories, maybe even a nightmare. It's been a long time since I've had one. The one where I'm going under the water with Harris and he's holding me hostage beneath the surface.

We'll be together forever, Lindee. I love you.

His voice is always a mixture of his teenage tenor and the gargle of water in his throat.

Pressing more firmly at Thad's lower belly, I lean in and kiss him again. And again. And again. Needing to feel his flesh and taste his skin and know that he is real.

I'm with Thad. *For now.*

"Need something, baby?"

"I want to get lost in you," I admit, mumbling to his midsection as I move lower.

A firm hand catches my chin and tips it upward. In the darkness, it's hard to see his eyes. At some point he must have gotten up and turned on the stove light again, providing soft illumination.

"Want something from me, climb up here and take it, sweet thing."

I want to be found.

My eyes prickle. The truth forms a clog in my throat. I'm tired of being lost.

But for tonight, I need to erase my thoughts and lose control.

With my hand on his belly, I press, and he rolls to his back. I straddle his lower body. Slithering up his middle, like a temptress ready to strike, I still when the bulge of his length is trapped in the heat of my center. I kiss him hard and deep, swirling my tongue with his, hoping to wash away memories and cleanse my head.

Guilt. Shame. Embarrassment.

Eventually, the kiss breaks and I rock back and forth over his covered length. His cotton briefs against my bare folds heightens the friction. Pressing on his shoulders, I hold myself upright. My hips have a will of their own, creating a dance where I'm the lead. Thad is my partner.

What would it be like for him to permanently be my other half?

"Get that sweet pussy wrapped around me, sweet thing. Take what you need from me." His hands move from my hips to the waistband of his briefs, where he shoves them down just enough to release his hard shaft.

We both hiss as my wetness hits the heat of his length, gliding up his stiffness until the tip catches on my clit.

"Condom," I groan.

Thad stretches over the edge of the mattress, fumbling for his pants before pulling out a packet and then covering himself.

Then I'm guiding him into me and taking him deep as I

close my eyes in relief. With his fullness seated inside me, I still, disappearing into hollow delight.

I want to be found.

Shaking the thought, I move over Thad, sliding up to his tip and then lowering to reel him back in. Up and down, I glide until I'm practically bouncing over him. His body taps mine in a spot that clicks me into overdrive. Bouncing up and down, that sensitive bundle of nerves finds a notch on Thad that sets me off. Gasping for air and racing toward a finish line, I draw him into me over and over until I slam down and still, throwing back my head and keening into the night.

There's nothing in my head but Thad and me, joined like this, in total bliss.

Thad jackknifes upward and kisses me hard, sweeping his tongue into my mouth before wrapping an arm around my back and flipping me over. I hit the mattress with a thud and Thad drives into me, chasing his own release.

"Fuck," he grunts as his hips surge forward, increasing the rhythm. He's as deep as any man has ever been when he suddenly stalls out, filling me with his seed.

I want you to stay planted, he'd said to me.

For half a second, I imagine Thad impregnating me. That's one way to ground me but the last thing I'd need. I never want to be an obligation to someone. And any hope of having children went over that bridge when I was twenty. I didn't believe I deserved to find another man and settle down, have a family and a home, when the dreams I'd once shared with someone else could never be fulfilled.

The idea of a baby blows away like dandelion seeds in a summer breeze, though.

Thad falls over me, breathing heavily on my neck before rolling us to our sides. "Fuck, I think you rung me out, sweetheart." He continues to his back and throws an arm over his face. His chest lowers and lifts, and I chuckle beside him.

Yeah, I'm lost . . . in this man.

But after my antics earlier, I don't deserve him.

"I don't want you to stay away from me," I whisper, apologetic that I'd said such a thing in the heat of my panic. Fear that he'd go into the water and never resurface. Fear he'd fall, but rise up a new man, a different man, a forever changed man. Fear that what happened to Harris could happen to anyone and I didn't want it to happen to someone I love again.

Love?

Thad quickly turns his head, and his hand cups the side of my face, his thumb smoothing over my skin. "I know, sweetheart. And I'm sorry again that we scared you."

I nod once, not wanting to discuss everything again.

"I think you rung me out, too," I say to deflect and return to his comment.

"I stink like river water and you, baby." He chuckles, slipping his arm behind my head and tugging me to his chest. "Never thought it'd be my favorite fragrance."

I roll my head, inhaling him again and note he does smell damp and musky, but he also smells like something else I haven't considered for a long, long time.

He smells like a safe place. Like home.

19

Playlist: "Sleep on The Floor" – The Lumineers

[Lindee]

Thad and I drift back to sleep, or at least, he sleeps, and I drift, floating through more memories of high school days, promises made, and all that was left behind.

Most times, my philosophy is to never look in the rearview mirror. There is nothing gained by going in reverse. But any good student of driving knows, you must glance backward once or twice in order to make sound decisions before moving forward, especially if you plan to change lanes.

And I felt like I was on the cusp of a major shift in my life.

Eventually, Thad leaves the bed in the early light of a new day, and I watch him slowly dress.

He offers me a warm smile. "Did you eat this weekend?"

I chuckle. This is what he has to say to me this morning. "Why are you so concerned about my meals?"

"Because I don't think you take care of yourself."

"I take care of me," I groggily scoff, a little offended.

Thad leans forward, resting his hands on the bed and staring down at me. "But I want to take care of you."

He bends down and presses a kiss to my forehead. "I'm headed out for Tiny Bites and coffee."

"You're gonna make me fat," I tease.

"They say the way to a woman's heart is through her stomach."

Feeding me will not win my heart. But taking care of me might. "Who is they? We need to chat." Laughter fills my throat and it feels strange after the tears of last night.

I don't deserve Thad's compassion.

Last night, I'd used him.

I'd needed to get out of my head and his body was the perfect escape. I hadn't slept with anyone since him and even before that night back in March, it'd been months. I ached in places I didn't recognize and a few I did, deep inside my chest cavity.

When Thad finally walks away, it is going to hurt. Because he is going to leave. Go back to his home and live out his days with his kids, maybe find a stable woman and settle down again.

My possessions might be light but the weight I carry is heavy and Thad does not need my baggage.

As he's left the camper, I heave a deep sigh and roll from the bed, stretching. Actually, I am starving, and I accredit the increase in hunger to the lack of food yesterday and my emotional state last night. I hadn't cried like that in decades.

The release was cathartic. With a sheepish smile on my face and a little ache between my legs, I make myself eggs deciding I need some protein on top of a donut and brew my goddess fuel.

Strangely, I find hazelnut creamers in my fridge along with a stack of sugar packets in the cabinet where I keep coffee.

Fresh from a shower and with a stomach full of energy, I prepare to face Duke, Manor, and Thad because apologies need to be made all around.

As I enter the lobby, which is our next project, the three men are already there. Duke slowly rises from kneeling on the floor near the original front desk, which we plan to tear out. Manor lets the tape measure he was using against the fireplace snap back into its container. And Thad pauses at the worktable, where the blueprints for this space had been the set of plans we last looked at together.

"Hey." His greeting is hesitant, leery even, but a Tiny Bites bag and a cup of coffee rests on the worktable near him.

Shame hits me in the chest as his whiskey eyes stare at me, questioning me.

I want to take care of you, he'd said this morning.

"I . . . uh . . ." I glance between Duke and Manor as silence fills the large vacant space. Slipping my hands into the back pockets of my jeans, I rock up on my toes. "I'm uh . . ."

Licking my lips, I close my eyes. *You can do this, dammit.*

"I'm not great at apologies." Because I don't do them often.

"But I just wanted to say I'm sorry for yesterday." *Having a total meltdown before all of you.*

"I kind of had a reason." I weakly smile and meet Thad's eyes, hoping he doesn't want me to repeat myself to his cousins, although I owe them some explanation. My gaze drops from his. "I had . . . a friend . . . who fell from a bridge like the one by the river and he was terribly hurt." I lift my head and glance from Duke to Manor. "*Permanently* hurt from the fall."

"Fuck," Manor mutters under his breath.

"You don't owe us an explanation," Duke offers, giving me a concerned look.

I ignore him and continue. "I don't like to talk about him,

but he . . . Harris." I swallow around his name. "He suffered a traumatic brain injury."

"Fuck," Manor mutters again.

Duke swipes a hand over his short hair and glances at Thad.

I shrug slightly. "He was only twenty when it happened. He died five years later."

Manor moves first, coming toward me. "Lindee, we're so sorry that happened to you, to him."

I want to ward him off. I don't need more hugs. Today, I need work and distraction like renovating this room. But when Manor wraps his long arms around me, I can't seem to help returning the embrace, circling my arms around his waist and holding onto him.

Duke remains where he's standing. "We won't do that again."

"We won't?" Manor questions, turning with me still trapped against his chest.

Thad narrows his eyes at his cousin. Duke shakes his head, disapproval in his rugged face.

"Oh, right. We won't," Manor corrects but the lie fills his compassionate voice.

"You can stop hugging me, now," I mutter into his soft shirt that smells like shaved wood and rugged man.

"But you're rather huggable."

"Manor, let go of her," Thad warns.

"She's so cute. I want to wrap her up and slip her in my pocket."

"Uh-uh," Duke drones rolling his eyes. "Her in your pocket. Or you in her pants. Same thing."

"Hey," Thad snaps, slamming his hand down on the worktable forcing the bakery bag and my coffee cup to jump.

"Someone's touchy today," Duke coos before meeting my

eyes and giving me a wink. A teasingly wicked smile crosses his face.

Manor gives me an extra squeeze, presses an exaggerated kiss to my temple, adding emphasis with, "Mwah," and then releases me.

I lightly laugh before catching Thad's gaze. All feels forgiven.

I just want to be found.

"I'm sorry," I mouth to him.

Thad dismisses my apology with a shake of his head. "Breakfast." He nods at the donut bag and coffee. "Then let's double check these plans and start on the new bar."

Intuitively, he seems to know what I need and I'm so grateful for the distraction he offers.

While the day passes with banter and curses between cousins, I remain stuck in my head, fighting through a slog of memories as I try to bury myself in helping Manor lay out a faux-stone pattern for the fireplace surround. The old façade was a dated red brick monstrosity that could be torn down but might pull down the wall behind it, which I couldn't afford to replace. The lightweight, fake river rocks were a modern alternative.

Manor and I will do the masonry work while Duke and Thad build a new bar. A semi-circular counter is intended to replicate the original bar that stood in the middle of this grand space in the late 50s. Old photographs found in the office and a few pictures Nessi brought when I'd first met her helped me finalize my vision for the space that would serve drinks by night and other treats by day.

I wanted this place to have activities for families, allowing them to linger in the evenings and relax during the warm afternoons. My assumption was most people would travel here in the summer for the hiking trails and in the winter for the skiing. The pool was going to have seasonal appeal.

My vision was based on an affinity for retro architecture and vintage green circa 1950. With updated décor based on old designs, I want to draw people into the thrill of a road trip. Stop where you will. Stay where you want. Travelers didn't need a high-priced resort for comfort and charm.

Thankfully, Thad, Duke, and Manor appreciated my mission. Maybe because they had fond memories of being here themselves.

I'd learned through their discourse that they'd visited this motel as kids. Thad's dad and the cousins' mom were siblings. Duke and Manor's father had been best friends with Thad's dad. From the sounds of it, other families came here at the same time as theirs, causing the entire place to be overrun by the collection of friends.

"How did Nessi end up with this place?"

For a moment, my question is met with cautious silence, like I'd asked something forbidden. I almost apologize for asking, but Thad scratches the back of his neck and answers.

"She came into some money later in life and decided real estate was the best investment for her. She bought places that had sentimental meaning to her."

He'd already told me how attached she was to this location.

I chuckle at the thought of the hippie-looking grandmother being a real estate mogul. "How many places does she own?"

Duke and Thad meet eyes before Thad continues. "About seven, I guess. This motel. The cabin in Tennessee."

"Land in Kentucky. With a huge house," Manor adds.

"Another house in North Carolina," Duke states, as if questioning the property. Manor nods to confirm.

"A bar in Georgia," Manor says.

"And her place in Kentucky." Thad ticks places off on his fingers.

"You already mentioned that one," Manor corrects. "Her house is on the land in Kentucky."

"And a spot in Sturgis, South Dakota." Duke finalizes the list.

"Why South Dakota?" I ask.

All three men look at one another before Duke answers. "Just a destination."

His simple explanation holds weight. The place was more than just a spot to visit but I don't press. Although a dribble has spilled from my jar of secrets, I don't need them to open the lid on theirs and tell me everything about their lives.

Still, I look at Thad, wondering what else I don't know about him. About this man who has entered my body and teases my heart into thinking he could be something more.

More than a thumbtack on the road map of my life.

20

———————

Playlist: "Ghost" – Justin Bieber

[Lindee]

The day had been long, but we accomplished much. Manor and I made a good start on the faux masonry work while Duke and Thad finished the bar in rough form. The countertop would need staining and coats of polyurethane to protect against liquid spills, but it was going to be beautiful. My vision for the lobby was coming together, one small piece at a time.

In silent celebration, I'm seated outside underneath a darkening summer sky, taking a moment to breathe in the fresh mountain air and appreciate what I have. It's been an emotional twenty-four hours.

Eyes forward, Lucinda Marie, I coach myself from my seat on the pine top of a picnic table near Karen the camper. Most nights, I hole up in the temporary home and read romance novels, living fictionally in other people's lives, but tonight, I brace my arms behind me and tip back my head, staring at the stars as they slowly prick into view and the sky shifts from muted blue to midnight navy.

"When we were kids, Nessi used to tell us our destiny was written in the stars."

I drop my gaze and turn my head in Thad's direction. He stands a few feet away, looking upward at the heavens himself. He chuckles deep and rich before glancing over at me. "Took Manor a while to admit he didn't think he could read because he didn't know what the stars spelled."

I quietly laugh. Poor Manor.

"This seat taken?" Thad steps up to the picnic table and helps himself to the space next to me. His feet hit the bench, and he leans forward, elbows on his thighs.

"Nessi had to explain she didn't mean words were written up there, but our fate was already decided. And that fate would test our will. Our will to live. Our drive to persevere. Our desire to love."

I hum. Nessi sounds like a wise woman.

Thad glances at me over his shoulder. "Can't say I believe in that stuff, but I do think there is a plan for each of us. Other people's plans collide with ours and sometimes we want to question *why me* when it's why them. Why did that accident happen to your boyfriend? His path set yours tail-spinning. Or did it? Did it send you on a journey that brought you right to this moment?"

He points a thick finger to a sliver of space between us.

I don't really want to talk about Harris again, but Thad continues. "Not saying that road was easier. When someone says leaving is the hardest thing to do or staying is the hardest, it's always a subjective statement. Leaving Harris was difficult. Me staying with Jaz was hard."

Thad turns his gaze back toward the sky, and I peer up at it as well.

"Sometimes the road isn't clear to us, but we take it anyway and just hold on tight for the ride."

Thad has no idea how much I relate to that statement.

A lump I don't want forms in my throat, and I ask a question I don't think is my place to ask, but I'm curious about anyway.

"May I ask...why didn't you and Jasmine work out?"

Thad bitterly chuckles. "Everything in Jaz's life has been a struggle. Tough girl from a rough family. She was wild, and a lot like the rest of us." He pauses a second, reflective maybe. "My brother Vic liked Jaz. She was ten years younger than him. But Jaz had her sights set on me. I kept her at arm's length, always telling her she was a kid compared to us, but Jaz was already a hard woman in her twenties. When she was twenty-five to my thirty-two, I was foolish enough to touch her one night, drinking too much and taking her to my bed. She got pregnant."

These things happen. "So, you married her," I add to complete his story.

"Something like that. We weren't legally married until after my second was born." Thad lowers his head, shaking it slowly. "Jaz and I were always tumultuous. A constant push and pull. We were each reckless in our own ways."

My mind races with what that might mean. Sometimes relationships are just like that—back and forth—and it's almost like an addiction, unhealthy in its own way.

Thad takes a deep breath and glances upward again as his hands come together between his knees.

"My older brother Vic . . . he'd been my best friend. Three years older than me. Manor and me are the same age. Duke is two years younger than us. The four of us were tight and always in trouble. But you kind of grow up and out of such things. Vic hadn't. Around the time Jaz and I hooked up, Vic and I started down different paths."

Thad pauses, squints at the night sky, and leans back, resting on his hands, mirroring my position.

"He fucking loved life." Thad softly chuckles. "Always a joke. A smirk. Thinking he was the shit. He was larger than life most days, but there was a darkness inside him."

Thad's expression tightens. His eyes narrow again. "I should have seen the signs, but I just didn't." His voice cracks, and he clears his throat.

Sitting up straight, I place a hand on his shoulder. "Thad," I whisper, emotion clogging my airway.

Still staring up at the sky, Thad drops a bomb. "My brother took his own life about ten years back."

My hand cascades down his arm, clutching at his wrist. "I'm so, so sorry." While I might have lost Harris by accident, I can't imagine losing someone on purpose.

Thad leans forward and takes my hand in his, lacing our fingers together and holding my hand on his thigh.

Gazing down at our entwined fingers, he continues. "I wasn't in a good place then. Vic's death. Victoria's birth. She was born shortly after his passing. Rumors among our friends said she wasn't mine." Thad tightens his hold on my hand, running the fingertips of his other hand over my knuckles. "Typically, I don't give into that gossipy shit, but something had me questioning the talk."

Thad told me Jasmine had been unfaithful to him. Had his wife slept with his brother? The question felt too painful to ask.

"When Vicki was about three, she climbed into my lap one day. Her tiny hands cupped my cheeks, so I was forced to look her in the eye. She said, *Daddy, I love you.*" Thad softly chuckles. "Made me hold her gaze, like she was imparting wisdom. Telling me a secret, like she knew the truth, and it wasn't going to matter. Vic was dead. I'd been raising her. She was mine."

He weakly smiles as his thumb strokes over my knuckles. "Out of the mouths of babes, they say."

"They say," I quietly tease. I still wanted a strong word with *they*.

Thad looks up at me. His whiskey eyes are the dull flame of candlelight, sad and somber like votives in a church lit to seek forgiveness.

"Anyway." He turns his head, staring out at the darkness that's filled in around us. "Jaz and I had been rocky for years. Got her pregnant again. I was damn near angry. We'd taken every precaution. She was my wife but sleeping with her had become a function of our marriage not a connection. I wasn't happy."

Thad turns back to me, catching on my eyes and holding. "Yet leaving felt impossible."

Staying can be difficult, too.

I imagine having kids was part of the decision to stick around. Not that his children were an excuse, just the reason he tried to remain in a marriage that was emotionally rough.

Marriages are hard work. I watched my sister Mae stick it out with her ex because of their two boys. Eventually, she reached her breaking point. We all have them. That threshold in our heart which has the amazing capacity to stretch and stretch and stretch before it unravels, or worse, snaps.

"What made you two finally decide to split?"

"Staying became unfair. To her. To me. I'd been unhappy for so long with Jaz. And I don't think I was doing her any favors either. I didn't love her. I tried to be good to her but loving her was difficult. When I turned forty-three, I had an epiphany. Kind of a life-affirming moment. This is *my* life. It's gonna sound selfish, but I need to live my life for me, and my kids. And me being happier was going to be better for them."

"I get that." My dad had left, and I imagined he'd thought it was better all around to leave us behind. Better for him even.

But I don't fault Thad for my father's decisions. We all have our human limits.

I'd had my own when I was younger.

"So, you divorced," I state, confirming what I already know of Thad's marital status.

"We divorced." A heavy sigh follows, one sounding full of relief.

Silence fills in around us again.

"I'm sorry again for what happened to your boyfriend when you were young, Lindee. That shit stings. I don't have advice for nineteen-year-old you," Thad says. "Thirty-nine-year-old Lindee is doing pretty well for herself, though. Happy looks good on you."

Was I happy?

I smile and squeeze his hand. "I'm sorry for yesterday. I might have overreacted. I just . . . I panicked." I didn't want to lose Thad in a similar manner to how I'd lost Harris. I didn't want him to ever be hurt.

"And I'm sorry about your brother. And Jasmine." I sigh, offering a playful shrug. "Just apologies all around, now let's move on." Hesitant laughter fills my voice as I nudge his shoulder, hoping to erase a bit of the sadness swirling around us.

"Also, I'm forty-two."

Thad winks as he pulls our locked hands higher up his leg. "Thought women were thirty-nine forever."

I scoff. "I actually looked forward to turning forty. I saw it as a milestone and wanted some big epiphany myself. The answer to the purpose of my life. Besides fixing up other people's properties, what was . . . written in the stars for me?" I wave toward the sky, waving my hand across it like the answer would magically appear, painted up there like a young Manor had suspected. "Surely my future wasn't only renovating places for other people."

"I think big things are coming your way, Lindee Fox."

"Nice to think about, even if unknown." The Universe will guide me. However, what was next for me? I was accustomed to the next project already on the docket. Being that I bought the motel for me, and intended to run it afterward, the future felt unsettled. Could I stay planted for a while? Did I really think I could manage this place and make a living here? Money wasn't my sole purpose. Contentment was what I sought. A home with a permanent address.

I want to be found.

"Sometimes an unknown path isn't a blind drive. It's a wise decision waiting to happen on an unfamiliar road. You never know what's around the bend. Could be a beautiful night." Thad lifts his head to gaze at the night sky which is polka-dotted with stars. Then he lowers and stares directly at me. "Or a pretty woman needing a rescue by a river."

"I didn't need rescuing." I playfully bump into his shoulder again.

"Then maybe I did."

We stare at one another before Thad leans toward me, and like a tide attracted to the moon, I lean toward him. Our lips meet for a slow, sweet kiss, reminiscent of younger days and lost promises. Harris. Thad's brother. Maybe even his marriage. There is sympathy in this kiss.

As our mouths move, our bodies remain still. Only our lips connect, sipping at the destiny of this moment, where I'm sitting here, next to a man I'm slowly learning about but already care about so much. He's compassion and comfort and assurance that a new day arises, night falls, and life moves on.

When Thad pulls away, I vow I won't take advantage of him again. Last night, I practically begged him to have sex with me, to make me forget myself and my past. We haven't spoken about it yet today.

"Last night—"

Thad covers my mouth with his fingers. Then he tugs at my lower lip and leans in to kiss me again as his hand slips to the side of my neck.

We stay like this another minute, kissing beneath a curtain of darkness with the moon as a spotlight. No tongue. No groping fingers. Just a tender kiss.

We break again. "It's late. Walk me home?" The flirtatious comment is an effort to lighten the heavy moment. It's been another emotional night, learning about Thad's brother and the state of his marriage. We all have a past filled with heavy burdens and bent moments. Thad and I are both proof that focusing forward is the only road to remain on, even if the route is unfamiliar.

Like he said, you never know what's around the bend.

Thad presses off the picnic table without releasing my hand. Then, he turns to face me and tugs me forward with enough force I crash into his body and slide down the length of him. Firm and solid, he's a good man beyond the muscular strength and sexy appearance.

Holding Thad's hand, we walk the few steps to the front of Karen.

I feel lighter after our talk. Maybe it was the admission about his brother and the shared sympathy over losing someone we loved. Maybe it was the revelation of his marriage or the fact he simply revealed some truth with me. Thad has been a mystery, but I certainly haven't been forthcoming either. I've often thought the past doesn't matter. I don't need to know someone's history, especially if they are only temporary in my life. But I liked that Thad had opened up to me and told me about his brother and his ex-wife.

I also felt different since confessing about Harris. It felt good to share my secret with someone. Someone who seemed to understand and didn't judge me. Thad simply listened. He held me. Then he offered me his body.

I want to invite him inside the camper, but I don't. I fight the desire to reel him in, offer him comfort, because that comfort would come from a selfish part of me that just wants to feel his body against mine, hear his heart beating, and connect us once again.

He might not feel the need to connect like I do.

We've spent over two weeks without physical contact until yesterday afternoon. Most nights, Thad disappears with his cousins, and I have no idea what they do together. Hang out? Head to a bar? Find women? The thought doesn't feel fair. Thad told me yesterday that I'd been his first in years.

How can I continue to rank number one with him?

"See you tomorrow," Thad says as we pause before my door.

"Night," I whisper.

Thad steps back, pulling open Karen's door, and I step into the camper. He'll wait until I've secured myself inside before he'll walk away, so I lock the door and press my forehead against the barrier.

Why do I always want people I can't have?

With that thought, I push away from the door and take a step toward the stove to turn on the low light. As the illumination flares, a soft rap comes against the camper door.

I close my eyes and fight a smile.

Stepping back to the door, I open it. Thad grabs the edge of the door and braces his other hand on the frame, reminding me of that first night together. Where he was holding himself back, offering me a choice. Let him in or tell him to walk away.

"Why am I always chasing after you, sweet thing?"

I lean against the back of the booth seat near the entrance and cross my arms. "Must be written in the stars."

"Good thing I know how to read. I have words I want to spell with my tongue all over you tonight."

"Thank God." I laugh, reaching out the opening and digging my fingers into his T-shirt to jerk him forward.

When the camper door slams shut, I'm already climbing his body, eager for what he'll imprint on me.

21

———

Playlist: "From Eden" - Hozier

[Thad]

The next weekend, I hated leaving Lindee. It wasn't officially my time with the kids, but Sam had a baseball picnic, and Vicki returned from camp. Sasha was giving Jaz all kinds of attitude that I didn't appreciate, and my ex was blowing up my phone over it. My girl was simply hurting with me gone. She'd been getting the brunt of Jaz's wrath, especially as the kids hinted their mom has been drinking.

When you're young and life revolves around partying, you don't see the signs of alcohol being a real issue for some. After all that happened with Vic, I tried to pay better attention. An occasional drunk night did not compare to a daily drinking binge that escalated into an entire bottle of booze every night. At first, I thought I was the problem and a part of me still thinks that I was. If I'd loved Jaz more, if I'd done better, she would not have felt so inadequate. But addiction isn't about other people; it's about the person addicted.

I couldn't make Jasmine get help. The decision had to be hers, and for now, she wasn't making smart choices. She knew the kids would be mine in a blink if she didn't shape up.

When I return to Mountain Motel at the end of my weekend, I'm in a piss-poor mood and I just want to lose myself in Lindee. We've been coming together every night since she told me about her boyfriend, and I told her about my brother. The sex is off the charts. Lindee is not shy about what she wants, and she lets me do what I will with her body.

The night before I left, we were twisted in a way her mouth had my dick to the back of her throat and my tongue slicked her heat. I hadn't been in that position in decades, and I fucking felt like a king when I finally entered her. Lindee acted like she was just as insatiable for me as I was for her, so I'm eager to return to her.

Only, when I pull around the back of the motel, both the camper and Lindee's Jeep are gone.

"What the fuck?" I park and step out of my truck as if magically both vehicles will appear. Lindee hadn't mentioned taking a trip. In fact, she worked every weekend the guys and I were gone, doing things that didn't involve heavy lifting or manual labor. She'd mentioned a shopping spree with her sister, Jane, who lived a few towns over. Lindee wanted to check out pool furniture as we were weeks into July, and sun loungers might be on sale.

The pool was an area that needed to be tackled soon. The smell of unattended water was ripe in the summer heat. The basin didn't look like it was in awful condition, but the standing liquid needed to be drained and the cement repainted. It would only be a seasonal draw to the motel but worth the effort to maintain in the future. However, the pool wasn't on the agenda for the guys and me, but the scope of this project had a life of its own, and somehow, we were getting dragged into all the extras.

Or maybe that was just me.

Because our boss had reeled me in, and I didn't want to be released.

I reenter my truck and pull around the main building to park in front of the duplex. Duke, Manor, and I have taken up residence there as the place was in the best condition, plus it offered a kitchen and two bathrooms which is necessary for three guys under one roof.

Duke happens to exit one unit of the duplex as I slam the driver's door behind me.

"Hey," he calls out.

I have no idea what he's done this weekend. He has his own issues as we all do, lingering from a past life we've been trying to dodge for over ten years.

"Hey. Have you seen Lindee?"

Duke pauses beside his bike. Eventually Manor, Duke, and I got our bikes here. Duke and I have pickup trucks while Manor drives a flashy Camaro.

"Yeah, she's up at the winter cabin. Got her all moved in this weekend."

"Lindee moved?" She didn't tell me she was moving into that place yet. "And you guys stayed around here?"

"Didn't have anywhere to be." Duke shrugs. "Lindee needed help hitching that camper to a service vehicle that picked it up. She moved her things into the cabin for the remainder of this job."

Why didn't she ask me if she needed help? *Just what the fuck?*

Admittedly, Lindee and I still don't know everything there is to know about each other and I'm okay with not needing every detail of her life. But something present day should be shared, like knowing my girlfriend was moving into a house.

Is Lindee my girlfriend? Aren't I a little old for such a thing? I'm certainly not considering her as *just* a lover, though, or a friend with benefits. She was important to me. She's funny and kind. She has a big heart she doesn't see in herself. And she's smart. She is going to have a great investment in this motel. She's a real entrepreneur with a solid vision.

"Thanks," I mumble to Duke before he hikes a leg over his bike and starts the engine. The roar is like a call to my soul. Maybe what I need is a ride. It's a warm summer evening and the sun will be dipping down soon. It's the perfect time to hit the road.

But first I need to find Lindee.

I stalk around the duplex and cross the lot in front of the main building. There's a slight incline as the gravel drive leads to the cabin tucked back in the woods. Once there, I notice Lindee's Jeep and a pickup with Wright Construction Co. on the driver's door.

Just what the hell? Is she thinking of hiring another construction company? Are we not enough?

Am I not enough?

My sour mood needs to settle down, so I swipe a palm down my face and knock a little too sharply on the cabin door.

"Come in," Lindee calls out in her smoky voice, calming my unease momentarily.

When I enter, the first thing I see is a man standing near the kitchen peninsula and my irritation flares again. Lindee is sitting on a stool by the counter, laughing. Her face is bright. Her smile wide. And her hand is resting on this guy's forearm in a show of affection.

"What the hell?" I snap.

Lindee pulls back her arm and the man by the counter turns to face me. Built rugged, like a construction worker, he wears jeans with heavy boots and a button up shirt with the sleeves rolled to his elbows. He's dressed like he might have just gone out to dinner. Or had a date.

My gaze slings from him to Lindee who is wearing a summer dress with large lemons printed on it. The outfit hits me. Lindee is so different from any woman I've known. While she doesn't mind getting down and dirty, wearing shorts, bib overalls, and worn T-shirts, there's another side to her that's a bit more proper, more feminine even, and this dress is showing off all her female curves.

"Thad." Lindee slips from the stool and takes a step toward me, but something stops her.

Maybe it's the expression on my face or the guy's hand as it comes to her waist, halting her movement. Heavy tension weaves around the dining table and swirls about the space.

"Thaddeus Rhode, this is Myles Wright." Lindee hitches her thumb at the man still holding her hip.

Normally, I'd approach a man, hold out my hand and grip it with a warning. My mood has me holding back, placing my hands at my hips, and tipping up my chin.

Old habits return and my voice cuts. "What's up?"

Myles gives me a long steady look before he says, "Nice to meet you, man. I've heard a lot about you."

Yeah? Like how my dick has been in this woman all week and I'd thought we had an agreement? I never did actually date before Jaz. When Jaz became my old lady, it was as simple as her being pregnant with my kid and me stating she belonged to me. So I don't know how to make a claim on this woman, whom I've only known a few weeks plus one night over four months ago.

"Lindee has told me about the great job you're doing here. Place is really shaping up." He glances around the kitchen area and looks toward the cozy living space. A ladder leads to the loft area Lindee had us build.

Were they up there? I hate the thought. I don't want to imagine her with his man. Or any other man for that fact.

"Thad." Lindee's sharp tone brings me back to her. She narrows her eyes. "Myles is my brother-in-law's brother. He lives in Wrightwood and owns a construction company."

"A Wright from Wrightwood? Bet there's a whole series of jokes about that." I huff.

Myles softly chuckles. "A few."

"His family owns the town. As in, his ancestors settled the land and built an entire town that his family still owns." Awe rings through her explanation. She admires him.

"Lindee," Myles moans, lowering his gaze as if he's embarrassed by how impressed she is with his status. "It's not exactly like that."

I used to fucking own towns. However, that was in a previous life and another part of me I haven't shared yet with this woman. A dark part. And now isn't the time for a pissing contest over town ownership. I guarantee my dick is bigger than his.

"It's exactly like that." Lindee sweetly laughs again, and I hate that she's looking at him, giggling in his direction, like they share a secret I'm not in on.

"I think I'll get going." I hitch my thumb over my shoulder. My mood has moved from piss-poor to shit-storm. "Just wanted to check in before tomorrow, boss, but we can talk in the morning."

I sound like a fucking moron but it's better than the alternative which is kicking this guy's ass for smiling at my girl. He still has his hand on her hip.

"You don't have to go." Lindee looks back at me, but something in her eyes suggests she isn't happy for me to stay.

Myles removes his hand and swipes his fist over his mouth like he's trying to contain a smirk. Maybe I won't leave after all.

"Nah, I'll see you in the morning, *boss*," I hiss, reminding both of us of my place. I work for her. We have a business contract but no personal agreement between us.

"No, I'll go." Myles reaches around the side of the peninsula cabinet. He shuffles a bit and pulls forward a walking cane.

Fuck.

He still could be wanting to sleep with my girl, but guilt slams me for being a dick when he might have only been reaching for Lindee to steady himself. Or maybe he was trying to protect her from me, and the angry vibe rolling off my skin.

He leans toward Lindee who places her hands on his chest, and he kisses her cheek. He must say something because her face flames pink as he pulls away.

Myles hobbles forward and I step back allowing him space to exit the house. I catch the door and turn toward Lindee a second before following him out onto the low stoop.

"Hey, man. I'm sorry. I was rude."

He pauses and turns toward me, leaning on that cane. "Ever hear the saying *beat you with my stick*?"

I'd laugh if I wasn't suddenly ashamed of myself. "Yeah."

"You mess with that woman, and it'll be my stick." Myles levels me with a steely stare. We have an understanding.

"Got it." Myles couldn't take me, but he's built like it'd be a fight. Maybe an unfair one because of his limp but he looks like a man that could hold his own for a few rounds.

I'm a dick.

He steps off the stoop and I watch him walk to his truck before I enter the cabin again. Lindee is still in the same spot she was standing in near the entrance to the kitchen area.

"What the hell was that?" She nods toward the door as I close it.

"I'm in a mood."

Her hands come to her hips. "Care to explain?"

I really don't want to talk about Jasmine and this weekend, so I start with, "I didn't know you were moving."

"I can't live in a camper forever. And as much as I liked Karen, it was time to part ways. I need a real bed and a larger shower."

I huff, agreeing with her.

"I'd always planned to move in here, and you know that. Until I figure out a home of my own, living here will be a sort of test of the amenities. To make sure I've got it right."

Glancing around the place, I tip my chin. "This place is going to be great."

"Yeah, well, we're working hard. All of us. Together." There's something underneath the emphasis.

"Are we together, sweetheart?" Our eyes lock. "You still with me?"

"I haven't been with someone else, if that's what you're asking?" Her tone deepens. Her chin juts up, defiant, strong. God, I want to lay her out right here on the floor.

"I'm asking," I admit. "I'm also curious what we are to each other."

"I thought we were having sex."

"Is that it?" My gaze holds on her flaming blue eyes. She could burn me with the wrong answer.

"I didn't think so, but sometimes I don't know. This is new to me." She waves between us.

"Me too." I step closer. "And I want it only to be us. No one else while we're here."

"I just told you there hasn't been anyone else." She lowers her arms.

The lemon print on her dress emphasizes the size of her breasts and suddenly I'm thirsty for something sugary and tart.

"What about after that night in North Carolina?" I brace for the answer. I have no right to be angry if she's been with someone between then and now. We were only going to be a one-night stand.

"No one, Thad." Her shoulders fall as well, like she's defeated by defending herself.

I take another step, cupping the sides of her neck. "I'm sorry. It's been a shit weekend and I just wanted to see you."

"What about you?" she asks, ignoring my confession. "Have you been with anyone since that night?" Her voice is hesitant.

"Not a soul, sweet thing. You've been my first in decades."

Slowly, the corner of her mouth lifts. Her eyes shift from flames to warm lights.

"If this is your first night in the cabin, I can think of a few other firsts."

"I slept here last night, but I'm not opposed to second-night shenanigans." She waggles her brows and I slide my hands down her arms, catching a finger on her bracelet. The bracelet that reminds her of me.

"Why didn't you tell me you were moving? I would have helped you."

"Because it was your time off and your kids need you." Her gaze lowers.

My fingers slide between hers, linking our hands together and I tug her toward me. "Sweet thing, I would have been here for you, though."

Her mouth falls open as she looks at me and I know the question she doesn't ask. *How would that have worked?* I didn't want to miss Sam's picnic or Vicki's return from camp, but Lindee needed me, too.

"I would have made it happen, if you'd have asked." Didn't she see I'd do anything for her?

"Thad," she groans. "Being with your kids is important. I don't want me or the motel to come between all of you. I already feel guilty that I kept you on as the construction team when your family is so far away."

"It isn't far, and we've made it work, right?" I pause. "Is that why Myles was here? Are you looking to hire him?"

Lindee shrugs out from our connected hands and takes a seat on the couch facing the fireplace. "Myles was here because he's a friend. We went to dinner to talk about *his* love life."

"You look mighty pretty for a friendly dinner."

Suddenly, I'm pissed off again. Lindee has refused to have dinner with me for weeks, but she went out with Myles. Her head snaps up as I cross my arms, glaring down at her seated position. I have a nice view down the valley between her breasts, conjuring up memories of my dick sliding there the night we met. We need a repeat of that position, once we resolve the present issue.

"I just felt like dressing up." She drops her gaze. "It's nice to remember I'm a woman once in a while."

Shit. We haven't done anything but work lately, nothing special just for us. And then I'm gone on the weekends. This isn't the way to build a relationship. Lindee needs dates and romantic moments. I haven't missed the romance novels littering her bedside with bare-chested men on the covers.

"How about we go out next weekend?"

"Don't you have your kids?" She sheepishly glances up at me.

Dammit. I'd promised Jaz I'd take the kids again as I hadn't been keeping up with the two nights a week. Dragging both hands over my face, I sigh. "Okay, how about during the week?"

Lindee watches me, maybe reading my conflict. I want to see my kids. I want to take Lindee on a date. I can make this work. However, doubt is written on her face.

"Maybe next weekend you could bring your kids here." Her voice is quiet with the suggestion as her hands fiddle in her lap.

"Could I do that?" *Would she want to meet them?* I step closer to Lindee, surprised by her suggestion. I've been taking the kids to Nessi's house because I don't have a permanent place yet. But I've been hoping to introduce my brood to Lindee.

"If you want." Lindee hesitates, peering up at me with innocent eyes, swimming in a blue color I want to dive into.

"That'd be awesome, but the rooms aren't really put together." The main hotel rooms are still in a heavy demolition stage. Not one has been renovated. The duplex that I share with my cousins is too tight for three more bodies.

"I mean here." Lindee pats the armrest of the couch. "At the winter cabin. I could take a room for the weekend or—"

"No," I interject, lowering to my knees and placing my hands on her thighs. "No, I don't want you to be displaced again. Sam would love the loft. Vicki might too. Sasha can have a bedroom to herself. I'll take another, if that's okay with you." I'd love to sleep with Lindee, but with my kids here, it might be best to keep separate bedrooms for a weekend.

"I'd like that." The corner of her mouth slowly curls. "I'd like to meet them."

"Yeah?" I shouldn't be surprised. I've been wanting to tell them about Lindee, but I've been treading lightly because of Jaz. She's volatile at best and ruthless at her worst.

Still, my heart hammers at the possibility of my kids meeting Lindee. They're going to love her.

"Yeah." Lindee gives me a big smile that rivals the one she gave Myles. I don't want to be jealous of her friendship with him, but I am.

"You have to promise me something."

Lindee tilts her head.

"Dinners this week. Every night. I'll cook."

Her brows lift. "You can cook?"

"I can grill. What more do I need?" There's an old metal upright outside the winter cabin, and Lindee cleaned it off weeks ago.

"Okay," Lindee whispers.

My heart does a little flip that she's conceding to me taking care of her.

"You're wearing my bracelet." I slip my finger over the silver cuff, feeling the dragonfly beneath my fingertip. She went out with him but she's wearing this reminder of our night, of us.

"Your bracelet, huh?"

"You wear it to remember me."

"Maybe." She nibbles at her lower lip, fighting a smile, but I want that grin on my lips. I lean up to kiss her, slipping my hands around her legs and reaching for her hips. Her hips, which are mine.

Her fingers fist in my hair, and I tug her to the edge of the couch, spreading her legs so my body fits between her thighs. Her thighs, also mine.

"Your lemony dress makes me want lemonade all of sudden." Her breasts are mine, too.

"Oh yeah?" Lindee tugs the side of her dress, teasingly lifting the skirt until it's pooled over her lap. Then she's reaching underneath it and tugging down her underwear while I sit back on my heels and watch until the thin material slips over her knees. When it falls to her ankles, she pulls one foot through the material and spreads her legs wide.

I'm so thirsty for her.

Taking the hem in her fist, she leans back and pulls the dress higher, exposing the lower half of her body and giving me a peek of something ripe and ready to be tasted.

"Lemonade for sale," she teases, reminding us both of neighborhood lemonade stands.

"How much for a cup?"

"What are you willing to spend?" The gleam in her eyes says she doesn't want monetary payment despite being impressed that Myles owns a fucking town.

"Will you take a payment plan?" Because the expense of my whole heart is too much to give her at once.

Lindee widens her knees. "Payment plan accepted." Her eyes dance until I lower between her spread legs and lick her seam. Then her lids flutter closed as her back arches. One of her hands comes to my hair again, combing into it and cupping the back of my head.

"God, I've missed you," she mutters.

It's only been two nights, but two nights feels like too many. I've missed her as well.

How eager her body is for me. How responsive she is to my touch. How much she wants me.

And I feel the same. This hunger for her. The magnetism of her. This desire for more.

The heat of her center as well as the wetness confirm how she feels about me. She's dripping onto the couch by the time I'm done with her, and a sweet whimper of my name graces her lips. Then she's pushing at my shoulders, and I'm tumbling to my back on the new area rug before the fireplace. With her hands making quick work of my belt and lowering my zipper, my jeans are below my hips in no time.

Then Lindee is over me, drawing me into her and she stills.

"You aren't wearing a condom." Her wide eyes stare down at me.

"Is this okay?" We've already discussed our sexual history, and I'm confident my little swimmers aren't effective anymore. Plus, she feels so damn good, but I'll follow her lead and pull out if she asks me.

Still, I want her to know, "You feel like heaven, sweet thing." Written in the stars maybe.

Lindee sighs as her lips slowly quirk. "You." Her breathless whisper still isn't an answer.

"Is that a yes?"

"Yes."

I tip up my hips, and she smiles wider before pulling herself up my dick and then slamming back down, taking me into her depths. I grunt at the force while my hips react again, surging upward. Then I'm jackknifing up and flipping her over, shoving her dress aside and barreling into her.

"I am so fucking jealous he took you out," I admit as I thrust forward.

"Are we really discussing Myles right now?"

I crash my mouth over hers, kissing her hard, shoving my tongue into her mouth before nipping at her lower lip.

"Do not ever speak another man's name when I'm buried inside you." The command is all grunts and puffs as I undulate into her body.

Her hands smooth over my head before fisting in the back of my shirt. She giggles as she says, "You're a little out of control when you're jealous."

I still. "Am I hurting you?"

"If you stop, I'm going to hurt you," she threatens with no bite.

I hook an arm under her knee and hitch it higher until her kneecap nearly kisses her shoulder. The position opens her up and I'm hammering home when she lifts her other leg on her own. Shifting to place my hands on her shins, Lindee is nearly folded in half and spread wide for me. The sound of us coming together fills the room. I'm loving the skin-to-skin friction.

"You," she whimpers like she did that first night, when her body started tightening and I sensed she was close. My pubic bone is hitting her clit in a way that she's bound to get off and when she does, she screams in a way I haven't heard before. Guttural and deep. Lindee's eyes roll back as she arches into the release. I let go of her lower legs and finish the race to spill inside her. Her orgasm set off mine, and I press up on my arms, arching my back as I drive myself as deep as I can into her.

We're a slippery mess but there's nowhere else I want to be than inside this woman's body.

With heavy breaths, I collapse to her side, inhaling her citrusy scent which smells a little more grapefruit than lemony.

"Want to shower?" Her breath is ragged.

My head pops up. We haven't been able to shower together because Karen's shower was so small. "Fuck yeah. Another first."

"Well…" The word recalls how we showered together on that night back in March. But showering with her here, in this cabin we restored together, will be a new kind of first, just like being inside her bare and raw.

And I can't wait for more firsts with her.

22

Playlist: "Secrets" – One Republic

[Lindee]

After another round in the shower, where Thad lifted me against the tile wall and showed me again how hungry he could be for me, we fall into my bed which is a little too small for a man the size of Thad. The camper bed was a king, but this bedroom only has a queen-sized bed in it, which keeps our bodies close.

Eventually I'm overheated and not feeling right. My stomach feels like a wrestling match is happening inside me, and I sneak from the bed as gingerly as I can, hoping not to disturb Thad. Or give away the embarrassing sounds coming from my body as I spend too long in the bathroom. After two attempts to slip back into bed, I give up and stay in the private space, leaning against the tile wall in quiet discomfort.

"You okay?" Thad asks at some point in the early hours when tears threaten to be released because of exhaustion.

"Just a stomach thing. I think it was something I ate."

Myles and I found a mom-and-pop place about a half-hour from the motel, and I ordered lasagna, a favorite of mine. However, my body is hating me for the cheese and tomato sauce decision, and I've been burping garlic. The fragrance seeps from my pours, and I languidly take a shower in the morning. I'm bone tired.

"Why don't you hang out a bit? Go back to bed for a little while." Thad stands in the kitchen looking refreshed as he sips a cup of coffee. My stomach twists at the rich scent.

"I'll rest later," I unintentionally snap at him. "It will pass."

But Thad demands I return to bed, going so far as to scoop me up and tuck me back beneath the covers.

Only, three days later I'm still not feeling great. I've just been tired, lacking appetite, and not sleeping well, despite the delicious meals Thad makes me and how much his body wears out mine. The other night, I spent an entire night reading a romance novel which makes no sense as I'm nearly living one.

I'm just stressed out. The excuse is only half-heartedly accepted.

With tunes in my ears, I'm in the lobby rolling paint on the freshly patched walls when the door opens. Glancing up, I see my sister-in-law, Dolores. She waves.

As I tug the headphones from my ears, I race to the door.

"Come in, come in," I encourage, reaching for Dolores despite my paint-speckled clothes. The tall, lithe woman with dark hair and Elvira like strips of purple and white hugs me back like I'm not a mess. My brother follows her, pulled together in a suit which leads me to believe this is more of a business meeting than a family visit.

"Garrett." I reach out for my brother who surprises me by

hugging me as well. When he brushes off paint that doesn't exist on his jacket, I chuckle to myself. Garrett is just as tall as his wife and has a trimmed beard that matches his dark hair and eyes. It isn't fair that he's crossed the line of fifty without a speck of gray while I spent time plucking the occasional one out of my hair.

Dolores gives me a wink in response to Garrett wiping non-existent paint off his expensive suit.

"Hey. We just wanted to case out the joint," Garrett explains.

"You mean check on your investment." I step back as they further enter the lobby, eyes checking out the new stonework around the fireplace and a long cement ledge before it. The newly built bar is stained a deep black on the bottom and a rich brown on the top. Earth tones abound in this circular room. The original place was a deep red and black combination I didn't want to replicate, but I still desired a classic vibe here. *Dirty Dancing* does West Virginia.

"How are things going?" Garrett asks, taking a walk around the room like an inspector. As if he'd know anything about construction. Garrett is a builder of businesses but not by physical labor.

I give him a brief rundown of what we've completed and where we're going next. The pool. The duplex. The motel rooms are a ripple effect of pressure washing the walk and exterior walls, painting window trim, and then interior work, which includes fresh paint, bathroom repairs, and final décor. I can't replace all the bathroom fixtures in the first year and the windows are still good enough for another year or two. There was a discussion about the roof. It's going to have to last another year as well.

Baby steps on a big project. Some things get removed; some get fixed. Some things get patched and disguised. I'm calling it charm.

As we finish reviewing my check list, the lobby door opens, and Thad and Duke walk in.

Duke stops in his tracks as Dolores looks up at him. Her head snaps around in a sharp double take and then she can't seem to take her eyes off him. At first, I can't tell if her interest is how attractive Duke is or just curiosity. Except, the two men with a bunch of tattoos are staring back at her like they've seen a ghost.

Thad slows and stalls a couple feet from where Dolores and I are in front of the bar. Garrett stands behind it with his arms spread like he's the bartender.

"What's going on here?" Thad's voice is rough, edgy even.

Oh God, not another Myles incident. Then again, he made up nicely for his overreaction.

However, when I glance between Garrett and Thad, Thad isn't looking at my brother. He's watching Dolores.

"Don't I know you?" Dolores squints and shifts where she stands to better face the two men. "Duke James, right?" She casually points at Duke. "You were a member of..." The fade of her voice has her turning toward Garrett. Her blue eyes widen before she glances at me.

When I look around, all eyes are aimed in different directions. Thad and Duke glare at Dolores. Garrett stares back at them. I'm the only one in the dark, and unease rolls down my back.

"A member of what?" My voice is too high.

"A motorcycle club." Dolores's blue eyes laser in on me.

"Excuse me?" I choke.

Dolores is from a small town named Blue Ridge, Georgia. She met my brother in California and it's a bit of a romance, but before she met Garrett, she had this loser boyfriend for ten years who was in a motorcycle . . .

I twist to look at Thad. His bike. His demeanor. The giant lion ring. The tattoos. I hadn't wanted to stereotype him. The ink is hot. His gruffness is sexy. Not everyone who rides a motorcycle is in a club.

The front door opens again, and Manor walks in. He stops quick and a huge smile brightens his face.

"Dolores fucking Chance." Without a thought, he rushes forward and pulls Dolores into an embrace.

She gingerly pats his broad back.

"Manor," she coughs as he releases her, and she peeks at my brother a second before looking back at the silver-haired guy with a man bun. "It's good to see you again."

"How the hell have you been?" Manor is now holding Dolores's hands and catches his finger on the huge rock she wears on her left hand. He pulls her hand up and admires the diamond. "Phew. Who is the lucky man? Don't tell me old Crusty Rusty got his head out of his ass finally."

Garrett subtly coughs, covering his mouth with a fist. Dolores hesitantly looks at Garrett before glancing back at Manor. "Uhm. No. Manor James meet my husband, Garrett Fox."

"Fox, huh?" Manor extends a hand toward Garrett who shakes over the bar. Manor then tips his head toward me. "Any relation to our girl here?"

"I'm her older brother," Garrett states with protective bravado he hasn't displayed in years. My brother and I are at opposite ends of the family. He's nearly nine years older than me and a true Fox sibling. I'm the fake one. Still, he's never treated me any differently than my sisters. He invested in Mae's flower shop. He offered to help Jane. And he loaned me the capital for the motel.

He used to claim he was an investor in things, not people, but then he met Dolores. She reformed him.

And she's different as well. She used to hang out with a motorcycle club. Or rather a band of bikers who were once a rough bunch but claim they are a riding club now. Rebel's Edge, or something like that.

My gaze falls back to Thad. "Garrett is also part investor in the motel."

"Fuck," Duke mutters, turning away his head.

Thad finally moves, stepping up to the bar and shaking hands with Garrett over the countertop. He leans in and gives Dolores a quick kiss on the check. "Nice to see you again, Lores."

"It's Dolores. I didn't change my name." She pauses, and I recall her once telling me how this Crusty Rusty character didn't like how old-fashioned her name sounded. He wanted to call her Lores. "It's nice to see you, too, Roadster."

My head swivels. Have I encountered another world? What is happening here? Dolores knows Thad's nickname. Which means . . .

"Were you all in a motorcycle gang?"

"We don't call them gangs," Manor responds, lifting his chest as pride fills his voice.

"Shut up," Duke mutters while I glare at Thad.

How many more secrets does this man have?

I DON'T GET an immediate answer to my question as Garrett asks to see the rest of the place, distracting us all from the heavy tension in the round room. Dolores follows but glances over her shoulder at the three men hovering near the lobby entrance. I lead Garrett along the walkway near the motel rooms where I point out what has been done. We circle back along the broken-up driveway and glance at the pool. Finally, Dolores and Garrett join me in the cabin.

Thad and his cousins have disappeared, back to work somewhere on the property.

In the privacy of the cabin, Garrett rounds on me. "What the fuck is going on?"

"Garrett," Dolores admonishes as my brother paces with his hands clasping the back of his head. She turns to me next. "Are you safe?"

"I didn't know I had anything to be unsafe about."

Dolores nods.

"A motorcycle gang?" Garrett sputters.

"I guess they don't call it a gang," I snark. They can call themselves a freaking pep squad for all I care.

What I did know was that the man I'd been sleeping with had another damn secret he hasn't shared with me.

First, I explain how it is that Thad and his cousins work for me and remind Garrett that while he thought it strange to include the stipulation in the purchase, he'd investigated their business and suggested I accept the deal.

"Yes, I looked into their business practices, but not their backgrounds. I didn't think to run a background check."

"Garrett," Dolores admonishes again before looking back at me. "I wasn't a biker chick, but I did hang around with a group of men who used to ride as a formal club. The most I know is the group was notorious in the mountains of Georgia and eventually splintered. Their president was killed, which triggered a series of incidents that killed other members, too. The local group decided to disband but some hangers-on keep a clubhouse in an old mansion near Blue Ridge."

Dolores pauses. While I might not have ever watched *Sons of Anarchy*, I'm familiar enough with the concept of motorcycle clubs, their hierarchy of government, and the idea of a central place for parties and meetings.

"The men who gather there now, or rather some stay there, are more like a bunch of lonely souls needing a place to call home. And they ride together as an unofficial club. No illegal stuff." Dolores glances at Garrett. "That I know of."

"I don't understand. So, Thad, Duke, and Manor were part of the riding club or the original gang?"

Dolores gives me a sympathetic glance. "It's probably best to ask them. I'd only see them a few times at parties after I started hanging out with members of the group."

Garrett snorts and Dolores narrows her eyes at him before turning back to me. "A man named Justice is their unofficial president now and he owns a legitimate bar just outside of Blue Ridge. Sometimes, one, or all three of them. . .Thad, Manor, or Duke . . .would be there."

"But Thad told me they live in Kentucky. Blue Ridge, Georgia is a bit of a distance."

Dolores shrugs. "Men love to ride their motorcycles. The bar. The clubhouse. They are destinations for guys like them."

I nod, placing a hand over my belly.

"Honey, are you okay?" Dolores asks, shifting toward me. "You look a little green."

"I just have a stomach bug. Something I ate a few days ago."

"You look exhausted," she adds causing Garrett to give me a long, hard stare.

"It's nothing. I just didn't sleep well last night."

Dolores hums, keeping her eyes on me a little longer than necessary. Garrett suggests we grab some lunch, but food just doesn't sound appealing right now. I'm hungry for answers instead.

Eventually, I walk Garrett and Dolores to his sporty car. They're traveling on to Jane's house in Wrightwood, and I promise that I'll join them for dinner tomorrow night.

Garrett opens Dolores's door, but she looks at him, cupping his jaw. "Can you give us a minute? Girl talk."

Garrett leans in to kiss his wife before stepping back toward me and offering me a brotherly hug. It's been a long time since the Fox clan spent as much time together as we do now. In our twenties and thirties, we only gathered for holidays, but now we meet more often, and the three sisters have our annual road trip together.

"Call me if you need anything," he stresses to me. He steps away and enters the driver's side, starting up the car and turning on some music.

Dolores shuts the passenger door. With an intense gaze, she assesses me. "I'm assuming you're sleeping with him."

"Who?" I counter. If Dolores wasn't like a fourth sister, easily blending into our fold and making attempts to build a relationship with Jane, Mae, and me, I'd be put off by her directness.

"Roadster."

"What makes you think I'm sleeping with Thad and not one of the other guys??" I ask wondering what kind of girl talk this is.

"The way he looked at you, like he was ready to shed blood and bury bodies."

"Well, that's graphic," I snort.

"It's how men like him are, though. The president who was killed years ago was somehow related to Thad. And before that, his grandfather was in charge at one point. All hell broke out before the local club disbanded."

My breath hitches. "When did they disband?"

"Maybe thirteen, fourteen years ago, I guess. Made the local papers when everything happened." Dolores pauses, tilting her head. "I thought Thad was married."

"He's divorced now." I hold my head higher, instantly upset that my sister-in-law would think I'd sleep with a married man.

"Be careful with a man like him, Lindee."

I could argue that nothing's going on between us. We're a fling until the renovations are done. When he'll go back to Kentucky and his ex and his kids.

But something holds my tongue. I don't want Thad to be just a fling, but every step is one forward and two back with him. He has so many sides and I'm always learning them from someone other than him. I trust him while at the same time I don't. It feels like he's got one foot out the door, while acting like he wants to set both feet inside my heart.

Dolores continues. "A man like him sucks you in, gives you promises, and then breaks your heart."

"And that's what happened to you?" I remind both of us of the long-standing relationship Dolores had before Garrett with Crusty Rusty. I shiver at the nickname, but I also know Dolores loved another man before him. A high school sweetheart and next-door neighbor named James Harrington. Dolores's brother is now married to James's sister and it's just too complicated for me to compute all this right now.

"That was history. I don't want to see it happen to you." Dolores cups my face like a mother instead of a woman not even ten years older than me. She's sweet while rough around the edges. She and Garrett couldn't be more opposite, but they work beautifully together.

"I can hold my own," I counter.

Dolores gives me a sharp nod before we embrace. She'd been alone a long time, like me, before she met my brother.

"Get some rest, honey. You look tired."

She has no idea how weary I am some days, and yet I keep moving on.

After my sister-in-law lowers into Garrett's car, her window automatically goes down and Garrett leans over the center.

"You feel unsafe, call me. I mean it. I'll get you out of the contract." There was a time my brother wasn't this present in my life but the strain in his voice tells me *he* might shed blood and bury bodies, or at least he knows a guy he can pay to do the dirty work, if I need him.

And it's kind of sweet to think my brother loves me like that.

23

Playlist: "Son of A Sinner" – Jelly Roll

[Thad]

uck.

I haven't been able to concentrate since seeing Dolores in the lobby. What a blast from the past. More like an explosion, and not a welcome one considering I hadn't told Lindee about the club. All in due time, I'd figured. But honestly, I wasn't certain how Lindee would handle this truth about me. We're different in enough ways that this part of my past could be a real deal breaker for someone sweet like her. I didn't know how to bring it up with us still new and a bit fragile. Quite frankly, I'd wanted a chance for her to know me as I am, not who I'd been.

What were the chances her sister-in-law was an acquaintance from a lifetime ago?

Hours have passed since Lindee gave her brother a tour and

then disappeared into the cabin with him and Dolores. I've threatened twice to go after her but both Manor and Duke demanded I let her handle her sibling.

Fuck, but I don't know what Dolores is telling her, or what Lindee must be thinking. The line between reality and fiction is so murky about motorcycle clubs and I gave up defending them once I walked away.

Stay or leave.

That had been the most difficult choice of my life and the decision forged a path that has been rocky and rough for thirteen years.

When I've hammered my own finger for the third time, I chuck my hammer across the motel room I'm working on, putting a nice dent in a wall that didn't need repairs, but now does, and stand to pace.

I catch a glimpse of Lindee and rush through the door to the pool area where she stands. Within seconds, I hear the thud of feet behind me. Duke and Manor intend to be backup.

If I thought telling Lindee about Vic was difficult, and spilling about Jasmine was easy, this falls outside the spectrum as the hardest part to explain about myself. And I didn't trust yet that she could handle what she now needs to know. I'd wanted more time. More time for her to know me as the man I am now, although the person I'd been will always reside inside me.

"I think I should put decorative tile around the pool's rim. Update it a bit." With her hands on her hips, she stares down at the murky water we haven't drained yet. Her hair is pulled up on top of her head in one of those messy knots she wears, sometimes losing a pen or two up there. She lifts her hands and spreads them apart to emphasize what she says next. "And a wrought iron fence around the perimeter instead of this gross chain link would do wonders as well."

"Sweet thing," I murmur, approaching her with caution as Duke and Manor slow up behind me.

"Oh, and condolences on the loss of your family member." She glances over her shoulder at me, eyes narrowing. "You know, the one you were related to when you were in *a motorcycle club*."

"It isn't what you think," I begin, but Lindee holds up a hand and spins to face me.

"Hmm." She taps her cheek and then points at me. "I think I've heard those words before from you." Taking a step to her right, intending to walk away from me, I block her retreat and grip her shoulders.

"Lindee, listen."

"No, you listen" A pointed finger jabs toward my chest.

Normally I love the fiery intensity of this woman, who looks good on the back of my bike, owns this motel, and has a vision for her future. But I'm not loving that fire currently directed at me.

"I'm done with all these secrets you have. I don't need to know everything about you but between the ex-wife, your kids, and now this doozy, I'm not sure what else can be sprung on me."

Her bright eyes hold on mine, and as if she reads my thoughts, her shoulders stiffen. "There's more isn't there."

I only have one additional thing left to tell her but now isn't the time for that. I need to tackle this new revelation first.

"You know, I didn't pass any judgement on the bikes or the tats. Even the broody attitude at times."

I'm not broody, am I?

"So why was this such a big secret?" Her shoulders fall beneath my touch and her head lowers like she's truly hurt I hadn't opened up about this history.

"This past isn't pretty."

"Is any?" she quickly interjects, lifting her head.

I release her shoulders and swipe over my head, removing my baseball cap to scratch my scalp before replacing the hat.

"I won't disrespect the club because what we did then we did out of loyalty. Out of dedication to the values we had then. For honor, for freedom. For living by our own rules." I heavily exhale. "But times turned dark. The danger to our families was getting to be too much."

I close my eyes a second and tip back my head before looking at her, willing her to understand and forgive me. "I've done things I'm not proud of, Lindee. Did things I thought I had to do, and I'd do them again to protect what's mine. What I love."

Lindee's eyes widen, perhaps reading in my expression exactly what I'm saying. I'd kill for family. For brotherhood. For love.

"I'll answer any questions you ask but some things might be better left unanswered." I don't want to give her the list of who I've hurt and how because I can't rectify the past. And some men just had the beating coming to them. Other people were killed for just cause, in the line of fire, like a battle during war. A private war, albeit, but one we were devoted to winning. Loyalty to the club above all else. We lived by that philosophy because we were born into it.

Lindee tilts her head, assessing me with ice-blue eyes, maybe processing what she sees. I'm a hard looking man with the tattoos and the scruff. I'm solid and tall, but I've been gentle as hell with her because she's special to me.

"Have you . . ." She swallows before squinting at me in the bright sunlight. "Have you killed people?"

How exactly do I answer her? Do I compare myself to a soldier, doing what he or she believes must be done in the name of pride and valor? Will she understand or see us as a wild bunch of menaces, like most people do?

She glances around me to Duke and Manor before lifting

her head in a long nod and rolling her lips inward. I'm taking too long to answer her.

"I'm going to take your non-answer as a yes to my question."

"Can you handle that?" Will she still be with me if I have crossed that line? I brace for her to tell me she never wants to see me again. To fire me on the spot and kick my ass off this property.

Duke, or Manor, shuffles behind me. Whoever moves is itching to explain.

We did things for protection and the rush of knowing we were part of something. Something we loved and loved us, like family. Hell, many of the members *were* blood family.

She doesn't answer my question but folds her arms over her middle and asks me something else. "How deeply were you involved? Is that the right term?" She looks past me to one of my cousins because Manor corrected Dolores earlier about the gang thing.

False hope fills me that Lindee's asking because she wants to understand.

"Yes," Duke chokes out. "Deep. Because it was our family. Literally. Our Pop was an original member in the seventies. Our ma and Thad's dad were both born into it."

Lindee's gaze swings back to me. "Your parents?" she cautiously whispers, knowing they were killed on a motorcycle.

I nod.

More processing in that beautiful brain of hers. I can practically see the gears turning, trying to piece things together.

"So Nessi was part of it, too." Her brows lift. "What about Jasmine?"

I sigh. "Jaz's dad was the most recent president. He was killed fourteen years ago."

Her eyes widen at the explanation. "Before the club disbanded." Then her eyes narrow. "Or causing the club to split."

What exactly has Dolores told her to know we dissolved the club fourteen years ago? And how do I explain the intricate details of what happened? Jasmine's dad's murder. The death of family from other members within the club. A senseless killing spree that was scaring the fuck out of all of us.

"After Ace was taken down, Pop begged me . . . us"—I gesture to my cousins—"to pull out. It wasn't the club he'd started with his buddies back in the seventies. Times had changed." Greatly changed. Weapons. Drugs. Life had been good, profitable, while not honest, and had grown literally deadly.

Lindee watches me before scrubbing the back of her neck with her fingers, tucking loose hair into her messy bun. Her gaze lowers. "And this is how you ended up with Jasmine."

Fell into bed with a woman full of heartache, feeling my own sorrow at the decision that needed to be made. I would walk away from all I'd known.

And suddenly, I was taking a woman and my future—*my kids*—with me.

"Yes," I admit.

"You just left." The surprise on her face has me surprised. Does she really think it was that easy? To leave friends I considered family? To take on a woman I'd known all my life, but didn't love, in order to protect her? To protect my first kid?

I get that Lindee has some abandonment issues, but this is different.

"It wasn't that simple," Duke snaps, stepping forward, but I hold up a hand to stop him.

For many guys, leaving behind the camaraderie was difficult. Like scraping off their tats, removing their vest was taking off a layer of skin. Some moved to other clubs, and the shift wasn't so hard. For those of us with our cut . . . a leather vest with our club insignis . . . stored in a closet, the separation had been much, much harder.

The symbol wasn't some souvenir on a shelf, long forgotten. Hardly forgotten was more like it.

"I'd given into Pop's request because Jaz was pregnant. I couldn't risk her because I couldn't risk Sasha." My throat thickens around my eldest's name. I don't like to consider what might have happened to Jasmine, thus what might have happened to my baby girl if I hadn't decided to walk away from the club.

Staying can be difficult. Leaving can be, too. The decision was subjective.

Pop's plea was easy enough to follow when I saw the fear in his eyes. He didn't for a second think I wasn't strong enough to be in the club, brave enough to fight alongside my brothers for what we believed in. What he feared was the loss of me, of my future, and my children. He didn't want me to suffer as he had, losing his son in a senseless accident and, eventually, his daughter to a terrible disease.

However, my brother Vic struggled with the clash between loyalty to Pop and the club. He wanted revenge. He wanted righteousness. He wanted to restore something so broken, many of us couldn't see how to fix it.

And the cycle would only continue. A life for a life. Who would be left standing? When would it end? Would I risk my own in the mayhem?

I wouldn't. I didn't. I walked away.

Vic didn't.

Lindee nods, agreement in those brilliant blue eyes of hers that my child had to come above all else.

"Was Jasmine your old lady?"

Duke snorts.

"She's learning," Manor says with pride without knowing why Lindee knows the term.

However, I shake my head. Jasmine had been a one-night

thing, but how do I say that to Lindee? Hadn't she been the same to me once? Now, she meant so much more to me.

"So, you felt obligated to her," Lindee asks.

"I wanted my child." I didn't want Jasmine running wild and she was at loose ends. Her entire family was gone. Her mom ran off when she was younger. Her dad was dead. She had a brother who stayed behind but agreed I needed to get his sister out of Georgia.

"So, you moved to Kentucky and the rest is history." Lindee's expression is pinched, almost angry.

"What are you upset about? The club? Me?" I tip my head. "Or Jasmine?"

Lindee looks away. "You were very devoted to her."

I had been, but I wasn't anymore. It was different in the beginning. Emotions in the way of reason. Sleeping with Jaz had been a mistake, but alcohol and sadness can lead to dumb decisions. Having Sasha wasn't a mistake, though.

I'd stuck with Jaz because Vicki came along, and as much as I hated Vic for what I was certain he'd done, he might have hated himself more knowing the truth. He was my brother, my best friend, and he'd not only slept with my wife, he'd gotten her pregnant. Even if he loved Jasmine, he wouldn't have taken Sasha from me. He might have known Vicki was his, but he gave her to me, too.

"Sweet thing," I murmur. "I am not going back to Jasmine, if that's what you're worried about."

Lindee lowers her head again and I step closer to her, tipping up her chin. "I'm with you," I emphasize, holding my breath, wanting her to tell me she is still with me.

Instead, she places her hand over her forehead, eyes widening again. "Do you legally and legitimately own this construction company or is it a front for something else?"

"Have you watched *Sons of Anarchy*?" Manor scoffs.

"Shut up," Duke mutters behind me.

"The construction company is legitimate. I have the paperwork to prove it." Lindee knows I'll use that paperwork as evidence if need be. "When I split from the club, I was lost at first. Didn't know what to do with myself. Nessi thought I needed to work with my hands to get out of my head. She had me work around her farmhouse, making repairs and renovating shit."

"Then, I started taking odd jobs, and like you..." I squeeze her chin still in my grip. "Word spread and projects grew. Duke and Manor joined me, and we formed the firm."

Duke and Manor had had their own struggles leaving the club behind and lingered for a while in hopes to re-organize something better. Their dad was still involved but that's their story to tell.

"Don't motorcycle people usually work as mechanics?" Lindee's brows pinch and I chuckle.

"You *have* been watching SOA," Manor guffaws.

"Actually, I was the club's accountant," I add.

Lindee looks at me long and hard for half a second, then she laughs. "You're kidding me."

"Nope. Certified CPA, actually."

"No shit?" Her laughter continues like I'd told the funniest joke. Tears actually fill her eyes, and I'm worried the drops will shift from streams of humor to rivers of disgust.

What is she thinking? How is she feeling about all this?

Again, I wish I could read her better. In the bedroom, Lindee is an open book, spread wide and willing to be enjoyed. But outside those walls, she's less easy for me to decipher.

She swipes at the corners of her eyes. "I've never seen SOA."

"Then how do you know anything about clubs?" Duke asks.

Lindee shrugs. "I read romance."

"What?" Manor chokes.

It's my turn to chuckle and I shake my head. *This woman.*

With my hands cupping her cheeks, I brush my thumbs

beneath her eyes to clear the final tears. "I'm sorry I hadn't told you about all this sooner. I thought I'd have a little more time with you, for you to get to know me as I am, not who I'd been."

The crunch of boots on cement tells me my cousins are walking away, giving Lindee and me the privacy we need now that the story is out, and she isn't screaming at me to go away.

"My upbringing is always going to be a part of me, but I'm a different man now. I'm just a man trying to live an honest life, live for my kids, and impress a good woman." I gently jostle her head, emphasizing my thoughts.

I'm not certain she finds this latest revelation impressive, but I'm being honest here.

She's the good I want to have in my life.

"You still with me, sweet thing."

She stares at me. What does she see? Does she see a man who did what he thought best for his family? Or does she see me as some monster, living a menacing life? Or worse, does she see me as a quitter? A man who walked away in what was the most difficult decision of my life.

Lindee tips forward, her forehead landing on my chest. Her messy bun tickles my neck.

"Am I safe with you?" she mutters, her words muffled by my shirt.

Pressing her head back so she'll look me in the eye, I say, "I would never let anyone hurt you. Never."

I'd take a bullet for her, and Duke and Manor feel the same way. They care about her.

"No," Lindee shakes her head and taps a fist over her heart. Her voice is stressed. "Am I *safe* with you?"

With her clenched fingers at her chest, I take her meaning. Will I break her heart? I can't say for certain, but I'll do everything in my power to make sure I'm not a person who harms her.

"Yes," I exhale, brushing loose hairs over her ears and cupping her neck as I repeat myself. "Yes."

"Then I'm still with you."

Relief washes over me like the waterfall near the cave I took Lindee to weeks ago. The sensation is shocking, refreshing, and awakening.

She's still with me. This piece of me isn't an issue for her.

Those sweet blue eyes meet mine. "Were you really an accountant?"

"Swear on a stack of twenties, I was." I'd been good at math, creative with money, and working my way to a future role in the club when everything fell apart.

I was destined to be president one day.

Now, I use my number skills for right angles, measurements, and keeping this woman's heart in one piece.

She chuckles and the vibration along her throat feels good beneath my hands at her neck.

"Well, Mr. Money, know anything about the cost of gallons of water, pool re-surfacing, and decorative fencing?"

I chuckle as I press a kiss to her forehead.

"For you, sweet thing, I'll figure it out."

I'll do anything for her, like make this pool work, and protect her heart.

24

Playlist: "Put Your Records On" – Corinne Bailey Rae
"You Don't Know Me" – Ray Charles

[Lindee]

Later that evening, I'm in the lobby again. Thad didn't want to let me out of his sight, but we had work to do, and I needed some space after all I'd learned about him.

A motorcycle club. An honest-to-God biker.

Pride filled his voice as he explained his dedication to his club, his brotherhood, his family, but intermixed was the pain of a difficult decision to walk away from all he'd known to start a new life.

A life newly devoted to a woman he didn't love and a child he did. Then another child and another one.

Thaddeus Rhode was a good man. Whether he felt obligated, or trapped, he hadn't let on. He simply did what he thought best for his family.

I admired his commitment. Hell, I was envious of it.

He hadn't walked away from Jasmine or the kids.

The wall I hadn't finished painting earlier beckoned. I hated leaving something unfinished. After all that happened with Harris, I promised myself I'd never be a quitter again of anything, even something as trivial as rolling paint on a wall.

Still, the day was growing dark, and I was losing my motivation tonight. I told myself I'd get to the corner and stop for the night. The wall was going to need two coats anyway.

The music blasting from my phone isn't helping my mood. In an effort to get lost in work, find the distraction of something so mundane as painting, my playlist shuffles through a collection of female vocalists, all with smoky sounds and sad songs. On any other night, these divas would be perfect for the ambiance I wish to create in this future space, but perhaps songs about love and loss aren't the most uplifting.

All that Thad gave up, all he'd lost, dominates my thoughts. His parents. His Pop. His brother. He's been through so much, and yet he smiles wide and genuine, like he's never been touched by absence.

I have much to learn from him. He's clearly moved on in his life, faced forward, and took the unfamiliar road to new destinations.

Husband. Father. Honest business owner.

As I roll final strokes up to the corner of the room closest to the fireplace, I pause. Did it matter if Thad had been part of a motorcycle club? I hadn't come to a firm conclusion.

I also didn't have a say. I couldn't change his past. I didn't dictate his life. He lived how he wanted to live, then and now. He was unapologetic for that time, but regret twinged his voice when he admitted he'd done things he wasn't always proud of.

It wasn't up to me to judge *or* forgive him. I didn't know what I would forgive. I didn't need to know either.

The biggest question had been the one I voiced to him.

Was I safe with Thad?

Physically, I didn't feel threatened. Being near him, I'd never felt safer in my life. Thad offered me strange comfort in the way he looked at me, the way he kissed me, the way he held me against his large body. My flesh and bones are not my concern.

My heart was the issue.

Jasmine is a huge part of the equation.

Thad already told me how their marriage was a push and pull. A reckless addiction, perhaps. He'd been loyal to her because of their children, which was no fault of his kids.

He made his choice. He picked her, protected her. My fear was he'd do it again. He'd go back to her if she needed him. Stranger things have happened between couples who share history and children. Who were once physically attracted to one another. Could they be that again?

Thad didn't need to love Jasmine to have sex with her. He didn't even have to always like her. As he'd admitted, sex was a function in their marriage, not a connection.

Still, he'd stayed with her. Over and over, back and forth, up and down.

He looked broken when I suggested he'd simply walked away from his club. His exit from Jasmine seemed equally tough. And yet, she was still present while his club was gone.

Jasmine could try to win him back, reel him in, and keep him again.

I didn't want to doubt Thad, but I didn't know what to think. He hadn't told me the truth on more than one occasion. Could I really trust him to stick with me? I had my own baggage full of shame and issues.

Abandonment was one I clearly recognized and quite

possibly a reason I walked away first. If I leave, someone else can't leave me.

But I also had a soul-wrenching fear that I wasn't lovable. I wasn't enough.

I hadn't been enough to bring Harris back, which was a ridiculous thought considering the extent of his injuries.

Still, the fear was real, complex, and complicated.

I set down the paint roller and pour the remaining paint from the angled tray back into the can, covering it for the night. Wrapping the paint tube in tinfoil, I set it aside and stand with the empty roller in hand.

A new, throaty feminine sound fills the lobby.

I'd definitely been born in the wrong era as I loved the classic sounds of female artists from the 50s and 60s, but Corinne Bailey Rae was a newer singer with a distinct voice, and I loved her song about female empowerment.

Turning toward the long cement hearth before the fireplace, I hop up on it like it's a miniature stage. Flipping the paint roller, the wiry end twirls around as I hold the handle toward my mouth, using it as a microphone to belt out lyrics about turning on records, losing myself in song, and accepting that I'd find myself one day.

I'd told Jane I'd been dating myself all these years. I liked me.

I hadn't admitted to Thad that as much as I lose myself in him, I want to be found.

Somehow, I wanted the two concepts to merge. I did like me, but I still wanted someone else to like me too. But it was more than liking who I was or what I stood for.

I wanted someone dedicated to loving me. Someone willing to stand by me no matter what. Someone who would protect me at all costs.

Thad's words come back to me.

Did things I thought I had to do, and I'd do them again to protect what's mine. What I love.

There was a fierceness in those words that sent a shiver up my spine and a ripple through my heart, causing it to skip a beat. What would it be like to have a man like him love me like that? To be loved that strongly, with such devotion and security?

I didn't feel worthy, though, as I'd walked away from dedicating my life to someone who needed me.

I spin on the fireplace ledge and continue to mimic the ballad, despite the wire roller swiveling and hitting me in the chest. Back in my theater days, I built sets for productions. I never wanted to act. I sang backup in montages.

So, Thad has a past. Who didn't? I prided myself on not looking in the rearview mirror and I shouldn't be looking into his either. The future drove me forward and he held the same philosophy. Unfamiliar routes, hidden roads, complicated paths. You never knew what was ahead of you, but the anticipation that something big lay just around the bend—that was powerful.

Somehow. Someway. I'd make it. He'd make it, too.

Thad and I didn't need to compare historical war wounds. The future was our battle and I'd love a warrior by my side. Despite what I've learned. Despite what I haven't. Despite any doubts, Thaddeus Rhode certainly is a man worth a fight.

He's this complex kaleidoscope of darkness and light, but not black and white. He's brilliant color with the love he has for his children and the hope in what lies ahead, but he's also muted shades, blurred and stained by a past he won't ever be able to completely put behind him.

We are kindred spirits in that aspect.

On that thought, the ending notes of the song fill the room and I follow the singers lead, tipping back my head like a queen lyricist. Arm up with a fist like I'm threatening the Universe to defy me.

A slow clap crackles through the dim room, startling me and I snap my neck righting myself. Lowering the paint roller before me, the wire cylinder hits my thigh and gives off a light *twing*. A phone flashlight nearly blinds me and hides my audience.

"Who's there?" I nervously chuckle, shielding my eyes from the blinding light. The flashlight clicks off and I blink as blue dots speckle my vision.

"I didn't know you could sing." Thad's rich tenor fills the sudden silence of such a large, echoey room.

"Guess we both have secrets." A tease fills my voice because my ability to hum a tune and his biker history do not compare.

Thad hesitantly steps forward. He scratches the back of his neck and sheepishly looks at me.

"Lindee." My name is too serious on his tongue. "If you have questions, ask me. I don't want you thinking I'm withholding answers. But it was such a long time ago, and I'm a different man now." His head lifts and our eyes meet. "I've been lost for a long time, but I feel ... found when I'm with you."

My heart does a like step-hop-skip.

Have we found each other? Sometimes we mirror one another so much it scares me.

"I feel found, too," I whisper. "And I don't have any questions right now."

What could I ask him? Did I really want the details? I didn't. His past was his. We didn't need to look back.

Thad steps closer to the fireplace and offers a sly smile, breaking up the loose tension between us. "Got another song in ya?"

I hop down from the ledge with a heavy thud and set the paint roller on the floor. "No, I'm good now."

"Can I request a song?" Quickly, he's close enough his hand

comes to my hip, and he tugs me toward him. His eyes still look cautious, questions filling them, maybe even concern.

"Sorry. I'm a one-woman act with a one-song set list." I attempt to keep things light. It's been a heavy day.

"How about a dance then?" With his arm wrapped around me, Thad pulls his phone from his pocket and clicks on a music app. He scrolls until he finds what he wants. He slips his hand into mine and sets his phone on the fireplace mantel beside mine.

Ray Charles' voice fills the room.

"What's this?" I giggle. Thad does not seem like a crooner lover.

"You want to restore the nostalgia of this place. Here's a classic I can respect."

Thad lifts my hand between us and wraps his other arm around my back, then spins me into the vacant space in front of the fireplace. With a gentle tug, he twirls me back to him while Ray sings about a couple who don't know each other well but he's dreaming of her, wanting to hold her each night.

As the lyrics surround us, Thad and I sway. I lean my head on his chest and he rests his cheek on my hair. As his heart beats through his T-shirt, I hum. The rhythm is safety and comfort. Sweet and desperate, the song continues.

"I know there's still plenty we don't know about each other," Thad murmurs over Ray's melody. "But, I want to know all the things about you, sweet thing. I want to be an honest man loving a pretty girl." He tips up my chin, so I look at him. "Say you're still with me, sweet thing."

Love? He can't mean it, but Thad has already told me he isn't a liar or a cheater. Maybe he's just a thief, stealing my heart.

"I'm still with you," I murmur and rest my head on his chest. Thad presses a kiss to my hair. With my eyes closed, and the light in the space dimming, plus the heat of Thad's body, I melt into a puddle of fantasy. Of a simpler time, before I was born, where a couple makes a roadside stop to enjoy a dance and a night.

The song ends and Thad pulls back. "Dinner time."

He still wants to feed me every day. Maybe he does want to love me.

Holding my head back, I stare up at him. "Maybe one more song?" Not for me to sing but us to hold onto this moment a little longer.

A memento for my heart.

25

Playlist: "That's Amore" – Dean Martin, Dick Stabile
and His Orchestra

[Lindee]

When Thad arrives at the cabin Friday evening with his kids, I'm a nervous wreck. I like kids. Other people's kids. But these kids are extra important because they are Thad's. I have the entire weekend planned and I initially wanted to run everything by Thad.

"You don't plan for kids. You go with the flow." He'd laughed and told me whatever I had on my agenda would be fine. He just wanted his kids to meet me.

The *flow* was rippling, though, when Thad opened the cabin door with a tense jaw and hard look in his eyes.

"Sweet thing, this is Sam." A dark-haired boy stepped forward, offering me a wide smile missing a tooth.

"Nice to meet you." He holds out a small hand and shakes mine before looking over at his dad. "How'd I do?"

"Perfect, little man." Thad winks at me.

He next places two hands on the shoulders of a slim girl, and says, "This is Vicki."

No matter what Thad might have thought at her birth, the girl clearly worships the man behind her because she glances up at him with a smile in her eyes before looking at me and offering a small wave.

I wave back. "Hi."

Thad sighs and steps to the side. "And this is Sasha." He reaches for a phone in her hand and tugs it free, slipping it into his back pocket.

"Hey," she snaps, looking up at him from her spot still on the front stoop.

"Manners," he grits and tips his head toward me.

"What's up?" She turns her head and surveys me with eyes that match Thad's. Her hair coloring and solid, tall form make her the mirror image of her father.

"Sash," he snipes.

I shake my head. She's thirteen and I remember being thirteen. Plus, she's angry at him, maybe me, possibly the entire stinking world.

"I'm Lindee." I step toward this girl whose protective armor is almost visible. Extending my hand, she touches mine but it's a limp, soggy rag shake, as if I might have cooties or something.

"Sasha," Thad growls, but I dismiss him with a wave.

"Who's hungry?" I ask.

No one answers.

"Pizza is on the menu," I announce with a little too much enthusiasm.

"I hate pizza," Sasha snarks, glancing toward the living room and wrinkling her nose like something smells bad.

"Since when?" Thad asks.

"Since we eat it a lot," Sasha states, turning a hard glare on her dad.

"I still like pizza," Sam says swinging his head from his sister and dad's stare-down to me.

Thad breaks free from his eldest daughter's glare and smiles at his sweet boy. "That's my man."

"We could always order something different," I weakly offer to Thad.

"We order out a lot at home," Sasha adds, saccharine sweet but full of sarcasm.

"We weren't ordering pizza." Keeping my voice steady, I defend my dinner option. "I have individual pizza crusts for each of you to create your own."

I bought mini pizza crusts and a ton of toppings with hopes the kids might enjoy making their own personal pizzas. Jane's daughter, Willow, loves them.

Sam's brows lift and his little eyes widen. "Do you have pepperoni?"

"Yes," I hesitate.

"Yes!" He makes a small fist and pumps his arm a few times. "Mom never orders pepperoni because the girls don't like it. It gives them the farts."

Vicki's face turns red.

Thad reaches forward and ruffles Sam's hair. "Well, Mom isn't here." While Thad's statement is said with good intention, it's the wrong thing to say. Sasha's shoulders slump and Vicki reaches out a hand for her sister.

I try to meet Thad's eyes but he's already lifting Sam's tiny frame by squeezing his thin upper arms and Sam squeals in delight. Then Thad hoists Sam over his shoulder and lightly smacks his butt.

"Pizza time!" Thad announces, marching toward the kitchen.

Since the kitchen itself is not big enough for five, the kids line up along the peninsula counter on stools and Thad turns on some music. I set out the pizza crusts for each of us and fill the middle of the countertop with bowls of toppings, shredded cheese, and pizza sauce.

"When can I have my phone back," Sasha grumbles, giving me a quick glance like I'm the one who took the device before looking at her dad.

"When you have a better attitude." Thad doesn't miss a beat. He doesn't give his daughter a look but dramatically swirls a spoon covered in tomato sauce around the pizza crust.

"Like this," Thad says to Sam.

Sam takes the spoon, swirls a glob of pizza sauce to spread it and flicks the spoon dramatically upward. Sauce flings into the air, lands on my cheek and dots my shirt, along with a plop on the counter.

Sam's eyes widen. Vicki's mouth falls open. Sasha looks like she's holding her breath.

The poor boy couldn't have timed this tomato-tornado tomato if he planned it. And suddenly, I laugh. Thad swipes the sauce off my cheek and puts his finger to his mouth, sucking it before pulling his finger free with a pop.

The kids still don't move.

"I'm so sorry." Sam's lower lip quivers and he looks to his dad with large apologetic eyes. "I didn't mean to do it."

"I know, Sammy." Thad's voice softens as does his gaze while he observes his son.

Something like fear rests in the younger set of eyes but that can't be right. Sam isn't afraid of his dad, is he?

Without thought, I rub a hand up Sam's back. He stiffens and I quickly retreat. I shouldn't have touched him, and I catch eyes with Thad. His brows pinch and he shakes his head, as if he doesn't understand the reaction either.

Not certain how to act next, I swipe my finger through the

tomato sauce in the bowl and dot the end of Sam's nose. His eyes cross before he giggles.

"No worries, Sam," I say. "Now we're twins."

His smile slowly returns as he assesses me. Whatever was in his head, expressed in those wide eyes, seems to settle.

"Food fight?" Vicki asks, lifting her spoon with a dollop of sauce on it and aiming the utensil toward her father.

"Not if you want to see tomorrow, kiddo," Thad teases, catching her wrist and tugging the spoon free with is other hand. His reflexes were fast, and Vicki laughs at the sudden movement.

"I'm going to change my shirt and be right back." I want to reach for Sam again, ruffle his thick hair like his father did to reassure him he hasn't upset me, but I resist. Instead, I give Thad a timid smile and head to my room at the end of the hallway. A quick change into something darker that won't stain if pizza sauce propels again, and I step back to the hall. Thad stands outside my room.

He cups each side of my neck, and he tugs me forward, pressing a fast, hard kiss to my mouth. I'm nearly dizzy when he pulls back.

"Thank you," he mutters.

"It's going to be fine." I've never met a man's kids before but how hard can it be? They're kids.

Thad hooks his forefinger around my pinky and leads me down the hallway.

"I don't have to like her," Sasha snaps, presumably said to her brother and sister, because Thad and I are not clear of the hallway nor in view from the kitchen. He takes a larger step forward, pulling at my finger but I grasp his forearm, holding him back. He turns to look at me.

"It doesn't matter," I whisper. I don't need them to like me, although it certainly would make things easier. I also understand. "As kids, I'm new to them. Their parents' divorce is still fresh and they're raw to the separation. Relationships take time and just like you and me are still new, so is this experience of seeing their dad with someone other than their mom."

Thad stares at me. "Why do you have to be so understanding? And why is Sasha being such a punk?"

I can't answer question number two and I don't want to explain question number one. Not tonight anyway.

"You go with the flow, right?" I remind Thad.

"Yeah." He sighs. "Flow." He leans forward, gives me another quick kiss, and then pulls back.

When we turn for the hallway entrance, Sasha stands at the end glaring at us.

AFTER PERSONAL PIZZAS turn out to be a hit, which even Sasha grumpily admitted was decent, I break out the bowling set I found in the cabin. I cleaned up the old wooden pins which are roughly half the size of normal bowling pins in both height and circumference. The skinnier, wooden pegs are a natural wood color with a faded red strip around the bottom. I didn't find a ball, so I bought a small rubber ball that easily rolls on wood floors and won't cause damage to all the newly painted trim.

"Bowling, anyone?" I say with the ball in one hand and the collection of pins underneath my arm.

"What's that?" Thad laughs seeing my wares.

"Hallway bowling." From the front door down the hall toward the bedrooms is the perfect length for indoor bowling.

"What's that?" Sam repeats with enthusiasm.

"We bowl from here." I step toward the front door. "To there." I point toward the end of the hallway opposite us. "We'll have to keep score by paper and pen, but I thought it would be fun."

"Yeah, fun," Sasha mutters under her breath. She's taken a seat on the couch and stares at the television set which isn't on.

"We can play boys versus girls," I state.

"That's politically incorrect now," Sasha mumbles.

"Hey." The sharpness of Thad's voice has all of us stiffening.

"Thad," I whisper, hoping to draw his attention from his daughter. She must feel his glare on the side of her face despite her efforts to keep her head steady, focused on the blank television.

He finally looks at me. "This is bullshit," he says a little too loudly.

"It's fine." Again, I shake my head, warning him to let it drop. "How about Sam and me against you and Vicki then. Sasha, you can turn on a movie or something."

"Do you even have reception out here?" Man, her attitude is a reminder of being young, but I could do without it as I'm older and wiser. Thinking back, I feel sorry for my mother having three girls so close in age, but we would have never made snarky comments to her, though. We'd be afraid she'd snap into a foggy state.

"Attitude," Thad barks again but I ignore him and walk to the stand where I keep the remote. Clicking on the television, I log into Netflix and hand the remote to Sasha. When she surprisingly thanks me for the device, I walk away, like a sullen teen myself.

"Okay." I shake off Sasha's brand of negativity and clap my hands once. "Thad and Vicki, ready to go down?"

"Yes!" Sam pumps his little arm again, and I hand him the pins to set up at the end of the hallway.

As the bowling game winds down, Thad glances at the television. "What the hell is this?"

I'm standing next to Sam and immediately clap my hands over his eyes. On screen, the teenage boy is kneeling between the teenage girl's legs as she sits at a desk chair in a bedroom. Her legs are spreading wider, and the boy blows at her center.

Thad steps toward the couch and picks up the remote next to Sasha. He clicks off the set at the same time Sasha yells, "Hey, I was watching that."

"That is not for you yet, young lady."

I almost giggle at the use of young lady directed at such a hard-shelled girl. The term is foreign to a modern child on the verge of being a woman but acting like a toddler.

"It's PG-13, and I'm thirteen. Plus, Mom lets me watch these kinds of movies."

Thad snorts. "Well, not everyone present is thirteen." He shifts his eyes to Sam, who has removed my hand from his face but still clutches at the edge of my fingers. I'm afraid to move. He's holding onto me like he doesn't want to let go.

"And your mom isn't here but I'll definitely be speaking to her about this." Thad nods toward the set.

"Lots of good that will do," Sasha states.

"I've had enough. Go to your room."

"I don't have one," Sasha snaps, pressing on the cushions and jerking upright to face her father.

I clear my throat as Thad and his daughter stare off again. "I've set you up in the green room. Your dad thought you might like privacy and you can have it all to yourself unless Vicki wants to sleep with you."

"Where would I sleep?" Vicki asks. Her voice is much quieter than her sister's, sweeter. She smiles a lot but also watches what's happening around her.

"You can sleep with Sasha, or your dad thought you might like to sleep in the loft with Sam."

"You have a loft?" Sam's voice rises, excitement filling the question.

"That ladder leads to a sleeping loft. It's like a little fort up there." We added dimmer lights and two miniature fans as the space can get warm. There aren't any windows for ventilation but the high ceiling fan in the main area cools off the space nicely.

"Can I see it?" Sam turns to me, still holding the edge of my fingers. I glance up at Thad who is watching his little man clutch my hand.

"Of course."

Sam lets go of me and races to the ladder, taking his time to climb. When he gets near the top, he calls back to his sister. "Vicki, you've got to see this."

Vicki looks at Sasha, caught between sister loyalty and a desire to grow up, while being only eleven and still on the edge of childhood. The temptation to see a niche carved out above us has her stepping toward the ladder.

"Room." Thad points toward the hallway.

Sasha storms forward, crossing her arms. Thad hangs his head a moment before looking at me. "Give us a minute."

"Take all the time you need." I nod toward the loft. "I'll watch out for them."

"*Thank you,*" he mouths, and stalks after his oldest child. The anger on his face hints I shouldn't envy her.

But, I do. Because her dad is trying when my dad simply disappeared.

26

***

Playlist: "Daughters" – John Mayer

[Thad]

In my former house, I respected privacy, but mouthy teenagers do not deserve the privilege. While Sasha walks in front of me, I reach around her and open the door to the room Lindee prepared. The space is neutral with green fern prints on the wall and a light green spread on the bed but it's also feminine. Lindee added a bouquet of bright pink flowers on the dresser, and I'd smile at the nice touch she's offering my child, if my offspring weren't being such a pain in the ass.

"What is your problem?" I snap the second we enter the room. The cabin isn't huge, and voices carry so I try to keep my tone low, but I'm pissed. Sasha has no right to behave the way she has, especially toward Lindee, when it's evident the issue is me.

"How could you bring us to the home of your sweet butt?"

My head flinches back at the use of a familiar term. A term my daughter wouldn't know unless a certain someone taught her such a thing.

"Where did you hear that?" I cross my arms, waiting out my daughter when I already know the answer. *Just what exactly is my ex telling my teen*? I'll tackle that movie she was watching in a minute.

Sasha doesn't answer me.

"First, I call that woman sweet *thing*." I point in the direction of the front of the cabin. "Because she's the sweetest woman I've ever known. She's important to me and she opened her home to you so we could spend a weekend together outside of always hanging at Gran's."

I love Nessi and my kids do too but being at her place isn't always easy. The kids feel like they're visiting their beloved grandmother not their old man.

"I don't want to hear you call her anything other than her name. Lindee." I lower my arm.

"Whatever," Sasha mumbles.

My blood boils. "You got a beef with me, baby girl, you lay it on me. Not her."

Sasha collapses on the edge of the bed and drops her head a bit. I reach for the door and close it, giving us the privacy this conversation might need.

"What's going on, Sasha. This isn't you." My kids are not perfect, but Sasha hasn't had this attitude in the past. She's tough like Jasmine, exerting her authority as the eldest sibling of three, but she isn't mean. She's direct and bossy but not hurtful.

"Yeah, well, we all change. I'm growing up. You can stop calling me baby girl."

I bristle at the thought. She's always going to be my baby

girl. From the moment she was born I was wrapped around her little finger, and I don't want her to ever let go of me.

Still, I'm angry. "Then stop acting like a child."

Her head snaps up and if looks could kill, I'd be bleeding on the hardwood floor. The challenge only spikes my irritation, though, and I step closer to her, towering over her.

"I know things are different and maybe they've been a bit tough for you—"

Sasha huffs, wraps her arms around her middle, and looks away from me. I cup her chin and gently make her look up at me.

"I can't help you if you don't tell me what's wrong. How you're hurting."

Divorce is going to sting any kid even if they understand the reasons behind their parents separating. Sasha is smart. She knows Jasmine and I were not a good fit for each other. The fights were out of control. One or the other of us was always storming out a door. It wasn't healthy for any of us. And the two years before we split, the stress wasn't good for me. I would have divorced Jasmine sooner if I hadn't been sick.

"You know I'm right here for you." I squeeze her chin, and her lower lip quivers. My girl is strong, and she rarely cries compared to the emotional side of Vicki. Tears filling eyes that match mine has me softening my touch and lowering to a knee before her. "I'm not going anywhere."

There's more than one reason for Sasha to worry that I'm leaving her. Me being sick scared her. But I'm healthy and strong again. It's just a new norm not seeing me every single day. Not saying I like it, but it's better for them that Jasmine and I aren't under the same roof or even in the same zip code.

"Are things bad at home?" I hesitantly ask.

"Nothing I can't handle." Sasha swallows hard and squeezes at her eyes to quell any tears.

"I can't help if I don't know what's going down."

Sasha lowers her gaze and nods. "Mom's just struggling."

I get that, but I also know my daughter shouldn't be making excuses for a grown woman. "You can call me. Anytime."

"But you won't be there." Her head lifts, and a fire returns to her eyes.

"When have I not answered a call, ba...I mean, Sasha?" *Nope*. Not gonna happen to stop calling her baby girl.

"It isn't answering the phone, Dad. It's being *there*."

"At the house?"

Sasha nods.

"You know why I can't. The house is for your mom and you guys now."

"But you could still live closer to us," Sasha whines when she's never been a whiner before.

"And I will. It's just this job . . ." Was it this job? Was this just work to make money so I can afford upkeep on the house for Jaz and the kids? From the moment I saw Lindee standing in the lobby of the motel I knew being here was going to be different. Something more. More than a paycheck. More than a project.

"Can't you find another one closer to home?" All traces of tears are gone, and Sasha's tone mimics my ex-wife's.

Why you got to work such long hours?

Why can't you be home more?

Are you fucking around on me?

The nagging was constant. The self-doubt overwhelming. The irony pathetic. The confident girl I'd first hooked up with was long gone. In its place was a self-absorbed, sad woman I'd lost sympathy for. The issues were hers, not mine, and that was a hard pill to swallow about the mother of my children.

"I can. And I will. But having a job like this one is a big commitment, and I can't leave until I'm finished."

"Because of *her*?" Sasha nearly growls.

Yes. "No, Sash, because that's what responsibility is. You don't leave until a job is done."

"So, you're done with your family? Responsibility over."

I stand so quickly my daughter flinches backward and catches herself on her elbows on the bed. I have never ever struck my child and I never would. I'm just done with this bullshit.

"You think about that one, Sasha Rose. Think long and hard about what you just said. And when you come to a conclusion, then we can talk about the cell phone that I pay for. And the roof over your head. And those designer jeans you're wearing. I don't even want to discuss that movie you were watching anymore. PG-13 means nothing when you're acting like a spoiled child and not a mature teen."

I step to the door and pause. Despite my anger, she still needs to know something. "Having children is a lifelong responsibility but that's not the word parents use. We call it love. I love you, baby girl."

On that note, I exit the bedroom. Sometimes shutting the door softly is stronger emphasis than slamming one and I've said my piece.

When I re-enter the living area, I don't see anyone.

"Lindee?" Her name is a strangled whisper. I need this woman right now.

A head appears from the sleeping loft. "Up here, Dad." Sam's voice is full of laughter.

I climb the ladder I built for Lindee's quirky idea to cut a sleeping space into the attic niche. The area turned out kind of cool with two mattresses on the floor, recessed lights, and personal miniature fans for air circulation. As I crest the floor of the space, Lindee is sitting between the two mattresses. A light is on over Vicki's bed and Lindee is holding a book.

"Dad, Lindee is reading to us, and she's doing all these voices." Sam's enthusiasm is bursting from this tight space.

"Oh yeah? Whatcha reading?" I'm not much of a book guy but reading is important. Lindee has romance novels scattered all over this cabin.

"*Harry Potter*," Vicki explains. "It's Sam's new favorite."

Vicki gives me a sympathetic smile before I glance back to Sam. "Really? Your mom reading that with you."

Sam lowers his head. "Nah. Sasha reads it with me."

Dammit. My oldest has a big heart, reading to her little brother every night. I want to ask why Jasmine isn't doing the reading, but I don't. Something deep inside me knows the answer but I don't have hard and fast proof. Jasmine is sneaky like that, functional as if at full capacity, while hiding a dangerous habit.

"But don't tell Sasha that Lindee does it better." Sam's head pops back up. His little eyes widen with concern. "That would hurt her feelings and I don't want to hurt her."

"Your secret is safe with me." I cross my arms on the floor, legs supporting me on the ladder.

Vicki asks, "Want to come up here, Daddy?"

"Don't think there's room for me." With Lindee between the mattresses on the floor, the space already looks cramped.

"We can make space." Sam wiggles toward Lindee, teetering on the edge of his mattress, and pats the narrow space behind him on the twin-sized bed.

Lindee and I meet eyes, and she smiles. "There's always room for daddies."

Yeah, I could love this woman. Listening to her read to my kids after I climb up the final rungs and crawl into the small bed with Sam. Watching her take Sasha's attitude. Seeing her smile sweetly at Vicki.

I'm in the very dangerous position of falling in love with her if she's good with my kids.

And I don't expect her to be otherwise as she's been so good for me.

27

———

Playlist: "Fancy Like" – Walker Hayes

[Lindee]

Once Sam is asleep, Vicki climbs down the ladder to brush her teeth and get ready for bed. She checks in with her sister before heading back to the loft.

"Everything okay, baby?" Thad asks her as we wait in the living room.

"She just wants to be alone." Vicki shrugs. "I'm kind of excited to sleep in the loft. It's like a fort up there."

I smile as that had been my intention—a cool place for kids to crawl into for privacy and fun.

"Okay, baby." Thad opens his arms and Vicki walks into his embrace before climbing back up the ladder. We wait another second for the light to go out up there. I promised Vicki we'd keep a light on down below so they could see the ladder if they needed to climb down for the bathroom during the night.

When the upper light goes out, I step over to the front door to check the lock and turn off the light over the kitchen table by a switch. But as I'm turning around, I'm flattened against the door.

"You," Thad whispers before kissing me hard and deep. His tongue savoring. His lips hungry. His hands cup my neck while his thumbs stroke up my throat and tip my head. "God, I want to fuck you."

Whoa.

"Thad," I groan. "The kids." We already discussed sleeping arrangements. Bringing the kids to the cabin, which is my temporary home, was one thing. The kids finding us sleeping together on their first visit was a completely different concern.

Thad's mouth cuts off my protest, kissing me with intention once more. His lower body presses against me and my leg hitches over his hip, drawing him closer to my center.

"Just let me touch you, sweet thing." He grinds against me, and I hum into his mouth as we kiss again. My hips flex forward, my core rubbing against the firmness of him. But one of us needs to be sensible.

And for the first time in my life, it might be me.

"Thad, we can't." With my fingers in his hair, I pull hard as I mutter against his mouth. "Not tonight, baby."

Thad stills. His forehead comes to mine, and he breathes heavily. "Call me that again."

"Baby?" I hesitantly whisper.

"Yeah. Just like that, sweetheart, all breathless and needy." His mouth seeks mine once more and I almost give in. He's grinding against me, and I just want to be close to him, but his kids . . .

"Thad." I slide my hands to his chest, feeling his heart race and press at him.

"Watching you be all sweet with Sam. And soft with Vicki. Even strong with Sasha. I just . . . I just want you." He kisses me once more, slowing to sip at my lips and lick at my tongue. He lowers for my jaw and sucks at my neck before pulling back. "I—"

He stops short, and our eyes lock.

I love you. I hear it as a whisper although the words never leave his mouth. And I wrestle with the panic that wants to settle in because love hurts. Love drills a hole in your heart. Love exits stage left.

Only with my hand on his chest, his heart hammering beneath soft fabric, I know I've done that to him. His heartbeat matches mine.

Maybe this time, there won't be a hole after all.

THAD DOES NOT TOUCH me by the front entry, and we do not sleep together. Instead, we kiss like horny teens before parting ways for separate bedrooms. Surprisingly, I sleep like a baby.

The next morning Thad makes a mess of the kitchen with a breakfast of pancakes and bacon, and chaos ensues. Sam's messiness. Vicki's eagerness. Even Sasha's attitude is chill, although she hasn't warmed to me. Hanging out with kids is foreign to me and yet not unwelcome. Strangely, I feel like a part of something. Something bigger than me and my one-woman roadshow.

This is a family.

Being part of something chaotic and messy like this is what I long for. However, I quickly push away the ache in my chest.

While Sasha does her best to sulk, she helps her dad without much begrudging.

Vicki is a chatterbox today when she hardly said five sentences last night. Her smiles are soft and her eyes observant. I don't fault her for wanting to scope me out before trusting me.

Sam, on the other hand, is suddenly my partner in crime.

After the pizza sauce mishap, bowling teams, and *Harry Potter*, we're big fans of each other and when we have a pancake eating contest that he wins, my heart expands like it never has.

I'd always hoped to have children, and I've accepted it didn't happen for obvious reasons. I don't stay put anywhere for long and I don't have relationships that last. Not that I need a man to raise a child, but it wasn't something I'd considered doing on my own. I'd known people who adopted later in life as single women, but in the back of my mind I also knew that having a dad would be important for a kid.

At least, it had seemed important to me.

Thad is a great dad. Despite his displeasure with Sasha last night, he hugged her this morning, holding her a little tighter although she squirmed to get away. She's a teenager. Hugging her dad probably isn't cool anymore. I wouldn't know about these things, though.

Once breakfast ends, I announce the plan for today. "We're going junkin'."

"We're what-*what*?" Thad laughs, wiping his hands on a towel. He did all the dishes after cooking, not allowing me to do a thing.

"Junkin'. There's a giant flea market and antique fair nearby, and I want to scope it out for items to put in the motel rooms. I'd like each room to have a theme."

"Like a honeymoon suite," Thad arches one brow.

"Not exactly." I turn to Sam. "Sam, what would be cool for a bedroom?"

"A Harry Potter room."

"On it," I say. "Your mission today, should you choose to accept it, is to find something that's Harry Potter-like to put in one of the future motel rooms."

Sam gives me the biggest tooth-missing grin. "I accept." Determination rings in his little voice as he nods once in confirmation.

"Vicki." I look to her next. "What do you think?"

"I don't know. But how about when I find something, I'll make that the theme."

I clap my hands once. "I love it. Spontaneity is the best."

Next, I gaze at Sasha. "And Sasha?"

Her face sobers from the smiles that have finally popped up during her dad's pancake shenanigans. "I like black."

Without missing a beat, I say, "Black works. How do you feel about white? If I paint an accent wall black, white items will pop against it. Or vice versa. I could do a wall of white with black items."

"Yeah, that'd be cool." She shrugs and tips up her chin, chewing at her lip. *Is that a smile she's fighting?* I doubt it but she seems to like the idea despite her brush off.

"Okay then. A junkin' we go."

Sam pumps his arm up and down like he's pulling a chain. "Whoot-whoot." With his little engine revved, he hops off his seat.

"Brush your teeth," Thad hollers as Sam rushes toward the hall.

"Gotta make number two first," he calls back.

"Boys," Vicki mutters, shaking her head and we all laugh. Even Sasha.

OUR DAY IS A HIT.

Vicki found an antique watering can painted bright red and decided on a geranium room with reds and greens to go with the iconic summer flower. Sasha started with a white iron gate piece that I explained would look great as a headboard and then found some other ironwork pieces to complement it. She had a good eye for what would work well together. Finally, Sam found a curtain with giant stars that he claimed looked like a cape, but he was discouraged when the only wand he could find was an old magician one. I told him we should look for sticks around the cabin and whittle wooden wands like Harry Potter and his friends have. I could hang them in shadow boxes and even make a curtain rod look like a giant broom stick if we found a thin sapling.

The kids ate their way through the day with popcorn and hot dogs from a stand. Food trucks at the fair gave me another idea for the motel. I could invite local trucks to the motel, offering visitors a special treat depending on who was available. Then I went down a rabbit hole of themed nights for the bar outside of the typical holiday ones.

"Hot chocolate night," I'd said in Thad's truck as he drove us all back to the motel with our treasures in the back.

"Marshmallow night," Sam calls out and we laugh.

"What would that be like, Sam-man?" Thad asks, glancing in the rearview mirror at his son.

"A night of fluff. When the first snow falls, serve fluff to visitors."

I glance at Thad and mock-whisper. "What's fluff?"

"It's a disgusting marshmallow spread. Sam likes it with peanut butter instead of jelly." Thad makes a gagging sound.

Sounds interesting and another reminder I don't know much about kids, but still . . .

"Not bad, Sammy," I say, glancing over my shoulder into the backseat and smiling at my new friend. "Noted." I lick at my finger before pinching it with my thumb and pretend to write down his idea in an invisible notepad in my other hand.

The windows are down as the day is warm, and Thad turns up a song the kids like about Applebee's, a restaurant franchise. They're singing along at the top of their lungs, making motions to dip fries and swirl whip cream as we pull onto the gravel drive beside the motel and climb the incline to the cabin.

However, their unified voices slowly die off as Thad rolls to a stop near a Honda CR-V I don't recognize. As he sets his truck into park, the driver's side door of the other vehicle opens, and Jasmine slinks out.

"Shit," Thad mutters as the silence inside the cab is like a mic drop on the day. He's quick to exit his side of the truck and as I pop open my door, a shrill voice bellows.

"Where the fuck have you been?"

28

Playlist: "American Woman" – Lenny Kravitz

[Thad]

The last thing I want is a scene, especially in front of Lindee. My kids had seen them often enough to know when to scatter but presently, everyone freezes like trapped mice about to be pounced on by a wild cat.

"Just where the fuck have you been?" Jasmine repeats as I slam my truck door. Another door opens and closes, then feet crunch on gravel but I don't take my eyes off Jaz. Her dark hair looks unwashed. Her eyes a little reckless and bright. Her skin is tight around her mouth, but her throat is thick.

"What are you doing here?" There's a reason I don't tell Jasmine the location of my job sites. After she showed up once all crazy-like, I almost lost the job when we were just starting the business.

"Sasha sent me a text."

Dammit. I'd had her phone since last night but that doesn't mean she didn't contact her mother between picking up the kids and arriving here. Especially when the text might have been sent when Sasha was standing underneath the address of this cabin.

"You can't cross state lines with my kids, Thad." Jasmine's snarl is all for show. How had I spent thirteen years of my life with this woman?

"*Our kids.* And I can take them where I want." We might have an agreement to be open about where the kids are but bringing them to Lindee's wasn't something I wanted to explain to my ex.

"You cannot bring our kids to your homewrecking whore's house." Jaz staggers toward me as she points over my shoulder at where I'm certain Lindee stands. "You cannot be in my bed one weekend and then take them to her the next."

A gasp happens behind me, but I can't take my eyes off Jasmine. I don't trust her not to spring as she's tried to do on occasion. There's no way she's taking me down and I refuse to fight her, but it doesn't mean I won't put her in a stronghold until she calms the fuck down.

"Don't lie," I growl because there isn't a chance in hell I was in her bed last weekend or the past two years. "And she isn't a whore."

My blood is boiling as I clench my hands into fists at my sides. I'm not doing this with this woman. Thirteen years of my life have been an ice-covered road with Jasmine's moods, and I'm done. The ride is over for me.

"Get out of here," I bark at her, pointing to the road.

"Kids, get in the car." Jasmine glances past me and waves at her SUV.

"You asked me to take them this weekend and they aren't going anywhere yet." I still have the remainder of today and all day tomorrow, and I'm not giving up my time. I'm also not dealing with this bullshit. "Get gone, Jaz."

"Kids!" Jasmine barks again.

The crunch of feet behind me suggests the kids are on the move. As I gaze right, Lindee is holding Sam's hand with Vicki on her other side. Sasha follows. They move as a unit, as if trying to ignore Jasmine's request.

"They aren't leaving with you," I state, stepping forward.

Then everything goes to hell.

Jasmine lunges for Sam, grabbing his little arm and pulling him free from Lindee's grasp.

"Lindee," Sam screams with his arm outstretched, reaching for the woman he was just forcefully pulled from, and desperate to recapture.

"Mom!" Sasha screams.

The cry doesn't stop Jasmine from nearly dragging Sam across the gravel, his little feet scrambling to keep him upright and out of the dirt, before I can get to my son. Lindee is closer, and she steps up to my ex, wedging herself between Sam and Jaz.

"Hey!" Lindee yells in Jaz's face.

Oh shit. I'm between the two women before the arm Jaz pulls back makes contact with Lindee. With Sam forgotten for the moment, he falls to the ground. My body blocks Jaz, holding her wrist tight in my hand over her head, and Lindee scoops Sam up. He clings to her like an oversized monkey. He's too big to be carried by such a petite woman but Lindee huddles him to her chest, hand protectively on the back of his head and another under his leg to keep him against her.

"He's *my* son," Jasmine screams as I'm moving her backward, separating her from the kids.

"He's not going anywhere with you." Gripping Jasmine's shoulders, I press her back, holding her arm's length away, before pinning her to the SUV. Sour wine breath slaps me in the face. "Have you been drinking?"

Jasmine freezes. "No." But her bloodshot eyes and suddenly clenched lips gives her away.

"You've been drinking, and you think I'd let the kids get in a car with you?" I can't believe this shit. I can't even put *her* in the car. She might kill herself or worse, someone else.

"Lindee, call Duke for me."

"What the fuck?" Jasmine spits, spray hitting my shirt.

"I warned you, Jaz. You put those kids in danger and you're out." I didn't want to do it, but my kids were not living with her brand of crazy in addition to her drinking.

"You can't take my kids from me." She holds her head high, but her eyes are so glazed she can't focus on me.

"I'm not. I'm keeping *my* kids safe." I didn't want Sasha, Vicki, and Sam to be raised missing their mother, but this wasn't the kind of mother they needed.

Thankfully, Duke arrives quickly, racing up the gravel drive on foot.

"Shit," he hisses when he sees me holding Jasmine back. I hadn't dared turn around at his approach, but I peek over my shoulder to find Lindee and the kids are gone. They've seen enough.

"Duke, can you get her out of here? I've got to check on the kids."

"*My* kids. Who are in that little whore's house." Vitriol and venom slither from this woman who is too hardened to see the beauty in her life. Her three children.

"So help me, Jaz . . ."

"Or what? You'll leave me. News flash, you're already gone from our lives."

"Not theirs. Not the kids." I'm present and about to get a hell of a lot more visible. I turn to Duke. "Get her home."

"Manor's right behind me." Duke turns to Jasmine. "Give me your keys."

"Search me for 'em." While she might have intended her tone to be seductive, it's not and Duke exaggeratedly shivers beside me.

"Wouldn't touch you for a million dollars, darlin'," he drawls.

"How 'bout a million and one. I have the buck."

Good God, she never stops. You'd think a woman like her would have learned her lesson but her standing here, drunk in front of her kids, making a scene, is only proof that she hasn't learned a thing.

And I'd feel sorry for her if I didn't hate her just a little bit more with every statement out of her mouth.

Once Duke has Jasmine in her car and he's driving her away, I take a deep breath and enter the cabin. Lindee is sitting on the couch with Sam sideways on her lap. Vicki sits beside her. Sasha stands near a window with her arms crossed, looking out at the side yard. She turns toward me as I shut the door.

I'm on fire.

"What the hell were you thinking?" I wheel on my oldest daughter. "You're typically so smart but this was the fucking stupidest—"

"Hey," Lindee interjects. Her voice loud and crystal clear. "You're not going to talk to her like that."

I'm ready to defend myself, ready to state I'll talk to my daughter any way I want, but the blaze in Lindee's eyes and the fear in Sam's has my tongue halting.

I swipe both hands down my face and turn to Sasha again. "Why would you text her?"

Tears slowly roll from my thirteen-year-old's eyes. She was

mad. She was upset. She was hurt. These could all be reasonable answers, but I don't want to listen.

"Your mom…" I exhale and catch on Lindee's hard expression. Her beautiful eyes are thunderous, and a grim frown thins her rosy lips. A face Jasmine almost struck. I glare back at Sasha. "She could have hurt Lindee."

The room falls quiet a second as Sasha's tears steamroll faster and Sam tucks against Lindee.

"She already hurt Sam," Vicki says, breaking the silence with her soft voice.

"She what?" My voice is loud like the crack of a whip.

Sam sits upright and glares at his sister sitting beside Lindee. "She didn't mean it. She said she was sorry."

"What?" I bellow again, voice rising like my temper.

"She was drinking," Sam says, turning his face toward me but lowering his eyes.

"She's always drinking," Vicki adds, straightening beside Lindee, like she's shoring up courage. "And she slapped Sam."

"Why?" I snap, barely holding myself together.

"I spilled my milk. I didn't mean to do it. The glass just knocked over and . . ."

I stare at my son with his dark hair and bright eyes, looking like his mother once did, only fragile and small. He's a child. *And she fucking hit him.*

"Why didn't you tell me?" I round on Sasha again, stepping toward her.

Out of the corner of my eye, Lindee shifts Sam off her lap and stands. "Alright. Out."

I spin toward her.

"Out." She points at the door and stalks toward me.

With her hand on my chest, she's pushing me backward and I willingly walk until we reach the door. She opens it and I pivot, stepping onto the stoop. Taking a few paces away from the cabin, I finally spin on the gravel drive with both hands on the back of my head. "She touched my son."

"I heard that," Lindee says, crossing her arms and giving me those blue eyes in a softer tone than the previous storm. "But that is *not* Sasha's fault."

"I never said it was." I drop my arms, slapping my hands on my thighs.

"Then stop yelling at her."

"Lindee, you don't—"

Before I continue, she holds up a hand and straightens her body, taking a step closer to me. "Before you lecture me on how I don't have kids and I don't know anything about raising them, let me tell you a thing or two I do know."

I hold still, though, my exaggerated breathing causes my chest to rise. Negative energy courses through my veins and I ball my hands into fists at my sides. I fucking hate Jasmine.

"I was a little girl without a father, and while I'd like to say my mom was all I needed, she wasn't. She curled into herself and fell apart after my father left and my siblings picked up the pieces along with my Grandad. I loved that man for who he was. My grandfather, but not my father. My dad left…" She swallows hard. "Because of me."

"Lindee," I sigh. While I want to hear about this, now isn't the time.

"I wasn't his kid."

"What?"

"My mom had an affair, got pregnant and tried to play me off as his kid but he knew I wasn't. And he left. He left behind his entire family because of me." She takes a heavy breath. "And I will not be the reason it happens again."

"Lindee, you have nothing to do with this." She wasn't even a blip in our lives when things were falling apart between Jasmine and me.

"But being part of your life is adding to the storm." She shivers and swallows again. "And I won't let you make your daughter feel like this is her fault. I couldn't stop this feeling for me, but I can stop it for her." Lindee points toward the house, implying Sasha.

I stiffen while my arms continue to vibrate with the desire to punch something, tear something down.

Lindee has no right. She has no idea how I feel. I'm not blaming my child for the shit show of my marriage. Taking another breath, I realize Lindee is defending Sasha while at the same time she understands Vicki's situation—not being my biological daughter. Still, I stuck around for my kids. I would never leave them.

"Now, you're going to cool off out here while I go in and pack a bag. Then I'm going to Jane's."

The suggestion lands in my gut like a punch and the wind whooshes out of me.

"I don't want you to leave." I need her. She's right. I need to calm down. I need a minute and I want that moment to be with her, chilling me out.

I take a step toward her, reaching out for her and cupping her shoulders. Her hand comes to my chest, pressing at me to keep some distance.

"Your kids need you, without me around, to be present for them with compassion and understanding. Not blame. It's not Sasha's fault."

I know this. *I know it*. Still. "She put you in danger."

"Jasmine put your kids in danger, and you need to rectify that with your wife."

"Ex," I snap, releasing her shoulders and standing tall again. "And I was not in her bed last weekend or any other weekend for years."

Lindee closes her eyes. "None of my business."

Covering her shoulders again, I smooth down her arms and

circle her wrists. Jasmine was fucking lying. "It is your business. You're my business."

Lindee sadly shakes her head. "No, I'm not." She tilts her head toward the cabin. "They are. "And they need you right now." She tips up on her toes and gives me the faintest kiss on my cheek before pulling away from me.

"I'll see you later." She slips into her cabin, and I take another minute to collect myself as my world slowly shatters.

Once again, because of Jasmine.

29

Playlist: "Old Soul" – The Highwomen

[Lindee]

When I arrive at Jane's beautiful colonial brick home in the hills surrounding Wrightwood, I'm shaky but calm until she opens the front door. With her arms spread wide, I step into my older sister's embrace and breakdown. It hits me that I've cried more in the last month than I have in years.

Jane ushers me inside and steers me directly to the couch. Her living room is old world charm with built-in bookcases around a red brick fireplace with a heavy mantel full of photographs. Her and Mach. Her and Willow. The three of them together. A three-paned bay window lets in tons of natural light contrasting with the dark accents in the room. As evening settles in, the space is somber and fits my mood.

"Start at the beginning," Jane says, brushing back my hair

like I'm still the child she practically raised. When our mother checked out, Jane was the one to change my diapers and feed me. From those early bonds, Jane's the one I've gone to with everything, especially when Harris was my first. First kiss. First love. First loss. By then Jane was in Chicago and wanted me to come live with her but I didn't want a big city for comfort. I needed something to keep my hands busy and my mind occupied.

Jane already knows about me sleeping with Thad that one night. She also knows about our re-meet. She's suggested that I let him give me orgasms, but I've kept our current connection quiet. I typically don't discuss the men passing through my life with my sister because those relationships are short-term.

My silence about Thad feels different, though. Like he's something special, like he's all mine.

However, I spill everything. How I confessed about Harris. How he told me about his brother. About the motorcycle club.

"Dolores might have mentioned that," Jane softly interjects, still angled toward me as I slouch into the thick cushions on her couch.

"Garrett wasn't pleased."

She arches her brow. "Does Garrett have a say in anything we do?"

My brother and oldest sister have memories of their parents as a couple. It was equally hard on Garrett to have his father leave him with a weak-willed mother and three younger sisters. While Grandad took over general maintenance around the house and offered financial assistance, Garrett was the one who felt responsible for us when he was younger. Then he left as well, seeking fortune in California.

"He has a little say when he's an investor."

Jane narrows her eyes. The tough businesswoman she'd become has softened in the past year, but old habits die hard when it comes to who is the boss of whom. Jane is still an independent woman despite her new husband and beautiful daughter.

"Garrett doesn't get a voice in your personal life. And it sounds like things have gotten very personal with Thad." Jane pauses a beat. "Does his past really matter? We all have one filled with things we aren't proud of. Things we wish had gone differently."

"It isn't the club." I heave a sharp breath before plunging on. "It's his wife and kids. She showed up today and demanded the kids leave with her and everything fell apart."

"What a minute? His wife, as in he's still married?" Jane has first-hand experience with how men can be deceiving in their relationship status.

"Ex. But she showed up and—"

"Back up. I'm missing a few details."

I backpedal to explain how Thad's kids were at the cabin and how we were having such a good time. Even Sasha's attitude had disappeared for a while. Then Jasmine appeared.

"She was drunk, and she almost hit me."

"Good God." Jane reaches for my arm. "Are you okay?"

As tears fill my eyes again, I clutch a fist to my chest, as if I can right the unsteady rhythm and banish the pain. "My heart hurts."

"Honey, you really like him, don't you?" Her hand strokes up and down my arm. "And his kids?"

I nod, focused on my lap. "But he went all *you don't know anything about having kids* when I tried to defend his daughter's actions." I glance up at my sister. "She's hurt, Jane. She's sad and I can relate."

"Because of Mom."

I chew at my lip. "Because of Dad."

Taking a deep breath, I continue. "It's obvious Thad loves his kids, and he doesn't like being separated from them, but he goes with what the system says works best. The kids live with their mom. It's heartwarming and heartbreaking at the same time."

I tip my head back.

"Is this because you've always thought you weren't one of us?"

Everyone knows I'm not a true Fox, but they've never treated me like an outsider. Yet, I've been an outlier compared to all their successes and I just want to belong in their club. The motel was going to be my redemption. I'd wanted to prove that I'm one of them.

"I'm not," I blurt.

"Did we ever give you a sense you weren't? Did we ever fault *you* for a weak man walking away from his wife? Or a sad woman sleeping with someone not her husband?" Jane pauses before answering her own question. "No. We didn't. Mom made her choice. And Dad made his. He walked away from all of us, left all of us, not just you, and not because of you. Because of Mom. But mainly because of he was a selfish SOB."

Jane has patience and forgiveness for our mother but maybe that's also because Jane has had decades of separation from her. Living in Chicago, and working a high-pressure job in corporate America, Jane didn't visit Mom as much as Mae and I had. Jane has always ignored Mom's a-woman-needs-a-man philosophy. But Mae suffered when she divorced that rotten apple ex-husband of hers, even though Mae proved she was capable of taking care of herself and her boys. For my part, Mom was quiet on the man-front when I was young and had Harris. She saw for me the same future I'd once wanted for myself. Marriage. Kids. Home.

When I don't respond to Jane, she wraps her arms around me again and pulls me to her for a long hug. We don't often discuss our parents and their past. Mom is just Mom. Dad is simply a name given to a man who wasn't present.

As I swipe at tears, I eventually pull back from Jane's embrace.

"Where are Mach and Willow?"

"Mach took Willow to town to distract her. I didn't tell her you'd be here." Jane gives me a soft smile knowing how attached Willow and I have become.

On cue, the front door flies open, and a tinkling giggle explodes in the entryway before Willow sees me.

"Aunt Lindee," she yells, racing for the couch where I sit.

Wrapping her in my arms, I tug her into my lap and already feel a little lighter.

"Did you come to see me?" Willow asks, pulling back and cupping my face in her small hands.

"Needed some couch cuddles with my favorite girl." Truth rests in the statement. I needed separation from the motel and time away from Thad to clear my thoughts. Plus, Thad needs time with his kids to soothe their fears and maybe figure out what to do about his ex.

"Can we watch *Frozen*?" Willow asks.

"My favorite," I exaggerate about the movie we watch every time we are together.

"Mind if I steal my wife for a little bit?" Mach asks in his deep voice. He braces a tattooed arm on the back of the couch and cups his other hand around the back of Jane's neck.

I cover Willow's ears and smile in response to the glow on my sister's face. "Are you two going to have s-e-x? Because we do not need to hear that down here."

Jane's mouth falls open, preparing to scold me like the mother hen she can be, but Mach winks. "Good thing we'll be leaving for a little while then."

"Get out of here, you two," I tease.

"Are you okay?" Jane asks, concern filling her voice.

"I'll be good as new after Elsa freezes the world," I joke, jiggling Willow on my legs as I mention the sister with an icy touch. That's me. I just need to get back to that point where I close myself off. My emotions have been out of control lately.

Jane still gives me questioning eyes while Mach leans for her ear and whispers something. Her face turns a soft pink color.

"If you're really sure." Her gaze shifts to Willow.

"I'm positive." Why should I deny the happy couple some alone time just because I'm sad? I have my best girl here and we're going to watch a movie about sisterly love and eat junk food.

It sounds perfect.

Later that night, I've just climbed into bed when Jane comes to the guest room. I'm exhausted.

"I've been thinking about something," Jane begins, and this never leads anywhere good. "You were sick about a month ago. Fever. Chills, right? Just a summer flu. But you haven't been the same since. Exhaustion. Stomach aches. Headaches."

"And?" I work hard. Sometimes I'm too tired to eat or drink. I get dehydrated or hangry. Although, Thad has been making certain I have three square meals a day and often reminds me to take breaks to at least chug some water.

"Do you think you might be pregnant?"

"God, no," I scoff while my hand protectively covers my lower belly. For a while I imagined I was gaining weight, but I brushed it off as muscle shift. I wasn't physically fit but I wasn't out of shape either. I didn't run five miles, practice morning yoga, or do CrossFit with weights and cardio. I worked on rehabs and then rested. Worked again and rested. I had a pattern, and this was the build muscle phase of renovations.

"When was your last period?"

"Jeez, *Mom.* I don't know." Flipping a mental calendar in my head, I recall having some light spotting back in May, but it didn't last long.

"What do you mean you don't know?"

"I mean, I'm irregular. My periods have never come twenty-eight days on the dot, and I assume missing one or two now is a sign of the change."

"The change?" Jane chuckles. "You're forty-two. I think you're still a little young to be in menopause."

"Well, at forty-two, I'm a little *old* to be pregnant."

Jane stares at me. "You know that's not true."

"Well, you'd need unprotected sex." Thad used condoms faithfully the first time we were together. Since our reunion, maybe not so committed to covering the masterpiece. "Besides, Thad says he shoots blanks."

"Because he's had a vasectomy?"

"I…" I didn't know. I'd only taken his word like I'd taken it so many times.

Glancing down at where my hand rubs over my belly, I stare at the fleshy bulge.

Could I be pregnant?

Surely, I would know, right? I'd feel different. Feel something inside me. Feel life within me.

What I feel instead is my heart hammering at the possibility. A whisper of hope I hadn't thought I'd have at the idea of being pregnant. I mean, I know I'd thought about it for a fleeting second a while back with Thad, but this could be a reality, not a blip of fantasy. I'm equally scared out of my mind that it is possible, and I don't know how Thad would feel about another child. Adrenaline races through my limbs and suddenly I'm shaking with the clash of emotions which includes a conflict between freaking out and wishful thinking.

When I glance up at Jane, her face is a cross between mother-hen-need-to-scold and sympathy. Jane always wanted to have her own child but can't. Now, she has Willow, and nothing else matters.

"Fuck," I whisper. "Have any late-night pharmacies around here?"

Wrightwood is a small town of boutique businesses, but the next town over has all the modern-day convenience stores like Target and CVS.

"I'll get my purse," Jane says, while I scramble out of bed.

Of all the late night runs I've made in my life, one for a pregnancy test has never been one of them.

30

Playlist: "Going, Going, Gone" – Luke Combs

[Thad]

After Lindee left, I needed to deal with my anger and face my children. I wasn't upset with them. I wasn't even mad at Sasha. I was just . . . livid at life and Jasmine.

How she thought she could drive drunk to West Virginia.

How she thought I'd let my kids leave with her in that condition or even let her drive herself home.

How she ruined the good day the kids and I had been having with Lindee.

How I'd let myself get involved with that woman in the first place.

Call it a moment of weakness. Call it sympathy. Call it stupidity. The bottom line was my dick got me in trouble with Trouble herself and I haven't been able to dig myself back out of the ditch that woman has dragged me into. Every time I think I can step away from Jasmine, something happens, but not this time.

Touching Sam, or any of my kids for that matter, the way she did in Lindee's drive isn't acceptable.

Then to learn she smacked my baby boy for spilt milk, when she'd been drinking . . . just fucking unbelievable.

Jaz and I had a mediator for our divorce. We didn't want lawyers because we thought we could work it out. I should have known better. We'd never been able to reasonably agree, and this was the final straw.

My ex needed help, and I needed to protect my kids. They were not going back to her.

When I reenter Lindee's cabin, the silence that greeted me was deafening. Lindee had given Sasha, Vicki, and Sam each a hug before she left.

"I'm going to see my sister and you three are going to enjoy the rest of your time with your dad." The unspoken was emphasized. *Without her.*

Sasha had tears in her eyes again when Lindee pulled back from hugging her. My girl had done wrong, and she knew it, but the way Lindee defended her had to mean something to Sasha. My thirteen-year-old was strong for the wrong reasons right now.

With the three kids lined up on the couch, I pulled a chair from the dining table into the living space, spun it backward and straddled it. My arms crossed the back of the chair and solemn faces avoided looking at me.

"I need to know everything. No protecting Mom. No worries that you'll hurt my feelings. Out with it all."

Vicki started, explaining that Jasmine had been drinking every night. Sometimes out in the open. Sometimes taking the garbage to the outdoor cans and lingering too long in the backyard.

"Sasha's been making us dinner and I've been helping keep the house clean." My girls are good about looking out for each other and their brother, but that isn't the way things should be.

"Sash, baby, why didn't you tell me?"

"I can handle it." She sits straighter on the couch.

"But you shouldn't have to. You shouldn't be handling anything. Your mom is the mom. And I'm Dad." I should be there, but I can't, and they know this. I cannot live in the house and be separated from their mom. It doesn't work like that.

"I need to know if she's hurt anyone else. Besides smacking Sammy." I swallow the bile climbing the back of my throat. My dad never knocked Vic and me around, although it was common practice between parents and their kids in the club. Dad didn't need his fist to get his point across. A disappointed look was worse than a punch ever would have been, and Vic and I aimed to please our parents. There was a mutual respect between all four of us.

All three of my kids shake their heads, but Sasha looks a little haunted. "What else? Has she said things? Called you names?" It isn't always bruises that harm a kid and Jasmine likes to sling dirt.

"I can handle it." Sasha lowers her voice while slowly shaking her head.

"Whaddid she say?"

Sasha rolls her lips inward. Shoulders tense, back straight, she holds still.

Fuck. Did I really need to know the words? I'm well aware of the venom my ex can spit. Was it Sasha's hair or her clothes? Was it her attitude? Was it something derogatory about boys?

"Whatever she said to you, you get out of that beautiful brain." I point at her. "I'm not going to excuse her behavior, but if she said those things under the influence, she didn't mean them."

"But there's always a little truth when someone's drunk," Sasha says. Her eyes narrow.

"Who told you that?"

Holding my gaze, she glares at me. "You said it once to Mom when you two were fighting."

Shit. I can't defend my words in any way that will disprove whatever Jasmine has said to our competent, intelligent, strong girl. Jasmine's words have been chipping away at the woman my daughter will be one day and I need to stop it. Or Sasha will be bitter and hurt like Jaz all her life.

Sliding my hands to the back of the chair, I sit taller. "Here's the deal. You're not going back there. I can't leave you three there knowing what she's like."

"But I love Mom," Sammy says, his voice trembling.

"I know you do, buddy. But Mom needs help. And only she can want to get it. If she doesn't get that help, I can't let you three be around her."

"You could come home," Sam adds.

"Sammy, little man, you know why I can't. Mom and I are divorced."

"Because you don't love each other."

Fuck, this is always so complicated. "Because we love you three more, and us being together isn't good. Mom and I are better apart, and it's better for you." But was it better for them? The shitshow in the driveway proves it hadn't been.

"Look. How about if you guys stay here the rest of the weekend like planned? Then we go to the house together. I'll talk to Mom. If she agrees to get help, she'll need to go away for a bit, and you can stay at Nessi's. If she doesn't agree to help, you'll be at Nessi's, and I'll come see you every weekend."

"I don't want to stay at Nessi's," Sam whines. "I want to be here. With you."

"I know, but . . ." This is Lindee's place, and I can't assume I can bring my three kids here. I don't even know if I'm welcome to remain in her bed every night. She'll honor the contract on the motel because we need one another, but when she walked away earlier, I swear my heart was being ripped right out of my chests.

Besides, this is currently a construction site, not a home. Even this cabin is temporary for Lindee. Eventually, she'll want to rent this place out. Then where will she go?

"I didn't mean to make Lindee leave," Sam says, his voice so small. His lips quiver.

"Sam-man, you didn't make Lindee go anywhere. She wanted us to have some time together." The lift I'm attempting in my tone isn't working to soothe his heart or mine.

"But we were having so much fun, and she left because I didn't want to go with Mom."

"Sam." I sigh. "Lindee was ready to get in a fight with Mom to protect you. That proves she didn't leave because of anything *you* did."

My gaze catches on Sasha.

"She left because of me, didn't she?"

Lindee was ready to fight for Sash, too.

I sigh again. "Look, she didn't leave because of anyone. She just wanted to see her sister and give us space."

"Will she be back?" Vicki asks as if she's holding her breath for a positive answer.

God, I hope so because I can't navigate all this on my own. I want Lindee by my side. Knowing she'd go to the mat for my kids was sexy as fuck and makes me want her even more.

"Yes. She'll be back."

I'll do everything in my power to bring her back to all of us.

"Hey," I softly greet Lindee when she answers her phone. "Did I wake you?"

It's after eleven. The kids are finally in bed. We went out to dinner and then watched a family-appropriate movie together. I don't think any of us had our minds on the screen, but we sat close together, just needing to be in each other's presence.

"I've just been laying here." Her voice is distant. She's too far away. I want her beside me in bed, letting me pillow talk with her.

"Whatcha thinking about?" I weakly flirt.

"You. How are the kids?" Lindee is good at deflecting, but I also appreciate she's asking about them first.

"Good. Better. I have a plan, but I need to talk to you about a few things first."

Lindee's quiet a second. "I need to talk to you, too."

"Oh yeah. Speak." The command is quiet, cautious even.

She's going to break up with me. Like a teenage boy, my heart races recognizing this is how it happens. Girl who didn't want to be seen with a biker's kid at school after she let me diddle with her beneath the bleachers. Another girl willing to fuck me at a party but wouldn't go on a date with me.

Stick to our kind, Vic had warned. But I wanted someone a little softer than the toughness of club women. Someone like our mom, who could hold her own with Dad, plus be patient and good. Someone like Lindee.

"We should probably talk in person." Lindee's tone is hollow.

I don't have any fight left in me today, although I want to snap. I want to demand she just get it over with. Rip off the damn bandage and pierce my heart. Instead, I scrub a palm down my face and exhale.

"Yeah, in person." The edge in my voice drives a deeper wedge between us. I hate the fucking phone. I can't see her face. I can't touch her skin. I can't reassure her that I want us to work.

Then again, she walked away earlier and I'm noticing a pattern. When things get tough, Lindee splits. The wanderer's soul she'd told me about was one of the first things that attracted me to her. Thought I'd found a kindred spirit in her. I didn't think she'd leave so easily. Still, she'd warned me that spirit makes her incapable of putting down roots and staying in one place. I hadn't listened, hoping I could be enough for her to stay. The thought I'm not, hurts.

"I'll see you tomorrow, okay?"

I'd like to hear hope in her voice, like she actually wants to see me, looks forward to it. But anticipation for her return is lacking, because my gut tells me we're over before we really began. I wasn't ever going to have nice things in my life. Not good, pure, easy things, like Lindee.

"Yeah, tomorrow."

"Good night, Thad."

"Night, sweet thing."

The night isn't going to be a good one with her missing from this bed, though, and tomorrow isn't going to be better when she tells me she never wants to see me again.

31

Playlist: "Will You Still Love Me Tomorrow?" – Amy Winehouse

[Lindee]

I arrive back at the motel at a time I consider late. I'd spent the day lost in my sister's new life with Willow and the cuddles of a six-year-old. Jane had always wanted to be a dancer as a child, and she found someone to open a ballet studio in Wrightwood. As the director of economic growth or something like that for the small town, Jane is friends with the local merchants and has access to all their locations. She asked permission to have a private dance party in which Willow tried to teach me ballet.

The distraction did me good.

The nerves dancing inside me started doing a jig on my trip home. By the time I pull onto the gravel drive leading to the cabin, my heart is in my throat. Then it drops to my belly at the absence of Thad's truck. I hadn't invited Thad to permanently stay in the cabin. The weekend plans were only to provide a place for his kids to visit with him, but I am still disappointed he isn't present. He's been here every night without me asking.

I should have called him, but I didn't really know what to say.

We should talk are three of the most prophetic words. And Thad isn't going to want to hear what I have to say.

I wasn't certain I should tell him, but Jane was adamant that would be wrong. Thad needed to know. My fear was he'd admitted his marriage was an obligation, one he didn't commit to until after baby number two, and I didn't want him thinking I intend to trap him.

After I unpack my overnight bag, I take a shower and then startle when I exit the bathroom to find Thad sitting on the edge of my bed.

"Jesus," I hiss, covering my chest with my palm and clutching the towel wrapped around my breasts. "You scared the hell out of me."

Thad looks up at me with a weary expression. His elbows balance on his thighs. "Sorry, sweetheart."

My shoulders relax. "What's wrong?"

He sits a little straighter. "Why don't you tell me what's on your mind?" There's an edge to his voice, similar to the gruff sound last night, when he mentioned we should talk.

"How are the kids?"

"Lindee," he snaps. "Out with it."

I gaze down at my feet, dragging one big toe against the wood floor. "I took a pregnancy test last night."

"What?" He chokes as his voice lifts, and I glance up at him. His eyes soften.

"I thought I was pregnant." The shrug I give isn't reflective of my spirit. A lump forms in my throat and deflation clogs my voice. "But I'm not."

"Sweet thing." Tenderness floats toward me. Thad stands and approaches, but I hold up a hand to stop him. He halts, eyes narrowing. "Talk to me."

"As you know, I haven't been feeling well. Just minor stomach issues and headaches here and there. Muscle ache that I believed was from manual labor. Total exhaustion." I pause and chew at my lips. "Jane suggested I might be pregnant, and I couldn't remember having a full period in a while. We went to Target last night and I took a test when we got back to her house."

"Lindee, baby. I told you I'm shooting blanks." He bends his knees a little, lowering his body so we're eye level. "Unless there's something else you want to tell me."

His smile is soft but instant hurt fills his eyes.

"I haven't been with anyone else." If anything, he's the one needing to explain his ex-wife's comment about him being in her bed last weekend.

"Same, sweet thing." He gently taps at my temple. "So, get that thought out of your head."

I start, like he has read my mind.

"I guess I hadn't considered when you said you were shooting blanks, you meant you had a vasectomy."

Thad sighs and scrubs a hand down his face. "Lindee." He reaches for my hand and pulls me to the bed, forcing me to sit side by side with him. Holding my hand, he flattens my palm and strokes along my fingers.

"Sweetheart, I was sick." His attention stays on my hand. "I had testicular cancer two years ago."

My eyes immediately prickle and my fingers curl against his hand, fighting the massage he's giving in an attempt to hold onto him. *Cancer?* After all he's battled, from leaving the brotherhood of his club, and sticking to a difficult marriage, to tackling cancer. It hits me hard that I almost didn't get the chance to know him, to experience this strong, wonderful man. I could have lost him before I had the chance to find him, to have him sitting beside me in this very moment.

Written in the stars.

He's overcome so much and I'm so thankful he's here.

Thad skims over my hand with his again, forcing my fingers to spread. I watch his fingers trail over mine.

"Jasmine and I were separated. I'd gone to the doctor for a vasectomy. Routine visit meant checking everything out. Doc found a lump. Fortunately, things were caught early. I had laparoscopic surgery and preventive chemotherapy treatments. Eventually, I got a clean bill of health, but I still had concerns."

Thad scoffs. "From all I'd read, I should be . . . okay." He swallows. "For sex."

My head lifts and I stare at his bowed head. The strain in his voice suggests this is a difficult subject for him.

Cupping his jaw, I lift his face, so he looks at me. "But you do have sex, and very well, I might add."

"Didn't know I could, though. I'd been leery. While Jaz and I were separated, we were still sharing the house while I recovered. She made advances, but I couldn't get it up." Thad tries to look away, but I hold his jaw, forcing him to stay with me.

"Do you take something?" While some men might brag about a little blue pill, others are deeply sensitive about using them. Pride conflicts with stereotypes of manliness.

Thad scoffs again. "No." His eyes finally meet mine. "I met this girl by a river near a hotel and I'd never been so hard in my life."

I softly laugh. "Thad." Leaning forward, I kiss his temple.

"You were the first woman I'd been with in years."

"I . . . What about Jasmine?"

"We were already heading for divorce. Cancer was the final epiphany. I didn't want to keep living the life I had with a woman who drove me mad. Told myself I'd figure out the two-household thing with my kids because we'd all be better off with Jaz and me separate from one another. Selfishly, I just wanted to be happy."

"It's not selfish," I tell him, leaning in to kiss his nose.

Thad bitterly chuckles. "Found out later that Jaz had slept with the dick doc. Burned any doubts I had that I'd be doing the wrong thing by leaving her."

Holy shit, again she'd cheated on him. "I'm so sorry." I pause. "Is she with him now?"

"He's married."

I don't even want to open that can of worms.

"Anyway, as for you being pregnant, I'm real sorry, sweet thing, but it can't happen with me."

Thad looks at me, watching my face a moment. "And I apologize that this is one more thing I hadn't told you, but cancer isn't sexy and as everything has been in working order with you it's one more thing I hadn't mentioned. Yet." Thad takes both my hands and brings them to his lips. "I keep fucking this up, sweet thing."

"You didn't fuck anything up." My voice is low, soft and soothing.

Thad's gaze finds my eyes. "Did you want to be pregnant?"

It's a question I've been grappling with for the past twenty-four hours. Having a baby hasn't been on my radar since Harris. I'd taken the pill for years, then stopped when it didn't seem to be helping my painful irregular periods. I'd moved to the birth control shot, something that's done every three months, but difficult to maintain when I didn't have a regular doctor since I moved around a lot. Eventually, I let every preventative measure slide, thinking I was growing too old despite knowing several stories of women holding off to have babies until later in life. I wasn't having sex enough to warrant carrying on with prevention other than condoms for sexual health reasons.

"I don't know," I whisper, while regret creeps into my head

again. "On one hand, it'd certainly be a surprise. I'm so busy with the motel, I don't think I could handle a child. Plus, I have to consider you. You'd told me about how you ended up with Jasmine and I didn't want you to feel trapped."

Thad squeezes my hands. "I would never feel caged by you."

"But you already have kids and—"

"I'd have more, if I could . . . with you." He's too sweet and almost eager, while remorse mingles in his eyes.

"Then, I considered how my sister always wanted a child and didn't have one. Willow is adopted. She's pure heaven and Jane loves her unconditionally, and it made me rethink my *plan*." I emphasize. "Children can be such a blessing. And while I'd written it off as not a possibility, last night, I might have hoped..."

From the moment Jane planted the seed to the time the single line told me I wasn't pregnant, I might have been wishing there'd be two lines, nine months and a little person in my life soon.

"I'm so sorry, sweetheart." Thad wraps his arms around me and tugs me to him. His lips linger on my head.

"But this is good." I press off him, unable to handle the sympathy in his embrace. "This is better."

"Don't do that," Thad softly demands, catching my wrist. "Don't push me away. And don't deflect your feelings. It's okay to be sad or disappointed or even hate me because it can't happen here." Thad waves at his lower region.

"I don't hate you." Cancer isn't his fault. And I can't blame my hope either. That was a teeny part of me I hadn't known existed inside me. "And I'm not deflecting."

I move to stand, as the damp towel is settling in and uncomfortably cooling my skin. But Thad tugs at my wrist, forcing me toward him, and pulling me on top of him as he falls back to the bed. Arms wrap around me like a vise, pinning me to his chest.

"Don't run away, either." Thad's chest rumbles beneath me.

"I wasn't." But his whiskey eyes read mine. This man knows me well enough after only weeks together. When I'm trapped, I run. When I'm scared, I walk away. When I'm hurt, I hide.

The run-in with Jasmine hadn't been the trigger. It was that Thad needed to be with his kids. They needed him after that scene, especially Sasha who felt at fault. And Sam who'd been frightened by his mother hurting him. Even Vicki was incredibly shaken.

"You still with me, sweet thing."

"Yeah." I sigh.

"That wasn't very reassuring." Thad rolls us to our sides then pushes me to my back, straddling my body and loosening the towel over my breasts. He tugs the material until my upper body is exposed, then rubs his hands over my belly.

"I'm sorry, baby," he whispers, watching his hands smooth over my stomach.

"I know." Emotion chokes my throat and I cough to clear it.

"I'm sorry," he says again, lowering his voice which only roughens it. Then he's leaning down, peppering my stomach with kisses.

I lift my hand to his hair, running my fingers through the tresses. As tears prickle my eyes again, I can't speak. A nod is the best I can offer. He's apologetic but it isn't his fault any more than mine that a baby isn't happening.

"I'm sorry," Thad says one more time, speaking to my belly before pressing a kiss there and lingering on my bare skin.

A tear leaks, but I'm quick to swipe at it. Another falls from my other eye and I brusquely brush it away. The movement makes Thad lift his head and his brows pinch.

"Fuck," he whispers before climbing my body and tugging

me to him again. We're back on our sides with my mostly naked body tucked against him. One hand cups the back of my head while his other hand palms my lower back. He kisses my forehead and temple.

"What can I do, sweet thing?"

I don't know how to answer him.

Suddenly, I'm on my back again and Thad is making his way down my body, kissing my neck, chest, and breasts. Reverent and worshipful, he covers my skin with his lips, taking his time to trail down my middle. He slides off the bed and tugs me to the edge.

"This alright?" he whispers to my center, using his thumbs to outline the sensitive area.

While I don't need an orgasm, I appreciate the attention Thad is giving me. He's physically paying me homage while hoping to distract me mentally. The relief he wants to give as he licks tender folds and teases my clit with his tongue takes time. Patiently, he explores me until my legs begin to quiver and I'm whimpering his name like a prayer.

When I finally come, I want to swim in the release that drags me from my thoughts and into the sensation of Thad. Like he alone is a sixth sense. *Taste, touch, sight, smell, sound, and Thad*. With my body languid and melting into the mattress, he climbs over me again. He's still fully dressed.

Our eyes meet and he runs his palm down my body once more. Between my breasts, over my belly, he skims my flesh before sitting back on his bent legs and tugging off his shirt.

"We don't need to do anything tonight, but I want to feel you against me, skin-to-skin." He shifts off the bed and lowers his jeans, kicking off his shoes before removing his pants and socks. His boxer briefs remain on.

Thad tugs free the towel that's been underneath me and tosses it to the floor. Then he pulls down the duvet and I crawl underneath the covers. He joins me and pulls me to him, holding me like I'm precious and breakable.

After Harris, I've always felt I'm strong enough to withstand anything on my own.

But for a little while, I let myself be fragile and this man to be the glue holding me together.

32

———————

Playlist: "I Don't Want to Miss a Thing" – Aerosmith

[Thad]

I couldn't sleep. With Lindee tucked into my side, I lay on my back staring up at the ceiling.

Between the look of hope and panic that withered to denial, she was disappointed that she wasn't pregnant. And I fucking hated that I'd disappointed her.

For the second time in my life, a woman wasn't satisfied with me.

When I'd taken the kids to Jasmine's to gather some of their things, I was having doubts again about removing my kids from their mother. She is their mom, and I didn't want them growing up without one, like I had. But when I arrived at the house earlier tonight, Jaz was already on her third glass of wine and primed for a fight. I doubled down on my resolve. I couldn't leave the kids with her.

Once more, I'd felt her dissatisfaction. I hadn't loved her like she wanted me to. I hadn't loved her like I'd wanted to love someone. Jaz had been a series of unfortunate conveniences. When the club broke up, she was lost like many of us. She clung to those she knew. When she had Sasha, I wanted to step up as a father, but I wasn't convinced I was the man for Jaz. Then Vic's death happened, and Vicki came along. Having Sam was such a fluke. A rare time when Jasmine and I felt good. Not great but good enough.

Six years later, I had cancer.

Had I used Jaz as she accused me of tonight? I'd stayed in my home to recover, trying to take comfort in familiar surroundings during a situation I found embarrassing as a man and sensitive. *Cancer?* Duke and Manor's mom passed away too young from the disease. Their dad was lost afterward.

I'd been given a second chance at life, and I wanted to do right by me. By Jasmine, too.

Still, I couldn't help her help herself. She had choices to make and right now she was selfishly choosing herself.

Nessi put things into perspective when I took the kids to her place.

"You can love an addict, but you can't help one. Only they can wrestle their demons. And only they can decide who is going to win the battle."

We'd all battled enough. I didn't expect life to be smooth sailing once the club dissolved but I hadn't expected the lingering troubles. The emotional ones. I'd moved to keep Jasmine safe, but she'd been doing harm to herself.

And my kids.

Rolling my head on the pillow, I kiss Lindee's head, holding my lips against her hair.

I'm sorry, baby. I can't be the man she needs, but God, she's the woman I want. Her citrusy scent. Her sweet smile. The way she'd been with my kids.

Sam's already in love with her. Vicki likes her a lot and even Sasha came around to being apologetic, not wanting someone to hurt Lindee. That someone being her mom.

The kids and I came to an agreement. Nessi's place during the week. I'd be back on Fridays. I'd have to do some shuffling with their schedules, arranging pickups and drop-offs that I didn't know how I was going to reciprocate. Jaz had been a good mother in many ways, but she was equally damaging to our children and that couldn't happen anymore.

The hurt to Sasha's fragile emotional state as a teen. The physical harm to Sam. Only Vicki didn't seem to have Jaz's wrath and it made me wonder once again if when she looked at Vicki, she saw Vic like I do. In the crook of her mouth. In the gleam of her eyes. Even her wiry frame reminds me of him.

Vic had been the man Jasmine needed. Not me.

Lindee's hand coasts down my chest and I rub my palm up her arm. My fingers float over the bracelet she wears that I consider mine. As in, she belongs with me and an engraved, silver dragonfly is a reminder.

"You have heavy thoughts." Her voice is a mixture of sleep and seduction even though she's not trying to be sexy.

"I do, but I don't want to think." I've been thinking for too long. Now, I just want to live. I thought that's what I was doing the night I met Lindee. That continued to be the plan when I was fortunate enough to have her in my life again. But what kind of living is this? Me with a crazy ex. Me with three kids. Me without a real home and a wandering job. Me who can't give her a baby.

Lindee props up next to me and cups my jaw. "Let me lighten your load." Her whisper is a siren's song.

"Yeah? How do you plan to do that?"

Her hand travels down my body and wraps around my dick. I'm not fully hard, but within seconds, she has me stiff and needy for her. However, I don't want to rush. I don't want to lose myself in her but linger in this moment.

I kiss her as she squeezes my length and teases the tip inside my waistband. "I don't want anything between us, sweet thing. No more secrets."

Our eyes lock a second while her brows pinch. "No more secrets."

"And I apologize again that I can't give you what you—" Her mouth cuts me off. The kiss hard at first. With a hand on her cheek, I slow her eager lips to tender sips. With her touching me, the desire for her grows to a frenzy I fight, allowing the tension to build and crackle.

Eventually, I press her to her back and shove down my briefs. Lindee never put anything on once we crawled into bed and I slip between her thighs, taking my time to kiss her again and again. I smooth a hand down her body, appreciating each curve and dip as I roam over her breasts and along her side. Sliding my fingers between her folds, I find her ready.

"Nothing between us," I whisper as I slip a finger inside her, coating it in her wetness. I don't want to just touch her. I want to feel her surrounding me.

Sliding my hand back up her body, I reach for her hand and lace our fingers together. With my tip at her entrance, I easily glide into her and squeeze our palms against each other. I lift her other hand, joining our fingers above her head as I drag in and out of her warm heat. I'm not racing, just taking my time to cherish this woman who has given me her body when I wasn't certain mine could respond. Then she wanted more of me, hoping a new life could form in hers.

I would give her all the babies, if I could.

With that thought, I kiss her long and slow while I glide forward and back, drawing out the sensation of her around me and me blanketing her.

"You," she whispers, so sweet. Puzzled while pleasantly content.

Yeah. "You," I counter, soft as I can. She's everything to me, and this right here, making love to her, is more than I ever imagined having in my life. She's good and deserving, even if she doesn't see it or want to accept it. I know as I've been in denial for a long time myself.

But I'm not denying how I feel or what I want anymore.

I want this woman.

SINCE THE NIGHT we made love, Lindee and I have been soft smiles and light touches during the day and then ravenous at night. I'm in her bed every night, practically living in the cabin. I'm aware the place is temporary, though, and not a home.

"Know what you're doing here?" Duke asks as we work on cutting new trim for the duplex. We're on the final phase of the project and a little over two weeks out from our projected end date. Time seems to be speeding up.

The motel rooms are mostly complete with new floors and fresh paint. Our plumbing contractor came in to thoroughly inspect all the bathroom fixtures and repair any minor issues. An HVAC guy tested all the heating and air-conditioning units. Three needed to be replaced.

"I know how to fucking cut trim," I snap, feeling Duke's eyes on me.

"I mean with her." Duke nods and I glance up, noticing Lindee speaking with a man near the pool.

Repairing the thing was not in our wheelhouse and while I would have taken a crack at it for her, it was better she had someone with the know-how to fix the lining and plumbing. The drain had damage from the long-standing water. A backhoe has torn a ditch from the street to the pool, ripping up the front yard of the motel. While Lindee's funds seem limitless, she's actually on a budget and keeping tabs on every dollar. She's a good businesswoman with a practical mind. And this setback has been a huge frustration in her goals.

"Yeah, I know what I'm doing," I mumble.

"You sure?" Duke questions.

"What's it to you?"

My cousin shrugs. "I like her. And I don't want her all love-sick hurt when we leave." His gaze catches mine. "Because we *are* leaving."

I hear him but don't like it. This job is already sixty minutes from home, but Nessi insisted we take it. The project will look good in a portfolio for our construction company. It would look better as my own property, but I didn't think I could tackle it with the divorce. Duke or Manor could have taken the place off Nessi's hands, but neither liked the idea of running a motel.

Lindee is going to be an excellent manager.

"I know," I mutter in response to us leaving. Then I amend my answer about Lindee. "As for her, I don't know if I'm so sure."

"You're not sure what you're doing?" Duke pauses and stares at me across the sawhorses we have set up.

"I don't know if I can leave her."

He watches me for a minute. "You know I want you to be happy, man. I want you to have everything after the crazy train you've been on with Jasmine but is this what you want?" He glances around the duplex. "Running an inn. Settling in the middle of nowhere. Being tied to a woman again."

We've always been on the edge of nowhere. Even Nessi's place is out of touch.

As for the woman, I don't feel tied. I feel bound, and there's a difference. I'm not trapped. If anything, I'm the one wound up in Lindee.

"I like it here." The area is quiet and peaceful with the

surrounding woods and river nearby, although I haven't been back to the river since Lindee freaked out. "And I like her, so don't make her out to be a ball and chain."

Duke continues to watch me. "You in love, cousin?"

I fight the smile that creeps onto my face every time I think about Lindee. "Don't know, but whatever it is, feels nice. Feels good."

"Happy for you, man. Just be careful." He points between me and Lindee in the distance. "Hearts and all that shit."

Yeah, hearts can be broken but I don't intend for that to happen here. To hers or mine.

33

Playlist: "Pick Me Up" – Gabby Barrett

[Lindee]

"Thanks, Hal. Let me have a day and I'll get back to you."

Dammit, the pool is turning out to be a cesspit of money. As is, it's an eyesore and I want it to be an enticing factor. The current issue is the drain and the giant ditch cut through the front yard of the motel.

"Here's my card." Hal hands over his business card and points. He's a slightly awkward man with a paunch beneath his professional polo that states his business. Hal The Pool Man is underscored with stitched waves and a flat line representing a pool. "I wrote my personal cell number on the back, in case you wanna get that drink together."

"Thanks, Hal." The stern tenor of a male voice resounds behind me, and I twist to find Thad only a few feet away. He closes the distance and places his hand on my lower back. "Are we all set today?"

Thad keeps his eyes on Hal for a moment before turning to me and giving me a tight smile.

"All good. Didn't know she was with someone."

"*She* is still standing here." I look back at Hal. However, Hal is watching Thad.

"Didn't see a ring or anything. Just assumed—"

"She's with me. No assumption," Thad states, his tone as tight as his smile. He rubs his hand up my spine and squeezes the back of my neck.

"Got it." Hal pauses before holding out his hand, formal and stiff. "Lindee, I look forward to talking soon."

After we shake, he heads to his truck, and I spin on Thad.

"What the hell was that?"

"Give me his business card." Thad drops his hand from my neck and holds out his wide palm.

"Excuse me?" I blink, fisting the card in my fingers.

"Give it to me. You are not calling him." The expression on his face warns me not to argue. Just to humor him, I slap the card into his outstretched hand.

Thad takes it and rips it in half and then half again. For good measure, he tears it one more time and then tosses the pieces in the wind. They quickly scatter to the pool deck.

"Feel better?" I cock my hip and cross my arms.

"Yes." His lips loosen and then return to the sexy smirk I'm familiar with.

"You know I have another business card for him." Hal's card is how I contacted him in the first place.

"With his *personal* cell phone number?" Thad mocks, arching a brow to test me.

When I don't answer, Thad gives me a victorious grin.

"He's already contracted, so I'll definitely be seeing him again. Personal phone number or not." My arms fall to my sides, and I straighten while glancing at the dirty basin and then the trench from the cement decking to the road. Slipping my hands through my hair, I tug it away from my face and cup the back of my neck.

What a mess.

"And I'm over budget on it." I exhale.

"How much do you need?"

I whistle and mutter, "Ten K."

"Done."

Twisting to look at Thad, he stands with his arms folded over his chest, casual and laid-back, like he didn't just say he'd give me ten thousand dollars.

"I can't take your money." He's such a generous man, always looking out for my welfare. He literally gave me the shirt off his back once to protect me from rain and now this.

"Why not? You need it."

"I have the money." I sigh, closing my eyes a second. I'd sunk most of my savings into the motel, plus the loan from Garrett. "It's just that I'd set some aside hoping to find a small house nearby." I can't afford something in Wrightwood where I'd be closer to Jane and have a longer commute to the motel, but I'd still like to find some place between here and there.

Now the pool needs my final funds.

"I'll just talk to Garrett." Only I don't want to ask for more money. I don't want to come across like I hadn't triple checked every penny and had the decimal points in all the right places. I'd been wanting to prove to my siblings I could do this. When past projects had involved other people's money, I didn't care as much about budgets although I respected the financial confines of a project. My reputation depended on not overspending. Still, issues come up and tweaks occur, and most owners never blinked at an additional expense.

Now I was the owner, and I was swimming from shallow

waters to the deep end where I couldn't touch and might possibly drown.

"Sweet thing?"

"Yeah?" I glance up aware I mentally checked out.

"Just take the money."

I shake my head but step up to Thad, placing my hands on his warm chest. "No. But thank you for offering, Mr. Money."

"Lindee, we said no more secrets between us. So let me clear the air that I'm really, really good with money and trust me when I tell you I have plenty. Nessi isn't the only Rhode with investments. If you need cash, I have it."

As secrets go, this isn't a dangerous one. Nor is it surprising. He'd told me he'd been an accountant and he'd most likely put those skills to good use before he left the club. Most motorcycle guys have the big bucks for expensive bikes and monster trucks. Still, I didn't want Thad's money.

Speaking of expenses, Thad was clearly in the credit column.

Since the night we talked about my pregnancy scare, and secret desire for a baby, we've been inseparable until he goes to visit his kids. He asked me to join him, but I used the motel as an excuse to stay behind. Too much to do was my consistent reason to avoid difficult situations. Sometimes, I'd use it to avoid the truth.

And the truth is I am growing attached to Thad. Too attached. And soon his work here will end, and he'll be gone. Thinking about his absence from my life makes me melancholy. Maybe things are different because this project is mine. I'm the owner. I'm in charge. I don't know how to keep Thad when his children need him. They are the most important factor. Thad needs to be present for them.

And I have a motel to finish renovating when I am running out of funds.

"Lindee." Thad chuckles as I'm lost in my head again. "You alright?"

His warm hands hold my jaw and he's looking at me as if he'd right all my wrongs. Throw himself between me and trouble. Give me ten thousand dollars. Hold my heart in his hands.

I don't deserve him.

"I'm good." In many ways, I've never been better, and I don't want this feeling to end. However, there are always limits, like a project calendar with an end date and a budget report with a bottom line.

I was overbudget on Thad, but being with him was one area I wasn't willing to make cuts.

Not yet.

Thad was a cost I didn't mind investing in a little longer.

LATER, I was on my way to the winter cabin with my tail between my legs, preparing to call my brother and explain my major fuck up with the pool. I didn't exactly know how the pool was my fault as I couldn't have predicted a faulty drain beneath the earth. But I still felt to blame.

However, Nessi shows up with Thad's kids as I'm crossing the busted-up parking lot in front of the motel, which is another thing I need to soon rectify.

"Surprise," Vicki hollers as she exits Nessi's SUV. A Porsche Cayenne is not what I'd expect a ninety-year-old grandmother to drive.

Sam exits next and races past me for Thad who easily catches him and lifts his son into the air.

"Have you grown since Sunday?" Thad lowers Sam and then raises him again, acting as if it's a struggle to lift him. "I swear you've gotten bigger."

To my surprise, Vicki walks up to me and wraps her arms

around my waist. I hug her back but give Thad a questioning look. *Is this okay?*

A wide smile and a wink answers me.

"Hi Dad." Sasha stands beside the passenger door and hesitantly waves at Thad. He told me about the conversation he had with his kids and then the disagreement he had with Jasmine when he took the kids to Nessi's. Last weekend was better when Thad saw his crew on neutral ground at her house.

Thad sets Sam down and tips his head. Sasha walks to him, falling into his chest as he wraps his arms around her. My insides are gooey as he leans down and says something to her before kissing her hair. After the kiss she looks up at him and smiles, while nodding.

I'm guessing it's been a good ten-plus days. No more cooking or looking after her brother and sister as much as she had before.

"What's the surprise for?" Thad asks, glancing at his grandmother.

"I'm cooking tonight." Nessi walks to the back of her SUV and pops the trunk. "You all have been working so hard and you deserve a break."

"Whatcha making?" I ask as Vicki releases me to help her great-grandmother.

"Spaghetti and meatballs," Nessi calls out from the back of her SUV.

"Better make enough for me," Manor says, approaching our group.

"Never can make enough for you," his grandmother teases, holding a large pot in her arms. "Put those muscles to use and get over here and help me."

"Yes, ma'am." Manor exaggerates a skip to Nessi's car, causing his man bun to bounce, before he grabs a bag of groceries.

"What's this?" Duke asks next, slapping Thad on the shoulder.

"Gran is cooking for us."

"Thank God," Duke sighs, walking toward his grandmother to help with additional bags.

"It wouldn't hurt for you to cook once in a while," Thad hollers after him.

"It would hurt. It would very much hurt," Duke calls back without glancing at his cousin. The three older men have such a good relationship and for a moment I'm nostalgic for my sisters.

Thad and I catch gazes, and he tips his head, questioning me.

I shake mine in response.

For the moment, I'm still good.

DINNER TAKES place in the lobby. Despite the meager workings of the kitchen, Nessi whips up homemade garlic bread, as in she made the bread and grew the garlic herself. She put the kids to work forming meatballs and Thad poured wine for the adults. An hour later, we were spread around the semi-circular bar, seated on stools, and teasing one another over the best spaghetti I've ever eaten.

Nessi grew the tomatoes for the sauce as well.

Thad's ability to cook must have come from his grandmother, and it's a touching thought to imagine them in the kitchen together. Her instructing him. Him taking pride in the meal he's created.

He's been so good to me, making me dinners for weeks now. Slipping in the occasional lunch, and still buying me Tiny Bites and coffee, although I've begged him to lessen the donut runs. It really is too much sugar every day.

As dinner winds down, Nessi puts the men on dishes duty. I stand up to help, but Nessi asks me to stay back in the lobby.

Quickly, I learn why when Sasha approaches me.

"I— I wanted to say I'm sorry for what happened the other weekend." Her eyes are lowered at first. She licks her lips, and finally looks up at me. "I didn't know Mom would react like that and I'm sorry she showed up drunk." She gnaws on her lower lip. "I'm sorry she almost hit you."

"Oh honey." I hesitate, wanting to draw her to me but not certain she'll allow a hug.

Sasha is a tough teenager. Not in the way teens can be mean but fierce because she's living like an adult, when she's still a kid. She's a big reason Thad removed his kids from Jasmine. At thirteen-years-old, Sasha is not the parent.

"Things . . . haven't been great since Dad left but it isn't his fault. Mom is just . . . difficult. And I shouldn't have egged her on by telling her where we were or implying . . ." She waves toward me.

I don't know exactly what she told her mom about me, but I heard what Jasmine called me in the driveway and I didn't like it. I did not wreck their home.

Am I a whore? I didn't want to believe that either. I'm a single, sexually active, forty-two-year-old woman. That makes me free spirited and independent, not what she called me.

"I understand." In fact, I might understand Sasha more than she knows. "My dad left when I was a baby. He never looked back so you're so lucky your dad wants to be around as much as he can. He loves you," I emphasize. "I also get it about your mom. Mine was depressed after my dad left and, for a while, my older brother and sisters had to take care of me. Change my diapers and feed me because my mom wasn't getting out of bed. Then my Grandad came along and shared in raising us, kind of like your Gran."

Sasha lowers her gaze and nods, but I have no idea if I'm

getting through to her with the comparisons. Being a teen is rough, no matter what era. It's even harder when you grow up too fast.

"I'd really like for us to be friends, but I get it if you just can't." I pause waiting for a response. When she doesn't answer, I add, "But I want you to know I like your dad. He's important to me. And I don't plan on going anywhere soon." We still have weeks to work together. "So maybe for his sake, we could at least get along. Not be more stress for him."

Sasha finally looks up at me. "I'd like to be friends, too." Her voice is quiet, sheepish even.

I don't suppose asking someone to be your friend is a norm, especially between someone in their forties and a teen.

"Good. Now, I'm a hugger, so I'd like to hug you, but I get if you—" *Oof.* Her body slams into mine. At thirteen, she's as tall as me and probably going to grow taller to match her dad's height. She hugs me hard and the strength surprises me, but I collect her in my arms. When she holds on a little longer, I gather her hair in my hand and stroke down her back.

How often does her mom hug her?

The affection with my mother had been lost when I was young. We missed out on bonding because she let other people raise me. We hug now as adults but it's the greeting kind of hug, not an embrace, not a hold that lingers.

"Everything okay?" Thad's voice is quiet from where he stands in the kitchen entrance.

Scooping Sasha's long, thick hair through my hand once more, I smooth down the length again as Sasha and I look at one another. Giving her a smile, I answer Thad.

"I think so."

Sasha nods, lids lowered. "Thank you for forgiving me."

"Of course." She's struggling while wanting to do right and I get that.

When Sasha steps away from me, she crosses to Thad. "Proud of you, baby girl."

"Dad," she groans. "I'm becoming a woman."

"Always going to be my baby, though." He pulls her to him for a side hug before she sneaks past him for the kitchen.

"Lindee, I—"

"Thaddeus, there're more dishes to be done." Nessi squeezes around him and gazes at me. "I'm glad you're free now. Let's take a walk while these guys clean up."

She steps up to me, loops her arm through mine and leads us toward the front door. I glance back at Thad, who is chuckling.

"Don't touch that dessert until we are back," Nessi hollers. "And I'll know if anything is missing."

She squeezes my arm in hers. "Those boys. They never learn that Gran knows everything."

34

Playlist: "Can't Help Falling in Love" – Elvis Presley

[Lindee]

With Nessi's arm looped with mine, she leads me out the lobby's main doors and down the covered walk along the motel rooms.

"Some days it seems like yesterday I was here." She glances from room to room with nostalgia in her eyes. With the curtains removed, she has a clear view of each room and the progress we've made. Beds are gone; new ones will be arriving this week. The salvageable dressers remain although I'm still working on my eclectic collection and themes per space.

Nessi sighs. "I was only a girl when I first came here. Ran off with a good man who did bad things for a living." She softly chuckles. "Sometimes your heart just takes a road trip and never comes back from the drive."

She stops walking and peers into a room. "Eventually, he brought me here. He took me to the waterfall first." Nessi glances at me but her gaze is faraway.

Thad took me to the dam in North Carolina on our first meeting. Seems the Rhode men have a thing for falling water on first dates.

"Thad told you that Pop got me pregnant in those waters. Telling the boys was his way of warning them about sex and babies, but he also wanted that place to remain sacred. Our secret. He proposed to me on that ridge by the river."

"I heard." I timidly smile at the reminder of the romantic setting and my breakdown when Thad jumped from the railway bridge.

Nessi focuses on me. I don't doubt she knows about my meltdown, and maybe even the reason why it happened. If Gran knows everything, Thad has filled her in on my past. I don't mind that he spoke with her. She isn't looking at me with pity or censure, just understanding.

When we are young, we make decisions that can affect which route we take in life.

She loops her arm in mine again and we continue at a slow pace down the sidewalk. "I'm a collector. I bought this place before my husband was gone. Wanted the reminder of good times. Times the club was a family of misfits and friends." Nessi smiles.

"I've heard you're quite the property owner."

Nessi chuckles. "What's the point of having money if I don't spend a little of it? Invest in the uncertainty of the future. Collect memories from the past." Her lips turn up in a mischievous grin. "This was one of my favorite places."

She sighs. "But we can't take places with us. Only the memories live in our heart and our heads."

We saunter to the end of the walk as her words settle in. There's no souvenir like a memory, even if we don't always remember correctly. Some places, some people, just make a permanent impact on us.

Thad is like that. Sasha, Vicki, and Sam, too. Even Nessi, Duke, and Manor will linger inside me once this project is complete.

Nessi pulls me toward the pool. There isn't much to show here other than a dirty basin stained from brackish standing water, and the ditch leading to the road. I could tell her about the changes I planned to make. The wrought iron fence and the decorative tile along the edge plus the lounge chairs I found during an end-of-summer sale although summer is still in full swing.

However, staring at the pool strangely feels like an admission of failure.

"A pool at a travel lodge was such a novelty once. Now families want resorts with lazy rivers, five-star restaurants, a day spa, and a plethora of activities."

I softly chuckle. "Well, I'm counting on the restoration of road trips and people making spontaneous stops along the way." Or planning ahead and making reservations for weekend getaways.

"Life is one spontaneous road trip, isn't it?"

"It is." I smile, but road trips eventually end. Vacations finish. Projects are completed.

"I heard you learned about the club and had a run-in with Jasmine." A weighty pause follows this abrupt statement. Uncertain how to respond as I don't know how Nessi feels about her former granddaughter-in-law, I'm grateful when she continues. "She's a woman who's dealt with a lot. Loss of friends. Loss of her parents. Lost her way, actually."

She pauses and glances at me. "Heard you had a loss or two yourself. We all do." She smiles with sympathy and pats my arm.

"Jasmine had Thad to pick up her pieces. My grandson is a

good man but he's no angel. He tried with her, for the sake of the children, which is always a terrible excuse." Nessi shakes her head. "I've been fortunate. Pop loved me above all else. It's why he eventually stepped away from a club he'd built with his friends. Most of them were gone already anyway. He had faith in the future with his grandsons at the helm, but the interim regime was the weak link in their legacy."

She softly chuckles. "Gonna admit I was surprised my boys left when Pop asked. Never saw that coming. Revenge and hate can run a man into the ground. I'm grateful three of four wised up, so they weren't all six-feet under like so many others. Or scattered into the breeze along some stretch of highway somewhere."

Nessi wistfully glances at the road in front of the motel as two cars pass by.

"A club breeds loyalty. It's engrained into the bones of the men. My boys were loyal to Pop. Thad especially. He's loyal to a fault. Jasmine is case in point."

I bite my tongue on a question I want to ask. *Will he go back to her?* It could happen. I've heard of divorced couples who still love each other. They discover the error of their ways and reconcile their relationship. Forgive. Forget.

From all I'd learned about Jasmine and Thad's relationship the push and pull between them sounds like an addiction in and of itself. He didn't love her like she wanted. She'd strike out by sleeping with someone else.

Was that the case for my parents?

Still, Thad stayed with Jasmine. He returned to her over and over again.

"Don't get me wrong. I feel sorry for the girl. She needs help and she might finally be seeing the light. Thad hung around a little too long and I'm glad he's free to be himself. I'm glad he has you."

"I—" I'm not certain what to say in response at first. "I'm fortunate to have him."

Nessi watches me. "Why do I sense a *but* in there?"

I shrug, not sure I should open up to this woman as a relative to Thad and yet unable to stop the words. "Everything comes to an end." Jasmine and Thad could be a prime example. His club another.

Thad's grandmother tips her head. "Are you waiting for the other shoe to drop?"

I glance back at the road, ignoring a sudden prickle in my eyes. "I've had a lot of people leave my life."

"And you think Thad is going to do that. Walk away from you?"

Would he? Could I blame him? He has his children. And a home somewhere other than a hotel room. His stay in the duplex is for an eight-week project, not a commitment of forever.

I shrug again.

"Silly girl, we can't spend our lives waiting for people to leave us. We'll never enjoy them while we have them."

My head snaps up. I've been enjoying Thad. I enjoy him a little too much and that's half the problem. I don't think I'll be happy when he's gone, and I never look at a situation like that. The end is simply the end, but this finale feels like permanent heartbreak.

We have less than two weeks left.

Nessi loops her arm with me again and leads me toward the duplex. "There's a reason I sold this place to you despite having a better offer."

"You had a better offer?" I didn't know that.

She tugs my arm into her side. "You saw the potential. You had sentimentality written in your business plan. You're a collector of memories as well."

We return to the broken driveway and continue toward the duplex. "But don't let the idea of chasing memories, even the haunting ones, prevent you from living for the future."

Harris. He haunted me. My father. He was a ghost as well.

I didn't want Thad to be one more lost presence in my life, but I still didn't believe I could keep him.

Jasmine whispers through my head, but she alone doesn't feel like the reason I'd lose Thad.

Nessi squints into the fading sunlight. "What's that saying? The past is behind us and our future is unknown, but today is a gift, that's why it's called a present." She softly chuckles. "Or something like that." We pause before the duplex. "Unwrap the gift, honey, and enjoy."

She steps away from me to investigate the duplex on her own. Reaching for the doorknob, she finds the place unlocked and enters. I remain outside letting her explore while I grapple with all she's said.

Thad has been the greatest present I've ever received. And gifts aren't intended to be returned.

But I still didn't trust that I could keep him long-term.

His loyalty wasn't the issue. I was afraid of mine.

Nessi returns and we walk side by side back to the lobby. I'm prepared to take her up to the winter cabin and show her the changes there, but she stops before the lobby doors.

"You've done real good here." Pride fills her voice and warms my heart. I want her to be pleased with my vision for her old place. As the new owner, it shouldn't matter how the previous one feels about changes, but Nessi's opinion matters to me. Because she's important to Thad but more so because I want her approval for some reason.

"Not disappointed in the least that I sold this place to you for less." Her confident statement assures me she means it. She's pleased that I'm the new owner.

"But don't disappoint me when it comes to Thad." Her wrinkled face turns stern, and those gleaming eyes harden to gems. Duke and Manor weren't wrong when they said Gran knows how to get things done.

She might be the pudding of proof, but she's no softy right now.

She has no idea how much I don't want to disappoint her or Thad.

Most of all, I hope not to disappoint myself.

AFTER DESSERT, which was a homemade apple pie and a collection of chocolate brownies, Nessi gathers Thad's kids to take them back to her home. Duke and Manor protest that a ninety-year-old woman shouldn't be driving in the dark with three kids, but Nessi holds her ground.

"I don't know who this ninety-year *old* woman is you are referring to." She winks at me before passing out hugs to everyone including me.

The kids each hug Thad and then me again, and my insides warm. Family. This is what it feels like.

I have my sisters and their kids, but I don't have a family of my own, and the hole in my heart at that absence became noticeable when I found out I wasn't pregnant. Not having a baby really was a good thing in my head, but my heart felt differently. It didn't mean I didn't want kids in my life somehow.

I'd been *that* aunt, who was happy to hang with kids and return them to their parents.

But what if I kept a sliver of kid-ness for myself? What if I shared parenting with someone? I'd never considered being a stepmom. Never thought about it because I was never in a situation where the man I'd been with was a package deal with an established family. I didn't get involved, until now. And of course, my thoughts would be contingent on a man wanting me to share parenting with him.

That man being Thad.

The subject isn't one I thought we'd ever discuss, especially when he practically yanks me into the cabin, slams the door behind him and drives his fingers into my hair before kissing me like I am that apple pie he couldn't seem to get enough of for dessert.

"Sweetheart," he exhales after the toe-curling kiss. "Seeing you with my kids. Vicki all snuggled up to you and Sasha wanting to apologize. And Sam being in so deep with you like me. I just—"

His mouth is on me again, cutting off his thought and distracting mine. We're moving slowly across the floor until I bump into a dining chair. Thad breaks the kiss and pulls the chair out of the way before lifting me by my hips and setting me on the table.

His mouth moves from my lips to my chin and down my neck.

"I don't think this table can hold me," I joke.

"Gonna have you for dessert because you are the sweetest thing I've ever had in my life."

I could argue that point when I consider Tiny Bites donuts and Nessi's brownies, but who can think when Thad has my shorts down to my ankles and places my feet on the edge of the table, forcing me to my back and spreading my knees. His head is between my thighs and the first lap causes me to drop my head to the table. I stare at the ceiling for a second as the man makes a delicacy of me. Quickly, my back arches and my legs quiver, giving into the delicious sensation of him feasting on me.

With my fingers digging into his hair and my hips thrusting up to match his tongue, I finally break. My legs collapse, falling to the sides. I'm melted chocolate over ice cream, all loose-limbed and replete.

Thad kisses my inner thigh and then leans forward, caging in my body. His eyes are flames as he stares down at me. His lips glisten from the attention he's paid my body.

"Lindee, I love—"

I reach for his cheeks and pull myself upward, cutting him off with a kiss of my own. One desperate to capture his words and erase them at the same time.

I love you whispers through my head but that can't be what he intended to say. It's too soon to consider love in this equation and we're running out of time. I always check out before my heart can be divided, so I don't think I can hear these words from him. But in many ways, I know I'm too late.

I love him too and that scares the hell out of me.

Thad pulls back while I cling to his scruffy jaw. He inspects my face, eyes shifting as they gaze from one of mine to the other, searching for something.

"So that's how it's going to be," he whispers.

I don't answer him, only lean upward for another kiss but a door feels like it's closing between us.

Thad lifts me awkwardly with my shorts at my ankles and I kick them off so I can wrap my legs around his hips. Silently, he carries me to my room and drops me on the bed.

"Roll over," he demands.

My skin pebbles as I do as he commands. I hear the sharp snap of Thad removing his belt and then the heavy unzip of his jeans. Turning my head to the side, I watch as he shoves down his pants to his thighs and bends over me. He pulls my hips upward and braces my knees at the edge of the bed.

With my hair fisted in his hand, I'm pinned to the mattress and loving it. Loving his control over my body when he places his tip at my entrance and leans toward my ear.

"I love you, sweet thing," he whispers, as he surges into me, filling me with those words. Once he's to the hilt he pauses. "And the next time I say those words to you, you're going to face 'em."

Then without another spoken sound between us, Thad hammers into me, as if stuffing me with his feelings.

He loves me, and I don't know what to do about that.

35

Playlist: "Heaven" – Kane Brown

[Thad]

Lindee didn't want to hear me tell her how I felt, and I wanted to be cool about that, but I wasn't. I got it, though. She was coming from a place where everyone left her. A man she'd never met didn't love her. A boy she'd been in love with left by accident. She'd been a wanderer all her life, and I wanted her to stay in one place.

Unfortunately, I also understood her wanderlust. I'd been that way myself when I was younger, wanting the road to take me where it would. Then the club disbanded, and Jasmine and the kids happened. I wouldn't say I was trapped but my nomadic soul had been caged. And I definitely didn't want to hold Lindee captive. Loving me had to be her choice.

Still, I wanted her to know where I was coming from with her.

As she lays beside me on her back, I'm on my side, trailing a finger down her middle. Her skin is so soft. Her body firm in some places, lush in others.

"I love . . ." Lindee stiffens beneath my roaming finger. Her eyes are wild when they meet mine. "Your body."

She narrows those blue gems, but I continue trailing over her flesh, around a breast and up to the tight nipple. Her mouth falls open.

I just took her a little rough, not in anger but frustration. I want this woman to let me in. Then again, I come with my own baggage.

How appropriate she plans to run a motel where visitors will never stay long enough to know her. Or her to really know them.

As my fingertip flicks over her nipple, I watch it pebble.

"I love . . ." I pause again. "How your body responds to me." With her nipples now tight, I lean down for a sip, swirling my tongue around one before sucking on the full swell. The moisture of my mouth wets the sharp peak and I blow on it, watching Lindee's eyes close at the sensation.

Hot and cold. We're in this lukewarm zone when I want us constantly heated for one another. Then again, maybe she doesn't feel the same about me. Maybe she doesn't want to love me, but she freely gives her love to others. It's there when she teases my cousins or smiles at my children. How she's patient with Gran.

Drawing my fingers along her neck and over her chin, I circle to her temple and tap once. "I love this creative mind of yours. The one full of vision and hope for this place."

The motel is her future even if she feels like a woman only living in the present because of her distant past. She's going to make a life for herself here and I want to be part of it.

I run my finger down her nose to her lips which open but I

don't stop there. I trace down her chin again, along her neck, and between the valley of her breasts.

"I love . . ." Emotion catches the words in my throat. "How you are with my kids. How you are with Gran. How you take to my cousins. They're my family and I want to make them yours."

"Thad," she whispers.

She has her own family but sometimes she thinks she's alone. Her brother has financially helped her. Her sisters have offered assistance. Even Myles has come around with a crew for floor installation and painting. She has people who care about her and I'm tossing myself into the ring.

"Let me love you, sweet thing."

"I—"

I cut her off with a kiss, not wanting to hear her rejection. I don't want her to feel pressured. I just want her to know where I'm at.

After losing Vic, I realized I didn't let my brother know how I felt about him often enough. If I had, maybe he'd still be here. Maybe I'm guilty of not being honest with Jasmine either. If I had, we wouldn't have wasted so many years together.

I don't want to wait with Lindee.

With my mouth still pressed to hers, I finish outlining her body, running my fingers down her middle and over her mound to find that sweet spot.

"You sore," I mumble against her mouth, recalling again how I took her hard only a few minutes ago.

"I ache for you in the best way."

Well, damn.

Slowly, I dip two fingers into her while staring into her eyes. Does she mean it? Is she saying the same thing I am, only in different words?

"Yeah?" I sigh, sliding my fingers in and out of her heat.

"You," she whispers.

Yeah. *You.*

Tired of talking, I let my body speak instead, hoping to explain with my touch how I feel about her and how she makes me feel about myself.

Like I'm a fucking dragon-king.

She's my treasure and I don't want to part with her.

THE NEXT DAY, Lindee is quiet and announces she's going on a scavenger hunt of sorts to find dressers. She's hoping for vintage pieces to match her themed rooms. In addition to the black and white room suggested by Sasha; the geranium room she created for Vicki; and the fun Harry Potter room for Sam, she has a mix of generic rooms with mountain-themes.

"I have one room left, and I've decided to make it a honeymoon suite," she tells Manor and me as we stand in the lot.

I stare at her long and hard, sensing deep down that she's running away. Even though our connection on a sexual level is out of this world, emotionally, she's closed off.

"You actually gave me the suggestion." She waves at me.

"I did?"

Manor arches a brow at me before asking, "What's the plan for this one?"

Lindee gets all excited when she starts describing the themed rooms with their color schemes and coordinating things. She's kind of a decorating geek.

"All white. White bed spread, white walls with the birch tree wallpaper as an accent. Then fairy lights across the ceiling. I want a couple to feel like they're sleeping outdoors under the stars but in the comfort of a king-sized bed." Lindee sighs, staring off at the last room of the motel. "It will be so romantic."

Manor wiggles his brows, eyes seeking mine again.

Lindee's dreamy gaze reminds me of when she told me how

she liked to dress up and feel like a woman at times. A dress with giant lemons on it did that for her, and so did a dinner with Myles. The scattering of romance novels tells me she has a romantic nature despite being closed off to the words *I love you*. Hell, she's wearing a bracelet that reminds her of a special night.

All of this rings a bell for me that we haven't been on a proper date since the waterfall. Sure, we share meals and spend time together each night, but we haven't carved out time away from the motel for just the two of us.

Duke calls out for Manor, and he heads toward his brother who is standing by the side of the duplex. We need to pick up the pace on the duplex if we plan to finish within the eight-week deadline. Lindee has a party planned for family and friends. The night won't be the grand opening or anything, but just a celebration of completion.

"We should go out," I blurt once Manor walks away.

"You don't need to go with me today," she counters.

"No, I mean, on a date. Just the two of us. Dinner. Or a movie." Is that what dates consist of? I hadn't been on a date in years. Instead, I've gone to family friendly movies or done kid appropriate activities, like bowling. But that wasn't what I wanted with Lindee. "We need a first date."

Lindee arches a brow. "Because a motorcycle ride along wooded roads and a waterfall swim wasn't good enough?"

When she puts it like that, I reconsider. However, we need another moment like those.

"Besides I never get the whole dinner at a restaurant for a date thing," Lindee states. "I eat out all the time. Maybe I'd prefer a home-cooked meal. Something that took effort. As for a movie, I don't know that I could sit still for one."

"You sit still to read romance novels." At least that's how she claimed to know about motorcycle clubs, as romanticized and fictionalized as those might be about the life.

Lindee sighs. "I haven't read in a while." After our bodies come together, she falls asleep with exhaustion lately.

"Are you trying to avoid a date with me?"

Her brows lift, surprise in her expression. "Is that what we're doing? Are we dating?"

"Aren't we?" We've spelled out our exclusivity and we've been together every night and see each other every day. There isn't time for either of us to be with someone else. And just last night I told her how I feel about her.

Lindee shrugs, narrows her eyes in the bright sunshine and glances away from me. "It's been a while since I've dated anyone." She's told me how she's had dates in the past but nothing with commitment.

"Then, sweet thing, go out with me." I glance at the dragonfly bracelet and tug on the silver cuff. "Still with me?"

Did I scare her away with my feelings? She's running away today, and I'll allow it if she needs to get lost outside of the motel for a bit, but she isn't going to outrun me. Because she's feeling something for me, she just won't admit it. She's wearing proof on her wrist right over that tattoo that once meant her life was on pause.

"I'm still with you," she whispers, flitting those sky-blues back to me. The same hesitation that was in her eyes last night flickers again. The way she looked when I was about to tell her how I felt. Maybe spread out on the dining room table wasn't the best time to spill my emotions. The words eventually came out when I had her bent over the bed and slid into her, but again, probably not the best timing if I wanted her to face the reality.

I am in love with her.

And I think she's in love with me.

I have staying power. I'm not leaving her behind like she thinks so many others have.

I always thought Lindee would be trouble, but she's more like a challenge.

The goal is to get her to admit she loves me, too.

THE NEXT NIGHT, I lead Lindee into the woods north of Wrightwood. The trail is well-worn although it leads somewhere private and protected.

While Lindee said she likes to dress up once in a while, I'm not exactly a suit and tie kind of guy. Plus, she said she didn't get the whole dinner and a movie thing, so I want something unique for this date.

We were hiking, and I'd told her she should pack for an overnight stay. She looked at me skeptically, but Lindee had lived in a camper for weeks. She wasn't opposed to the great outdoors.

As we near our spot, Lindee stalls. "What is this?" Her voice rises like a giddy girl.

"It's a geodesic dome." Before us stands a dome that's partially transparent. The opaque canvas side allows for privacy, while the clear plastic provides a view of the woods and the sky.

"I've heard of these but have never seen one up close." Lindee looks at me over her shoulder and her smile suggests I've done well so far.

Once we approach, I enter the code on a lock, then pop the latch, allowing us to unzip the door and enter. The space is a bit opulent for camping, thus the word *glamping*. With a solid wood floor and a king-sized bed, the space is sturdy and surprisingly spacious. It even has a private bathroom.

"This is incredible." Lindee spins in a circle, taking in the dome over our heads. "You can see the sky."

I glance up at the circular window at the top of the dome,

like a giant skylight wondering if she'll make the connection between what she said the other day and where we are.

When a slow smile curls her lips, I realize I don't need her to connect the dots. That smile on her face is enough for me. Looking at me like I hung the moon for her is all I ever want.

After a sheepish smile back at her, I lower my backpack and make quick work of emptying the contents.

"What are we doing? How can I help?" she asks, stepping closer to me and inspecting a few of the items I pull from my pack.

"Nothing. This is my date for you. I brought a bottle of wine, and we can start with that." I pull out the red I'd selected and hold it up.

Her smile grows.

"I'll pop the cork on this and then while you hang out, I'll cook."

A stone-edged fire pit is outside the dome, and I've already reviewed all the requirements for leaving no trace behind and campfire safety. A grill grate is supposed to be available, and I quickly find it propped up near the door.

"I have steak and potatoes, and even vegetables." I prepped everything before we left, knowing room temperature steak cooks better than cold meat. Our hike didn't harm our future meal.

Lindee's brows lift. "I'm impressed."

"Good." I want to impress her, and I want to impress upon her how I feel about her. She's important to me.

Lindee follows me back outside where I uncork the wine and pour her a glass in an insulated cup.

She lifts up the wine holder and inspects it. "I should have some of these made as souvenirs for the motel."

"I thought you didn't believe in souvenirs." My gaze falls to the bracelet on her wrist. Then I change course. "And sweet thing, for this one night we are not discussing the motel."

She glances up at me all innocent and maybe even a little hurt. Then she lifts her glass to salute me and drinks. I take a sip from my own cup and get to work on building a fire.

When we were kids, my family camped. The memory is distant and faded and while I'd always thought it'd be something I did with my kids, I hadn't. This dome is a bit fancy compared to what I had in mind, but maybe I could find a happy medium to share with the kids. We could even camp in Nessi's backyard, and I don't know why I never thought of it until now.

Glancing up at Lindee, who is watching me from her seat on a tree stump, I have an answer. It's because of her that I'm thinking differently, wanting different for my kids and me. I want her in our lives.

"Penny for your thoughts," she teases.

"I'll give them for free." She doesn't want to hear how I really feel so I'm hoping to show her instead. "I was thinking how I haven't been camping since I was a boy, and I don't know why I haven't done it more often as an adult."

Lindee hums. "We didn't travel much as a family. Just local places. Nothing spectacular like Disney or the Grand Canyon."

"Never been to Disney myself." Can't say it's a place I long to visit. "I've seen the Grand Canyon, though. Took a ride out there once."

It was a long haul on a bike but worth the trip. I'd needed space after the club had fallen apart. I was as lost as everyone else. Took me, Duke, and Manor three weeks. Jasmine was pissed.

Lindee watches me as I work the low flame, waiting for it to really heat up before setting the grate over the pit for the steaks.

"My sisters and I made a deal to road trip somewhere new each year. Just the three of us. The idea sparked after my middle sister Mae took a road trip down Route 66 last summer. It's the reason we were in Tennessee at Nessi's cabin."

I fall back to my heels, kneeling beside the fire. "You don't mention Mae much."

"Mae is awesome but we're just different. She's free spirited in a different way than me. She owns a flower shop in Michigan." Lindee huffs while the corner of her mouth crooks upward. "And fell in love on that Route 66 road trip, giving her a second chance at such a thing after her divorce."

Our eyes lock. Lindee's my second chance. I already know it but is she willing to love again? Being in love at nineteen isn't the same as being in love in our forties. Life has happened for both of us which I'd like to think has made us wiser, not just older.

"Sounds nice."

"Tucker is a great guy." Lindee sips her wine. "My sister Jane worked with him and Mach, before he was her husband. They actually pretended to be married and then married for real."

"Sounds like something out of a romance novel."

Lindee laughs as she teases. "Read many lately?"

"Never read one in my life." But there's always a first time, right?

Our night continues with idle chatter, telling each other stories about our siblings and families. I imagine this is how a first date goes, filling in the cracks and holes of history.

We eat grilled steak, fire-baked potatoes, and butter drenched vegetables under the sky as it grows dark. Lindee cleans up while I scrub off the grill grate and set it against a tree to cool.

Turning back for the dome, Lindee sits on a blanket beside the lingering flames as I excuse myself and return with something in my back pocket. I take a seat beside her and pull out the bulky wedge jammed against my ass.

"What's this?" Lindee giggles, sweet and coyish, as she tugs the book from my hands. Her fingers thumb through the pages.

"You said you didn't think you could sit still for a movie but you can read for hours. I thought we could read this together."

"*The Outlaw's Confession*." Lindee reads the title and flips the book to read the back. She chuckles. "Is this . . . a motorcycle romance?"

"I want to know how inaccurate they are." I shrug, bracing my arm behind her back.

"Where did you get this?" Laughter and disbelief fill her voice.

"A bookstore."

Lindee's brows lift. "And you want to read this together?"

"Out loud. Right now."

"What if I told you I already read this one?"

"Have you?" My brows lift.

Lindee chews her lower lip, fighting a smile while her eyes brighten with mischief.

"Then just skip to a good part."

Her smile grows almost devilish as she turns the pages, seeking out a passage. When she starts reading to me about the main character's hunger for a woman and how he goes down on her, I'm nearly sweating with desire. I tug the book from Lindee's hands and slap it down on the other side of me.

"Do not tell me that was too much for you." Her expression is flirtatious and evil. She knew what she was doing picking that scene.

"I'm trying to be good tonight. First dates are not for fucking."

"Says who?" Lindee laughs, twisting her body toward mine.

I glare at her. But she's so darn cute.

She laughs harder. "We threw that out the window the first night we met."

"Only that wasn't an official date, and this is."

"Do they need to be official?"

Why was I trying to label everything with her? If she

wanted casual, I should respect that. I should relish it as a newly single man, but I don't. I want her as mine. And I want her to claim me as hers.

I don't answer her. Instead, I bump her shoulder with mine like a nervous teen who's never been with a girl before. "Just humor me."

Lindee softens her smile and gazes up at the stars. "It's so pretty here. Peaceful even."

"Yeah, I like this area." I glance around like I haven't seen dark woods or starry nights before. It's the company I'm keeping that makes this place special.

Like Pop bringing Gran to the waterfall the first time and proposing to her on that river ridge. Some places seem ordinary until they aren't. I'm putting a pinprick in this place as a must-revisit with this woman.

Lindee and I hang out beside the fire until the flames disappear. I cover the embers and douse the pit before we enter the geodome. I've slept with Lindee plenty of nights but like I told her, I want to be patient tonight. We prepare for bed and then crawl in and stare up at the circular skylight.

Lindee lays still for a moment before turning to me. "You did this because of what I said about the honeymoon suite? Sleeping underneath the stars in a king-sized bed."

"Don't know what you're talking about." The smirk on my lips gives me away.

"Thad." She props up on her elbow. "This is so . . . romantic."

"Yeah?" I roll my head on the pillow to face her. Her eyes glow in the natural light of night around us. The moon is out there somewhere.

Lindee cups my face. "You," she whispers like she's done before.

I don't want to read more in one word than I should but

every time she says it, I feel like she's saying something else to me.

"You," I say back, fighting a sudden anxious feeling in the pit of my stomach that I'm not going to be able to keep her.

She's a moment but not forever.

"Thank you," she says, before falling to my side and tucking her head on my shoulder. My hand skates up her back and I press a kiss to her forehead.

"I used to dream of getting married. When I was young." Her voice is soft. "When it never happened, it didn't mean I didn't believe in happily ever after. Every hotel I've redone has a honeymoon suite that can double as a romantic getaway for a couple."

My woman has a heart for others, but I want her to know her heart can be open to me.

"Nothing I've ever created tops this, though." She grows quieter. "It's kind of like a fairy tale."

As I glance up, the stars prick to life above us and despite our shelter the view gets clearer overhead.

I don't really believe in fairy tales, but I'd like to give one to her.

We could be our own story where the motorcycle man turns good, and the woman he loves doesn't mind a little bad.

The Outlaw's Confession is more likely our plot, though, and I'm not liking the odds that a romance novel about a woman loving a MC guy might not end so happily ever after.

36

Playlist: "Wild as Her" - Corey Kent

[Thad]

True to my word, I did not have sex with Lindee. We laid underneath the stars in the geodome and talked through the night, learning more about each other. The conversation wasn't awkward. We weren't filling in gaps, just dropping bits and pieces about ourselves. Once we finally slept, the night was too short.

We drive back to the motel just after dawn. It's going to be a long day as I'll be heading to Nessi's after work for the weekend with my kids.

"Just going to kiss you by the front door," I say, once I walk Lindee to the front stoop of the winter cabin. Isn't that how a date ends? "Don't want to be presumptuous on our first *official* date."

"Think we might be a little bit past presumptions," she teases. "And firsts."

"I have more firsts in mind for you." However, I don't want to make any assumptions about this woman.

I'm a knot of desire for her despite daylight and standing outside her cabin, though, and when my mouth hits Lindee's, I'm unleashed, despite the effort to keep it chaste and sweet. The kiss is hot and heavy, imparting words she won't let me say and things I'm afraid to mention. Like how I don't want to ever let her go.

Her back hits the front door with a soft thud and I release her lips, resting my forehead against her.

"Well." She sighs. "You certainly know how to kiss on the first date." Her hand slaps the front door at her back. "And when you said at the front door, you meant literally."

We both laugh and the deep rumble from my body travels against the fine curves of hers.

"That sweet mouth of yours is going to get you in trouble." I swipe both hands into her hair, brushing it over her ears.

"I like trouble." Her eyes gleam with promise.

I groan. I'm trying to be good for just one night with her. "I'm going to walk away now before I spoil the romance of a first date."

"Who needs romance?" She smiles, before chewing at her lower lip.

"Trouble," I groan. "From the moment I saw you by that river."

We stare at one another, neither of us moving, longing in both our eyes at the reminder of that day.

"We should probably get to work," she whispers.

I release her hair and scrub a hand down my face. Exhaling is a failed attempt to bring my body under control. "Yeah."

Then her fingers are fisted in my T-shirt and she's tugging

me toward her. "Then again, I know the boss. Maybe we can be a little late."

My mouth is back on hers, kissing her with everything in me. When she breaks free and spins for the door, my mouth hits her neck, kissing up the column while my hands outline her body. Her hands shake as she struggles to get the key in the lock.

"Thad," she whimpers when I bite her a little harder than normal at the juncture of her neck and shoulder.

"I don't even know if I can wait before we are inside to touch you." Reaching around her waist, I find the button on her shorts and pop it. The zipper is next and my hand slides between her thighs, cupping where she's warm and damp against her panties.

Lindee hums and arches her back, forcing her backside against my front. While sucking at her neck, I slip my fingers underneath the band of her underwear and dive into her.

We both groan. Her at the intrusion; me at the heat. She's sunshine and moonbeams and low flames beneath a dark sky. I never want to lose the light she is in my life.

"I don't want to say goodbye to you. Ever."

Her breath hitches and I nip her neck again as I work my fingers in and out of her.

"Someone might see us," she whimpers as my thumb swipes over that sweet spot on her.

"Never gonna let anyone get a look at what belongs to me, sweet thing."

The winter cabin has a little alcove before the entrance, and we're well protected from anyone seeing what I'm doing to her. The direction I'm going to take her before we enter this house and I finish us both by burying myself deep inside her.

Because she is mine and I am hers.

With her hand smacking lightly at the front door, Lindee rushes like a river over my fingers, coating them in her sweetness as she falls apart. When I swiftly remove them, she glances over her shoulder and I stick my fingers in my mouth, sucking at her honey-essence.

Our eyes lock a second before Lindee is fighting with the key again, slipping it into the lock and nudging the front door open. It's hardly closed behind me when she's climbing my body, tightening her thighs around my hips. We stumble to the couch. In seconds, her shorts are off, and my jeans are lowered and I'm sliding home.

I want to live in this woman. In her heart, and her head. I want to share in her body and her future.

"Come with me this weekend," I say as I thrust into her, winding her up for another release and coming to the edge of my restraint.

"What?" she chokes as I bury myself in her. Her ankle is propped on the back of the couch. Her other leg dangles off the edge. I cover her shin and press her leg upward, opening her up in a new way to me.

"Thad," she whimpers as I hammer harder.

We're both panting. Sweat trickles along my brow.

"Say yes," I strain as my movements come faster, sharper, taking her like I'm afraid she'll disappear before me.

Her hand swipes over my hair before cupping my jaw and I slow despite the racing of my heart.

"Okay," she whispers, eyes bright while hesitant.

"Yeah?" I still, smiling down at her. My dick aches deep within her, but I want to be certain I've heard her correctly. "You'll go with me."

"I'm with you," she says, and my smile grows to a fucking cheesy grin.

Yeah, she's with me and I plan to keep it that way.

Despite our late start, we call it a day early and head to Kentucky for the weekend. It's a beautiful summer evening and Lindee agrees to take my bike. There is nothing better than open road, summer breeze, and a girl behind me, squeezing my thighs with hers. Lindee holds tight on my waist and when I can, I rub my hand up her forearm, loving the feel of her clinging to me.

For a moment, my past rumbles with my future. The bike beneath me with Lindee at my back. And for the first time in a long time, I feel something I'm not certain I've ever felt.

Hope.

Then we pull into Nessi's driveway, and I see a familiar vehicle.

"Fuck," I grumble as I bring the bike to a slow halt and park alongside the SUV I'd bought my ex-wife.

Checking in with the kids every night is second nature. After Sasha apologized to Lindee, I was extra proud of my girl, and I made a strong effort to double check her emotions. Not that the other kids weren't hurting with the absence of Jasmine or me working so much, but Sasha had taken the brunt of Jaz's bitterness. The kids collectively told me they hadn't seen Jaz in weeks.

But my ex-wife was presently sitting on Nessi's front porch and that does not make me happy.

Lindee slips off my bike and waits beside me as I cut the engine and climb off myself. I take her hand, making a statement as we near the steps leading up to the porch.

Jasmine stands. She looks jittery. Eyes too big. Hands shaky as they rub down her skinny jeans-covered thighs. Jaz looks on edge while fragile at the same time. Guilt stabs deep, reminding me that I haven't always done right by her. We had three kids, a house, time together, and none of it made a difference.

"I was wondering if I could talk to you," she calls down from where she stands at the top of the porch, like she's blocking the entrance to my grandmother's home.

I sigh, shaking my head slowly as I glance down at my feet. Lindee squeezes my hand.

Lifting my head, I stare up at my ex. "Jaz, I just don't know what's left to say." We've been talked to death, rehashing shit for years, and it doesn't get us anywhere but fighting.

I turn to look at Lindee. Her face all fresh and her hair a bit windblown despite a helmet. She's my second wind and I just want to breathe her in. Not cyclone through the past again.

"Just a few minutes," Jasmine says, slowly descending the wooden stairs I built when I helped fix this place up. Jaz's wild gaze skips from me to Lindee and down to our hands. "Alone."

I tighten my hold. Jaz isn't getting anywhere near this woman and the last thing I want to do is be alone with my ex.

Lindee turns to me, and whispers, "I'll give you some space."

Space is the last thing I want, but with an extra squeeze at my bicep from her other hand, she loosens her fingers. Because I want to make a point, I turn to face her, slipping my fingers into her hair and kissing her a little deeper than necessary before releasing her.

Lindee chews her lower lip, meets my eyes a second, and then turns away from me, giving Jasmine a wide berth before she climbs the stairs to the porch.

"Knock, knock," Lindee calls out as she raps on the screen door.

A squeal comes from somewhere inside the house. Feet gallop down the hardwood hallway before Sam shrieks, "Lindee!"

I smile and glance at Jaz who has her back to the house. Her eyes are closed.

"What do you want Jasmine?"

Her lids flip open. "I'm going away for a while. At least six weeks." She swallows hard. "I won't be allowed to contact the kids."

I stare at her, uncertain what she's saying. "You going to rehab?"

"It's the only way." Her glassy eyes are cautious.

"Just like that, huh?" The decision sounds too easy.

"It's been a long time coming." She sighs, swiping a shaky hand through her long, dark hair. "I can't do it alone." She pointedly looks at me.

My shoulders sag and empathy fills my veins. We couldn't do it together. We weren't good for one another. "I'm sorry, Jaz. You know I'm so fucking sorry."

She shrugs. "I've always known it would be like this. My mother loved my father more than he loved her." The reminder of her dad and his infidelities does not settle well with me. We've been over this. I never touched another woman when we were together.

I could argue with her at the assumption—just one of a million jealous streaks she rolled on—but I don't have the energy to fight with Jaz anymore. It wasn't worth the effort.

Besides, she's the one who cheated on me . . . more than once.

"Someone always loves more in a relationship."

My mouth pops open, prepping to ask what she means, but I clamp my lips shut, not wanting to prompt an argument. I don't agree with her, but I don't dispute her either.

"I'm sorry I wasn't always there for you, Jaz." I sigh. "And I really hope going to rehab helps you find what you need. Helps you find out who you want to be."

Jasmine was too wrapped up in being my wife and a mother to our kids to get a sense of herself. She was the daughter of a motorcycle club president but when the princess identity was gone, she didn't know who she was anymore.

"I already said goodbye to the kids. Told them I was taking a long vacation."

I scowl, not certain I like the explanation and equally certain I'll be telling the kids the truth. They need to understand their mom is sick and needs help, not that she's run off for margaritas and stray men.

She'd already done that during our marriage.

"I just wanted to tell you what I was doing. Face to face." She stares at me, watching my face, but what she's looking for she isn't going to find. Jasmine is always going to have my sympathy but not my heart. We clung to one another for too long, for the wrong reasons, and it was time we both did right by ourselves. Separately.

"Best of luck to you, Jaz." I step forward and offer her a hug. She wraps her arms around my waist, inhaling deeply. I press a kiss to the crown of her head and quickly pull back while she hesitates to release me. A part of me is always going to be defined by her but not owned by her. We hurt each other in our years together. It was time for the hurting to stop, for both of us.

A soft sob comes from her before she covers her mouth and glances back at the house. "I love them so much."

"Then get better for them. But most of all, do it for yourself."

She turns back to me and swipes away a tear. This woman could cry on a dime, but they were always angry, bitter, hate-filled tears. Never broken ones like the stream rippling down her cheeks now.

She nods once and heads for her car.

I step toward the porch and climb the stairs, knowing it's best not to look back.

My path is forward inside Gran's house where my kids are filling it with laughter and the woman I love waits for me.

37

Playlist: "In God's Country" – U2

[Thad]

I'm nearly giddy as I enter the house and find Lindee near the large kitchen island. Vicki is helping Gran make something that smells delicious near the stove and Sam is on his knees on a stool, on the verge of falling off it. Sasha holds her phone on the countertop but looks up.

I'll need to be checking in with each of them and their feelings about the bomb their mom just dropped on us but for tonight I have other plans.

"Dad," Sam squeals as my fingers dig into his sides, tickling him and righting him before he falls off the stool.

"Hey Daddy." Vicki glances over her shoulder at me but quickly turns back to whatever she's stirring with Gran.

"Hey." Sasha gives me a soft smile.

"You good?" I ask, settling Sam on the stool. Sasha nods.

Later, I tell myself.

I glance over at Lindee, watching me. *"Are you good?"* she mouths.

She has no idea how good I am and it's all due to her.

"Yep," I pop and clap my hands. "Guys, I got a plan for tonight."

Vicki pauses while continuing to hold the spoon over the pot. Sam twists on the stool and Sasha even sets her phone down. Nessi turns to face me.

"We're going camping." My announcement is met with stunned silence. Only Nessi's face lights up.

"Where?" Sasha hesitantly asks.

"Here. There are old tents in the bunkhouse, and we can set them up in Gran's yard. We'll make a campfire and roast hot dogs."

"Can we cook marshmallows?" Sam asks. I can always count on him for enthusiasm.

"Definitely." I glance up at Nessi. "I might need to use your car to make a run to the store."

"Anything you need." She gives me the same smile she's given since I was twelve. She's always been here for me, and right now, pride fills her face.

"Okay. Sasha, start a list." I point at her and her phone.

"Marshmallows," Sam calls out.

I look at Vicki and she lists off other items including the remaining ingredients for s'mores.

Finally, I gaze at Lindee. "This okay with you?"

Lindee offers me that soft sweet smile that makes my chest ache for her. Her voice is equally tender while her eyes say everything. She wants to do this with me. With us.

"Sounds perfect."

∽

NESSI TAKES stock of anything she might have that we'd need. Then, Lindee and I head to the store with Sasha and Sam. Vicki stays back to finish her cooking lesson with Gran.

"I should have told you my plans with the kids," I say as Lindee stares at the numerous options of hot dog buns available in the bread aisle. Sasha has taken Sam to find chocolate bars and graham crackers.

Lindee pauses her inspection and turns to me. "Nah, with kids you just go with the flow, right?"

Jesus. I love this woman. Tugging her to me, I kiss her a bit inappropriately in the bread section, wanting to take her up against the shelves despite the public location.

When I pull back, I feel the eyes of an audience and look up to find Sasha near the end of the aisle. Her hand is over Sam's eyes and she's shaking her head at me with a disapproving glare but struggling to hide the smile on her lips.

"Are they done kissing yet?" Sam calls out, pulling at his sister's hand.

"Yeah, they're done."

Nah, I'm never going to be done kissing this woman.

Sasha gives me another oldest-sister scowl like I'm the child and she's the parent but I only chuckle. However, Lindee pulls free from me and faces the hot dog buns again like she needs to research every ingredient in them. As Sasha and Sam approach the cart, I reach around Lindee to pull two packages off the shelf without giving them a second thought.

"That kiss was definitely not PG-13," Sasha mutters as she offers me a sassy smirk. And if I didn't see me in that expression on her face or the twinkle in her eye, I'd be upset.

Instead, I reach for my girl and tug her to my chest, pressing a quick kiss to her head, watching all forms of reproach wash away.

Once we return to Nessi's, finding the tents is a hunt, then setting them up takes some mastery. The old things smell a bit musty from years of disuse, but the canvas is still in good condition. I wish we had a giant one that fits all five of us, but I settle for two small tents side-by-side.

"Boys and girls," I point between them before catching on Sasha and teasingly reminding her of her snide comment weeks back at Lindee's. "Or do you want to rearrange us?"

I'd happily sleep with Lindee, but that isn't the point if I want to spend time with everyone.

Sasha rolls her eyes. "Girls and guys works."

"We forgot sleeping bags," Sam calls out, and starts racing for the house. It feels like there are a hundred details I hadn't considered.

"I got him," Lindee says before jogging after him. Watching them, it appears they are suddenly in a race which Lindee is letting Sam win. They're both laughing as they reach Nessi's back door and I smile to myself. She's so good with my boy.

Looking back at the tents, both my girls observing me. I clear my throat.

"How you doing with what your mom told you?" As long as we have a few minutes, now seems like a good time to check in with them.

"She's not really going on a vacation, is she?" Sasha's question is full of wisdom.

"No, baby girl. She's checking into rehab."

Vicki's eyes widen and cloud with wobbly tears. "Will she be okay?"

"That's the plan. Rehab should help her quit drinking. And be a better mom." As long as she sticks with it, Jasmine should be a better person, too.

"She wasn't terrible," Vicki defends.

"Not saying she was. She's your mom, and she loves you. All three of you. She's doing this to be better."

"And she'll be back when she's done?" Vicki asks, blinking her eyes and swallowing to settle the unshed tears.

"She'll be back." At least, I think so.

"Are we going to live with her again?" Sasha's voice is full of hesitation, caught between wanting a better mother and still hurt from the things Jasmine said to her.

"I think that will be up to your mom. When she's back, and better, we can talk then."

"Being at Nessi's isn't so bad," Sasha quietly says.

"She's teaching me to cook." Vicki's voice rises with excitement.

"I saw that. Maybe tomorrow night you can make us something."

Her eyes light up, reminding me again of my brother, only the mischief and danger isn't present. She's just eager to please.

"I'll talk to Gran," Vicki says with enthusiasm.

I nod. "How about Lindee? You guys okay with her being here?" This might be the more difficult question.

"I like her," Vicki easily admits.

"Yeah, I'm okay with her." There's no sass or sarcasm in Sasha's tone. She isn't indifferent, just taking her time to warm up. Lindee has asked me to give Sasha patience. My baby girl has no idea how much my big girl understands her and her attitude.

As the back door slams, Sam waddles toward us with his arms full of two sleeping bags. Lindee holds three more.

"We still need pillows," Sam calls out as he struggles with his load.

I'll need to check in with him later as well, but for now, I'm on pillow duty. Then it's campfire, hot dogs, and s'mores time.

THE NIGHT PASSES with games of tag, in which a few times, I'm it and go straight for Lindee, pulling her into me and giving her ass a quick squeeze or sneaking in a too-brief kiss before chasing my kids around Nessi's yard. There are acres to roam but we stick close to the house tonight.

Eventually, we hang out around the campfire and Lindee teaches the kids a few songs. She has a decent voice and I wish she'd sing more often. The night I caught her in the lobby I wanted to hear more, but she brushed off her ability.

She's amazing in so many ways.

Sam is dozing off beside me while we sit around the fire, watching it burn down to crackling sparks and low embers, when I announce it's time for bed.

The girls give me hugs and head for their tent while Lindee stands and pours water over the fire. We've already collected all the trash and extra food has been returned to Nessi's kitchen, so we don't have unwanted nighttime visitors, like raccoons. Or even a bear.

Sam heads for the designated boys' tent, and I pause outside, taking a final look at the stars lighting up the sky.

"It's been a good night," Lindee says beside me, and I tug her into my side, kissing her head.

"Gonna miss sleeping with you," I mutter to her hair.

"You'll survive." She teasingly pats my chest and glances up at me. Her eyes are bright. Her smile wide.

She has no idea. I don't want to survive without her. I've been surviving for so long and now I just want to live. I want more nights underneath the stars with my kids and this woman in my arms.

Telling her I love her is on the tip of my tongue again, but I hold back.

Her hand fans out on my chest, pressing over my heart.

Does she feel that? Does she know the beat is erratic because of her? Does she realize she makes me feel alive?

"I'll miss you, too," she whispers before tipping up to offer me a sweet kiss, like a good night kiss on a first date.

She's right, we jumped ahead, but I don't ever want to go backwards with her.

INSIDE MY TENT, Sam is a squirrelly mess. He's rumpled up his sleeping bag and he's spinning around on his knees.

"What's up, little man?"

"I'm looking for my book. I can't find it." With a camp lamp illuminating the space, it should be easy enough to find, only we don't.

"We'll find it tomorrow." We've shifted the sleeping bags twice, but it isn't in here.

"I can't sleep unless you read me a chapter."

Embarrassingly, I'm not the one who reads to my kid. Sasha handles that each night still, even when I am present.

"Not tonight, Sam." Since we don't have the book, he'll have to go without.

"I can't, Dad. Maybe Sasha has it."

Why the hell Sasha would have Sam's book, I don't know, but I offer to check. Only Sam follows me over to the other tent.

"Knock, knock," he calls out before opening the flap without waiting on a response. The girls already wore pajama shorts and sweatshirts around the campfire. In the warmth of the tent, I'm assuming they'll be down to tees. Sure enough, the three of them are sitting cross-legged on top of their bags like a slumber party is happening in here.

While I remain hunched over at the entrance, Sam crawls in between all of them. "I can't find my book." His watery voice hints at exhaustion. He needs to hit the hay, but he's still wound up.

Vicki and Sasha both start looking around until Sasha finds it underneath her pillow. Her brows pinch like she isn't certain how the book got in their tent or under her pillow.

"Okay, Sam-man. Out we go to read."

"Can Lindee read to me?"

"Sam," I groan, glancing at Sasha. Sam said before he doesn't want to hurt her feelings about him thinking Lindee reads better.

"I don't mind, if it's okay with you." Lindee isn't looking at me but Sasha for permission.

With a subtle nod, Sasha gives Lindee the okay and Lindee reaches out for Sam, pulling him to her side. Sasha stretches out beside Sam. With Vicki on Lindee's other side, there isn't much space in the tent, and I finally kneel down on one knee as leaning over was killing my back. Sleeping on the ground might not be the smartest idea I've had but being with Lindee last night reminded me how much I'd missed doing something like this and how sorry I am I haven't shared this experience with my kids sooner.

"Come on in, Daddy," Vicki invites me.

"Looks a little cramped in there." Three sleeping bags. Four bodies.

Lindee glances up at me. "There is always room for daddies," she says, like she said the night she read to Sam in the loft.

After the four of them huddle closer because Lindee scoots her and Sam to the right, I slip into the tight space, stretching out beside Vicki.

Then Lindee starts reading about Harry Potter, and she really does have the voices going, hinting once again at her theater background.

And my kids and I drift off to sleep under the spell of a woman full of love with a good cackle and warm octaves that hint at love.

38

Playlist: "Leather and Lace" – Stevie Nicks and Don Henley

[Lindee]

The night camping in Nessi's yard had been incredible. Almost as wonderful as glamping with Thad.

After staying up all night on Thursday and the rustic sleeping of five people in one tent on Friday, Thad said no to another night in tents despite protests from his kids.

"Maybe we can actually take a trip and go camping somewhere else," Sasha says as a way to pacify her siblings but also in question to her dad.

We've had a lazy day just hanging out, playing in the yard, or watching the kids chase each other. Sasha wasn't always involved in the shenanigans, but she didn't separate herself very far from our cluster of five.

Falling asleep together in the close quarters of the tent wasn't what I'd expected to happen, but surrounded by Thad and his kids felt nice, like I was part of something special. Part of their family.

"Sure, we can take a road trip." Thad looks up and winks at me as we gather around Nessi's kitchen island. The room is a dream kitchen with industrial appliances and a farmhouse sink plus pretty light-green cabinets and white granite countertops. Vicki is going to make us dinner tonight under Gran's guidance.

"Why don't you search places you'd like to visit, and we'll see how we can make it happen."

"Can we go to Hawaii?" Sam asks, his wide eyes hopeful.

"You can't road trip to Hawaii, silly. It's an island and you need to cross an ocean," Vicki explains.

"Why do you want to go to Hawaii, Sam?" Thad curiously asks.

"That's where Mom said she was going."

Oh boy. Thad has already told me what Jasmine said and how he talked to his girls about the truth.

Looking up at me again, Thad sighs. "Sam-man, let's take a little walk."

Sam slides off the stool he'd been kneeling on and follows his dad who leads them toward the screen door for the backyard.

"Am I in trouble?" Sam quietly asks as Thad holds the door open. He swipes a hand over his son's hair and gently tugs at the back, so Sam looks up at him.

"No trouble, little man."

So much love for that boy. It just exudes out of Thad.

I've quickly developed a strong attachment to Sam myself. Just like his dad, he's sneaking into my heart.

With the boys gone, I ask to help Nessi but she says the star of the night will be Vicki. Instead, she pours me a glass of wine and I casually sip it, watching Nessi give her great-granddaughter a cooking lesson. Sasha sits beside me on a stool and as much as she isn't engaged in the instructions happening around her, she's still present.

This little cluster of women, sharing generational knowledge, and enjoying each other's company is how I envisioned my life being. I wouldn't have structured my life around temporary-stay locations but a house, turning it into a home. The blueprint would have included a partner in a lasting, loving relationship. We'd have children that centered our lives, bringing us comfort and joy. I'd have rooms to gather friends and additional family, like Nessi's large kitchen. Warmth would exude from the walls as we painted our lives in daily routines and special occasions. Brightness would illuminate the space as we linger at the kitchen table, or collapse on a comfortable sofa, and just spend time with the people I loved most in my life.

The dream didn't feel like it would ever be a reality but a hint of hope whispers through my head.

Could I be part of this with Thad?

Nessi is an amazing great-grandmother, and I imagine she was a tough matriarch to her grandsons. Their love for her is in every smile and tease.

Thinking of Duke and Manor makes me feel guilty as I sit on a stool, drinking wine in their grandmother's house while they work the weekend on the motel. We're only a little more than a week out from the deadline for their part of the project.

Eight weeks has certainly flown by. In another ten days, it will be September and Labor Day weekend. I have a party planned for Monday evening to celebrate the opening of Mountain Motel. Hal promised me the pool would be done but then we'd have to wait two seasons before opening it as fall and winter are dead zones on outdoor swimming.

Jane has helped set up a website and she's connecting the motel with the travel apps and hotel-seeking services. I'm listed with the West Virginia Tourism Department and set up advertisements in their winter magazine as I was too late for the fall issues. Jane designed a new logo for the place and had a neon sign made as well, to replicate the iconic feel of classic roadside travel lodges.

Everything was falling into place, almost too easily.

The only thing that still felt complicated and unsure was Thad. He'd been consistently by me for weeks. I was here, spending time with him and his kids, and yet a sickening sensation low in my belly told me it wouldn't last.

Life was *too* good.

Thad told me he loved me. I hadn't meant to dismiss his declaration, but panic took over. Loving me was dangerous. I was trouble, as I'd told him, and I didn't want to hurt Thad. He wasn't safe with me, despite me asking him if I was safe with him. I was *afraid* to love him back. Like stomach-clenching, boulder-in-my-throat frightened that I'd mess everything up and then Thad would leave me.

I wouldn't be able to take that kind of heartbreak. I might be a survivor by nature, but it doesn't mean I don't feel things. When my emotions kick in, they cling, and I didn't want to hang onto Thad. I didn't want to feel like I had sharp talons, digging into him, like Jasmine had done to him.

While I'd heard the loving phrase uttered by Thad, it was so hard to believe that he could love me. Love me like I need someone to love me, with a promise to never leave me behind.

I wanted to think Thad wouldn't do that. I'd hoped in the depths of my soul he couldn't, but something still held me back and I couldn't pin down what it was.

When the screen door squeaks open, Thad returns with a hand on Sam's shoulder. His son still looks puzzled and his eyes a little red-rimmed. Still, he offers Sasha a smile and when I look at Thad, I mouth, *"All good?"*

Thad gives me a wide grin and a wink. "Never better," he answers loud and clear.

I've never felt better myself and that scares me.

AT NIGHT, I can't sleep. Thad and I are in separate rooms despite Nessi's teasing that we could sleep together. I was the one uncomfortable because of the kids. We'd watched a family-friendly movie after Vicki made us a delicious dinner of chicken, mashed potatoes, and steamed vegetables. Thad looked exhausted, but I was wound up once I'd showered and slipped into a guest room down the hall from him. Nessi's farmhouse had several bedrooms on the second floor accommodating her great-grandchildren. Her room was on the main level.

"My grandsons don't trust me with those stairs," she'd teased. I didn't think a staircase would stop her from doing what she pleased, where she pleased.

With another sigh and a toss of the unnecessary covers in the warmth of the August night, I slip out of bed and down the hall to Thad's room.

I shouldn't be doing this, but I just need to see him.

As the door shuts quietly behind me, I tiptoe to the side of the bed, noting the large tattoo over his broad back. He's sleeping on his stomach with his thick and colorful arms beneath his pillow. The sheet is pushed to his lower back, giving me a clear view of his skin and the firm mound of his backside. He's such a spectacular man.

I slip out of my underwear, wearing only a T-shirt, and gently lift the sheet. Thad shifts. His head flips from one side of the pillow to the other without him opening his eyes.

"Whatcha need, sweet thing?" he groggily mumbles.

"Nothing," I lie, as the desire to be close to him vibrates through me. I slip underneath the cool covering and roll to my side, running my hand down his spine.

Thad hums. His eyes remain closed. His skin is warm. The ink a contrast of angry black against tan flesh. I watch as I drag my hand over him. The curve of his shoulder blades. The dip of his lower back. The hill of his ass.

"Lindee." My name is seduction. Or maybe he's dreaming. I'd like to know if I fill his nighttime thoughts like he fills mine.

Leaning closer to him, I kiss his shoulder while my hand still skims his back. Slowly, I pepper him with kisses, outlining the large tat with my fingertip and tongue.

"Sweetheart." He groans as I slip a leg over one of his, forcing his thighs to spread. I straddle his thick leg while continuing my exploration of his summer-sticky flesh. My fingertips coast along the dip of his spine to the base of his back. My tongue follows the trail.

Instantly, I'm turned on. Who am I kidding? I was desperate for him before I snuck in here.

Thad spreads his legs more, allowing my achy core to straddle the heat of his thigh.

"I can feel your hot pussy," he grumbles without opening his eyes. "You're dripping on me."

He's right. I'm wet and overheated. I rock against him.

"Fuck, sweet thing, that's hot." A smile fills his sleepy voice as I press against him, finding the friction a tease. Sliding along the back of his leg, I work myself into a lather. My fingers massage his strong back while I grind on him, squeezing my thighs over his singular leg and rubbing sensitive folds against his skin.

"Gonna come on me, baby," he mutters, his voice a little stronger while he hasn't opened his eyes or shifted positions.

I don't answer him, continuing to find a rhythm that makes my center pulse and my skin prickle. My fingernails score down his back.

"Fuck," he growls, rubbing his nose against the pillowcase before returning his head to the side.

I rock faster, running my hands down to his ass and squeezing at the firm globes. Thad flexes, tightening the muscle before releasing and allowing me to play. I spread his cheeks.

"Lindee," he warns as my thumbs squeeze him apart. He tightens again beneath my hold. Massaging into the solid flesh, I roll my hips and rub my clit against him. Easily, I glide over his skin, moistening him with my desire.

I'm out of control and the ripple rushes so quickly up my center I gasp before I still, letting the release wash over me and flow down my core like a dive into a cool body of water. Like I've jumped off a bridge into a river. Only I'm not drowning. I'm letting the rush swallow me, comfort me, draw me under and then spit me back up with a gentle push.

Thad flips beneath me and I'm suddenly straddling his lap.

"That was so fucking hot. Get on my dick." He's already hoisting me up by my hips and setting me down on his tip, and with one gentle thrust, he's buried to the hilt inside me.

There's no pause in my orgasm and as my clit hits his pubic bone, I'm off again, rubbing the sensitive spot against him.

"Sweet thing," Thad groans, fighting off his own release as his body reads mine, knowing I'm building up again, like climbing a river ravine. Only I'm not certain I ever came down and I clutch at Thad's body. Digging my fingertips into his abs. Then running my hands up his chest. Squeezing his pecs.

My hips lift and lower, drawing him into me over and over again.

"Lindee," he warns.

I'm lost in my head, chasing my own release, growing eager to give him his. The way he'll pulse inside me. The way he'll fill me up. The way he'll hold me tight to him as we connect.

The thought sets me off and I still. Only Thad surges upward, bucking his hips as I come around him, squeezing him inside me until he gives me what I want.

He gives me all of him until he's spent and then I'm collapsing to his chest.

Thad brushes back my hair, swiping at the sweat along the edges. The room is warm. His body hotter.

"Jesus, sweet thing. Promise me you'll never leave me. We'll never stop being like this."

"You," I whisper instead, every emotion in a single word. The truth is on my tongue because Thad has made all the difference.

Him.

He's been the one to crack open my heart and make me long for things I'd pushed so far down inside me I didn't think they existed anymore. He brought to light what I've been yearning for and what I needed to feel whole.

He found me, and I never want to be lost again.

As the sun is rising, I sneak out of Thad's room. The pastel fade of light pink and warm purple fills the sky outside the window. I'm just shutting the door to his room when I turn and find Sam standing in the hallway. He's wearing underwear that look suspiciously like something from Harry Potter, and a Hufflepuff T-shirt.

My hand comes to my chest as I start at his presence. "Sam, honey, why are you awake?"

He shrugs. "I was hungry."

The answer is so simple. Thankfully, he doesn't ask me why I'm awake or why I'm coming out of his dad's bedroom.

"Why don't you go put on some pants and I'll change and meet you in the kitchen in five," I whisper, attempting to keep my voice low.

He gives me a sleepy nod and turns back to his room.

When we meet in the kitchen, he's slipped on a patterned

pair of shorts that clash with his tee. Thankfully, the coffee pot clinks to life, and I find cereal in the cabinet for Sam.

"Have you had a good weekend?" I ask after filling a bowl with Frosted Flakes and adding milk for him.

He hums around the first spoonful and nods.

"What was your favorite thing?" I lean across the island, my upper half on the counter while my hands wrap around a coffee mug. I'd slipped into my bib overall shorts.

Sam shrugs, still chewing his cereal. "I liked it all but I'm hoping we can sleep in a tent again when Mom and Dad get back together."

I freeze. My body grows cold despite the warm mug in my grasp. Treading lightly and knowing it is not my place to ask, I still question, "Why would you say that, Sam? About your mom and dad?"

He lifts another spoonful for his mouth and then talks while chomping. "Mom told me. She says her and Daddy always get back together. Fightin's what they do." He swallows. "And when she comes back from her vacation, her and Daddy will be together again."

Oh boy. I want to believe Thad and Jasmine getting back together isn't true. But Sam has a valid point, confirmed by his mother. Thad and Jasmine have had a push-pull relationship. Forgive and forget. Hiccups and makeups.

"What did your dad say to that?" Knowing Thad talked to Sam yesterday, I'm hoping to trigger his young memory. Thad has been rather adamant that Jasmine and he will never be together again, and he's mentioned how it's been difficult for Sam to understand.

"Dad says we're going to be a better family, too."

My heart shatters, like a fragile stone dropped from a high point, breaking on contact with a hard surface. Or maybe the depth of a fierce river. Slowly, I lift off the countertop, still clutching at the coffee mug like it's the only thing that can hold me afloat. My entire body vibrates, and I struggle to regulate my breathing.

"You can be part of our family, too." Sam shrugs, watching as he spoons up another scoop of cereal and shoves it in his mouth. "When Mom and Dad get back together, we can all be a family."

I could interpret this in many ways but the only thing drifting through my head is Sam believing full-heartedly that Thad and Jasmine will be together again. They will be a family once more.

Young Sam wants this for his parents.

He needs the family unit I never had.

He deserves to have a mother *and a father* who love him, making them better, together.

He will not be me—a kid raised without his dad.

Suddenly, like a wave of reality, what's been holding me back from admitting my true feelings for Thad becomes clear.

Jasmine was not Harris. She could heal. She could get better. Thad could love her.

And I will not take that beautiful, kind, loving man away from this sweet, innocent boy who just wants his family back together.

I cannot be the reason they remain split apart.

And I can no longer risk my heart when Thad will return to Jasmine.

"Sounds nice," I choke.

Because I'll never be part of this family and I don't know why I ever thought I could be.

39

Playlist: "Last Night" – Morgan Wallen

[Thad]

When I find Lindee in the kitchen with Sam, something is wrong. She only offers me a weak smile as she sips her coffee and Sam rambles about Legos. Eventually, Lindee excuses herself to take a shower. When she comes back down, Sasha and Vicki are awake, and Nessi is making waffles for everyone. Sam is thrilled to have a second breakfast.

Lindee keeps her distance, offering to help Nessi cook, or serve food, or do dishes. She's looking for any way to be busy and avoid glancing at me.

There's no way she's embarrassed about last night. Last night was fucking hot with her getting off on me, taking what she needed and then bringing me to the brink, driving me out of my mind.

Something else must have happened, but I can't figure out what.

By mid-afternoon, Lindee is asking if we can return to the motel, citing that she has something she needs to do. I'm eager to snap *like what*, but I hold my tongue.

Hugging the kids goodbye is always hard, especially when five days will separate us. While I hate the phone, I'm grateful for the convenience of video calls, so I can actually see the kids each day.

Lindee passes out hugs as well and when she holds on a little longer to each of my kids and then clings to Nessi a bit, I'm feeling only slightly better. She loves my family and I'm so grateful. We had a great weekend together.

My bike doesn't offer us a chance to talk and once we pull up to the winter cabin, she's quick to hop off the back.

"Hey." I catch her arm without dismounting and hold her still. "You're so quiet."

Her eyes avoid mine again. "Long weekend." She falsely smiles, finally lifting her gaze but then quickly glancing away again.

"Was it too much? Was it the kids?" Fuck, it's a lot to take on a divorced man with a ton of baggage and three children.

Her head finally pops up and she blinks. "No! God, no." She licks her lips. "Your kids are amazing, Thad. I mean, Sasha might be a little hard-shelled but she's still a good kid. And Vicki. She's just so bright and eager. Watching her with your Gran . . ." Lindee sighs.

"And Sam." She swallows hard. "*Your* Sam-man is just the best."

There isn't a doubt in my mind that Lindee isn't being heartfelt. Her admiration of my kids is evident in the wistful expression on her face. She really adores them, and they adore her.

"Is it me?" I question, feeling unsure of myself for the first time.

Lindee shakes her head, finally keeping her eyes on me. "You have it all, Thad."

"That isn't what I asked." I cheekily smile. "But, I am a lucky man." Great kids. A beautiful woman in my bed.

"I'm tired." Her eyes hold still, and something tells me she's lying. "Maybe a stomach thing again." She waves at her lower belly.

"Maybe you should get that checked out by a doctor." I'm one to talk as I put off seeing a doc for years and then finally gave in once I wanted a vasectomy. *Cancer* hadn't been what I expected the doctor to say at a routine physical and the treatment hadn't been a picnic either. I swore I would never take my health for granted again.

"It's probably my period."

Lindee hasn't had one since we've been together. She told me she was just irregular, thus the pregnancy scare.

"You should definitely get that checked out." I playfully laugh, squeezing her arm in hopes to lessen the tension between us.

"Yeah, it's probably just stress that keeps it away."

I'm not liking that answer any more than I'm liking her avoidance of whatever is the real issue today.

"Did Sam say something to you this morning?" My brows pinch while I continue poking for answers.

Lindee stills. "Why would you ask that?"

"What did he say?"

"He didn't say anything." Her voice softens and slows as her eyes lower again. She's lying to me, and I don't know why.

"I need to call my brother." The shift in topic is so abrupt I release her arm.

"Yeah, you do that." Whatever is happening here, I'm not liking it, but I'm not in the mood to fight for answers.

We had a great weekend and last night was incredible, but I can't make her talk to me.

With a twist of my wrist and a kick of my foot, I rev my bike and Lindee steps back. I walk the Harley backward a second and then turn for the highway, not glancing back at the woman suddenly pulling away from me.

THE NEXT FIVE days are a rush of one final project after another. Then it's all Lindee and touch ups. Jane comes to stay for days to help make every bed, hang curtains and pictures, and fold towels over rods in the bathrooms. Jane brings her daughter, Willow, with her, and as the two take up residence in the winter cabin with Lindee, I'm out a bed partner.

But it isn't only the mattress I'm missing. I miss Lindee, and I don't understand what happened.

With her sister present and endless tasks to be done, Lindee is good at avoiding me. Even Duke and Manor give me questioning looks from time to time.

"She on the rag?" Manor asked one day.

"Don't talk about her like that," I snapped.

Duke watched me, shaking his head.

When the weekend came, there wasn't much for me to do, but I was hesitant to leave Lindee.

"Put me to work," I begged on Friday afternoon.

Lindee finally paused from fluffing pillows in the room Vicki suggested with geranium prints on the wall and the red watering can as an accent by an oversized lamp on a freshly scrubbed dresser. This piece of furniture made the cut to remain. The bed is new and covered in a light green coverlet. I only know the term because of Lindee.

"Can't," she says, offering me a weak smile. "You have weekends off."

There's no disapproval in her tone or even sarcasm, and I'd welcome either just to have some spark from her. We haven't connected all week and it isn't just the sex that's on hold. She's shut down.

Duke says it could be the stress of finalizing the renovation and finally opening the motel, and I want to believe him, but I just don't.

"I could bring the kids here. They'd love to help." I can't miss the weekend with the kids, but I don't want to go anywhere without Lindee.

She stands tall and sets her hands on her hips. "Thad, really. Go spend time with them. You've worked so hard this week."

We've worked some long hours to finish the duplex which needed more work than anticipated. Lindee had the guys and me move into finished hotel rooms to give us rest from the duplex construction zone.

"I don't want to leave you." A sudden gasp behind me has me spinning to find Jane in the open doorway.

"Just go," Lindee prods. "I'll be fine." She softens her expression, but the smile she offers doesn't light up her blue eyes.

With Jane still lingering in the doorway, I'm dismissed, and I want to punch my fist through the freshly painted wall.

Instead, I head for my truck and take off for the weekend.

IN THE FINAL days of the motel renovations, the trench for the pool was filled in and the busted driveway was dug up. Instead of replacing the drive, Lindee had gravel laid in a semi-circle around the pool as a driveway and then added grass along the sidewalk in front of the motel rooms. A green space, she called it.

When I'd left on Friday, the sod was being heavily watered.

The pool was being filled, and the pebbled drive was being smoothed out.

Duke and Manor stayed the weekend to help in any way they could, and I hated that I'd been absent during the last days of our contract.

On Sunday morning, Lindee sent a text telling me not to worry about coming back early. Just bring Nessi and the kids to the party the next night. I'd been dismissed again.

Everything in me screamed that I should hop on my bike to head back to the motel, but Vicki had a stomachache Sunday night, and she was crying over it. When I checked in with Duke, he told me things really were being handled.

On Monday, Nessi drives the kids to the party while I drive my truck. I don't plan on leaving the motel. Not until Lindee and I have talked.

When I pull onto Mountain Motel's drive, it's like an entirely new place. In the glow of a summer evening coming to a close a little sooner with each passing day, the place gleams white with freshly painted evergreen-colored trim around the windows and on each guest room door. A lit sign advertises the place by the highway and a neon light spelling out Mountain Motel flickers above the lobby.

The green space, which is a glorified name for the added lawn, holds a few picnic tables and some yard games like cornhole, ladder toss, and a giant ring set. The pool glistens while lights beneath the surface illuminate the water. A food truck with Bob's Bar-B-Que on the side is parked beneath the canopy by the lobby.

I park near the duplex and linger. Dolores and Garrett are here. I recognize Jane and assume the man beside her is Mach. Three kids I don't know are running over the grass with Jane's daughter Willow. Myles stands near a blonde-headed woman.

Nessi pulls up shortly after me and my kids pile out of the Cayenne. Sam races for Lindee and she separates from the people she's chatting with to meet him, lifting him up in a spinning hug.

Laughter filters toward me. The night is a celebration of a job well done. Lindee is fucking radiant in her lemon print dress. She should be sparkling. Look what she's accomplished.

Finally, I make my way down the new gravel drive. Lindee meets me halfway before I've neared the other adults. Some sit in Adirondack chairs on the grass. Others stand nearby eating barbeque.

She offers me the first smile she's given me in days and for a minute I think we might be okay.

"I have something for you."

"Oh yeah?" Thinking it's a kiss or maybe something deeper like an apology and then an admission that she loves me, I feel momentarily lighter.

Instead, she hands me an envelope. "Here."

"What's this?" I'm strangely reminded how I copied my divorce papers and left them on her camper table as proof that I'd been divorced hours after I met her.

Lindee sheepishly smiles as I flip over the container and open the flap. Then I pull out a rectangular piece of paper and my teeth clench.

"It's your last check. I wish I could have given you guys a bonus. You worked so hard, and everything turned out perfect. But I'll write you the highest review and you can use me as a reference for any future projects."

Is she fucking kidding me? I don't want a reference. I want her.

Lindee's hand covers her stomach. I swear she's giving herself an ulcer.

"I don't know what I was thinking." She exhales, fisting the fabric of her dress, and then inhales as if she can't catch her breath. "I've decided to sell."

"You what?" The shock in my voice echoes around us. With the final check in my hand, I crush it in my fist and stand taller.

"When I was little, I had this play motel. It was a square that unlatched at the roof and opened at a right angle." She uses her hands to outline a square and then mimic opening the latch. "The outside had motel room doors on two levels and a lobby while the inside was open to the motel rooms with these plastic beds and little square people."

She smiles fondly as she recalls the toy. "There was a pool on a board, like a board game, and it lay flat and snug against the hotel when it was open." Again, her hands motion as if she can feel the object before her, spread out on a floor.

She blows out a breath and swipes at her forehead. "But this isn't pretend. I'm not some four-sided doll jumping into a board game pool. The only real part is motels are meant for visits. Temporary stays along the highway."

Lindee waves toward the street behind us, like a model on a fucking game show. But I am not willing to play along.

"I can't do this." With her body facing the motel again, she takes another breath, like she's on the verge of hyperventilating. Her fingers fist against her belly. "I don't know the first thing about hotel management or the hospitality industry. I'm not the person who stays in one place."

She finally turns to me. "I understand there is a clause in the purchase agreement. You have first right of refusal to purchase if I sell and—"

"Whoa. Slow down." I interject, holding up both hands, one still clutching a crumbled check. "This is your dream. You've got this, sweet thing."

I reach for her shoulders, but she steps back, putting space between us.

"So, this is how it's going to be," I growl, low and hurt. My chest feels like I'm being fucking stabbed.

Lindee doesn't answer me. She holds my gaze for the first time in weeks and her eyes swim with liquid like the pool behind her.

My shoulders fall. "You can do this, sweetheart." *It's stress.* She's freaking out and overwhelmed. She's worked too hard and she's just spiraling.

"I don't have this. I'm the fixer upper. The renovator. I make things pretty for other people, but not for me." Her voice shrinks.

"You've got this." I repeat, emphasizing every word as I step closer to her, filling in her space as her eyes lower to our feet.

"I— I don't want it." She lifts her head high as her hands fall in clenched fists to her sides. She meets my eyes.

I don't believe her. "You've been living and breathing this place for eight weeks. It's finally ready. You're ready." I stare at her, wanting her to accept that the place is incredible and so is she. She can do anything she sets her mind to.

"That's what I do. Projects. On deadlines. And it's time to move on."

"What do you mean you don't want it?" The pressure on my chest is like my bike has rolled over me. I puzzle through what she's just said but then piece together the truth. Through gritted teeth, I say, "You mean you don't want us."

Lindee doesn't respond. She can't—or won't—meet my gaze, and I want to demand she does. *Look me in the damn eye and say that to me.* Instead, I ask, "What will you do? Where will you go?"

"Wherever the road leads me next." She isn't being flippant, only sad, so pathetically sad.

But I'm unbelievably angry. *Is she shitting me?*

"So . . . that's it?" I lift my fist with the crushed check. "You just . . . leave."

Lindee doesn't answer.

"What happened between last weekend and today?"

"You don't want to know," Lindee mutters, her voice still quiet. She looks everywhere but at me.

"No, I really do want to know. Because the woman I love is

breaking up with me and I want to know what the fuck happened."

Lindee's head lifts as my voice rises. She peers to her left, but I don't give a fuck if we have an audience.

Glancing back at me, she sighs. "Sam told me Jasmine was coming back. And when she did, you two would be back together. You'd be a family again." Sorrow fills her voice as she weakly smiles, as if what she's saying is a good thing. As if there is even an iota of truth in that statement.

I stare at her, perplexed and downright pissed off. "What?"

"You're so loyal. Dedicated. Your kids come first, as they should. And you have this whole push and pull thing with Jasmine."

"Do *not* bring her into this," I snap.

Lindee continues. "It's like a different kind of addiction. A drug of love and hate."

I lift my hands and place them on the back of my head, spinning in a circle a second, uncertain I'm really hearing what she's saying.

"You're telling me, because of an eight year old, you're running away from me? From us?" I huff. "Because that's what you're doing. You're running. You're fucking scared that I'll leave even as you're standing here, telling me how devoted I am." With a heavy exhale, I drop my arms. "You have time limits on everything. Schedules and calendars and budgets on your emotions."

Squeezing the crushed check in my fist, I hold it up between us again. "Time's up and I'm out?" *Un-fucking-believable.*

"Sam said you were going to be a better family when she returns." Lindee's voice lowers, soft and flickering like candle-light in the darkest of nights.

"I said we were going to be better because of *you*. I told Sam I planned to make you part of our family. And while Jasmine would always be his mother, *you* were going to be one of us. Belong to us. And *we'd* be better for it."

Lindee stares up at me, tears filling her eyes, but I can tell my words still aren't getting through to her.

"I'm telling you I love you. I want you." I sigh heavily and stare at this beautiful woman. "You're brave and fierce, so what are you so afraid of with me? You don't have to keep going it alone, sweet thing. I'm here." I slap at my chest, the envelope and check crinkling against me. "Taking on this project, I'm here for you." I wave out at the motel. "Tearing down walls, building new ones, I'm here. Demolition and construction shouldn't apply to people, though, Lindee. You don't have to be strong with me. I'm with you."

Lindee lowers her head, her lip quivering and her eyes leaking.

"There's no time limit on feelings." I stand tall as her silence feels like a gate crashing down between us. "But you want a time limit, sweetheart? Forever, Lindee. That's what I want with you. Forever. Time infinity."

Lindee covers her face and sobs harder.

"Dude," Duke softly calls out, and I turn toward my cousin, noting the audience, awkwardly trying to avoid looking in our direction as Lindee and I fall apart before them. She's crumbling before me and as much as I want to pull her to me, the thin space between us tells me I'm too close to her. She doesn't want my touch anymore. She doesn't want me.

"This is your dream, sweet thing," I say lowering my voice. As much as I want her to stay for us, I don't want her to stay for me alone. She needs to stay for *her*.

"Yours." I pause, then whisper. "You."

With Duke nearing, and Lindee crying, my body vibrates with the need to hold her, to press her to me and never let her go, but I can't do it if she won't meet me in the middle. I won't cage her in. I know the feeling too well myself.

Lindee is a free spirit like the dragonfly on her bracelet. The one she's wearing because it reminds her of us.

With jerky movements, I shred the check in my hands. I'll pay the guys out of my own savings.

"What's going on?" A male voice interrupts, drawing close as well, and I turn to Myles, leaning on his cane and watching me. He doesn't need to beat me with his stick. I'll take it from him and beat myself.

"We're done," I mutter, dropping the pieces between us.

"Thad." Lindee reaches for my wrist, but I can't handle her touch. One stroke and she'll incinerate me more than I'm already burned. Something that looks like panic flickers in her eyes before I turn away from her. I need to get gone before I break.

Crossing the gravel drive, I head toward the duplex.

Lindee said she'd go where the highway took her. I need the same thing.

The mountain mist and warm asphalt beneath me with a hint of gasoline and oil in my nose to clear away the scent of citrusy sweetness, lemon print dresses, and a fantasy of something I can't have.

When I reach my bike, it roars to life, cutting into the festive night that's been severed like a buzz saw. The sound overtakes my racing heart and the sour taste in my mouth. Duke calls out to me as he's followed me, but I don't pay him any mind. I don't even think of my kids who are going home with Nessi tonight anyway because I'd had a plan.

I came here tonight determined to prove I was who Lindee needed.

Instead, I'm rolling away from the motel like an interim guest.

Checking out, please.

Stay over.

40

─────────

Playlist: "I'm Sorry" – Brenda Lee

[Lindee]

We'd made quite a scene and when strong arms wrap around me, I fall apart in Jane's familiar hold. She presses her lips to my head and walks me away from everyone. She doesn't ask me what happened, she simply guides me to the winter cabin where I only cry harder as I've done every night since I walked away after the weekend at Nessi's.

I couldn't rip a father away from a boy so hopeful for his family to reunite and yet I missed Thad terribly. His mountain-male scent was everywhere in the cabin and every spot held a reminder of him. I didn't need the dragonfly on my wrist as a memento. I owned an entire freaking motel full of memories.

And I'd panicked. I'd meant what I said to him. I didn't know the first thing about hotel management or the hospitality industry. I wasn't a person who stayed planted but someone constantly uprooted and moved. From what Mae tells me, you can only transplant a plant so many times before the roots die off and the plant won't bloom anymore.

I am withered and spent.

Jane tucked me into bed fully clothed, pulling the covers over me, before rubbing my back. The position felt familiar to when Harris fell. When his prognosis was still uncertain. When my future was on hold.

"I ruined the party," I eventually whimper as my sobs subside.

Jane doesn't respond. She's not one to soothe when her words would be a lie.

"I heard him say forever," she says instead.

I nod into the pillow, turning my face into the scent of him still lingering on it.

"As someone who thought I had a time limit on my relationship, let me say, forever is better than weeks, or months, or only a year."

The tears begin to leak again. Jane isn't helping but she isn't wrong.

"You can run forever, Lindee-girl."

The use of my nickname causes me to catch my breath.

"But eventually, you're going to run out of steam."

I'm already there. My engine is tired. I've worked so hard the past ten days, burying myself in all the details of the motel in order to rid my thoughts of Sam's little voice in my head and Thad's body imprinted on my skin, and it's been exhausting. And no help.

I'm lonelier than ever.

I roll to face Jane. "He deserves his family."

Her brows crease. "He deserves you." She pauses and tilts her head. "But what am I missing?"

I've already filled Jane in on how I thought he might go

back to his ex. How stranger things have happened between couples. Jane repeatedly argued she didn't believe it. The percentage of reunited divorced couples was small and Thad didn't seem like a man to turn back on a decision once made.

She'd only met him this week, but she'd been watching him. And she claimed he was always watching me.

"He loves you, Lindee. But I'm worried you don't love yourself enough. You won't trust yourself to take the risk to love him." Her tone softens. "You don't trust him to love you."

"I do trust him." *But did I?* If I thought he'd easily go back to his ex, didn't that say I didn't believe him when he insisted they were over? Or was it my fear getting in the way? Was I projecting an excuse on him, so I could walk away?

"You aren't showing it." Jane gives me an admonishing look, stern but not reproachful. Still the mothering-hen.

"I told him I was selling the motel."

"But you're not." Jane narrows her eyes.

I'm not. Thad was right. This has been my dream. I've worked hard, and while I'm scared, I have Garrett who understands what it takes to start a business, and Jane in marketing to help me promote it. Even Mae who runs her own small business can offer me advice. My family isn't going to let me fail. And as much as I wanted to prove I was one of them, they're simply proving to me I've been one of them all along. They are sticking by me.

"I fucked up," I whisper.

"Probably. But I don't think all is lost yet."

I've been lost for so long and Thad found me. Or I found him. The particulars didn't seem to matter.

"What am I going to do?" I cover my forehead with my arm, a headache forming from the strong tears and a week of exhaustion.

"I'd give it the night. You'll think of something creative. You always do." She pats my thigh like I'm a teenager again and leaves me to my thoughts. The flash of memory. The pain etched in Thad's expression. The moment I finally realized what a stupid thing I was doing.

I was throwing away the best person I'd known, scattering our time together in the wind, like that torn up check he dropped at our feet.

At the last minute, I reached for him. I couldn't hurt him like I was. I couldn't hurt us. I didn't want us to turn into the tug-of-war Thad had with his ex. If I wanted him, I had to surrender in the game and tell him how I felt.

Only, I was too late.

He stormed away. And while I could accuse him of leaving me, his exit isn't what happened.

I'd pushed him to go.

HOURS PASS and the night turns dark. Eventually, I slip out of bed and dress in comfy pants and Thad's flannel shirt. The nights are cooling considerably as fall tiptoes closer.

Jane went home with Mach and Willow. Mae and Tucker are spending two nights in the motel. Even Garrett and Dolores are sleeping here tonight. Garrett demanded the honeymoon suite.

Because of the darkness, I take a flashlight and walk toward the main building. My feet crunch over the freshly laid gravel. As I pass the lobby, I pause, glancing inside at the semi-circular bar plus the couch and two chairs near the fireplace. I can almost hear the music in my head, and the laughter of guests enjoying a drink. Or kids playing board games on the low table, fighting over the rules like I did with my siblings when I was younger.

Next, I walk along the covered walkway before the rooms. All is quiet here with the curtains drawn on the occupied spaces. I cross the new lawn area until I reach the pool where I stop and stare toward the highway.

Mountain Motel. The sign is illuminated by the road, announcing to travelers who we were.

My thoughts leap to the toy motel I told Thad about. I don't know why I mentioned it or where the memory even came from. The hours of enjoyment it gave me, offering fantasies of running away. In my head, I could travel the world, discover new places, and meet interesting people. I'd long forgotten about the toy but as I stood before the motel, telling Thad how I didn't want to run it and planned to sell it, the memory returned.

A souvenir of childhood, probably in a closet, or forgotten on a shelf.

A reminder of escape when I no longer wanted to run.

With the flashlight in one hand and another item in the other, I lift my arm to look at my wrist, finding the dragonfly bracelet that reminds me of Thad. I rarely take it off unless I'm worried it will catch on something and break while I work.

Why have I worn it so much if memories are fleeting? Because I didn't want to forget Thad. Not that night. Not the later nights. And not the days either. Not that I thought I ever would.

I turn back toward the motel and stare at the darkness of most rooms minus the soft glow from the honeymoon suite. I don't want to think about what my brother is doing in there with his wife, but that's the purpose of the room. A retreat for couples. A getaway. A brief stay.

I wasn't leaving this time and it scared the crap out of me.

The soft buzz of a motorcycle echoes down the highway and my heart hammers in my chest.

Is Thad coming back?

The fact that's my first thought at the sound of a motorcycle should tell me everything. As I said to Jane, I've made a mistake, and I need to fix it.

This isn't like the roof I'll eventually need to replace. Or the bathroom fixtures that need an update. This is an overhaul of my heart.

The motel holds everything I wanted. The themed rooms. The modernized lobby. The family yard space.

But the thing I'm missing most here is the family itself.

I have Jane and Mach. Mae and Tucker. Even Garrett and Dolores, but the absent piece is a family of my own.

And a permanent place to call home. My life can no longer be a temporary stay but a fixed space. I wasn't going to live in the winter cabin. I needed separation from work, or I'd let it drag me under again, and I didn't want to be buried in renovations. There was always going to be something with the motel. I was giving it time. I was giving myself time as well.

Forever, Thad had said. *Infinity.*

The motorcycle draws closer, and I hold my breath, anticipating it will simply pass by the motel, while hoping it might pull into the drive. The biker does slow and pull in. He rolls forward and parks by the duplex.

Thad?

I race toward the separate building, clutching the flashlight in one hand and the gift in my other. As I turn the corner, a tall man lifts his leg over his bike and takes off his helmet, but I don't have to see his face to know he isn't Thad. He's a little thinner, a little leaner.

Duke turns and stalls a second as I stand in the space before the duplex, breathing heavily from running here.

Slowly he approaches. "Lindee." The sharp curtness of my name should send bristles up my spine, but I hold my ground.

I have no right to question where Thad went or what he's doing, but I still have one ask. "Can you give this to him?"

Duke takes the book from my hand and turns it over, brows creasing as he stares at it.

"Thad will understand."

"Will he?" Duke lifts his head, eyes burning at me. "He's already been through a lot."

"I know." I lick my lips. "And I want to make it right."

Duke stares at me for a long minute before slapping the book on his other palm. "Yeah, I'll pass this along."

From the tone of his voice, I'm not convinced, but other than tear-filled phone messages and begging texts, this is my only chance to reach Thad.

And I'm thinking I'm only going to get one more chance with him before he's lost to me.

Forever.

41

Playlist: "Chances Are" – Johnny Mathis

[Lindee]

Two nights after the failed party, I'm pacing the lobby of the motel. We still aren't officially open for business, but our website is up and our information available on hotel apps. Our rooms open this coming weekend and we're half-full. Between all the renovation work, I hired housekeeping and a bartender plus an overnight manager. I'll be on the day shift.

Which means the motel is still vacant as Garrett and Dolores left, and Mae and Tucker went to Jane's place.

I'm wearing a path across the new hardwood flooring and the area rug underneath the new couch and two chairs. The evening has grown dim as autumn slowly settles in, making the day shorter and the nights much cooler.

The space is lit, though, with forty-three candles exactly. Thick luminaries fill decorative lanterns by the front door. Tall pillars are scattered all over the fireplace ledge with shorter, squattier ones on the mantel. Votives decorate the low table before the couch and cover the bar. The scene is probably a fire hazard and I'm holding my breath for two reasons.

I don't want the smoke detector to go off and drench the fresh room in water.

And Thad isn't here.

I've been checking my watch for the past hour every ten minutes and coming up with excuses. My mind spirals between he didn't get my message to he didn't want to give me another chance to something extreme, like he's hurt, or worse the kids are.

As time passes into the next hour, I accept defeat.

He isn't going to show.

Kicking off my heels, I walk barefoot across the floor and start at the bar, slowly blowing out candles and waving at the smoke, again in fear the detector might trigger.

Sorrow settles on my shoulders, but I have no one to blame but me. I did this to myself, pushing Thad away when I only wanted to pull him closer.

I cross the floor to the low table and blow on the candles there. Reaching for the ones on the mantel first. The front door flies open, and a gust of wind sends the remaining candlelight flickering.

I spin and stare as Thad stands in the doorway, looking a little windblown himself and a bit harried.

"You," I whisper as if he wasn't the person I was expecting. My head is slowly catching up to my heart which is hammering at his sudden presence.

"Am I late?"

I blink, almost laughing at the question. *Yeah, he's late...*

"No," I stammer. "You aren't too late."

He pulls the book from his back pocket and holds it up, cover facing outward. *The Outlaw's Confession.* I've read it a few times, but never owned a physical copy until Thad gifted it to me. Handing the book over to Duke, I was worried he wouldn't pass it on to Thad or worse, throw it away and the book would be a lost memento.

Thad pulls a slip of paper from the book and unfolds it.

"I got your note." This, too, he holds facing out to me where I remain frozen by the fireplace, and he hasn't ventured further into the lobby.

"Did you read it?" I sound like him when he asked me if I'd read the date on his divorce papers.

Thad flips the paper back around and reads it out loud.

Let's be our own romance novel. We write the story. I'm hoping it's happily ever after.

The bottom of the note gave him the date and time to meet me.

"You wanted to talk." He tips his chin. He isn't cold but standoffish, hesitant, and I don't blame him.

If we write the story, I need to start the first line.

"I am scared," I admit. "And you know all my reasons." Harris. My father. A thickness clogs my throat. "But I don't want to be scared anymore."

Thad continues to watch me.

"I want to love you." His eyes widen and I add, "I do love you. I love you, Thad." My voice cracks. "And it frightens me."

I lift my wrist. "I'm a dragonfly, always buzzing about, but I'm ready to stand still, and I'd like to stand with you, if you'll still have me."

Thad steps forward but then stops himself. "What does this mean?"

"I'm not going anywhere. I'm not selling the motel." If I thought he'd be angry that I'd said I was selling and now I'm not, he isn't. He also doesn't seem surprised that the place isn't up for sale.

"You were right . . . I'm a runner." I lift a shoulder. "But I don't want to run anymore. I've been lost for a long time, Thad. And I just want to be found. By you."

Thad lowers his head, and I can't exactly make out his face. He's still holding the book in one hand, and he slips the note back into the pages like a bookmark. A pause in the story.

Slowly, he lifts his head and glances around. "Quite the setup here." He arches a brow, still not acknowledging that I just told him I love him, or that I'm scared, or that I'm staying.

I shrug and gaze at some of the still glowing candles. "I was going for a grand gesture. All the best novels have one in them."

Thad dips his head. "A grand gesture, huh?"

"It's when the main character grovels, asks for forgiveness for being an idiot, and then admits all her feelings."

His mouth fights a curl at the corner.

"And I'm sorry, Thad. I'm so sorry I pushed you away when all I wanted was to pull you closer. I'm sorry I listened to Sam when he's only a child with hopes. I didn't want to rip apart your family."

Thad nods once.

"I'm envious of what you have." I wave out at him. "You're so close to your cousins. And you have Nessi. Plus, Sasha, Vicki, and Sam. It's everything I could have hoped for." Everything I still wanted.

Thad closes his eyes a second and I think we're both reminded of the baby I didn't have, that he was willing to give me, and I'd wished for despite the fact he couldn't.

"You once said sometimes the road isn't clear, but we take it anyway and just hold on tight for the ride." I swallow again, sure I'm botching this up, but now that the dam on my emotions has been set free, it's like a river of feelings I can't seem to stop. I want him to know everything. "I don't want to be in the fog, but if I am, there isn't anyone else I want to hold onto more than you."

Thad still hasn't said anything, and the lump forming in my throat feels like a boulder, but it isn't holding back the overwhelming love I have for him, or the sadness that I must be too late.

Thad finally comes closer to me but still not close enough, using the couch as a barrier between us.

"Take a ride with me."

I almost laugh. It's the same way he propositioned me the first night we met, only it's said with seriousness not flirtation.

He reaches into his back pocket and pulls out his wallet. He tugs his ID from the leather and holds it up. "I'll even show you my driver's license."

"Thad," I lightly laugh. He doesn't need to prove anything to me. "I trust you. Completely."

He slips the placard back in his wallet and tucks everything back in his pocket. Holding out his hand, he says, "If we're writing our own love story, then do something completely out of character. Something unexpected."

"Falling in love was unexpected," I reply.

"Exactly." Thad waits, his hand still out for mine. "You with me, sweet thing?"

"I'm with you." I step toward him then stop, pointing at the candles. "I'll just need to finish blowing them out." I also need sixty-seconds to collect myself as I've just spilled my heart and he hasn't responded to any of what I've said.

Still, Thad watches me as I move from candle to candle, blowing out each low flame. He doesn't help and I don't ask him, too. This was my failed grand gesture. My lips quiver and tears sting my eyes, but eventually I reach the ones by the door, leaning over and giving the final ones a hefty puff.

"How many were there?" Thad asks, a tease in his voice.

"Forty-three," I admit. One for every year I've been alone.

I was hoping the start of my forty-third year would be beside this man, but right now, I'm not so certain.

42

―――――

Playlist: "Buy Dirt" – Jordan Davis ft. Luke Bryan

[Thad]

Lindee was sweating, but I didn't intend to make her sweat too long. When I got her note late Monday night, I was ready to race back to the motel, but I didn't. She needed time to collect herself and so did I. I'd said some things I hadn't meant to say so harshly. I'd spilled some things I meant to say but not in anger.

I love her. I want infinity with her.

But Lindee is a woman who needs proof, not just the words, so I had to think big. And I had to pull in some resources. Mainly her brother and her oldest sister.

I hadn't made the best first impression on either of them. With Garrett, it was the revelation of the club. With Jane, it was the quiet cold front from Lindee. However, they both heard me loud and clear when I announced what I wanted from her. *Forever.*

In the days before I could return to Lindee, I also needed to have a little talk with Sam about being careful what we repeated to others and how Lindee misunderstood him because Sam mixed up what we talked about.

As I told Lindee, I said we'd be a better family *with her*. Jasmine was always going to be part of the unit, but her role in it was going to be her decision when she returned . . . if she returned. We had weeks before we'd learn how rehab went for her.

For now, Lindee was my only priority and as she followed me out to my bike in a sweet, light purple dress, my body hummed. She was going to be behind me again. Her thighs would grace the outside of my legs and her arms would be wrapped around my waist.

I heard what she said, but I didn't respond because Lindee needed something substantial, not just my word for how I felt.

I wanted her to stay planted, and I had the best solution I could think of.

With her on my bike, we slowly roll off the drive and onto the highway, heading toward Wrightwood. I'd been through the small town a few times but hadn't given it much thought. A week before Lindee came to Nessi's and camped out with us, a place caught my eye, and I want Lindee's opinion.

The drive is thirty minutes from the motel through forest-surrounded roads. Soon the leaves will change color and drop but the view is still a summer bloom of deep greens.

We eventually slip off the road onto a private drive until a house comes into view.

I pull up close to the home and cut the engine.

Lindee remains on the back of my bike, and I take a second to rub my hand along her arm still wrapped around my waist.

"Want to hop off, sweet thing?" I can't see her behind me, so

I check the rearview mirror. She shakes her head but slowly slides off the seat anyway. "Careful of the sides. I don't want you to get burned."

Lindee nods, remaining quiet as she pulls the helmet off her head. She's so pretty in her purple dress. Her hair a little wild. Her eyes a touch sad, but I plan to change all that, if she'll let me.

"What do you think?" I wave toward the house a long, flat ranch. The landscaping needs some work and I'd like to put in some new windows allowing for more natural light, but the structure is good and the roof sound. The interior can be torn out for all I care.

Lindee stares at the place. "It has character. Who lives here?"

"I was thinking I might."

Lindee turns her head toward me.

"A motel isn't really a home, and the winter cabin is a little small for five, so I'd like to buy this place." I pause and glance at her. Her eyes are wide. Tears swimming in them. "Actually, I already did."

"You bought a house. Near Wrightwood." Lindee restates the obvious then blinks and stares back at the place.

"It's going to need some work, but I happen to know someone a little excited about decorating. I figure she could theme each room."

Her head sharply turns back to me.

"But I'd like the overall theme to just be home." I look directly at her. "Because you need a place to permanently plant, sweet thing. And I'd like it to be here with me."

"You," she whispers, and I hear it in her voice. The love she has for me.

I tilt my head, swirling the sound around and then stare at her. I point at her. "That right there." My throat thickens. "You've been saying it all along."

You. It was as simple as one word.

Tears slip from her face, and I cup her jaw, swiping at the spill. "Say it all, sweet thing. Let me hear it again."

She said it in the lobby, but I want the words once more.

"I love you, Thad. I love you so much." The tears fall a little harder.

"I'm going to love you forever, sweetheart." No time limit, like I'd told her.

Leaning toward her, she meets me halfway, eager for me like I am for her, and we kiss on the lawn of our new home. She's going to have a permanent address, a family of her own, and love. So much love from me.

"No more rearview mirrors." I rest my forehead against hers as I slide my fingers down to her neck. She covers my wrists with her hands, and I see the bracelet on her arm.

A dragonfly. A transformation happened for both of us that night by the river lodge. And I'm never looking back.

"Wherever the road might lead," she whispers. "I'm with you."

Yeah, she's with me.

"Happy Birthday, sweet thing."

Lindee pulls back and stares up at me. "How did you know?"

I shrug. "Checked out your driver's license. In case you were an ax murderer."

Lindee laughs loud and strong despite the tears still on her cheeks.

I swipe at them again. "How about we go celebrate?"

"Yeah?"

"Yeah." I pull back and take her hand in mine, leading her to the front door. The key is in my pocket next to the ring I plan to give her once we're inside our new home.

EPILOGUE
TWO MONTHS LATER

Playlist: "You" – Dan + Shay

[Lindee]

"Are you sure about this?" Thad asks me. I glance to the right but the path we need to take is to the left.

Holding out my hand, I wiggle my fingers for his. "I'm sure." With him beside me, I can tackle anything, and this was something I felt I needed to do.

Thad hesitates before leading me through the woods and into the opening that overlooks a river canyon and a railway bridge. We stop on the plateau and I breathe in the crisp fall air. The leaves have changed in the mountain forests. The motel has been full of leaf-peepers. The lobby is decorated with autumn décor.

But the view I need to see is this one.

The sharp colors of yellow and orange blend with the stark

bark of trunks prepping for a long winter's nap. However, the bright sunshine and a hint of heat as summer makes a momentary resurgence suggests winter is aways off in this region. The air is fresh. The rocks warm to the touch. The river ruggedly flows down below echoing off the boulders holding up this bluff.

We drove Thad's truck today so we could bring a picnic. He spreads out a blanket and lowers to his side.

"Mind if I sit here?" I ask.

He gives me a warm smile as he pats the blanket before him. "Sure, sugar."

It's a weekday and the kids are in their new school. Jasmine did return from rehab a new person. A quieter woman still fragile but stronger in many ways. She asked Thad if he'd keep the kids for a little longer, reversing their visitation schedule to allow her only one night a week and one day on the weekends. No overnights. Jasmine needs more time to figure out who she is after another major life shift.

For her, I hope she maintains her sobriety. For her children, I hope she can get back to being their mother.

For now, Thad and I have them twenty-four-seven and I love every second of the chaos and mess that comes from running a household . . . and a motel.

However, today is a day off, and I've asked Thad to bring me to the river.

It's too cool to venture into the waterfall. We'll have future days to return there and make new memories.

But this spot, this romantic location where his Pop asked his Gran to marry him, needed a new forever tale.

We met beside a river. We needed a re-do by this one.

"Have you ever done something so unexpected?" I begin.

Thad slowly smiles. The corner of his mouth quirking up first. He's giving me that same whiskey stare he did the first day, like he isn't certain what I'm asking, but he's listening. He isn't looking away from me.

"Something completely out of character? Something extreme."

He softly chuckles, looks out over the river, and then back at me. "Sure." His smile says he'll play along.

He knows I won't be asking him to jump from a bridge. He knows not to ask me to do it either. But he also knows, I'll do anything else for him.

"What about you?" he asks, leaning on his elbow as he rests on his side. I sit straighter, staring out at the canyon a second before looking at him.

"I fell in love."

"Did you now?" His smile grows as he reaches for my left hand and pulls it between us. We both glance down at the diamond ring he gave me. The dragonfly silver cuff is also on my left wrist, covering the semi-colon tattoo because my life is no longer on pause. Soon, I'll be getting another tattoo. A dragonfly, of course. A sign of transformation and change. Hope and love.

"Yep. I met a man by a river. He walked away."

Thad lifts his gaze. "I did not."

"But then he came back for me." My lips curl, giving him a soft look. He came back on that day. Out of character for him, perhaps, but completely unexpected by me. "He rescued me."

While twisting the diamond on my finger, Thad stares at me. "She rescued him."

We sound like we're telling a story in third person. He and she are him and me. Our new romance goes like this.

Woman meets man. Man falls in love first. Woman is an idiot. Man forgives her.

Although it's never that simple because life is complex. The journey is full of twists and turns, speed bumps and sharp bends, maybe even a fork in the road. Which path you select can change everything. The stars confirm it, and Thad and I are convinced our destiny was to meet how we did, where we did, when we did.

The Universe pointed the way, but it wasn't straight and narrow from where we were to where we are.

Glancing back at the river a second, I know that I'll always love Harris. He was my teenage heart and my future dreams, but he wasn't the plan. The plan was foggy when I was young. Around the bend was something else, only I took a lot of bends before I arrived here.

Sitting beside a man by a river wearing his ring.

"So, Pop proposed to Gran here, right?" This story is ingrained backward and forward in me by now.

"Yep," Thad says with pride, gazing at the railway bridge. A whistle blows. A train is coming. The rickety-rickety of it clacking over the steel structure soon breaks into the peace around us and we wait it out as it passes.

Sometimes, something just can't stand still. Like a dragon-fly. Like a freight train. Like a woman a little lost.

But there's a destination somewhere. Not every stop needs to be temporary.

I shift and face Thad, still angled on his side watching me. "Thaddeus Rhode. I don't ever want to climb another mountain without you."

Thad chuckles at first. We haven't really climbed mountains despite living in them. Despite occasional hikes. We're more road people, taking rides over the hills and through the valleys on his bike.

But slowly, Thad sits upright. His expression shifts from jovial to puzzled. He tips his head, watching me as he braces himself on his straightened arm.

"What are you saying?" His typically rugged voice is a little choked.

I reach into the bag I brought and pull something out.

"I was wondering if you'd marry me." I hold up the silver cuff bracelet I had made with a dragonfly engraved on it in a more masculine design. "I've learned that bikers don't always exchange rings. They don't officially marry sometimes either. A gift is given as a symbol of connection. Typically, that would be a leather vest with a patch on it, stating I was your property. Your old lady."

With wide eyes, Thad stares at me.

"Okay, maybe I read too many romance novels. Still, I want a way to claim you as mine. You belong to me, like I belong to you."

"Lindee." When Thad says my name like that, it's either that he's serious about something or overwhelmed. I'm thinking it's the latter.

"I told you I'd wear a ring." Thad didn't wear one during his first marriage, opting to wear his grandfather's heavy lion ring as a sign of commitment to something bigger than him. Loyalty to the brotherhood. A vow to protect a woman who had been part of the club. He's never worn a wedding band but he's going to wear mine once we marry.

"I know. And I'm honored, but I still want you to have something now. Think of it as an engagement bracelet."

That might have sounded cooler in my head but as I wrap it around Thad's thick wrist and he holds his arm up, straightening the cuff to see the dragonfly, he swallows several times and blinks twice.

"Thad," I whisper.

He shakes his head before swiping at his eyes with one hand and pinching at the bridge of his nose. I reach for the wrist that wears the silver band.

Thad lifts his head. "I love you so much." Emotion fills every word.

"You," I whisper.

He exhales. "You."

Knowing Thad needs all the words, I state, "I love you, baby."

He leans forward so fast I catch myself on the rock behind me as our mouths come together. We kiss like we're hungry for one another and didn't have a little early morning snack of each other before taking the kids to school. While I work the day shift at the motel, Thad only takes jobs within the immediate area sometimes sharing projects with Myles. Other times they trade, if one or the other of them is in demand.

He abruptly releases me, but his hands are in my hair, and he tugs my forehead to his. "Look me in the eye and say that again."

I pull back so we can meet eye to eye, and I repeat myself. "I love you more than I ever expected."

"Out of character, yeah?" he teases.

"I wrote a new heroine for my story. It's completely *in* character for her to love you."

Thad chuckles before pulling me back to him and taking my mouth once more, telling me he loves me with every pull of my lip and swipe of his tongue.

"You know what isn't going to be extreme?" he says as he slowly presses me, so I lay back on the blanket. "Me having you on this rock. With the sunshine and blue sky as a witness."

"Thought you weren't ever going to share me with anyone." I chuckle as Thad is already tugging up my shirt and reaching around my back for my bra.

"Only sharing you with the kids and even that's on a time limit."

"A time limit, huh?" Our eyes meet.

"Yep. You're mine all the time."

With my bra off and his hand cupping my breast, I gasp. "But I love the kids, too."

"And I love you for it, but this time, right here, right now, is my time, so we aren't talking about kids. Or calendars or schedules or budgets."

His mouth covers my breast and I gasp at the sharp suction. Okay, he has all my attention.

"Forever, sweet thing," he murmurs before moving to my other breast and sucking it just as hard.

With my fingers in his hair, I tug his head upward so he can look me in the eye. "Forever."

His mouth comes back to mine before the rest of our clothes are removed and Thad loves me on a rock plateau beside a river, where his Pop asked his Gran to be his forever, and I promise Thad I'm going to love him for time infinite.

Thank you for reading *Rhode Trip*.
Please leave a review where ebooks and paperbacks are sold and discussed.

Want a little more of Lindee and Thad?
Click here for a bonus scene.

Rhode Trip BONUS

Want to read about Garrett Fox (Lindee's brother) and Dolores? Check out WINE & DINE.

Wine & Dine

Start the Road Trips & Romance collection:

HAULING ASHE.

PLAYLIST

Listen to Lindee and Thad's playlist on: SPOTIFY

1. "Girl On Fire" – Alicia Keyes
2. "Sweet Thing" – Hozier (Van Morrison cover)
3. "Born to Be Wild" - Steppenwolf
4. "Hotel California" – The Eagles
5. "Unforgettable" – Nat King Cole
6. "Take Your Time" – Sam Hunt
7. "Chasing You" – Morgan Wallen
8. "I Hope" – Gabby Barrett
9. "Never Wanted to Be That Girl" – Carly Pearce & Ashley McBryde
10. "Back To Black" – Amy Winehouse
11. "The Good Ones" – Gabby Barrett
12. "The Night We Met" – Lord Huron
13. "Suspicious Minds" – Elvis Presley
14. "If I Told You" – Darius Rucker
15. "Layla" – Eric Clapton
16. "Simple Man" – Lynyrd Skynyrd
17. "River" – Leon Bridges

18. "Heart Like a Truck" – Lainey Wilson
19. "Sleep On The Floor" – The Lumineers
20. "Ghost" – Justin Bieber
21. "From Eden" – Hozier
22. "Secrets" – One Republic
23. "Son Of A Sinner" – Jelly Roll
24. "Put Your Records On" – Corinne Bailey Rae & "You Don't Know Me" – Ray Charles
25. "That's Amore" – Dean Martin, Dick Stabile and His Orchestra
26. "Daughters" – John Mayer
27. "Fancy Like" – Walker Hayes
28. "American Woman" – Lenny Kravitz
29. "Old Soul" – The Highwomen
30. "Going, Going, Gone" – Luke Combs
31. "Will You Still Love Me Tomorrow?" – Amy Winehouse
32. "I Don't Want to Miss a Thing" – Aerosmith
33. "Pick Me Up" – Gabby Barrett
34. "Can't Help Falling in Love" – Elvis Presley
35. "Heaven" – Kane Brown
36. "Wild As Her" – Corey Kent
37. "In God's Country" – U2
38. "Leather and Lace" – Stevie Nicks and Don Henley
39. "Last Night" – Morgan Wallen
40. "I'm Sorry" – Brenda Lee
41. "Chances Are" – Johnny Mathis
42. "Buy Dirt" – Jordan Davis ft. Luke Bryan
43. Epilogue: "You" – Dan + Shay

MORE BY L.B. DUNBAR

<u>Sterling Falls</u>
Seven small-town siblings muddle their way through love
over 40.
Sterling Heat
Sterling Brick
Sterling Streak
Sterling Clay
Sterling Fight
Sterling Touch
Sterling Stone

<u>Chicago Anchors</u>
When your eyes are on the silver fox coach more than the ball.
Elevator Pitch
Catch the Kiss

Parentmoon
When the mother of the groom goes head-to-head with the
single father of the bride.

Holiday Hotties (Christmas novellas)

Holiday novellas certain to heat the season.

Scrooge-ish

Naughty-ish

Grouch-ish

Road Trips & Romance

Three sisters. Three destinations. All second chances at love over 40.

Hauling Ashe

Merging Wright

Rhode Trip

Lakeside Cottage

Four friends. Four summers. Shenanigans and love happen at the lake.

Living at 40

Loving at 40

Learning at 40

Letting Go at 40

The Silver Foxes of Blue Ridge

Small mountain town, silver fox brothers seeking love over 40.

Silver Brewer

Silver Player

Silver Mayor

Silver Biker

Sexy Silver Foxes

When sexy silver foxes meet the feisty vixens of their dreams.

After Care

Midlife Crisis

Restored Dreams

Second Chance

Wine&Dine

Collision novellas
A spin-off from *After Care* – the younger set/rock stars
Collide
Caught

The Sex Education of M.E.
The original sexy silver fox.
When a widowed professor decides she'd like to date again,
and a local fireman volunteers to give her lessons.

The Heart Collection
Small town, big hearts - stories of family and love.
Speak from the Heart
Read with your Heart
Look with your Heart
Fight from the Heart
View with your Heart

A Heart Collection Spin-off
The Heart Remembers

BOOKS IN OTHER AUTHOR WORLDS

Smartypants Romance (an imprint of Penny Reid)
Tales of the Winters sisters set in Green Valley.
Love in Due Time
Love in Deed
Love in a Pickle

The World of True North (an imprint of Sarina Bowen)
Welcome to Vermont! And the Busy Bean Café.
Cowboy

Studfinder

THE EARLY YEARS

<u>Legendary Rock Stars Series</u>
A classic tale with a modern twist of rockstar romance and suspense.

<u>Paradise Stories</u>
MMA romance. Two brothers. One fight.

<u>The Island Duet</u>
Intrigue and suspense. The island knows what you've done.

<u>Modern Descendants – writing as elda lore</u>
Magical realism. Modern myths of Greek gods.

ABOUT THE AUTHOR

www.lbdunbar.com

L.B. Dunbar loves sexy silver foxes, second chances, and small towns. If you enjoy older characters in your romance reads, including a hero with a little silver in his scruff and a heroine rediscovering her worth, then welcome to romance for those over 40. L.B. Dunbar's signature works include women and men in their prime taking another turn at love and happily ever after. She's a *USA TODAY* Bestseller as well as #1 Bestseller on Amazon in Later in Life Romance with her Sterling Falls, Lakeside Cottage, and Road Trips & Romance series. L.B. lives in Chicago with her own sexy silver fox.

To get all the scoop about the self-proclaimed queen of silver fox romance, join her on Facebook at Loving L.B. (Dunbar) or receive her monthly newsletter, Love Notes.

+ + +

CONNECT WITH L.B. DUNBAR

9 781956 337273